www.booksattransworld.co.uk

The Business
'A compulsive, intriguing and perceptive read'
Sunday Express

'Compulsively readable'
Options

In Sunshine or in Shadow
'Superbly written . . . A romantic novel that is romantic
in the true sense of the word'
Daily Mail

Stardust
'Charlotte Bingham has produced a long, absorbing read, perfect
for holidays, which I found hard to lay aside as the plot twisted
and turned with intriguing results'
Sunday Express

'Irresistible . . . A treat that's not to be missed'
Prima

Nanny
'It's deckchair season once again, and Charlotte Bingham's
spellbinding saga is required reading'
Cosmopolitan

'Excellent stuff'
Company

Grand Affair
'Extremely popular'
Daily Mail

'A stirring tale of a woman struggling to overcome her past'
Ideal Home and Lifestyle

Debutantes
'A big, wallowy, delicious read'
The Times

'Compulsively readable'
Daily Express

The Blue Note
'Will satisfy all of Bingham's fans'
Sunday Mirror

'Another offering of powerful romance and emotional
entanglement from an author on whom I am most keen'
Sarah Broadhurst, *The Bookseller*

Change of Heart
'Charlotte Bingham's devotees will recognise her supreme skill
as a storyteller . . . A heartwarming romance which is full of
emotion'
Independent on Sunday

'A fairy tale, which is all the more delightful as it is not
something one expects from a modern novel . . . It's heady stuff'
Daily Mail

The Season
'Her imagination is thoroughly original'
Daily Mail

Summertime
'Destined to become one of the season's bestsellers, this is great
summer escapism'
Choice

Distant Music
'Bingham's characters are warm, empathetic, and endearingly
cosy. Their unfolding story is as comforting and nourishing as a
hot milky drink on a stormy night. Her legions of fans will not
be disappointed'
Daily Express

The Chestnut Tree
'As compelling as ever'
Woman and Home

Also by Charlotte Bingham:

CORONET AMONG THE WEEDS
LUCINDA
CORONET AMONG THE GRASS
BELGRAVIA
COUNTRY LIFE
AT HOME
BY INVITATION
TO HEAR A NIGHTINGALE
THE BUSINESS
IN SUNSHINE OR IN SHADOW
STARDUST
NANNY
CHANGE OF HEART
DEBUTANTES
THE NIGHTINGALE SINGS
GRAND AFFAIR
LOVE SONG
THE KISSING GARDEN
THE LOVE KNOT
THE BLUE NOTE
THE SEASON
SUMMERTIME
DISTANT MUSIC
THE CHESTNUT TREE
THE WIND OFF THE SEA

Novels with Terence Brady:
VICTORIA
VICTORIA AND COMPANY
ROSE'S STORY
YES HONESTLY

THE MOON
AT MIDNIGHT

Charlotte Bingham

BANTAM BOOKS

LONDON · NEW YORK · TORONTO · SYDNEY · AUCKLAND

THE MOON AT MIDNIGHT
A BANTAM BOOK: 0 553 81399 4

Simultaneously published in Great Britain by Doubleday,
a division of Transworld Publishers

PRINTING HISTORY
Doubleday edition published 2003
Bantam edition published 2003

1 3 5 7 9 10 8 6 4 2

Set in 11/13pt Palatino
by Phoenix Typesetting, Burley-in-Wharfedale, West Yorkshire.

Bantam Books are published by Transworld Publishers,
61–63 Uxbridge Road, London W5 5SA,
a division of The Random House Group Ltd,
in Australia by Random House, Australia (Pty) Ltd,
20 Alfred Street, Milsons Point, Sydney, NSW 2061, Australia,
in New Zealand by Random House New Zealand Ltd,
18 Poland Road, Glenfield, Auckland 10, New Zealand
and in South Africa by Random House (Pty) Ltd,
Endulini, 5a Jubilee Road, Parktown 2193, South Africa.

Printed and bound in Great Britain by
Elsnerdruck, Berlin.

THE MOON AT MIDNIGHT

'We met on VJ night, supposedly celebrating victory. The cloud over Hiroshima cast turbid reflections in the beer. We have lived in that shadow ever since.'

John Heath-Stubbs

MAGNOLIAS   SHELBORNE   THE MANOR

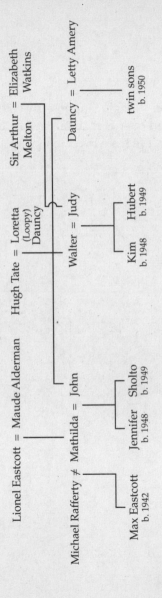

Lionel Eastcott = Maude Alderman   Hugh Tate = Loretta   Sir Arthur = Elizabeth
                                                  (Loopy)   Melton   Watkins
                                                  Dauncy

Michael Rafferty ≠ Mathilda = John   Walter = Judy   Dauncy = Letty Amery

Max Eastcott   Jennifer   Sholto   Kim   Hubert   twin sons
b. 1942   b. 1948   b. 1949   b. 1948   b. 1949   b. 1950

CUCKLINGTON HOUSE

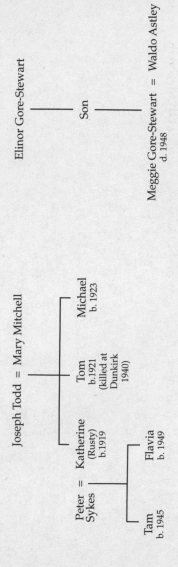

Elinor Gore-Stewart

Son

Meggie Gore-Stewart = Waldo Astley
d. 1948

THE BOATYARD

Joseph Todd = Mary Mitchell

Katherine
(Rusty)
b.1919

Tom
b.1921
(killed at
Dunkirk
1940)

Michael
b. 1923

Peter =
Sykes

Tam
b. 1945

Flavia
b. 1949

Prologue

The time is twelve o'clock of a summer night, a time that is always particular, but add to it a dark sea, boats bobbing gently, the sleeping village of Bexham, and you will see that the midnight hour is not just a time for wolves to howl, witches to start to mutter incantations, or lovers to be revealed, but a time when everything can be seen clothed in a suddenly magical light. A time when familiar houses, the village green, the church, the old inn, take on a shining bridal look, when cottage doors open and figures slip out into the now brilliant scene, meeting under the trees on the green, or on the rolling Downs, or beside the water, for when a full moon is shining at midnight, madness is most definitely abroad.

BEXHAM, ENGLAND, OCTOBER 1962

Chapter One

The moon was so bright that, when a dark cloud
started to pass slowly over it, inevitably it seemed
to be bringing with it a sense of doom. As the cloud
obliterated the brilliant light the whole village
appeared to be sliding silently not into night,
but into everlasting darkness. First the houses set
about the village green, next the old Saxon church,
then the pub on the quays, finally the boats
bobbing gently on the water, so that in the end it
seemed to those few who were watching it that not
just Bexham but the whole world might soon, with
the moon, be about to disappear.

At Shelborne, the Tates' house overlooking the
estuary, Hugh was playing the piano to his wife,
as he did every evening. Loopy knew that she
should be finding the music soothing, but this
evening it was having quite the opposite effect.
She lit a cigarette and stared out of the window
down the garden towards the village harbour
where they still kept a boat moored. She would
have liked to put the television on and watch the

latest news bulletin, but the fact that Hugh was playing for her made this impossible. She thought of her grandchildren and hoped that they were not wide awake and worried. She tapped her cigarette nervously, and too often, on the side of the ashtray and sipped her dry martini too fast, and at the same time hated herself for doing both. She should have more control over her nerves – she had lived through the last war, after all.

The truth was, however, that whatever Loopy had lived through, and however toughened she'd imagined herself to have become, the fact was that for the past few days each hour had appeared to be not moving forward normally, but melting one into the other.

It seemed that Hugh had at last finished his piece because he was looking round at her from his piano. Failing her saying anything about his playing, he stood up.

'Another martini, darling?'

Loopy nodded. Another martini might, after all, help the time to go quicker, or was it slower that she wanted it to go?

Waiting to go on stage that night Max Eastcott suffered a sudden attack of such severe stage fright that he found himself running headlong through the Green Room into the arms of the tall, dapper, dinner-jacketed company manager.

'I think I'm going to be sick, Henry,' Max muttered.

20

'About turn,' Henry Robinson told him, imperturbable as ever. 'If we played through the Blitz we can play through this.'

'I really don't think I can go on, not tonight, really I don't.'

Henry held Max's arm and nodded towards the stage manager.

'When you're ready, Johnny,' he called to him. 'Cue the band.'

The cue lights flicked on and the quintet in the pit struck up. Henry firmly propelled Max back to the brightly lit stage in front of him, on which the curtain was now rising.

'We are dying the death out there, Henry!' Max hissed, before drawing a deep breath. 'No one out there feels like laughing, and you can't blame them, besides which my stepfather's brother and his wife are out front tonight,' he added, inconsequently.

'You're doing a first class job, Max, all of you are doing a first class job. Remember what we say—'

'The show must go on,' Maisie Stirling sighed, as she appeared at Max's side, rubbing her perfect white teeth with the end of one moistened finger to make sure they were lipstick free. 'There's no business like it, remember?'

'Stand by—' Henry warned.

'We're going up,' Johnny called.

'Hope to God not, dear!' Maisie moaned, and she adjusted her costume and tossed back her hair.

'And cue—'

Henry tapped them on their backs.

Max and Maisie stepped on stage to join their two colleagues who were entering stage right opposite them in the opening number of Act Two of the hit musical revue *I Say Look Here*. Normally the satirical number 'Just Four Minutes' had the audience in stitches, but, understandably perhaps, not tonight.

'Give me a matinée on a wet Wednesday in Wilmslow any day,' the tall and mournful Joe Martino sighed as he traipsed up the stone steps to his dressing room at the end of the number. Max, who had the quicker change, pushed past him.

'You can't blame them, Joe,' he said as he went.

'Ours not to reason why, ours but to act and die!' Joe called after Max's fast disappearing figure.

'I can't imagine how anyone could find that funny,' Walter Tate hissed at his wife from behind his programme.

'It's not exactly an ideal time to be in comedy,' Judy whispered, realising at once from Walter's frowning expression that he was obviously determined to be stuffy about Max's show.

'Don't know how Max has the nerve—'

'Please – Walter.' Judy waved her programme like a fan in front of her face, concentrating on the show.

On stage the fourth member of the cast of five was bemoaning all the obscenity on television, pointing out that if that was what he wanted he could get it from the Bible.

Judy gently nudged Walter.

'You must admit *that*'s funny.' But Walter only shook his head mournfully, as if saying he had quite given up on his elder brother's stepson.

He sat silent for the rest of the show, and when they went backstage to see Max, even though he shook his sister-in-law's son by the hand, and patted him in an avuncular way on the shoulder, he left all the complimenting to Judy who, besides being very good at that type of thing, managed to sound passably sincere. As for Walter, he couldn't wait to drive down to Bexham and put the whole experience behind him. Satirical revues were quite simply not his kind of thing.

Later, as he parked the car in the new garage further up the lane, Judy put her key in the lock of Owl Cottage, pushed the door open and bent down to greet their two West Highland terriers before snicking back the lock and leaving the door ajar for Walter, following which she went straight to the kitchen to make them both a cup of tea.

There was no doubt about it, London had been a shock, and not just because darling Walter had been so stuffy about poor young Max's show. It had been the strange, uncertain atmosphere of unreality, reminding her of the days just before the war. As they'd driven out of the city she'd found herself looking for some sign of activity, her eyes constantly searching for the reassuring sight of couples passing by laughing and talking, or walking their dogs slowly through the leaf-strewn parks, in the time-old way. Inside the car they'd hardly exchanged a word, listening for news bulletins on the radio, Judy staring mutely out of the window as they drove past ribbon developments, new petrol stations neon lit, vast advertisement hoardings, all the time wondering, silently, if they would still be there in the morning. Thankfully, and at last, the countryside started to appear, and they came to Owl Cottage and Bexham, and the feelings passed as they always seemed to when they reached home, as if war and bombs were more to do with cities, which of course they weren't.

Now Judy pushed open the double doors to the garden. The star-scattered night sky was as clear as it had ever been, and the moon so bright that it lit up each part of the cottage garden's neatly tended beds. As the dogs busied themselves among the shrubs, she stared up at the beauty of the heavens above her and wondered at their loveliness, at the galaxies and the stars, searching as for some kind of comfort in the mystic shapes of Orion, the Great Bear and the Little Bear.

'A bomber's moon tonight, I see.'

Walter stepped into the garden and he too stared up at the night sky. As he did so, Judy turned and smiled. So many of Walter's expressions were hangovers from the last war. A bomber's moon had always been thought to bring good luck for the RAF because it meant it was easier to carry out precision bombing.

She pulled her tweed coat with its fur collar and cuffs tighter round her, thinking of their children, Kim and Hubert, fast asleep at their schools. At least she hoped they were fast asleep, or, in Kim's case, just looking forward to half term which was coming up, not dwelling on the crisis.

'Has it all come to this?' she asked Walter suddenly, as he wandered round the garden, staring at the last of the autumn flowers. 'Someone being able to pick up a telephone and start a nuclear war, just like that?'

'Kennedy's got to stand up to Khrushchev the way Churchill stood up to Hitler – America's got to stand up to Russia, or it will truly be the end.' Walter was still staring up at the sky, his arm round her.

'But it's so different now – nuclear weapons, the end of everything.'

'Death and sorrow will be the companions of our journey; hardship our garment; constancy and valour our only shield.'

This was Walter's favourite Churchillian quotation, and for some reason it always made Judy want to block her ears and sing loudly so as not to hear it, probably because it seemed so doom-laden. Instead she fell silent, continuing to stare up at the sky, wondering to herself, as she so often did, whether, if men had been made to go through childbirth, they wouldn't have put their talents to better use than building atom bombs to end the world.

Walter turned to face her, and as if from nowhere, his indignation obviously having built up on the drive home, it now burst out of him.

'You see, Judy, my point is this, it's that—' He paused, breathing out, and in, and then, seeing Judy's startled look, began again more calmly. 'My point is, if this lot – if young men like Max Eastcott had fought in the last war they could not possibly put those sketches on stage and expect people like us to laugh at them. They couldn't, really, they couldn't. I mean. Tonight, they were making fun of the war, of everything we fought for, our friends died for. It's just not on, really it's not.'

'No, I know what you mean. But. But I thought *Max* was jolly good, Walter. Actually, I thought it was all really jolly good. Max did say it was war *films* they were poking fun at, and really when you see some of them nowadays, they are a bit – well, a bit silly, not real at all. No one laughs and jokes in them in the way we used to, no one gets on with it, and I just can't believe in Noel Coward as an admiral, or whatever he was meant to be, whatever anyone says. So, I'm with Max on that, really I am, Walter.'

Judy was determined to defend Max, if only because she and her friend Rusty Sykes had helped to bring him into the world during a bombing raid on Bexham. And anyway, not only was Max's mother, Mattie, Walter's sister-in-law, but she was also one of Judy's oldest friends. In light of all that it would be ridiculous to be stuffy about Max's show.

26

'Mmm. Well, maybe you're right, if war films is all they were getting at, that's different.'

As Judy looked round for one of the dogs, Walter stared up once more at the night sky, frowning, only to begin again.

'I'm sorry, Judy, but I found the whole thing utterly facetious, and what's more even if it was only war films they were poking fun at, it was damned unpatriotic. If it hadn't been for Max up there being – well, Max; if he wasn't Mattie's boy, my sister-in-law's boy, frankly, I'd have walked out. It was insulting to England, to the war, to everything we stood for, and heaven only knows what the rest of Bexham will make of it. Frankly, it doesn't bear thinking of.'

Flavia Sykes stared at herself in the mirror. She had just put on a stiff nylon petticoat with a layered net underskirt, teamed with a tight-fitting brand new Shetland wool twinset, the property, alas, of her mother. She twirled in front of the mirror before sinking gracefully down in front of it, all the time watching herself in the looking glass, mesmerised by her own beauty. After a few seconds of contemplation, and perhaps for want of knowing what else to do, she put her arms above her head and executed a few swaying movements. She had always been good at ballet, the proud possessor of long and slender arms, so now she watched in fascination as she moved them correctly in swan-like gestures before leaning forward and slowly kissing her own image.

'God, you are so, so beautiful, Flavia,' she told herself, in a low voice.

'Flavia! Flavia!'

Her mother's voice, edged with anxiety, interrupted her orgy of narcissism.

Flavia stood up, panic-struck, and knowing that she'd be in a boiling cauldron of hot water if her mother found her trying on her precious new twinset. She tore the pullover and cardigan off and stuffed them back into their tissue paper and under her bed, until such time as she could secretly replace them in her mother's wardrobe.

'Flav*ia*! Ah, there you are!' Rusty Sykes sighed and stopped halfway up the stairs as she saw Flavia coming out of her bedroom. 'Lunch is served in the dining room today.' She stared at her daughter. 'Your dad has insisted that I entertain four members of the Empire League for Ladies, and I'm afraid the Empire League for Ladies would not understand your being dressed like that, Flave.'

Flavia nodded. She knew how much her mother hated formal entertaining, quite as much as she hated everything else to do with the social life of Churchester. Ever since they had moved to their bigger, grander house, Rusty had worn an expression of resignation close to martyrdom. Part of Flavia understood this, because her mother had always lived in nearby Bexham, by the sea, and had sailed boats – even been to Dunkirk several times on rescue missions, her grandad had told Flavia, although Mum never would talk about it nowadays. So Flavia knew that Rusty found town life claustrophobic, and she sympathised with her; on the other hand, another part of her sympathised with her father who wanted his wife to toe the line and make a proper social life, mix with the right people, if only for the sake of his business.

'OK, I'll put on proper things, don't worry.'

Flavia turned on her heel and went back to her room, sighing, as Rusty in her turn went back down to the ground floor of their large Victorian house clicking her tongue.

'And try not to say "OK", Flavia. It's not nice.'

Flavia turned to address her mother's departing back.

'Mrs Perkins our English teacher says we shouldn't say "nice",' she called down to the hall, tossing back her hair.

Flavia quickly went from her bedroom to her parents' room, replacing the precious twinset in the new mahogany wardrobe. Rusty loved clothes, because, as she was always explaining to Flavia, not having had any during the war, what with clothes rationing and the rest, she was only too appreciative of them now.

Having carefully removed the tulle-lined petticoat with a regretful little sigh, Flavia went to her own newly made mahogany wardrobe, opened the doors and stared in. She knew that if there were members of the Empire League for Ladies coming, she would be expected to wear a pleated tweed skirt, a silk crêpe blouse with long sleeves, nylon stockings with a light brown seam, and a pair of slip-on shoes in a discreet dark colour. A single row of pearls – never two – and a dark matching cardigan with small pearl buttons draped across her shoulders would complete her ensemble.

Once appropriately dressed she turned yet again to her dressing mirror to check her clothes, anxious to make sure that she looked every inch the well-brought-up young lady, which, thanks to her parents' new-found prosperity, she truly thought she might be. Flavia really liked to examine herself objectively at every point of the day, because she was increasingly aware that, if she was to get on, she had to study herself as if she were a subject she was taking at school. She was after all her own greatest asset, and likely to be able to make more from herself than she was ever going to make from geography or Latin.

She studied her straight red hair and green eyes, her tall, slender figure, and her thankfully freckle-free skin every time she passed a mirror, or even a shop window, and, while she took care to always be critical of what she saw, she was none the less also aware that the reflection she saw was of a gratifyingly beautiful young woman.

She heard the bell downstairs being rung, and turned regretfully from her mirror. It was time to be ladylike.

*   *   *

Nowadays the more proper ladies of Churchester were only too happy to come to the Sykeses' large Victorian house in its few acres of carefully manicured grounds, because not only was the food at Lowfield House quite a cut above that to which they might be used, but since their move into Churchester Mr and Mrs Sykes were proving an unexpected asset to such organisations as the Empire League for Ladies. Peter Sykes had taken care to donate generously to the League, and was in the way of lending them cars, and drivers, whenever it was necessary for the ladies to travel round the country in the course of their League work. As a consequence of all of this, the ladies were kindly prepared to ignore the fact that Peter Sykes was in trade.

After the statutory greetings, and the serving of before-lunch sherry, Flavia sat silently throughout the meal, contributing nothing except 'please' and 'thank you' and 'would you like' and listening to the to and fro of conversation, which always seemed to centre around improving the world, and women's role in it, by placing rallying articles in newspapers or magazines. As far as Flavia could gather, even such things as recipes for bottling beetroot could produce a better, healthier nation, something which greatly concerned the League. Today the menu in the dining room at Lowfield House consisted of the cold jellied soup known as 'consommé' – which Flavia ate dutifully, but privately found quite revolting – chicken in white

31

sauce with rice, and Queen of Puddings, which when served, which it was with monotonous regularity, was always greeted with a murmur of appreciation. Happily for Flavia she knew that it was not her place to contribute to the general conversation, which was just as well, since she found the word 'empire' as pathetically old-fashioned as the ladies themselves. For, what with their tightly corseted figures encased in neat suits whose lapels were inevitably decorated with regimental brooches, they seemed to be as much part of the past as the League itself.

It was not that Flavia herself was political, because she certainly was not. It was just that she could not see what the Empire League for Ladies could possibly have to do with the modern world, particularly when they all knew that Kennedy was probably just about to chuck an atom bomb at Russia, and Khrushchev quite ready to return the compliment. Also, the very fact that the subject of Cuba was not even raised once over lunch seemed really so peculiar. It was just as if none of the ladies present had ever heard the news on the television or the radio, or even read a newspaper, for the past heavens only knew how long, as if their lives had stopped in 1945.

Not that Flavia herself cared too much what happened to the world at that moment, just so long as whatever was going to happen manifested itself *after* she had been to see Max Eastcott in his West End show. It was to be her half term treat, and if an atom bomb ended the world before that she would be really, truly furious.

Before the Cuban crisis came to a head that week Lionel Eastcott had already been to see his grandson Max in his show. He had made sure to attend the first night in London, taking along his old friend Waldo Astley, and, as he told the boy afterwards, thoroughly enjoyed it.

'Some of it's a bit left wing, and so on, but nothing wrong with that, that after all is what being young is all about. Left wing before forty, right wing after, I think you'll find,' he told Max, patting him affectionately on the shoulder before turning quickly to leave the boy's dressing room and make way for the next visitors. 'Just make sure you get down to Bexham for a game of golf before too long.'

'You bet, Pops,' Max called back, his eyes drifting over his grandfather's head to the next in line.

'Jolly good show, wasn't it?' Lionel asked Waldo as they walked back to spend the night in Waldo's London flat.

'I thought so.' It was Waldo's turn to pat his old friend reassuringly on the back. 'I really thought so. Clever boy, Max. Should go far I would have thought. Acted and sang like a real pro. You must be proud of him – you *should* be proud of him.'

'I *am* proud of him. I just hope the critics don't devour it.'

'They can't, not after a reception like that,' Waldo stated, and for a while the two of them walked on in happy silence, as friends do after they've enjoyed an evening out.

'I don't know,' Lionel went on, after a bit. 'These critics, you know, they can get their knives out and carve up the young, make mincemeat of them, just like that, and all of a sudden they're finished, at the bottom of the barrel.'

As it happened Lionel's fears had not been realised. Far from devouring the show the London critics adored it, which was just fine, and had delighted Lionel. Now, as he looked round his late autumn garden taking in the few things that still needed tidying up, he could still remember the reviews for Max's show, which was hardly surprising because he had not only rushed them round to Waldo at Cucklington House, but had re-read them time after time, after time, until he knew them by heart and the print seemed to be fading from the warmth of his hands.

'Stunning tour de force by Max Eastcott' and *'A star is born'* and *'Run to see Max Eastcott because not to do so is to miss the performance of a lifetime.'*

The reviews had been well beyond the wildest dreams of any grandfather for his twenty-year-old grandson, which was more than gratifying, because young Max had always been a bit of a handful, although that was only to be expected, what with having been born out of wedlock to Lionel's daughter Mattie during the war.

Not that Mattie didn't love Max with all her heart, because of course she did; she just didn't

34

appear to love him quite as much as Jenny and Sholto, the children she'd subsequently had with his stepfather, John Tate. Lionel knew that of course Mattie had meant to love Max quite as much, but it had become increasingly hard for her not to appear impatient with the boy, simply because Max was already growing into a stroppy adolescent when the others were still young and angelic.

It was then that the game of golf had come in so handy, because Lionel, only too happy to have a young companion on the links, had been able to take his grandson under his wing and whisk him off to the golf club at every opportunity that presented itself. Not only did their regular games do them both the world of good, but it also gave Lionel an opportunity to listen to Max airing what he considered to be his problems, while Max was forced to listen to an older more reasonable point of view.

However, hard as Lionel tried to be a peace-maker between the two generations, the fact that Max's mother and stepfather had, for various reasons, been unable to go with Lionel to Max's first night in London had not made family relations any smoother, which was why, quite against his better judgement, Lionel found himself ringing Mattie to confirm that she and John *were* actually going to Max's show, albeit a week late.

'I told you, we are *going* to Max's show, Daddy,' Mathilda sounded irritated, as if Lionel was nagging her to do something for the hundredth time, which was so far from being the case that her father found himself feeling almost virtuous. 'I already told you, we *are* going, but John had to rush up to Scotland for *his* opening of his new factory which has been having terrible teething problems, and I, as you well know, have had the most God-awful flu.' She paused, preparing to list a catalogue of emotional achievements which would cancel out any hurt that her son might have suffered on their account. 'We *sent* him a first night telegram. I've *spoken* to him on the phone, and we're *booked* to take the children on their half term to see the show next week. We're even taking the Sykeses and *their* children, so we'll be a big Bexham party. Only Hubert will be missing because his half term's different. So, we *are* going, really we are, and I've *told* Max. There's no need to fuss, really there isn't.'

Lionel replaced the telephone. He was not fussed. He knew he wasn't fussed. He just didn't want the boy hurt. Although, come to think of it, it was a bit late for that kind of talk. His grandfather knew that Max had been hurt, was hurt, and so far as Lionel could see would remain hurt. For, whatever the reasons for his mother and stepfather's having missed the opening night of his first success on the West End stage, Lionel knew that they could never now make it up to the boy. It would have been better if they'd attended it and hated it, rather than just not gone, whatever the excuses. Not to have gone looked like disapproval, and both the

good Lord, and Lionel Eastcott, knew that disapproval was the last thing young Max needed.

Max stared at himself in his dressing room mirror,
wondering for the hundredth time what *it* would
be like? Would he feel anything? Would he know
anything? What. Would. It. Be. Like. What would
the Big Bang be like?

The door of the dressing room was pushed open.
Max turned to see the dark, curly-haired head of
Joe Martino. He was unshaven. He had bags under
his eyes, and he had not even started to change into
his dark suit for the first act.

'You look awful.'

'What else should I look? I spent the night in the
theatre basement.'

'You didn't.'

'I did.'

Max started to laugh. Henry Robinson had
suggested that Max and Maisie and the rest of the
cast do the same thing, but neither he, nor the other
three, had taken the idea seriously. Hiding from the
impact of atomic warfare in a theatre basement
seemed somehow perfectly hilarious.

'I just don't believe it.' Max lit a cigarette and
immediately puffed the smoke out, at the same
time doing up his tie in front of his mirror. 'That's
about as clever as taking refuge in a broom
cupboard when an incendiary bomb is about to
drop on your house, Joe.' Max laughed again.
'What did you sleep on, for heaven's sake?'

'There's a sofa down there, but I didn't sleep,' Joe said hoarsely. 'I took a bottle of Scotch and a blanket, and drank myself into a stupor.'

'Overture and beginners, please.' The announcement came over the tannoy.

'You'd better scarper, my friend.' Max looked at Joe affectionately. 'Henry is on the war path. We went up two minutes late yesterday.'

'Rather an unfortunate phrase in the circumstances, I should have thought, Max,' Joe grumbled, but he hurried off to his own dressing room nevertheless.

Kim Tate was waiting impatiently by the school gates for her cousin Jenny to arrive. They were being let off early for half term so that they could drive up to town with Jenny's parents, John and Mattie Tate, to see Jenny's half-brother Max in his musical revue.

All the time they were growing up Kim had never bothered to conceal from Jenny that she found Max both big-headed and patronising. However, this did not stop her feeling excited at the idea of seeing him on stage in a professional West End revue, his name in lights, the lot.

When they all looked back to their childhood, growing up in and around the little fishing harbour of Bexham, the fact that Max Eastcott was starring in a show when he was not yet twenty-one did not surprise the young of Bexham. They had all long ago accepted that Max stood apart from the rest of the Tate clan, not just because he was not a Tate, but because he was Max, tall, dark, handsome, edgy, and highly strung, looking out on the world with what Kim always thought of as being an unnecessary and really rather tiring cynicism.

'Oh, God, Jenny, do stop fussing with your hair. You look fine, really you do.'

Kim groaned, and both fourteen-year-olds hurried towards the school gates. They were dressed not in their school uniform but in home clothes, and feeling happily confident they would be able to mix with the most sophisticated in the West End theatre audience, since beneath their navy blue winter coats they were both wearing borrowed black cocktail-type dresses with the new fashionably shortened hem lengths.

'What on *earth* have you both got *on*?'

Mattie stared at Kim and Jenny, and then shrugged her shoulders as both girls, their eyes watering from the excessive amount of Woolworth's mascara they had plastered on their eyelashes, stared miserably back at her, trying not to look deeply hurt at her reaction to their carefully chosen high fashion look and succeeding only in looking painfully guilty. Kim had thought that it would be quite difficult to get the length of their skirts past her Aunt Mattie, while Jenny, knowing her mother's sharp eyes, had judged it to be impossible, while hoping against hope that she was wrong.

'Really, I don't know.' Mattie stared at both girls

in some despair, wondering what on earth to do about them. 'Look, it's too late for you to go back and change, so just keep your coats done up, and for heaven's sake, whatever you do, don't undo them when we get to London.' She looked at Kim and shook her head. 'Walter and Judy will have a fit, young lady, if they find out I let you go to the theatre dressed like that! As for your uncle. You know what *he's* like when it comes to skirt lengths. Just as well your parents saw the show earlier in the week. If they saw what you were wearing they'd send you straight back to St George's to change.'

Kim climbed glumly into the back of the car, followed by Jenny, both of them muttering 'Hiya, Sholt' to Jenny's brother, Sholto, who was already sitting in the front of the old Rover.

'Mummy says that Daddy only likes women to look like old Queen Mary. You know, skirts down to your ankles, and hair in a bun,' Sholto opined, looking back at his sister from his front seat.

Kim peered out from under her dark fringe of hair at the road ahead of them. The thought of having to keep her wool coat done up for the rest of the evening was enough to make her want to burst into tears. She turned and looked at her cousin, but Jenny seemed oblivious of disappointment, merely staring ahead, a faraway look on her face.

In Kim's eyes at any rate, Jenny was looking really pretty. Her long blond hair was held back decorously by a velvet bow at the back, a black velvet ribbon around her neck giving her what they had both imagined, when they were dressing, would be a sophisticated woman-of-the-world air. OK, so her mascara was a bit smudged, but otherwise in Kim's opinion her cousin looked so wonderful, someone might actually mistake her for a model, and sign her up.

'Is anyone else coming to the show, Aunt Mattie?'

Mattie pulled up at the traffic lights and looked back at the two of them sitting together on the back seats.

'Yes, as a matter of fact, Peter and Rusty Sykes are both coming. And they're bringing Tam and Flavia.'

Kim and Jenny turned towards each other. This time both their eyes registered exactly the same thought – that was all they needed. First they had to keep their coats buttoned up to stop John Tate seeing the length of their skirts and telling Kim's parents, and now they would have to compete for attention with blasted Flavia Sykes – always and ever known as the Beauty of Bexham even though she now lived in Churchester.

'Oh no, not Flah-viah.'

Kim pulled a face at Jenny. No one could compete with Flavia Sykes. She was not just beautiful, she was stunning, possessing as she did the kind of beauty that made people stop talking and stare at her whenever she came into a room. When

41

she walked along the quays at Bexham, tossing back her red hair, and pretending to stare out to sea at some faraway ship on the horizon, the whole of the harbour came to a standstill, and that was no exaggeration.

'By the way, no one's to mention Cuba tonight, do you understand?' Once again Mattie glanced in her driving mirror as she addressed the girls in the back seat. 'Did you hear that, Sholto? No mention of the crisis,' she added, looking sideways at her son, and he nodded slowly.

'Why can't we mention Cuba, Aunt Mattie?' Kim asked, all innocence.

'Because it will spoil the evening, Kim darling, that's why.'

'A prefect at school told me we were either very brave, or very stupid, going to the theatre tonight,' Sholto informed his mother after a short pause. 'He said that most people want to stay at home in case there's a nuclear war. He told everyone in my form to say goodbye to me – for ever. "Tate's going up to London to be sure to be in the middle of the Big Bang," he said to everyone.'

'What nonsense, Sholt.' Mattie changed gear over-loudly. 'Such talk is – that is just cowardly talk. War should never stop one doing things, not ever. During the last war we always went straight ahead with whatever we wanted to do. We wouldn't let Hitler and the Nazis stop us going to the theatre, or out to dinner, and when bombs dropped one just carried on dancing and singing.

That's what you do, you just carry on with what you're doing, no matter what. To do otherwise is to give in to the enemy.'

There was a much longer silence in the car now during which Kim bossed her eyes at Jenny. She found she could hear just so much about the last war. Her parents, Walter and Judy, hardly seemed to mention anything else. And, really, when all was said and done what did the war have to do with anything? Kim stared at Jenny and then taking a handkerchief out of her pocket she rubbed it lightly under one of her cousin's eyes.

'Smudge!' she hissed as Jenny tried to dodge her ministrations, before rubbing the handkerchief lightly under her own eyes. Really, they would both have to learn how to deal with mascara better.

Happily once they arrived at the theatre the foyer was so crowded John Tate didn't seem to notice that both the girls were remaining firmly buttoned up in their winter coats, seeming simply relieved to see them arrive safely and on time. As his daughter, Jenny lived in dread of her father's conservatism, and as his niece Kim was only too impatient of it, but even so, after Mattie's reaction to the length of their cocktail dresses, they did not dare risk taking off their coats. Instead they edged into their seats and sat back, waiting excitedly for the curtain to go up, Kim finding herself half hoping that Max would be so bad she would, at long, long last, be able to cut him down to size.

* * *

Max peered through the spyhole at the side of the stage. The last few nights had proved to be more awful than ever, the audiences sitting staring quietly at the stage, giving every appearance of attending a funeral rather than a comedy. They actually seemed physically unable to do anything except titter politely, until finally, and astonishingly, getting to their feet at the end, and cheering the cast to the echo.

It was as if, while they themselves were unable to find anything in the show remotely funny at a time of such crisis, the audiences were nevertheless determined to sit out this new much praised musical revue, sketch after sketch, no matter what, in true British style. Of course the cast realised that the thunder of applause at the end could not possibly result from enjoyment, but from recognition of the strain through which the silent reception had put the five young performers on stage. It was not the cast's fault, the end of show applause of the past days seemed to be saying to Max and Joe and Maisie and the others, *they* could not be blamed for the fact that the show was busy satirising a life which, now that they were faced with losing the world to nuclear war, seemed even more precious than anyone could possibly have imagined.

'You're looking a trifle grey, dear boy. Heard or seen something we haven't?'

Max turned from the spyhole and smiled at Guy Litton, the oldest member of the cast, who was still busying himself with his silk knitted tie.

'No, no, not at all.' Max cleared his throat nervously, then breathed in and out very, very slowly. 'No, actually, Guy, the reason for my deathly shade of white is that my whole family's in tonight.' He nodded at the spyhole through which he had been busy observing what seemed like half of Bexham making their way to their seats. 'Of course they couldn't come to the first night when it was still funny, could they? Oh no, they had to come tonight when the bomb's about to drop and the show's about as funny as nuclear fallout.'

'I don't think it matters which night one's family comes,' Joe opined gloomily. 'The whole Martino family came to the first night, and they didn't just hate it, they loathed it. My father's now cut me off without a penny and will have nothing more to do with me, and my mother and brothers all think I'm depraved.' He took Max's place at the spyhole. 'So all in all, my living has not been in vain. *God*, they look a right lot tonight, don't they? Is there anyone out there *not* dressed in black?'

'Not that I could see.' Max cleared his throat once more, and adjusted his tie. 'Oh well, here goes, plenty to look forward to.'

'Or, as my father would say being foreign and therefore speaking English correctly – ' Joe assumed a thick Italian accent, ' "plenty to *which* to look forward, dear boy".'

'Quite so.'

*   *   *

45

God bless all the young from Bexham, that's all Max could think as he played and sang sketch after sketch to the sound of their enthusiastic youthful laughter. The two boys, Tam Sykes and Sholto, Max's half-brother, appeared to be busting their guts, they were laughing so much.

The only trouble was that the theatre was so small that it was also too apparent who wasn't laughing, and he could see that among those with the stoniest faces were his stepfather and mother.

Oh come on, Ma, laugh, just once, won't you?

Max stared down at his mother as he performed a sketch entitled 'Not With A Whimper If We Can Help It', doing it probably better than he'd ever done it, so determined was he not to be thrown by the all-enveloping gloom in the auditorium.

Of a sudden he saw Mattie beginning to crack up, and finally start to laugh. She laughed and laughed, and laughed, and gradually the rest of the audience, obviously becoming infected by her, started to join in, until their laughter became one great gale of mirth. For the first time for days, it seemed that the people out front were seeing the joke on stage, in all its stark entirety.

'At least someone's still alive out there,' Will Roger, the shortest and tubbiest of the cast ad-libbed. 'There's hope for tomorrow. If we're still here.'

Not surprisingly this silenced the audience once again, and the curtain slowly fell, still to silence. Behind its cover the five actors pulled over-sombre faces at each other.

46

'Well done, Will,' Maisie congratulated him, sighing theatrically. 'Just when we had them, too.'

She had hardly finished speaking when a tumult of applause broke out quite spontaneously, unheralded by any particular group or claque, and when the curtain rose again for their calls, to their intense amazement the audience was on its feet.

'Would you believe it?' Joe said under his breath as he took a bow. 'I thought they'd all gone home.'

It seemed as if they were going to take even more calls than usual, so unceasing was the applause, as if the audience was unwilling to leave, preferring to remain in the theatre, in the land of never-never, rather than face the terrifying prospect of a future that promised extinction. Then as suddenly and surprisingly as it had begun it stopped, and all at once the theatre emptied, not as usual to the sound of excited conversation but only to the tread of hundreds of pairs of feet hurrying to the nearest exit.

As the audience left, rather than amble off to their dressing rooms to discuss the night's performance the quintet of performers stood their ground, remaining in line behind the dropped curtain, staying there even as the safety curtain slowly descended and its final thump as it hit the stage announced the close of play. It was, for a few seconds, as if the players had become statues, as if molten lava had encased them, and they were doomed to stay as they were, for ever.

*　　*　　*

At home in Bexham Lionel sat in front of his television not really taking in anything, hoping only that his daughter and son-in-law were enjoying Max's musical revue as much as he had, while secretly dreading that they might not, and by not being able to do so would once again wound Max.

He did not want his grandson hurt, couldn't help it: what hurt Max hurt Lionel. He sighed, thinking of how much his late wife Maude would have loved the boy. Max and Maude would have been cracking together. He would probably have had to prevent Maude climbing up on stage to dance the Black Bottom or something with Max. Given her head Maude could be irrepressible. He stared ahead of him, not really concentrating.

And then suddenly – there it was.

There before him was film of the ship in which the world's fortunes were vested, a large but otherwise quite unremarkable freighter steaming slowly but remorselessly across the ocean, its deadly cargo all but out of sight, except – according to the news-reader – for what appeared on deck to be the nose cone of one ICBM protruding from its huge canvas covering. As Lionel sat watching these fateful images, he felt his blood run cold.

Mattie knew that John had really done his very best to enjoy Max's show, laughing whenever he found it remotely possible, but it was quite clear, even at the interval, that he was also profoundly shocked by it, and it wasn't difficult to see why. There were

48

sketches in it that made fun of the war, of the pathetic nature of civil defence, of boring vicars; indeed when the show wasn't making fun of everything that the Tates themselves happened to hold sacred, it was making fun of their whole way of life.

In John's defence even Mattie thought it rather shocking, most especially to anyone who had fought in the war, and lost their friends fighting the Nazis. And yet, another part of her thought that the new generation *must* be allowed to have a go at all that the middle-aged, middle-browed professed to hold dear, or else there really wasn't much point to being young. Surely *they* would have been just the same had there not been a war?

Certainly it was quite clear from their delighted expressions that all the rest of their party, while not understanding everything, had nevertheless determinedly enjoyed every minute, and the fact that they were now eagerly crowding backstage to congratulate Max made Mattie feel really quite proud. One thing was quite clear, to his mother anyway, no matter what John or the rest of the audience felt about the material in the show: Max had proved that he was really talented. He had been right to take the gamble and leave university early. This must prove to be an opportunity in a lifetime. As she walked round to the stage door Mattie made a mental note to tell him so, but then his dressing room was so crowded, she was finally swept away to meet the rest of the cast without having been able to say what she really felt. Only

Rusty's son, Tam Sykes, bringing up the rear, seemed able to express what he thought.

'Fantastic, Max. Really.' Tam shook Max by the hand. He was only seventeen, younger by quite a bit than Max, which meant that while they were all growing up in Bexham, Max had become Tam's total hero.

'I'm just so sorry you all came tonight.' Max's expression was doleful. 'It's gone so much better than tonight – but, you know, the Cuban crisis – it really hasn't helped one bit. Actually, apart from you lot, I really thought the audience was made up of corpses.'

'But they really enjoyed it, Max, really.'

Max stared at Tam in his dressing room mirror. 'You should have been here at the first night, really you should. It went like a bomb – I didn't say that.' He pulled a face, and as they both laughed they could hear the rest of the Bexham party calling in at the other dressing rooms, congratulating the rest of the cast.

'They loved it, Max, really.' Tam managed to look both earnest and protective of his older friend at the same time. 'Really, they did, they loved it.'

'You wouldn't have known it, not if you were on stage, Tam, really you wouldn't. I just wish you'd been here on another night.'

'They loved it, really they did. I'm telling you. Your mum bust a gut, I thought she'd be carried out, and so did Flavia, she laughed that much.'

'Sounded more like hysteria to me.' Max

towelled his face off, and stared at himself in the mirror.

'Look, Max, the man sitting next to me – I thought he'd be sick he laughed so much. It just took a bit longer for them, you know, for the penny to drop, because they're all so much older. The girls loved it, Kim and Jenny, they told you, didn't they? They laughed, and laughed, all the way through.'

'They were alone, my friend, quite alone.'

'I laughed.'

Tam was beginning to both look and sound desperate. He scratched his auburn-haired head and stared at Max in the mirror. God, he so admired Max, he didn't want him to think that none of them had enjoyed the show, that would be so *awful*. But he could see Max was looking unconvinced, pale, tired, taking down a clean shirt from his wardrobe while sporting a vest that looked as dejected as its owner.

'I really wanted you all to see the show at its best.'

'We did, really we did.'

Max shook his head. 'No, Tam, you didn't. If only you'd been here on the first night.'

'I was at school, we were all at school. We came as soon as we could, half term – we weren't allowed out for the first night. I asked our head of house, but there was no way we were going to be allowed out until half term.'

'You weren't alone, don't worry. Even my mother and John didn't bother to come to the first night.'

Tam dropped his eyes. He and Max had grown up together so he knew all too well of the ongoing battle for approval that Max had waged within his family, but younger though he was by three years, Tam had always sensed that Max would never, ever win that particular battle. Max's stepfather and mother were nice people, but everyone could see Jenny and Sholto would always come first with them, and Max second, because John and Mattie didn't share Max. Max had only ever been part of Mattie, the baby she'd had during the war, long before she'd married John Tate.

'Your mother was really ill with the flu, Max, really she was. I know she was, because my mum told me. For a moment, Farnsworth thought she was going to be a goner, she was that bad.'

Tam was improvising madly, and they both knew it, which was probably why Max was looking determinedly unconvinced.

'Yes, I heard. My grandfather told me.'

He said nothing more, but once again Tam sensed that if Max had chosen to go on to say something more it would have been *but even so, even if she did have flu she might at least have made an effort to come to the first night, flu or no flu.*

'Come on, let's go to the pub.'

'Can't – still under age.' Tam looked embarrassed. At seventeen he was so tall he knew he would pass as older, but his father would have a twin fit at just the thought of it. Nowadays, Peter Sykes was a respected member of Churchester

52

society. Tam owed it to him to behave, and he knew it.

'I'll get you in.'

'The parents would have a fit. Anyway, they're setting up a lot of wine and sandwiches at the Savoy. Come and join us, won't you?'

'No, really. I can't.'

'Please? Everyone's going to be there.'

'If only they'd been in last week.'

Out of the blue, Tam pulled his tie round so it lay across his back, after which he put his arm under his left leg, stretching his hand out to Max.

'I've been sent here, sir, to ask the President of the Bar Sinister Club to join us all at the hotel. My mum said specially to tell you. Won't be the same without you, really it won't.'

Tam always knew that finally he could get Max by going through their Sinister Club routine.

When he was growing up in Bexham Max had found out from Tam's mother that Tam, like Max, had been born, as the old people in the village still called it, *out of wedlock*. So as the old coats of arms proudly displayed a 'bar sinister' proclaiming royal bastardy, Max formed a club for two – the Bar Sinister Club. They would meet under the chestnut tree on the village green, and having exchanged strange and sinister handshakes they would go off to Max's house to eat toasted marshmallows – which never quite seemed to – and drink ginger beer laced with lager, which usually made Tam feel quite sick. Despite this, and also because of it, Tam had grown up hero-worshipping the older boy. They were as close to each other as it was possible to be, each feeling for the other in a way that Tam sometimes thought they might never feel for anyone in their own families. It was not just that they were both 'born bastards', as Max always loved to put it, seeming to relish the word, but also because they both seemed to look at the world in the same odd, upside down sort of fashion, loving to turn everything on its head, irreverence their creed.

'Come on then.' Seeing the acute disappointment hovering in Tam's eyes, of a sudden Max relented, knowing that he couldn't let him down. He put his arm round the younger boy's shoulders. 'Lead the way, if you must. After all, the world may not be here tomorrow.'

When they reached the alleyway outside the theatre, Tam rewarded Max with a beautifully executed cartwheel. Max watched him affectionately.

'Any more of that nonsense and you'll be joining the profession, my boy.'

They walked along together towards the Savoy.

'My dad would have a heart attack if I became an actor.'

Tam stared thoughtfully ahead. Max was lucky in that way. His father was a non-runner, having never showed at any point in his life, and his grandfather, like Tam's grandfather, more or less went along with anything that Max wanted, just so long as he didn't take the pants off him at golf too often.

'Your dad's made a great success of his cars. You'll go into cars like him, and have a ball,' Max prophesied. He smiled at Tam. 'You forget I remember you when you were driving better than Stirling Moss and you were all of ten, mate. You'll be winning the British Grand Prix by the time you're my age, see if you won't. Besides, someone like you, you don't want to be an actor.'

'I'd love to be an actor.'

'No, you wouldn't.'

'How do you know I wouldn't?'

They were outside the Savoy now, and Max turned to Tam.

'Because, dear boy,' he drawled, 'because you are, and always will be, Tam Sykes. You are you. It's only someone like me who has to become someone else, someone who doesn't know who he is.'

Max strode ahead of Tam, his head thrown back, his long dark hair lit of a sudden by the overhead lights of the hotel foyer.

'Someone who fears that they are really no one, that's who has to become an actor, Tam. We can play a king, or a duke, a poet or a prince, and in those hours we are them! What could be better? Nine to five in an office? Not on your nelly. I shall be who I want, when I want.'

Tam quickly followed his hero across the hotel foyer, hoping that by the time they found the rest of their party he might have twigged what the great Max was on about.

*   *   *

Flavia threw one last look in the becomingly pink mirror of the Savoy ladies' loo and then followed the rest of her party out of the doors into the hotel corridor. She was wearing a beautiful pink dress that Mattie had bought her, right out of the blue, that afternoon. It was silk, with a matching jacket, and it made her look so sophisticated that Flavia knew that the moment she walked up to Max Eastcott, and all the rest of them, they would not be able to take their eyes off her. The new shorter style of skirt was serving to make her already long legs look even longer, while the crisp cut of the boxy long-sleeved jacket showed off her nineteen-inch waist to such a flattering degree that it would make every man in the room long to put both their hands around it to see if they could span it.

'I am beautiful, I am beautiful, I am beautiful.'

Flavia always said that, silently of course, to herself as she walked along. She had read in a book that the exquisite Regency buck, Beau Brummell, never checked his clothes once his valet had finished dressing him. It seemed that the famous dandy had opined that once you left the hands of your valet you should never once check your dress, or glance in a looking glass. So now, as she walked across to the rest of her party determined not to glance in any mirror that she passed, Flavia gave herself social strength by silently reassuring herself of her beauty. Belief after all was everything. If she stopped believing that she was beautiful she might stop being beautiful, and that would be the end, because, as her father often teased her, she was certainly never going to have brains. 'Thick as a plank, our Flavia,' Peter would say proudly, to anyone who would listen. Thinking of this, Flavia tossed her auburn hair back, and thrust her hips forward in imitation of a top model.

'Hallo, Max.'

'Ah, Flah-viah!'

Flavia stared up at Max Eastcott, her face deliberately expressionless. What a pity he hadn't changed at all since he'd left Bexham for London, and her family'd left it for Churchester. He knew that Flavia always found her name embarrassing. It wasn't *her* fault that her mother had seen *The Prisoner of Zenda*, not once, but nine times.

She sighed loudly, tossing her hair back yet again. Max was quite obviously just the same as he'd been when they were all young, and he was always to be found sitting on the harbour wall, or on the village green, making fun of everyone and everything. So here he was again, still the same old Max Eastcott, waiting to squash Flavia by making fun of her name, just as he had been satirising everything on stage tonight.

'Actually, you were very good, Max,' Flavia told him in her cold, oddly mature way. 'Really, very good. Very funny.'

Max nodded. Holding a French cigarette between his teeth he lit it with a Zippo lighter while smiling back in an equally patronising way at Flavia.

'Oh, I was very good, was I, Flah-viah?'

'Yes.' She paused. 'You're really quite talented you know.'

'How would you know how talented I was?'

Flavia shrugged her shoulders. 'Because *boys* like you . . .' she allowed a cruel pause, before finishing, 'usually are, aren't they, Max?'

Once again Flavia tossed her beautiful auburn head of hair and moved away from him with the kind of smile that Max felt would have done credit to the Snow Queen. Happily at that precise moment John Tate arrived at his stepson's shoulder and pushed a glass of champagne into his hand.

'Well done, old chap.'

John was trying so hard to look enthusiastic that Max found himself feeling almost sorry for his stepfather.

'Did you really like it?'

'Yes, I really enjoyed it, Max, really.' John nodded vigorously.

'It was such a pity that you couldn't be at the first night. It went so well, the first night, it was un-believable.' Max stared past his stepfather, his expression sad to the point of misery. 'People were being taken out. The *Daily Mail* said that someone actually had a heart attack they laughed so much. It put – the laughter – it put something like ten or twelve minutes on the running time.'

John patted Max on the shoulder with his free hand.

'We both wanted to be at your first night, Max,

but you know what happened, don't you? Mummy told you, didn't she? I had the Scottish opening of the new shop, arranged months ago, and Mummy had really bad influenza.' John frowned, remembering how ill Mattie had been. 'Still, here we are now, and thoroughly enjoyed ourselves tonight, really we did.'

'Mmm, well, I'm glad you enjoyed it, because up there, for us, it was really, really hard work. The point is the audiences are so nervous – they can hardly bring themselves to even smile. You get the feeling they're just listening for the sirens, or something. But I have to say "Not With A Whimper" went better tonight than it has for a long while.'

Max stared into this stepfather's eyes, realising that the poor man was in such shock over what he had been put through that evening that he couldn't take in a word of what Max was saying. Worse than that, Max had the feeling that John wasn't even very interested in how well the show had gone on the first night, or indeed any other night. Max stubbed out his cigarette and promptly lit another as John nodded and smiled, but moved quickly away.

'Hanging, drawing and quartering's too good for you. Daddy's thinking of brand new things to do to someone who stands up and makes fun of everything he holds sacred, Max Eastcott.'

Max turned to see who it was, although suspecting already that it had to be Walter Tate's daughter Kim. Greatly daring she'd crept up behind Max and tapped him on the shoulder.

'You don't have to tell me. I saw your father's face, after the show. What about Judy? She feel the same?' Max took a deep draught of his wine, and stared so miserably at Kim that for the first time in her life she started to feel sorry for him.

'Not so much, no. Mummy just keeps saying it's difficult for the old folks to understand you making fun of the war, and all that – you know, because of losing all their friends, and so on.' Kim wriggled her feet in her new shoes, staring up at Max, who she always felt was almost a cousin, even though strictly speaking he wasn't really.

'We're not making fun of *the* war,' Max insisted. 'We're making fun of *war*, and the hypocrisies, and war films, and all that. That's what we're making fun of, not the people who died, or fought. No one in your family seems to understand that. It's just humour, ha, ha, ha, not a political statement for God's sake. Just meant to make people laugh, but no one seems to have twigged that.'

'I do.' Jenny, who now joined them, smiled up at Max. 'I thought it was wonderful,' she told him diffidently, because she always found that there was something about Max that was a little awe-inspiring. 'Really, really wonderful. I laughed till I cried.'

'Did you, did you really?'

Max's anxious expression reminded Jenny of young Sholto at the beginning of term when he was about to go back to school, trying to pretend to himself that everything was going to be all right.

'Yes, I did. Everyone did. Everyone from Bexham loved it, didn't they, Kim?'

Kim nodded. 'Yes, they did,' she agreed, her own expression serious for once. 'Everyone.'

Max was prepared to believe them both until he looked across the room and noted that his mother and stepfather were standing on their own looking nothing if not dismal.

'That's good,' he said abruptly, and once again he drank his glass of champagne far too quickly, not caring. Best to blot everything out and hope for the best, although he had very little of that particular commodity left in the locker. He squinted surreptitiously down at his watch. By now Maisie would be singing at the Place as she usually did after the show. If she was, he had a funny feeling he might just be in luck with her tonight. That after all, at the end of the famous day, was one helluva way to go, with Maisie wrapped around you.

Chapter Two

Waldo Astley was standing in front of Meggie's portrait, as he nearly always did late at night. It was over fourteen years since the love of his life had died in his arms. Despite the length of time that had passed between that terrible moment and the present, it was rare that a few hours elapsed when he didn't think of her and send news, and love, to his darling Meggie. She was as much with him as ever, and always would be, perhaps even more now. He tried to imagine how she would take the present crisis, the world faced with its own ending, and it seemed to him that she would be as courageous as she'd always been, hating to show fear, even should she be feeling it.

The ringing of the telephone interrupted the loving intensity of his thoughts. He quickly went to it, for despite the fact that he had no real family or dependants the sound of a telephone ringing late at night was always worrying.

'Waldo?'

'Lionel.'

'Can I come round?' Lionel sounded vague and uncertain as if he didn't quite know why he was ringing, and at the same time embarrassed that he was disturbing Waldo so late.

'Can't sleep?'

'No, I can't.'

'I can't, either. Come round, do.'

Waldo replaced the telephone. The Cuban crisis, the idea of the world *teetering* on the edge of nuclear war, as the newspapers kept describing it, must be much worse for his old friend Lionel, for unlike Waldo he must fear terribly for his daughter Mattie, and his grandson, Max.

'Jolly decent of you, old chap. I'm feeling a bit wobbly, on my own, I don't know why.'

Lionel touched his thin white moustache lightly as Waldo put an arm round the old man's shoulder and shepherded him into the drawing room.

'Come and be wobbly with me, Lionel, over a whisky and soda.'

All at once, standing in Waldo's drawing room with its beautiful furnishings, its silk wallpaper and pale eau-de-Nil curtains, its cerise brocade Knole sofa, and velvet buttoned chairs, and last but not least its beautiful, posthumous portrait of Meggie Gore-Stewart, Waldo's wife of only a few days, or was it hours – Lionel couldn't quite remember – was like stepping into heaven.

Everything in the room was so beautiful and inviting, it made him catch his breath. The fire burning brightly, despite its being nearly midnight when most people's fires would be out, the cut glass decanters, the Irish Waterford crystal whisky glass that Waldo was putting into Lionel's hand – everything, every damn thing in that room, including Waldo, was a reason for living, and not dying, a reason for loving the world, not hating it so much you couldn't wait to destroy it.

'Cheers.' Lionel raised his glass. 'Awfully good of you to have me round. I must admit I was beginning to feel a bit odd on my own.'

'Been listening or watching for the news?'

'Both,' Lionel admitted. 'Just can't sleep,' he added rather unnecessarily.

'I keep wondering when, in the whole history of mankind, this has happened before, and I can't remember a single instance. I mean we all thought Hiroshima was a one off, didn't we?' Waldo frowned vaguely up at the ceiling as Lionel stared into his whisky glass.

'The way I see it, it's quite possible that one or other of these politicos will make a mistake. Didn't someone say that the last time the famous red telephone rang in the President's Oval office he picked it up and it was a Chinese laundry?'

'That wasn't someone, Lionel, that was me.'

'Oh, yes, it was you, of course it was you, Waldo. You're one of the few people who tells me anything interesting – you, and young Max. Everyone else talks down to me, I don't know why. I get fed up with it sometimes, really I do.'

Waldo decided to ignore this, instead staring up

once again at Meggie's portrait over the fireplace.

'Do you remember how wonderful Meggie's laugh was, Lionel?'

'What did you say?'

Waldo knew that nowadays Lionel always pretended not to hear something he thought might be upsetting.

'I said—' Waldo smiled, knowing exactly. 'I said – do you remember how wonderful Meggie's laugh was?' He went back to staring up at the portrait. 'She had a wonderful, wonderful laugh, didn't she?'

Now Lionel too looked up at the painting of Meggie. She had been so beautiful, and so brave, and for once he could honestly say that the portrait actually did justice to the sitter. The artist had depicted Meggie staring out at the rest of the world with more than a hint of amusement in her large blue eyes, one hand resting on a model of the racing yacht she'd loved so much – the aptly named *Lightheart*.

'She did have a wonderful laugh,' Lionel agreed. 'So full of gaiety.'

But after staring up at the painting for a good minute he suddenly burst into tears.

'I'm so sorry, really, so sorry,' he said, quickly putting his glass down on a side table, and taking out an immaculate silk handkerchief to dry his eyes. 'Really, I am so sorry. I used to be better than this. It's just that I can't bear to think of all the young not having a go at life. I'm so afraid of them being taken early like poor Meggie. Whatever's happened to us, at least we've been given a chance to take a pot shot at living.' He wiped his eyes on his handkerchief, and shook his head. 'It's all so dreadful, really it is.'

'Refill needed.' Waldo leaned forward and picking up Lionel's glass he went to the drinks table to refresh both their drinks. 'Here's to tomorrow.' He raised his glass encouragingly once more, as Lionel shook his head.

'I'm sorry, Waldo old chap, I think I must've been listening to the news too much.'

'We've all been listening to the news too much.'

'Worrying times—'

'They are indeed.'

They both drank deeply.

'Heard anything on your American grapevine, old boy?'

'Nothing except there's a vast increase in the sale of fall-out shelters, and a large number of people have disappeared into caves, which I think sounds quite sensible really. I think I might hide in a cave somewhere round here, if they weren't all water-logged.'

'It's coming up to twelve o'clock – shall we?' Lionel's eyes switched mournfully towards the large mahogany radio set in the corner of the room.

'Why not?' Waldo stood up. 'After all, we're still alive; Bexham's still here, so that must mean some-thing. Not only that, but there's always the risk we might hear some good news.'

But there was none. The Russian convoy carrying nuclear warheads had not turned back. Indeed far from turning back it seemed they were still set securely en route for Cuba. The only hopeful news was that while neither Kennedy nor Khrushchev had made a move towards conciliation, they had not made one of aggression either.

'It's not quite stalemate, at least not yet, I wouldn't have thought.' Waldo's darkly handsome, middle-aged face looked across at his old bridge-playing partner.

'No, it's not stalemate,' Lionel agreed. 'But there's still no sign of Russia backing down, and if she was going to, I would have thought that she would have done so by now. Kipling said that the Russians are a wonderful people – until they take off their jackets.'

'I would hate to be Kennedy. Russia is not bullied. Remember Churchill said the only man who ever succeeded in frightening him was Stalin.'

Waldo paused for a moment, thinking this statement over, while at the same time lighting a large cigar.

'Do you know something, Lionel? You've actually cheered me up.' As Lionel said nothing in reply to this, he went on, 'I'm now going to go to sleep tonight thanking God that at least it's not Kennedy versus *Stalin*. It may be clutching at straws but that at least is something.'

Soon after that, both cheered and comforted by his old friend, Lionel took his leave of Cucklington

House and walked home alone. Since giving way to his emotions in front of Waldo, it seemed to him that he had at last discovered just what kind of an old fool he actually was. No wonder John and Mattie were always talking down to him as if he was a child of nine. He must have really embarrassed Waldo giving way like that. He hoped he hadn't, but he was sure he probably had. He put his front door key in the lock of his house, finding that as soon as he did so the telephone was ringing. This time it was Waldo telephoning to him.

'I've just heard from a friend in America – they think the convoy's turning back. They think Khrushchev might be climbing down. No one can believe it, but they think the Russian ships are turning back.' His voice sounded so excited and boyish that Lionel was quite tempted to go straight back round to Cucklington House again, but he was stopped by the sight of his old spaniel waiting to be taken out.

'If only it was true, eh?' he told the old dog. 'What we two old boys wouldn't give for it to be true, eh?'

After which he walked into the garden, ending the evening staring up at the night sky, hoping, wishing with all his being, that it might be.

As it turned out it was true. At the eleventh hour the Russians had a change of heart. Kennedy never dropped his eyes and so finally Khrushchev took his finger off the button.

And the world breathed again.

Max sat halfway down the bed, the sheet pulled up over his knees, smoking a cigarette and watching the television he had pulled into view in the corner of the bedroom. They were running a special news bulletin on the Cuba crisis, and as far as he could gather there was now no doubt in anyone's mind that the heat was off.

'For the time being,' Max muttered, squashing his smoke out in the top of an old coffee jar.

'What's up?' a sleepy cockney voice said from the other side of the bed. 'We all still 'ere, then?'

'It would appear so.' Max stretched his arms above his head. 'Dear old Nikita turned his boats back at the last throw of the dice.'

'Wasn't *that* close, surely?' Maisie wondered, now making a somewhat dishevelled appearance from under the bedclothes. 'Come on, he was only bluffing, surely?'

Two worried, mascara-smudged eyes blinked at Max. To reassure her Max leaned forward and kissed her lightly on the cheek, wondering as he did whether he would have found himself waking up in her bed if the world hadn't been teetering on the verge of extinction the night before and deciding that the answer would definitely be in the negative.

'Coffee?' Max slid out from between the sheets, pulling the counterpane off the bed for cover.

'No, thanks – champagne.'

Max turned and raised one lazy eyebrow at her.

'I put it in the fridge last night, love. Time to

celebrate, innit? No need for Joe to sleep in the basement with his bottle of Jack Daniel's, audiences are going to laugh again without us having to put a stick of dynamite up 'em, and best of all – no need for you to take me to bed in case it's your very last chance to make love, ever. Now if that's not a reason to celebrate with a bottle of shampoo, what is?'

Maisie squinted up at Max from the sea of pillows upon which she had draped herself, and they both laughed.

'Don't you take anything seriously, mate?'

'Nah.' Maisie rolled over on to her front. 'Would I be an actress if I did?'

Max hooted with laughter, and went to fetch Maisie's champagne, and two glasses, and what with one thing and another their breakfast turned into quite a celebration.

The mood was considerably more sombre round the lunch table at John and Mattie Tate's house overlooking the estuary at Bexham, John, like his younger brother Walter, still being obsessed with the idea that Max and his fellow thespians in the cast of the musical revue had deliberately set themselves up to destroy everything that his stepfather held dear.

'Is nothing sacred? Everything decent that we fought for, everything – they made fun of in skit after skit. I simply don't understand it, really I don't. Nothing positive, nothing constructive, they've just set about tearing down the world we fought to save, and what have they put in its place? Nothing, absolutely nothing.'

Lionel, who was doing his best to enjoy Mattie's cooking, sighed inwardly at his son-in-law's statement, while keeping his eyes fixed steadily on his plate.

One of the great problems of getting older was having to sit on your tongue in front of younger people. When he remembered how irreverent John and Mattie's generation had been during the war – the jokes, the wild behaviour – it was ludicrous to pull a face because Max's generation were having a bit of a go at their elders and far-from-betters.

'Point is, John,' Lionel said after allowing a few seconds to pass. 'Point is, that's what we fought the war for, at least that was how I've always understood it.'

His son-in-law stared at him and the words 'Et tu Brute?' came into Lionel's mind as he did so. Nevertheless Lionel persisted with his thought. He had to; to do otherwise would be to fail in his duty to the young.

'We fought the war, both world wars, precisely so that young people like Max could grow up in a world where they could have a bit of a go. Imagine a world where you could be arrested for making a joke, or putting a skit on the stage, or daring to disagree with some politico. I mean, that's what winning the war was all about, I should have thought. It was all about freedom of speech, and

71

doing skits about your elders' obsessions. Surely that's why we had to flatten the Nazis, so that our young people could do that, grow up with that kind of freedom? I understand that no Nazi was ever found to have a sense of humour, and still can't be, and that is for certain.'

'I think Daddy's got a point, John.' Mattie picked the plum crumble out of the serving hatch where her Spanish au pair had placed it and put it on the sideboard.

'It's all so destructive,' John moaned, not taking any notice of either of them, wallowing in self-pity for his generation obviously being the order of the day. 'Anyway, it's not just me who found it far too much. I understand Walter had a fit, apparently.'

'Apparently, as I understand it, it doesn't take much to give your darling brother Walter a fit nowadays, John.' Mattie bossed her eyes comically behind John's back to make her father laugh, at which Lionel immediately dropped his own, afraid of laughing at her in front of John.

Although he didn't see Mattie perhaps John felt what his wife was doing, because he suddenly stood up abruptly, and putting his napkin in the middle of his pudding plate prepared to leave the room.

'No pudding for me, thank you, Mattie. See you at the pub tonight, Lionel. There's going to be a helluva darts game on – Bexham versus Littleton. We need you to cheer us on, and that's an order.'

He smiled sadly round at them both before leaving the dining room to Mattie and Lionel, who, if the truth were known, were more than thankful that they could finish their lunch without him.

'Don't take any notice of him, Daddy.' Mattie sighed. 'He's in one of his older-man-respectable-person moods. I keep waiting for him to start everything he says with "young people nowadays". Honestly, what happens to us when we get older? We all get so pompous, forget all about the wild and woolly things that we used to be.'

'Yes, I agree, we do get pompous.' Lionel nodded, relishing his plum crumble, wiping his moustache appreciatively between mouthfuls. 'War or no war, you were all quite as dotty as Max and his lot. It's just that John's quite blanked out all the fun you had – despite the war – just blanked it out of his memory. He only remembers the sacrifices, the pain, and I understand that, but he must also remember what it was all *for*. Freedom of speech, freedom and democracy, so that young men like Max can act up a bit, and pull everyone's legs about war films and so on.'

Mattie smiled. 'Yes, we *were* all a bit mad, weren't we? Jitterbugging and heaven only knows what, despite everything. But I'm not a Tate, Daddy, I'm an Eastcott. John's a Tate, and the Tates were all born a tiny bit on the stuffy side, bless them. I'm dreadfully afraid Max takes after me, poor love.'

*   *   *

The following morning Jenny stared into the large, old-fashioned bath. Mattie had not only thoughtfully removed the spider from it, placing it outside the window, but she had also drawn the water for Jenny, as was her careful maternal custom – all six inches of it.

Not only that but she had laid out Jenny's towel for her, a much-mended affair with a great deal of tape stitched round the edges, which Jenny now held up in front of her. Crikey! It must be about nine hundred years old. She climbed into the few inches of water thinking that even at boarding school they were allowed deeper baths. Downstairs she knew her parents were still talking about Max Eastcott and the satirical revue. Sholto and she had adored it, but their dad had hated it.

All the way home in the car after the show her father'd gone on and on about knocking the values for which people had fought and died in the war, until a really fed-up Sholto had slid down his seat and, well out of sight of their parents, blocked his ears.

'I don't care what they say, I *liked* it,' he'd hissed at Jenny when they parted at their bedroom doors late that night.

Jenny stared at the old chrome bath taps with their black Victorian writing remembering Sholto's suppressed indignation. She'd felt exactly the same as Sholt. After all, Max's show was meant to make people laugh. And it *had* made all of them laugh, all the young from Bexham, even Flavia Sykes who was never really interested in anything except how she looked, even Flave had killed herself laughing at some of the sketches.

'They've talked more about it – more even than Cuba – do you know that?' Jenny told Kim when they met on the village green the following lunchtime. 'I mean the world's about to end and all they seem to be worried about is Max's sketch about war films. Honestly.'

'Who?' Kim was too busy staring across at Tam Sykes to pay much attention to Jenny.

'My parents. They just haven't stopped going on about Max's revue letting down the side, knocking the war, and all that.'

Kim quickly turned and looked at Jenny with utter, concentrated fascination.

'I know, mine were the same,' she said, flicking back her dark hair and giving Jenny a deeply sympathetic look. 'They all think Max has let the side down, which is just plum stupid. Why shouldn't he make fun of the war in his show? It's been over long enough, although you really wouldn't think so the way they all go on about it still. And I mean my parents . . .' She sighed. 'They still toast bread with mildew on it, and water down the milk. I keep trying to tell them – *the war is over!* You should have seen *my* bath water this morning.' She held up her hand, and narrowed two of her fingers. 'Half an inch. Hardly covered my big toe.'

'Really? Mine was just the same. It's pathetic, really. I mean, how long since the war stopped, seventeen years? Really, you'd think they would have put it behind them by now, wouldn't you?' Jenny was pleased. It wasn't like Kim to even listen to anything she said, let alone carry on an intelligent conversation with her. She soon saw the reason for the change, though, when Tam Sykes, dressed in a black and green striped shirt with brass buttons, his hair flicked back in the newest American style, arrived at Kim's elbow.

'Want to come for a spin?' he asked Kim.

Kim tossed her hair back. 'Dunno, really. Don't think so.'

'Why not?'

'You know why not, Tam,' Jenny put in, frowning. Frowning at Tam Sykes was actually a hobby of hers, he was just such a goer, thought far too much of himself, in her opinion.

'No, I don't.' Tam assumed an innocent expression.

'Because you haven't passed your test, Tam Sykes, and you shouldn't be driving on your own until you do, you know that.'

'It's not against the law.'

'The way you drive, it should be against the law.' Jenny hooked her long, blond hair back behind her ears, and swung her legs in front of her, kicking the back of the wall they were sitting on as she did so.

'My parents let me drive where I want on my own, it's all right in fields and things, it's not against the law, Jenny Tate.'

'Just because your parents let you, doesn't mean ours *would*.'

Jenny stood up, but Kim didn't. Instead she turned and looked at Tam.

'OK. I'll come,' she said, with yet another toss of her dark hair. She turned to Jenny. 'You can tell my parents that I've gone for a walk, sketching or something, if you don't want to come.'

'No, I don't want to come.'

'Well then – stay behind.' She walked a few paces and then turned and said softly, 'Chicken.'

'I'm not chicken, I just think it's wrong.'

Kim was following Tam across the green. Reluctantly Jenny found herself following them both. She didn't know why but she always felt responsible for Kim. OK, they were only cousins, but being brought up in Bexham and being so close in age, they were more like sisters, really.

As she trailed slowly and reluctantly after the other two, Jenny found herself wishing that half term was over, that she was back at school with her books and her music, most of all that her reckless cousin Kim was someone else's blasted responsibility.

Kim turned and grinned down at Jenny as she climbed over the stile into the field towards which Tam and she had been heading.

'I say, we'll be able to boast about this when we get back to school, won't we?'

Jenny's eyes drifted past Kim's mischievous face towards what lay in the field beyond them. It might be old, but she knew just from looking at it that it must be fast. It was a two-seater sports special with bright red painted mudguards, and it was waiting for them on a dirt track cut in the field.

'You can't go in that, Kim, not with Tam Sykes, Kim, you can't, really. It looks as if it's been put together with cardboard and string. You can't go in it, your mum would have a fit, really she would. Aunt Judy would have a complete fit.'

'Why ever not?' Kim protested, but she eyed the little car nervously.

'Anyway, Tam probably doesn't even know how to drive it.' Jenny caught at Kim's arm, but Kim shook her off.

'Course I know how to drive it!' Tam protested crossly, overhearing her. 'Why do you think it's here? Not just to look at, you bet. Besides, I'm going to be a racing driver. My dad's going to be my manager, I'm going to be as big as Stirling Moss. I'm going to be the best.' He looked proudly from one face to the other. Jenny frowned.

'Where did you get it, Tam?'

'I didn't get it. I've borrowed it. My old man bought this field, see.' Tam looked proudly round the large grassy area. 'My dad's making a track round here for me to practise, see?' He pointed out the beginnings of the track around the field. 'He's building a couple of dirt trackers at the moment. Now they're *really* hairy.'

'So what's this?' Jenny demanded. 'It's not exactly built for weddings and funerals, Tam Sykes.'

'It's for hill climbs really. We're going to use it for speed tests and hill climbs.'

'It looks pretty fragile, and it's so low on the ground. Are you sure it's all right to go in?' Kim stepped back. 'I don't think I fancy going in that, actually, Tam, not one bit. It's not like a normal car.'

'Course it is! It goes fifty, I swear.'

'Fifty in that thing?' Kim backed right off down the field. 'You can keep your speeding tea tray, Tam Sykes, thanks all the same.'

'Now who's chicken?' Tam called after her. 'Tell you what, just to show you how safe it is, I'll take Jenny in it.'

'Oh no you won't,' Jenny protested, and she too backed off down the field. 'I'm not going in that thing. Not with you driving.'

'Well you drive it, then.'

'Don't be silly.'

'I promise I won't go over forty.'

'Thirty.'

'Thirty-five. Any slower and we'll be pushing it ourselves,' Tam protested, obviously in his element. 'It's OK, really it is. It's private land, I can drive here. Dad wouldn't let me otherwise, really.'

Jenny looked from Kim to the car and then back again to Tam, trying not to show her anxiety.

'Promise me you won't go over thirty, Tam?'

'I promise. I just want to show Kim how well the little car goes, that's all.'

Tam's eyes were dancing with mischief. He longed, as always, for Kim's admiration, longed for

79

her to see him as a bit of a hero, a bit of a lad, not just old Tam Sykes, the garage owner's son, no one much, not as smart as Kim, not as classy.

'OK, so long as you don't go over thirty.'

Jenny didn't want to get in one bit, but she wanted to show Kim that she truly wasn't chicken. Out of the two Tate cousins Kim had always been a bit of a daredevil, Jenny the more gentle and bookish one.

'OK. Hop in.' Tam opened the car door, and Jenny climbed in feeling sick to her stomach, grabbing hold of the side door with one hand and under the seat with the other.

'Wagons roll!' Tam shouted as he engaged gear, and he waved back at Kim.

Jenny too turned back and waved, letting go of the seat for a second before grabbing it again. Seconds later Tam accelerated away, but not at thirty, not at thirty-five, but at forty-five, nearing fifty. Jenny had embarked on the shortest of journeys, but it was one that would change her life for ever.

Loopy was enjoying Hugh playing 'Blue Room' to her, so much so that she hardly heard Waldo coming into the sitting room.

'Isn't that the best?'

Waldo had managed to slip in unannounced by Gwen, who nowadays always seemed to be too busy watching a quiz show on television to hear the front doorbell.

'Oh, Waldo, darling. You let yourself in. Good man. I'm so glad.' Loopy kissed Waldo affectionately on both cheeks and stood back from him, still holding his hands tightly, while Hugh called greetings from the piano.

'Have you heard the news?' she went on, shaking both their hands up and down to emphasise her excitement. 'The convoys are on their way home and the Russians are dismantling the sites!'

'Isn't that the best?'

'Do you know, this time I really thought we might have had it, really, I did. I just couldn't see a way out.' Loopy let go Waldo's hands and drifted towards the drinks table. 'Whisky sour?' She started to make it, watched intently by her newly arrived guest. 'Really, I thought we had well and truly *had* it. And so bad for the young, growing up thinking all the time that there's no point to anything when the world is about to blow up. So difficult to explain that each day is for living, the same as it's always been.'

'Not being a father I have escaped that problem.' Waldo sighed without sadness. 'But I do know one thing, Loopy, no one makes a whisky sour like you, do you know that?' Waldo sighed again, this time with satisfaction. 'Do you think it's because, just might be, because you're American, maybe?'

'Just might be, darlin'. Or,' Loopy handed him the freshly made drink, 'maybe you have to be an American to know how to enjoy it?'

Their feelings of relief at the good news was such

81

that they both laughed more heartily than the remark deserved.

'God, it's just wonderful to be able to laugh, or have a drink, without feeling guilty, do you know that?'

'It's a moral victory for all time.'

'You're right, Waldo, it is.' She indicated for him to sit down, just as the telephone in the hall started to ring. 'I'm sorry, I won't be a minute.'

Waldo watched her going to answer the old, black Bakelite telephone, which must have been put in when the house was built. Despite her age, everything about Loopy was still elegant, still easy on the eye, but more than that, she was just about the kindest person around. An instance of this was that she regularly asked Waldo round to dinner once a week when she knew his maid was off – to save him having the bother of cooking for himself.

He was just beginning to feel pleasantly relaxed, talking to Hugh, laughing with him about his next choice of number, when they both overheard Loopy saying, more loudly, 'Oh, dear God, no. No, no, of course. I'll come at once.'

She came back into the room again, her face pale with disbelief.

'What's the matter? Not bad news, I hope—'

Even as he finished speaking Waldo could not help wondering why there wasn't a better way of expressing anxiety to someone. It was so obvious that the news Loopy had just received was bad, if it wasn't she would not be looking as she was, her face having gone from sparkling happiness to complete shock.

She went straight up to Hugh, and touched him on the arm.

'It's Jenny, Hugh. She's had a car accident. She's going to be all right, just a few broken bones and so on. But I must go at once. She's in Churchester General. Oh, poor Mattie and John, how simply terrible for them.'

Hugh stood up, his own face now paling. Loopy looked up at him, all concern. Although Hugh never said as much, Jenny had always been his favourite grandchild, probably because she was the most like him. They shared the same sense of humour and love of music, and naturally – since Jenny had grown up in Bexham – they were both dotty about sailing. On top of which it always seemed to Loopy that Jenny had inherited Hugh's admirable intransigence, as well as his cautious nature.

'I'm coming—' Hugh braced himself, clearing his throat.

Loopy stopped him.

'No,' she said firmly, putting a hand on his shoulder. 'There's no point in us both going. You stay here with Waldo, Hugh. I'll ring you as soon as I have any news.'

'I'll drive you—'

'I don't want to be rude, darling, but after two whiskies – I'd really rather drive myself.'

'Understood. You drive then.'

'No, no, I will. I've hardly touched my drink.' Waldo stepped forward, taking his car keys out of his pocket, and putting his glass down.

They all caught up their winter coats from the downstairs cloakroom and made their way quickly to Waldo's magnificent old Bentley. As they hurried towards the car Loopy began to explain the nature of the crisis. It seemed that Tam Sykes had been driving one of his father's cars in a field, and had crashed. On hearing this, it was Waldo's turn for his heart to sink. Tam was almost like a son to him. Quite apart from his great affection for the boy, Waldo'd been in business with Tam's father for years.

'I kept trying to tell Peter that the boy was too young to be mucking about on his own with those motorised tin trays of his,' he muttered to Hugh, once they were driving out on to the road and towards the hospital. 'Just because he's in a field might make him legal, but it doesn't stop him from being dangerous.'

All the way to Churchester, staring out of the back window in a numbed silent way, Loopy tried not to imagine what she would find when she reached the hospital. To stop her imagination taking off in all the wrong directions she asked Waldo to put the radio on, only to find it was playing a song that Jenny had always loved to sing to her grandfather's playing. *It's a lovely day today. . .*

* * *

The first person they saw when they'd managed to find the correct ward was Mattie standing at a window where the corridor gave way to the doors of the ward. Loopy went up to her at once, knowing what an agony she must be in.

'Mattie.'

She hugged her. As she did so she could feel the tension in her daughter-in-law's body, and immediately feared the worst.

'The doctor's in with the surgeon. They've done their best but it's much, much worse than we all thought. She's alive, but—'

Loopy's heart sank as she heard the pallid, grey, hopeless words. 'But?'

'It will be months before she's better, or even out of hospital.'

'But she *will* live?'

'Oh, she'll live all right.' Mattie shot a look at Waldo. 'She'll live all right, but not thanks to Tam Sykes!'

Loopy stepped back. 'How do you mean?'

'You *know* Peter Sykes's one ambition is to have Tam become the next Stirling Moss? He's spent the last God knows how long busying himself making a racing track round Bottom Field, if you please, and breathing on a lot of old bangers for the wretched boy to drive.'

'No—'

'Oh yes! So what must he do, he persuades Kim and Jenny to go along with him – I don't know why – and he lost control, and crashed. He walked away unscathed – and if it hadn't been for the motorist that Kim flagged down I actually don't think Jenny would have even survived.'

'I don't understand what Jenny was doing in the car,' Loopy muttered, sounding vague even to herself. 'Jenny doesn't like cars.'

Tears appeared in Mattie's eyes. It was true. Her gentle bookish Jenny didn't like things like fast cars at all. She liked music, and sailing. Seeing her distress Waldo stepped forward.

'So what happened?' he asked carefully. 'Did Tam hit something?'

Mattie eyed him carefully, wiping the fresh tears from her face with her handkerchief before replying.

'Kim said he just appeared to lose control. One minute they were speeding round this wretched makeshift racetrack and the next the car headed for the trees. Jenny. Jenny . . .' She stopped and took a deep breath before continuing. 'Jenny was thrown forward through the windscreen, and then out of the car altogether.'

'I'm so sorry.'

Mattie stared up at Waldo.

'What is the point of that?' she asked flatly, but before Waldo could say anything her eyes drifted past his and Loopy's faces to the entrance to the outpatients' area.

'What's she doing here?' she muttered, turning away. 'How could she even come?'

Loopy turned, and seeing who it was she murmured to Waldo, 'Take Mattie away, would you? Take her over to the window.'

She herself walked over to greet a white-faced Rusty Sykes.

'Tell her to go away! Leave us alone, won't you?' Mattie was still muttering as Waldo dutifully led her towards the window, where they stood sparely staring out at nothing more than a cluster of hospital buildings. 'Her and her bloody family, it's all their fault!'

'I had to come—'

Rusty's whole body emanated misery as she stood tying and untying the knot in her headscarf. She seemed so deathly frightened that Loopy thought she might actually pass out.

'I've tried to stay away, but the waiting was such agony, and the hospital wouldn't tell us anything, seeing we're not family.'

'She's going to live, Rusty dear, she will live.' As she heard her voice asserting that Jenny was going to survive Loopy couldn't help thinking *but in what fashion?* before she went on, 'It's just going to take an awful long time to mend her, that's all. She's not going to die.' She touched Rusty lightly on the arm as she finished speaking.

'I kept warning Peter that Tam was too young to be allowed to drive those stupid cars on his own,' Rusty said, in a sad, weary voice. 'I kept telling him, over and over again. Tam's only seventeen, however brilliant his driving, he's still only seventeen. But you know men, listening isn't something they do a great deal, is it?'

'It was very good of you to come.' Fearing that Mattie might come over and make a scene Loopy quickly took Rusty's arm and turning her round marched her back through the double doors and down the corridors to the car park. 'I know that Jenny, and John, of course, will appreciate that you came, but as you may imagine Mattie's a bit overwrought at the moment. It's understandable.'

'I feel so terrible, you've no idea. I keep feeling if only I'd stood up to Peter. If only I'd made sure that Tam never went out on his own, unsupervised like that.'

Rusty's voice was flat and dulled and she kept tugging at her scarf as they walked along, pulling the knot up on her chin, and then back under it, time and time again.

'It's not your fault. Really, it's young people. They never think it's going to happen to them, until it does. We're all the same when we're young, it just never occurs to us that we could kill overselves in a matter of seconds, doing something not just stupid, but quite unnecessary.'

Even as they mouthed the usual platitudes at each other they both knew that possibly the worst aspect of the accident was that young Jenny was the last person to do anything dangerous. Jenny was the last one to want to be driven like a bat out of hell. It would never be something that she'd want to do. Driving in an old banger round a field would be Kim, not Jenny Tate's idea of fun. Kim had always been the daredevil, always falling off ponies, or out of boats. She was the goer, gentle Jenny the bookish, musical one.

Rusty turned towards her car, her body sunk into hopelessness. 'For this to happen to Jenny of all people.' Her voice tailed off, and she stood by her car with the keys swinging from their silver ring, reluctant to climb into it in front of Loopy, as if she feared that by doing so she would remind Loopy of the accident.

Loopy patted Rusty quickly on the arm and turned on her heel and left her, but just as she did so it seemed to her that she heard a sound which was something between a sigh and a sob, and following that the noise of a car starting up, which in the quiet of a Sussex town seemed strangely violent.

'What did *she* think she was doing here?' Mattie's mouth was a thin line of fury.

'I know, I know, she shouldn't have come, but she feels terrible, Mattie.' Loopy put a protective arm round her daughter-in-law.

'If I thought it would do any good I would go to the Sykeses' house and tell them what I think of them.' Mattie sank down suddenly on one of the side benches. She looked up at Loopy, and said in a much lowered voice, 'It's her face, Loopy. Jenny's pretty little face, it's smashed to pieces.'

Mattie was still sitting down, her head held in her hands, when the doctor came through. She immediately stood up, wiping her hands down the skirt of her suit as a cook might wipe her hands on her apron, her eyes staring fixedly at the young doctor, as if trying to learn something from his expression before he even opened his mouth.

'I'm Dr Rankin, Mrs Tate. I've just come from the recovery room where I was talking to Mr Barton, the surgeon. I'm afraid Jenny's injuries, while not life threatening, are nevertheless very serious. Cosmetically more than anything.'

Loopy turned to Hugh, instinctively sensing the despair, while Mattie just stared blankly at the doctor. John had gone up north the day before to visit the new factory, but he was driving down as fast as he could. He would be with her by midnight, but until then she had to cope, she must cope.

'Jenny has sustained deep cuts and lacerations to both cheeks, her upper lip and her nose. She has also broken a cheekbone and her nose, and there's a hairline fracture to her jaw. But by some miracle the glass missed both eyes entirely, for which, I think you will agree, we must all be very grateful. As you doubtless know, the problem with glass injuries is that you are injured twice. First you fall through the glass, sustaining one set of injuries, and then you come back, once again through the glass, suffering a second set. That is why car accidents are so lethal. Mr Barton has however managed to removed all the glass shards and splinters and has done a good job on the wounds, but I'm afraid an initial assessment of the injuries tells us that there's going to be some pretty serious scarring.'

There was a long silence, so long that Waldo, realising the shock waves with which he was surrounded, felt he must break it.

'Plastic surgery is wearing seven league boots nowadays, I believe. Surely there's every chance that Jenny's face can be repaired?'

'Of course,' Luke Rankin agreed. 'But it will take time. A great deal of time. However, she has been a very lucky girl, of that there is no doubt. The very fact that Mr Barton happened to be at the hospital when he was, in itself, was very fortunate. There are few better than he, in my opinion.'

'You're too kind.' The surgeon now appeared at Dr Rankin's side, and proceeded to explain in some depth the exact procedure that he envisaged would be necessary before plastic surgery would be effective.

'Most importantly,' he finished, speaking in a lowered tone to Mattie, 'Jenny herself must be handled with kid gloves. We don't have to emphasise why. Looking in the mirror is going to be a daily trauma for her, until such time as she can be treated cosmetically. It will be a daily battle to keep depression at bay.' He fell silent, staring round at the small family group.

'Thank you so much, Mr Barton.' Hugh stepped forward, shook his hand and, nodding curtly to Loopy and Waldo, turned to Mattie.

'If you don't mind we'll leave you to wait for John and your father, Mattie.'

He beckoned to Waldo to follow him as if he was a junior officer, and Waldo, taking his cue, kissed Mattie gently on the cheek, as they all did, before making their way miserably back to the car park.

'I don't think I shall ever get over this,' Hugh announced as he buttoned up his overcoat and slid into the front passenger seat. 'I shall never forgive those wretched Sykeses, not ever. Not to my dying day.' He shut the car door abruptly.

Loopy and Waldo stared at each other briefly, before opening their own doors.

'He doesn't mean it,' Loopy whispered. 'He really doesn't.'

But Waldo, knowing Hugh of old, from the days when he'd happily sent Waldo on dangerous government missions to Berlin, risking life and limb in the interests of world democracy, sensed at once that Hugh meant every word.

Tam's grandfather, Mr Todd, was standing facing Tam and Peter Sykes.

'Waldo's right, you'll have to leave the area for a while, Tam, there's nothing else you can do,' the old man told his grandson sadly. 'There's so much to the accident, so many sides to it, you can't stay on here at the moment, not when feelings in Bexham are running so high. The Tates are such a popular family. Always have been.'

'He hasn't murdered anyone – Tam hasn't committed a murder.'

'That's not the point. It's a scandal. The boy'll suffer.'

Mr Todd shook his head at his son-in-law.

'I know Bexham as well as you know Bexham, Father-in-law,' Peter stated. 'And all right we don't live here any more, but I still don't believe it's necessary for Tam to be sent away.'

'Begging your pardon, you don't know Bexham any more, Peter, and that's the truth, and more's the pity, in my opinion. You had to go grand and buy Tam here big boys' toys he'd no business to be playing with, not to the mind of this old man. If it'd been a sailing boat he'd been in, young Jenny Tate would not be lying in Churchester General. No, she wouldn't, and if there's any more to be said on the matter, it's me that's going to have the saying of it.'

Despite this outburst, Peter remained looking recalcitrant and unconvinced.

'The accident happened in Bottom Field,' his father-in-law continued relentlessly. 'And Bottom Field, that's Bexham, and mark my words if we don't get young Tam out of the area double quick, as Waldo advises, we'll find it'll be the worse for us. Village feelings can run high. It's happened before – barns on fire, cars set alight on forecourts. You know as well as I do, these things happen, and there's naught anyone can do. That's life when feelings run high – things happen.'

'He hasn't killed anyone,' Peter protested yet

again. 'He's had an accident, that's all. Young people have accidents in tractors, in boats, not just cars. Look at young Dick Fallow, he died under his granddad's tractor, his own grandfather ran him over, remember? It was an accident. Dick's grandfather didn't have to leave Bexham, did he? People fall off their horses and get killed out hunting all the time, because some young thruster's jumped in front of them, and no one leaves the area, now do they?'

Tam, his freshly plastered wrist held in a sling, shook his head.

'No, Dad, he's right. Granddad's right. I'll have to go somewhere else for a bit, I will really. Besides, I think I should.'

'You haven't done a murder. You've had an *accident*, Tam. Accidents happen, that's all there is to it. Besides, it looks like running away, and that's no damn good.'

'No, Granddad's right, and so is Mum.' Tam shook his head again. 'Mum thinks the same as Granddad.' He looked across at his father, suddenly feeling older than him. 'Besides, as Mum says, we don't want business affected. Remember when Dulcie Newton's father got copped in the red light district in Brighton? Well, the Newtons, their trade went to nothing. They had to close all their local newsagents, and start up again somewhere else. And that wouldn't be fair to Flavia, would it? We've got to think of her, haven't we?'

Peter sighed, knowing that everything that Tam

was saying had to have come from Rusty. He might be able to fight his father-in-law, but he couldn't fight Rusty, not once her mind was made up.

'Where will you go, though, Tam? What about school? Where can we send you? You'll have A-levels soon, you can't just flee the place, start over. It's ridiculous. What about school?'

'Mum's already asked Mr Astley.'

Peter felt his mouth going dry. If Rusty had approached Waldo already it must mean that she meant business. She wouldn't go to Waldo otherwise. It would be her last resort, but if she'd done that, then she really was set on getting Tam not just out of Bexham, but out of England.

'And what did he say? What did Waldo say?'

Peter had never felt more useless as he heard his son pronounce his own fate.

'Mr Astley's got friends in America. He told Mum he's only got to pick up the telephone and he can find me somewhere where I can go and work in Texas. He has family there, and all.'

'Texas is a long way away, Tam. You're only seventeen.'

'Old enough to harm, old enough to go abroad, my father used to say,' Mr Todd chipped in bitterly.

'Texas likes young people. Mr Astley told Mum.' To placate his father's ambitions for him, Tam added, 'and I'll take my driving test there. I can drive cars and work, Mr Astley says.'

'Blasted cars.' Mr Todd looked round at his

son-in-law, a bitter look in his eyes. 'That's what I said. If you'd come in with our family business, you and Rusty, if you'd stuck by Mickey and myself, if you'd stuck to boats, stuck to the water, we'd have none of this come-over, would we? But no, you had to go in for fancy motor cars, and now look what's happened. I'll be dead before I see young Tam again, so I will be. Dead as a nail, I tell you. Lying in the churchyard alongside Grandma, poor soul.'

He gave a great shuddering sigh and sat down suddenly, and although his walking stick crashed to the ground he paid no attention to it, leaving it lying on the floor and sinking his head in his hands in a sudden display of misery.

'It had to be the Tates' child that you injured, didn't it, Tam? Couldn't have been someone we never heard of, or who never heard of us, it had to be the *Tates*.'

Tam sat down beside his grandfather and put a hand on his knee. He loved his grandfather so much, and now he'd disgraced him. His father's despair, his grandfather's misery, the Tates' grief and anger, poor little Jenny suffering in hospital, everything, it was all his fault, everything was his fault, and he knew it. Never mind that it was the first accident that he'd ever had. Never mind that his hero, Max, had always said that he never felt nervous driving with Tam, not ever. Max always said he'd put his life in Tam's hands, he was that good at driving, but never mind all that now, look where his driving had brought him.

'Mr Astley's right. I'll have to go to America.'

'It was an *accident*!' The words burst out of Peter Sykes so forcibly he felt they were actually coming out of his chest rather than his mouth.

'No, Dad.' Tam looked up at his father. 'It wasn't an accident, it was a crime. We have to face it. What I did was criminal. I should never have been driving that fast.'

'He should never have been driving that fast.'

Hugh stared across the pub table at Waldo. They were seated in the Three Tuns pretending to eat lunch, while mine host, a retired butler, the now old and venerated Mr Richards, moved slowly round the dining room checking that everything was all right. Although he was still the landlord everyone knew that this was actually all that he did do nowadays.

Fond as he was of old Richards, in view of the bad news about Jenny, Hugh had been hoping that the old chap would walk on past, not hover, but Richards, as was his custom when Hugh was in, came up to the table.

'I'm very sorry to hear about your little grand-daughter, Mr Tate. What a shocking thing to happen.'

'Thank you, Richards, but in the event she *is* going to be all right, eventually.' Hugh pushed his lamb cutlet to one side of his plate, half eaten. He was miserable, and they all knew it.

'They can do wonders with plastic surgery now,'

Waldo said, for what seemed, even to him, to be perhaps the hundredth time.

'Young Tam Sykes will never forgive himself.' Richards spoke factually. 'And his mother will never forgive his father for indulging him. The problem is Rusty's never approved of his father's ambitions for him. She never wanted the boy to be encouraged to become a racing driver.'

'No, I dare say she didn't.' Hugh got up abruptly. 'I say, Richards, I think I'll have another gin and tonic, if you don't mind?'

Waldo watched the two older men making their way back to the bar with a feeling of relief. It gave him time to think out how exactly to phrase what he had to say to Hugh. It was not going to be easy to break the news to him that he was sending Tam to America. It would not be the kind of news that the older Tates would take well. Impossible for them to prevent themselves from seeing Waldo as taking sides, and while Jenny would be paying the price for the accident for years to come, it would appear to them that Tam was being not just let off without a punishment, but given his liberty to boot.

'Hugh.' Once Waldo could see that the older man was looking better for two gin and tonics and a glass of wine, not to mention his lunch, which he had eventually managed to eat, he felt brave enough to broach the subject. 'You know how I feel about what has happened to Jenny, don't you?'

Hugh, whose eyes had been drifting towards the window of the Three Tuns, and from there out to the estuary beyond, to the waters that he had been sailing in now for half a century, turned his attention reluctantly back from the view to Waldo.

'Yes, yes, of course,' he said mechanically. 'Of course I know how you feel about Jenny. This particular grandfather perhaps most of all; Sir Arthur – you know, Judy's father – because of not really getting on with children, not as much as he would like, at any rate, I've been more of a grandfather to her. Doesn't mean Arthur doesn't love her, you know. Bit shy, that's all.'

'Exactly so.' Waldo took out his cigar case and removed an expensive cigar from it, lighting the end, and sucking long and hard on the delicious Havana. 'Exactly.' He paused, thinking how best to continue, knowing that whatever happened he was going to be in hot water. 'We all love Jenny.' His brilliant dark eyes stared at Hugh through the cigar smoke as he puffed. 'But some of us also love Tam. I'm actually his proxy, pretend godfather, you know,' he added conversationally, while he too diplomatically fixed his gaze on the view of the sea beyond the window.

'Tam Sykes? Your godson? Please don't attempt to have a good word to say about that boy, not around me, Waldo. He's obviously rotten. The Sykeses have always indulged him, fast cars and garish clothes – and now look at the result. It doesn't bear thinking of, really it doesn't.'

Waldo put up his hand. 'I'm sure everything you say is true, Hugh, and no doubt more than true, too, but Tam is still only seventeen. Very well he was showing off in front of Kim, because he's got a crush on her. Young men do those sorts of things. I know I did those sorts of things. I just never had that kind of accident, but the fact that I didn't, when I look back, the fact that I didn't was just luck. That's all, just luck.'

'Are you trying to tell me that Jenny's accident was just *bad* luck, Waldo? Because if so, I'm afraid I can't agree with you. What we are facing here is an indulged boy, indulgent parents, and now – disaster.'

'No, what I'm trying to tell you is that I'm sending Tam to America, because I want to try to help him, and Jenny, of course. But I've known Tam since he was a little fellow living in the flat in my house just after the war, and Rusty was cleaning for me. I can't desert him now. The reason I'm telling you about this is I don't want to deceive you, Hugh. I know how dear Jenny is to you, and how much she means to us all, but Tam is Rusty and Peter's son, and I am very fond of him too. I can see that while he has done wrong, to stay here would be suicidal for him. There's only one way for him, and that's out, and I'm helping him to take that way out, because not to help him, in my opinion, would be wrong.'

Hugh looked at Waldo. 'You must do as you wish, Waldo.'

'Hugh . . .'

Hugh stood up. 'No, Waldo. There's no more to

be said. You must do as you wish, but frankly if you could see Jenny as I've just seen her I dare say you might not feel quite so generous towards Tam Sykes.'

After which he took out his wallet and, placing some money for his lunch on the table, left abruptly.

Hardly a minute had gone by when Richards returned. 'Not a good time for all the Tates, then?'

Waldo shook his head miserably, and indicated for Richards to sit down in the vacated seat. 'Not a good time for the Sykeses either.'

'Tam will recover. Will Jenny though?'

'After plastic surgery, yes.'

'Don't expect Mr Tate to be comforted by that, Mr Astley, will you? Jenny is his precious little flower, always has been.'

'I will help Jenny in every way I can, but I have to help Tam too, Richards.'

Richards looked across at Waldo and sighed. 'Aren't you ever going to give up trying to help people, Mr Astley?'

'No, at least not if I can help it!'

They both laughed, and the moment having lightened Richards returned to his usual seat behind the bar, and Waldo went to meet Rusty and Tam who were waiting for him to drive them to London Airport.

As he drove to the Sykeses house in Churchester, Waldo became more and more aware that this newest calamity that had hit Bexham would probably divide it, because he'd seen it happen in his home town when he was growing up. It was always the same with the aftermath of accidents that involved young people: everyone took sides, families were set against each other, nothing was ever the same again.

The Tates' favourite grandchild had been horribly injured. As far as the rest of Bexham was concerned, blame would be duly apportioned, sides taken, and no one would condone Waldo's helping to find Tam a safe haven. It would be seen as being partial. It would not be understood.

In going to the aid of Tam Sykes, Waldo must be seen, not just by the Tates but possibly by Lionel Eastcott too, as being utterly wrong. Nevertheless he continued on his journey, driving to the Sykeses' house in Churchester. After all he had his conscience, other people had theirs, and if it left him friendless there was nothing else that he could do.

Had Waldo been standing by Jenny's hospital bed at that moment he might have felt less sure of his position, and been even more sympathetic to Hugh's private grief.

Had he felt the pain that Jenny was feeling at that moment, been conscious of it, he might have been as anguished as her grandfather. For the fact was that no matter how kind the nurses, how caring the surgeons and doctors, how often they filled her with painkillers, Jenny was now knowing pain as she had never imagined it to be. There was, after

102

all, a limit to the painkillers she could have administered to her, and in between there was nothing but agony, an agony which she felt could never ever be relieved, until the next life-saving injection.

Ever afterwards, if anyone asked her, Jenny would always tell them that she could not remember much about the accident, when the truth was she could remember far too much. She could remember turning and smiling back at Kim as she settled in the car. She could remember Tam whistling and shouting above the sound of the revving engine. She could hear his laughter and see the daredevil light in his eye as he boasted that he was going to drive faster than sound, and she could remember her hand going over the brake, ready to pull it up, if necessary, and how frightened she felt. Then she remembered the car going forward, the mown grass on the rough track flattening in front of the old banger, Tam laughing while the car was going faster and faster. Finally had come the sound of her screaming, and then, darkness.

It was the waking time that was the agony. The being awake and not wanting to be, because being awake meant enduring the terrible pain. The anxious faces of her parents, vaguely appearing in front of her, the sound of everyone's voices. The kindness in the eyes of the doctors and nurses, the endless injections, while all the time knowing, as she could not help doing, that it was not just now that the pain was going to be there. It must be going to go on and on. She knew this because everyone kept telling her that she mustn't worry about her face, that it would not be long before they would be able to repair it. They were going to make it like new.

'As soon as they can they'll be sending you to Bristol or London, and they will start to make good the damage. You'd be amazed what they will be able to do, really you will.'

After that, although she was coming and going so much, lapsing into unconsciousness, while still for some reason able to hear, Jenny remembered the distant sound of her poor mother's crying and her father's comforting words to her, usually followed by one of the doctors talking to them, or the nurses offering tea.

Sholto's voice was always the best. Sholto who was always so four square, full of the kind of marvellous energy with which boys who can't stand to be indoors always seem to be brimming over.

'I've come to tell you about my sailing lesson today. I went out with Grandpa's friend Captain Bettington. We took a picnic. Captain Bettington took a leather case with gin in it, and we sailed Chummy to the point, and round the lighthouse, and back again, and I did it, all by myself.'

As he finished his account of his day on this particular afternoon Sholto saw his sister's lips moving. He leaned forward to try to hear what she was saying.

'Don't you mean "*by my own*"?'

As soon as he realised what Jenny was saying

Sholto's own lips started to tremble, which he jolly well didn't want them to do, so he quickly swiped his arm across his eyes to stop the tears coming, hoping against hope that no one would come into Jenny's room, and see him.

When he was little he had never said 'by myself', he'd always said 'by my own'. He knew Jenny was making a jokey reference to this. She must be in agony, but she was trying to make him laugh in the old way.

'Hurry up and get better soon, Jenny!' he told her, having thought he had successfully swallowed the lump in his throat away. He tried to say something else, but failed. Finally giving in to his grief, Sholto shoved his head under the counterpane on his sister's bed, and sobbed his heart out.

'I don't think you'd better go again. Not for the moment.'

'I want to.'

Waldo shook his head firmly. He had asked Lionel to meet him in the Three Tuns to have an early lunch, knowing that the poor old chap, as he himself had just put it, had been 'a little untidy medically' over the past days.

'No, Lionel, it's bad enough for you imagining what young Jenny's going through, but at your age, to drive there every day, it's too much of a strain. No wonder you've had a bad turn.'

'It wasn't a bad turn. It was a small turn – nothing to speak of.'

'It was not nothing, and it was not something – but it was a bit of a warning. You must take care of yourself, really you must. It won't help Jenny, if you're taken ill. Besides, I need you for bridge at the weekend. We need to put in some practice for the challenge match in the spring. We shall be right up against it, I'm telling you.'

Lionel sighed, staring into Waldo's handsome, tanned, middle-aged face with its still brilliant eyes. He knew only too well that Waldo had been going through torture about the accident that Tam Sykes had caused, and not least because he was so fond of Lionel's granddaughter. Lionel also knew that his fellow grandparents, Hugh and Loopy, were finding it well nigh impossible to socialise with him at the moment, for the simple reason that Waldo had refused to take sides over the accident.

Much as Lionel appreciated the intensity of the Tates' feelings, and despite the fact that they shared two grandchildren, in all honesty he simply couldn't sympathise with them, and this despite knowing what Jenny was going through.

Lionel's point of view was that they had all known Tam since he was a nipper, and that he had always been a bit of a goer, but there was no knowing now what Tam too was suffering, and would always suffer, on account of his foolhardiness that afternoon. No one could take back the moment, that was certain; on the other hand, to Lionel's way of thinking, no good was going to come from apportioning blame.

'I don't want the poor child to think I've forgotten her. I don't want Jenny missing my coming to see her. I don't want to leave her lying there all alone in that great big hospital.' Lionel turned his head and looked out of the inn window towards the estuary. 'Her face, you know. The surgeon told me that to begin with, when the bandages come off, we mustn't be too shocked. She'll look a bit like a cracked cup.' He stopped, and sighed again. 'She's had everything in life you could want, has young Jenny. Her parents loved her from the moment she arrived in this world. She has a golden nature, gets on with everyone, loves music and books, is good at sailing, and then one moment, one stupid, stupid moment, and bang – everything's ruined for her. Not her fault, not necessarily anyone's *fault*, young people do these things; they do stupid things without thinking.'

'Apparently, in America, it's called the *it won't happen to me* syndrome. It's a whole subject in psychology. People even take degrees in it—'

'Oh, I understand you can take a degree in anything nowadays,' Lionel put in, interrupting him. 'The flight of birds, drawing insects, Egyptian art, anything you like. In my day it was called hobbies – now you take a degree in it.'

Waldo laughed. This was better, this was more like the old Lionel, sitting in his favourite Windsor oak chair by the window of the Three Tuns, sipping a gin and tonic, and making cracks about modern life.

'So you'll come Saturday night, then. To Gloria's?'

Lionel nodded. 'Rather. Who's hosting the challenge match, by the way?'

'Philip Basnett – remember I told you about him? He plays for very high stakes at the Clarendon – oh, and Mrs Marcia Farrow.'

'Not Marcia Farrow? She's the tops.' Lionel looked impressed. 'I remember my friend, you remember, Mrs Van?' As Waldo nodded he went on, 'I remember her telling me about Marcia Farrow, and that was years ago now. Marcia Farrow could only have been young then, but by George she could play.'

'Well, she's certainly older, and apparently she's also dead keen on coming, so Gloria says.'

'Dear old Gloria.' Lionel's gaze drifted towards the window, and he was silent for a while. 'I was in love with her, once, you know, when I was a young man.' Waldo, who had heard this fact quite a few times before, smiled, and encouraged by this Lionel went on, 'Thought the sun shone when she smiled, and the rain fell when she frowned, and now look at her.'

'She's fantastic for her age.'

'We're all fantastic for our age, old boy. What we certainly are not any more is *young*.' He paused, his thoughts suddenly returning once more to his granddaughter in Churchester General. 'Speaking of which I really must order my lunch, and then go and see young Jenny.'

'Tomorrow perhaps, but not today. Jenny won't miss you not visiting her today. Quite apart from anything else, the weather's too bad.' Waldo nodded towards the window. 'It's sheeting down. You really shouldn't go to Churchester today. Go tomorrow.' He didn't add *because you look worn out*.

Lionel stared out of the window. It was true. It was pouring with rain, heavy rain, coming down in stair-rods in fact. Perhaps he *would* leave visiting Jenny until tomorrow, after all.

'Tell me, what do you know of Mrs Farrow's game?'

Inwardly Waldo sighed with relief as he realised that he had succeeded in distracting Lionel's attention away from Jenny.

'She's bold, a bit of a gambler, not like a woman, no caution, but she has a phenomenal memory for cards played, and can hold a game in her head for years. Never forgets everyone else's game, and as a consequence she manages to scare the life out of most of them, but she is also the greatest gas.'

'Fancy our chances?'

'Not for a second,' Waldo smiled at his old bridge-playing partner. 'But at least we can have a bit of joy out of it. Try and squeeze her game until the pips squeak.'

'Yes, we can, can't we?'

'Another gin and tonic?'

'Of course, dear boy, of course.'

As Waldo strode off towards the bar, Lionel stared out of the window. The rain was stopping and a bit of light was showing between the clouds. He'd visit Jenny tomorrow. Waldo was right. His thoughts turned back to the bridge match in the spring. It promised to be quite something.

'Cheers!'

'Cheers.'

They touched glasses, and Waldo was able to note with some satisfaction that there was a bit of colour in Lionel's old cheeks and what was more the look in his eyes was less tired.

'By the way, Lionel, I do appreciate you being here with me, you know that, don't you?'

They both knew what Waldo was saying, without his having to say it. They both knew that with the whole of Bexham taking sides about the accident, the fact that Lionel was refusing to do so, having lunch at the Three Tuns with Waldo, in the usual way, was doubly appreciated.

Lionel never said as much, and never would, but in his opinion Hugh Tate was making an ass of himself, getting on his high horse. Tam Sykes had always been a bit of a scamp, but good-hearted to a degree, and not a bad bone in his body.

'I've always liked being with you, dear boy, and always will.' Lionel touched his thin, white moustache briefly, and smiled.

For no reason he could think Waldo's heart sank. It was Lionel's smile. He knew it was telling Waldo something that he really didn't want to know, but they walked along by the estuary in companionable silence nevertheless.

'Apparently, according to Richards, there are some very strange rumours flying about the place. Have you heard anything?' Lionel drew hard on his pipe and at the same time glanced down the estuary.

'Yes, I have heard as much from Gloria, of course. London friends tell of orgies in high places – but when weren't there orgies in high places?'

Lionel puffed hard to keep his pipe alight. 'Perhaps it's Jenny's accident, perhaps it's just my age, but I keep having the feeling that the house of cards is just about to come tumbling around our ears, everything's going to fall apart. Don't need the A bomb or the H bomb, nothing like that, for our destruction, got it here already, beneath us – something insidious, something rotten in the foundations.'

'I know what you mean.' To distract Lionel from such gloomy thoughts Waldo nodded towards the horizon. 'That liner out there,' he nodded towards it. 'I always think when they pass in the distance they look as though they're being drawn along by a piece of string.'

He turned to Lionel for corroboration, only to see him staggering and seconds later falling forward on to the grass to the side of the path.

Chapter Three

Kim looked cautiously round the newel post of the staircase at Owl Cottage hoping against hope that her father had left for London and the station, which he should have done ages ago, but not quite trusting that he had, which meant that she was now waiting for Hubert to give her the signal.

'All clear!' Hubert hissed up the stairs. 'All clear! You can come down now.'

Kim walked slowly down the stairs to the hall, not quite trusting that brother and sister were really alone.

'Where's Mummy? She's not here, is she?' she asked, anxiety etched on every inch of her tense young face, while at the same time she pulled down her cardigan sleeves to cover the wretched eczema on her arms.

'It's all right, Kim, she's gone off to Churchester. Left ages ago. She's having lunch with someone or another.'

Kim nodded. 'Thank God. I thought she might be going to be in all day.'

She looked across at Hubert, suddenly at a loss as to what to do, where to go.

'Kim.'

Hubert stared at her. Despite being a year younger than his sister, he had always been taller, and since the accident he felt not just taller, but somehow much older.

When the accident had first happened and they'd brought Kim home and sent her to her room, Hubert had thought he'd never heard anyone crying so loudly, or so long. Kim's crying had been the kind of crying that had a sort of despairing hollow sound to it, which was perfectly horrible to hear, and made Hubert want to run out of the house and down to the other end of the village rather than listen to it, although even there it seemed to him he might still not be out of earshot.

It was when their parents had driven Kim back to school in funereal silence that Hubert had come to realise exactly what was going to happen to his sister when Walter and Judy left her at school.

The headmistress would know all about Jenny's accident so Kim would be made to feel even worse by all Jenny's school friends, and her teachers, and all that. So now he knew why she'd become such a frightened person, always pretending to be in her room studying, anything rather than see yet another person who would stare at her as if she'd tried to *kill* Jenny. He knew his sister's life was going to be one long hell, and that was before he'd seen the insides of her arms and the backs of her legs, all of which were now covered in nervous eczema.

Hubert knew of course when the eczema had started. It was the day Kim had visited Jenny in hospital. Seeing her much loved cousin there, covered in bandages, in dreadful agony, had actually turned Kim's mind; he really thought it had. She hadn't been the same since that day. Hubert had said as much – not to their father, of course, but to their mother, but for once in her life it seemed to Hubert that Judy – who was usually pretty good – hadn't seemed to understand at all.

'I'm sorry, Hubert, but it was so important that Kim saw what had happened to Jenny on account of Tam's and Kim's stupidity. It's no good, I know it was terrible for her, but it *was* important, it was something that Kim had to go through,' she kept insisting, whenever Hubert dared to bring the subject up.

Hubert hadn't seen it like that, and as a matter of fact he still didn't. He only saw that, from that day to this moment, his beloved sister had seemed to be disintegrating, little by little in front of his eyes, and it was frightening, most of all because he seemed to be the only person who *could* see it.

First her voice. Nowadays it always seemed to have a kind of dulled quality so that she sounded to Hubert as if she had a permanent headache. Next her eyes, which had always been quite pretty, but nowadays never seemed to be looking directly at anything, just always looking down. And after that

114

her appetite, which had always been so healthy – it was now completely gone; and no one but Hubert seemed to notice that she was always pushing her food under lettuce leaves to hide it, never settling to anything, not even things she used to like before the accident. And now, here they were on holiday again, and she was still the same, and he hated it.

'What shall we do now, Hubert?'

Before it had always been Kim who thought things up during the holidays, now it was Hubert she turned to for ideas. It was as if, by being treated like an outcast, all her imagination and zest had left her.

'We could go to the shop and buy some pies and then take them up the Downs for a picnic, with a bottle of pop, couldn't we?'

'It's too cold for a picnic, Hubert.'

'We could eat it walking along and try and see things, you know, hares and things.'

'Oh, all right. But you go to the shop. Here's some of my Christmas present money – OK?' Kim turned to go back upstairs for her coat and gloves. 'I'll meet you up by the beech trees.'

Hubert ran off to the village shop watched by Kim from the upper window. He was tall for his age, which made him look awkward when he ran, because he still ran like a boy, his tie flapping in the breeze, his fair hair flopping into his frowning eyes.

They both knew without having to say anything to each other exactly why it was that Hubert had to go to the shop on his own. It was because Kim was

115

afraid that if she went with him Mrs Salter who sat behind the counter would make unkind remarks, because that was how much the village blamed Kim for Jenny's terrible accident, they still made remarks in her hearing, even when they were coming out of church.

They were walking up the Downs, the chalky soil showing bare under the tufts of grass, a little out of breath, but feeling better for being in the air, away from the oppressive atmosphere of the house, when Kim made her announcement.

'I'm going to do something so that no one need be bothered with me again, Hubert.'

Hubert, who was leaning against a tree, and just beginning to feel better about everything, meat pie in one hand, tomato in the other, swallowed hard and stared at her mid-mouthful.

'Please, Kim, don't do anything silly.'

'Nothing could be much worse than this, Hubie.' Kim looked across at Hubert. She was in the process of unwrapping her meat pie, which was difficult when you were wearing woollen gloves. 'Nothing could be much worse than now, with Jenny still in hospital. I heard Daddy saying last night that Christmas is ruined for all of us, that because of the accident we can't visit each other in our houses.'

Kim stared out to the wide horizon in front of them. When they were children they used to call the place where they were now standing and eating their pies 'the top of the world', probably because they always felt so on top of the world once they'd managed to climb up there. At that moment it seemed to her that she was standing beside the child she'd once been, wearing her navy blue coat with the tartan tam o'shanter, hearing everyone around her laughing and talking, and thinking she was the luckiest girl alive to be growing up in Bexham. Now she found herself longing to be that other Kim, happy, carefree Kim, whom her parents had loved so, so much, and yet at the same time knowing, without any doubt at all, that the happy, carefree child inside her was gone for ever.

'It's all so stupid everyone trying to blame you!' Hubert shouted suddenly, his voice losing power against the wind. 'It wasn't your fault. Oh, all right you were there, but if you ask me they're only all blaming you because Tam's not here to blame. He's got off scot free, gone to Texas to be a cowboy, Sholto told me. But if you ask me that's why they're all being so beastly to you, Kim, because Tam Sykes's not here, because he's gone, and there's no one else to blame.'

'But don't you see, that's just it? If I'm not here, everyone else would be better off too? Daddy and Mummy, and Uncle John and Aunt Mattie, and Sholto, and Grandpa and Grandma, they'd all be better for me not being here.'

'That's not true, Kim.' Hubert bit into another pie, and chewed hard on it to stop himself getting too upset.

'You're the only one, Hubert, that still talks to me same as always, do you know that? You're the only one that doesn't pretend I'm not there when I come into a room, you and Mummy, but even she – I can see she feels awkward. She doesn't know what to say to me any more, and we used to talk. A lot. We really did. We talked. A lot.'

Kim frowned hard. They had used to talk. A lot.

'They're just stupid,' Hubert said helplessly, still furious with everyone, their family, the village, everyone. 'Really, they're just stupid.' He turned to Kim, a desperate, pleading look in his eyes. 'Promise me, whatever you do, promise me you'll tell me before you do anything, Kim?'

'Look, look, Hubie! – a hare, over there—'

Kim distracted him. She didn't want to talk about what she was going to do, she was just going to do it.

Waldo was staring into the fire, memories crowding his mind, bumping into each other, seeming to him to be kaleidoscoping one long life into a few short moments, as they often did now he was older, and all the moments were centred around Meggie. Meggie sailing, Meggie wearing a wonderful red dress, Meggie dancing. Seated in front of his fire, staring into the flames, he could conjure up a thousand Meggies at will, and love every one of them. It was a winter pastime, and a fine and splendid one when you were seated in your own home in front of a roaring log fire.

'There's someone to see you, Mr Astley – a Meester Tate.'

His Spanish housekeeper interrupted his reveries, at the same time placing a tea tray on the sofa table. Without meaning to Waldo found his face breaking into a relieved smile.

'Please show him in, Maria, whichever Meester Tate it is!'

Waldo stood up, straightening his tie in anticipation of greeting his guest. He was just about to say 'Hugh, just in time for a toasted crumpet' when in place of Hugh Tate his housekeeper ushered in a tall young man with a shock of dark hair, in grey flannels and a sports jacket, the sleeves of which already threatened to become far too short for him.

'Hubie.'

'Hallo, sir.'

'How – unexpected.'

They both stared at each other, knowing that strictly speaking, because of the rift caused by Jenny's accident, Hubert shouldn't really be at Cucklington House, although Waldo was too much the gentleman to say so.

'Would you like a cup of tea?'

'Not really, sir. If you don't mind.'

'Crumpet?' Waldo lifted the lid of the muffin dish.

'No, thank you, sir.'

'You don't mind if I do, then?'

'Course not, sir.'

Hubert stood staring round the room as he

119

waited for Waldo to pour himself a cup of tea and butter a crumpet, and remained standing until Waldo nodded for him to sit down. He tried not to look at Mr Astley eating his crumpet and sipping his tea, letting his eyes continue to rove round the room, taking in the beautiful silk curtains which seemed to have been sculpted rather than sewn, the faded chintz cloths on the tables, the photographs in silver frames. As he did so it occurred to him that the room was strangely feminine. He puzzled over this until his eyes rested on the portrait over the chimneypiece and he took in the beautiful blonde with her hand resting on a model of a racing yacht, her slender figure in a pale blue chiffon dress, the look in her eyes one of amusement, as if she had seen quite a bit of life, but still found it delightful. Whoever she was, it was obviously *her* room.

'So, Hubert, how can I help you?'

On arrival Hubert had looked so nervous, his eyes so large in his face, that Waldo had deliberately cooled the atmosphere by eating his tea with slow relish, for he had quickly realised that whatever was making young Hubert so anxious must be something pretty serious for him to come calling on Waldo.

'Well, sir, you know about the accident? You know that my cousin Jenny is hurt so badly she'll need lots of operations on her face, and all that? You know about that?'

'Yes, I do, Hubie. As you may guess it has been on everyone's minds.'

120

Feeling that nothing more could or indeed should be said on the subject, Waldo stood up and went back to Maria's carefully laid tea tray.

'Are you sure that you don't want anything, Hubie?'

'Yes, thank you, sir.' A pause and then, 'Well, perhaps a muffin.'

'Good man – jam or honey?'

'Honey, thank you, sir.'

Following this small but effective exchange Waldo sat back opposite his young visitor and once again sipped his tea, and ate yet another honeyed crumpet, buying time as he did so. He was not just buying time, however, he was also remembering the pain and anguish of what it was like to be thirteen years of age, and trying to put behind him his father's furies, his mother's permanent absence, his feelings of loss and bewilderment. Looking across the short space between them he knew that in reality he could only imagine everything that Hubert was going through, but of one thing he thought he could be quite sure, and that was that young Hubert would be seeing, quite clearly, everything that everyone was doing to each other, and yet knowing he was helpless to do anything, too young to be of any account.

'The thing is, sir.' Hubert put his flower-patterned tea plate down very carefully on the tea tray and then returned to the fireplace and his seat on the sofa opposite Waldo. Following the ingestion of the muffin he was looking less pallid, his

121

voice stronger, the look in his eye more assertive. 'The thing is, sir,' he said again, clearing his throat. 'I have to tell someone, because I'm so worried.'

'Naturally.' Waldo's brilliant eyes stared back at the young man opposite him, serious, listening, knowing that to say nothing was always better than saying something.

'It's Kim, sir, my sister. I'm so worried about her.'

'Kim would be a worry.'

'Our parents won't really see just how bad it is for her. It's not something that's meant to get out, but – but last term she ran away from school because she was so unhappy about Jenny, trying to get to see her in hospital, but a policeman spotted her and when she went back she was put in Coventry for the whole term, and she's covered in eczema, at least on her arms and legs, really bad. And now she's got it into her head that she's going to – she's going to . . .' Waldo leaned forward as Hubert stopped. 'Someone's going to have to talk to her, to stop her.'

Judy's mother, Lady Melton, was feeling her age, which was, unlike the temperatures outside, in the high seventies. Sir Arthur was asleep in the chair opposite her, the *Daily Telegraph* covering his tweed waistcoat, and a china cup beside him. All in all it was a typical scene for late winter in the old house at the top of Bexham, when old Ellen scratched at the drawing room door, and her daughter Judy was shown in.

Before she could speak her mother put her fingers to her lips, nodding to indicate Judy's sleeping father, and the two of them silently tiptoed out of the room, leaving Ellen to quietly stoke up the fire.

'How is poor little Jenny?' Lady Melton asked at once, as they settled down in the morning room where another fire was blazing.

'She's going to be all right, as far as her body is concerned, but her face is terribly damaged.'

Lady Melton's expression became grave. She came from a generation which believed that the slightest flaw could influence a girl's chances of marrying, and so the idea that John and Mattie's daughter would have a scarred face was perhaps even more terrible to her than it was to Judy.

'Poor child.' Her face clouded, and she looked away from her daughter and stared into the fire. 'So much worse for a girl, I always think.'

'I don't know what to do for the best, I don't really.' Judy felt free to look as worried as she felt in front of her mother.

'There is nothing that you can do.'

'That's why I don't know what to do. And of course with Kim home, everything seems so much worse. She skulks about the house, won't even come downstairs when Walter's home for the weekends. She pretends she's feeling sick, anything rather than face her father nowadays.'

Lady Melton straightened up, and smoothed her tweed skirt over her knees.

'She can't be blamed for that, Judy. The guilt of what has happened must be terrible for the poor girl. And Walter, you know, has rather got it in for her just lately.'

'He hasn't got it in for Kim, Mama—'

'He most certainly has. The last time he came to Sunday lunch here your father and I were quite shocked at his attitudes about the accident, and about Kim – of course she was bound to have some sort of reaction to what had happened, and although we all know that her eczema is not the end of the world, nevertheless Walter's treating it as if it's just a mild irritation, which it certainly is not.'

There was a pause as Judy saw Walter from her mother's point of view, and was vaguely shocked.

'Walter can be a bit much when he's got a bee in his bonnet,' she conceded finally. 'As a matter of fact so can John. Loopy says that the way John keeps going on and on about poor Max's show you would honestly have thought that he was at the Windmill Theatre in a nude revue.'

'It's rude to move! I always remember that sketch about the dear old Windmill.' Lady Melton gave a sudden smile. 'I believe some quite good people got their chances there, you know, at the Windmill.'

Judy nodded, knowing that if she waited patiently enough, her mother would give her advice.

'Kim is going through a bad time in the village,

too. People make remarks when she's in the shop, that sort of thing.'

'That is only to be expected, the village is always very narrow, full of hen roost gossip, when it comes to these things. That has to be shrugged off, but so much worse for Kim that her father's embarrassed by her.'

'But he's not embarrassed by her!' Judy protested. 'Walter's not embarrassed by Kim.'

'Of course he is, Judy, you'd have to be blind not to notice. Walter is embarrassed by Kim's letting him down publicly, by her letting down the Tates, by the permanency of the damage done to her cousin, but most of all by the fact that he himself has been caught out. He doesn't know how to go on in this situation. Everything that has ever happened to Walter has had some sort of understandable code, some set of rules that he could follow, until now.'

Lady Melton shrugged her shoulders and Judy stared at her mother, knowing that inevitably the old lady had put her finger on the reality of the situation. It was true, everything that had ever happened to Walter, whether it was to do with the Navy, or the law, his family, the yacht club, the golf club – everything that he had done, or would do, was governed by a recognisable code. He was a gentleman. He knew how to go on. But now Kim, his beloved daughter, had been involved with a tragedy, for the first time in his life he didn't know how to go on, because there was no specified code of conduct for him to follow, no rules to learn and obey.

'What do you think I should say to him? To Walter?'

'You must point out that it's not up to him to be judge and jury on an accident. That to cold-shoulder his daughter over – put quite simply – a motor car foolishness is simply neither Christian nor acceptable. You must tell him that he has to face up to what she is going through, not think so much of himself and the loss of face *he* is feeling.'

Judy turned away. 'You're right, Mama.'

And she was, she was right, Judy knew that, but being right is one thing, doing and saying the right thing at the right time was quite another.

Left with his problem, which, little though he knew it, was the same problem that Judy was facing, Waldo immediately telephoned to Peter Sykes and asked him round to Cucklington House.

Standing in the genteel surroundings of Waldo's house and despite his smartly tailored suit and perfect manners, Peter still looked very much the ex-mechanic tough guy, Bexham's very own war hero. It wasn't just that he'd lost a leg in the war, it was his whole demeanour. No matter what he wore he always looked as if he was just about to jump into a mechanic's pit, or an armoured car. He bristled with activity. Perhaps it was because of this restless quality that he and Waldo had become instant friends. Certainly without Waldo's help,

Peter could never have set himself up in business just after the war, at a time when most cars were still on blocks, and there was nothing to put in them that wasn't rationed, except hope.

Despite this he had forged ahead, building for himself and Waldo, his one and only investor, a lucrative motor car business, which in due course had turned into a franchise worth thousands. It was for this reason, and many others, but most of all because they respected each other, that Peter had come round to Cucklington House the moment Waldo had telephoned.

'I'm sorry to eat into your day this way, Peter, but I really need you to be here for the next hour.'

Waldo was looking so worried that Peter put out one of his big, strong, calm hands and placed it on the sleeve of the other man's Shetland wool pullover.

'What's the matter, Waldo? Has Jenny taken a turn for the worse?'

'No, no, at least not that I know of, no, but Walter and Judy's – Kim – she seems to have, and we have to act now, in unison, before another tragedy occurs.' He went to the window overlooking the drive. 'Ah,' he said, after a minute or so of watching. 'Here she comes. Just follow me, would you? I'll take the lead.'

They both knew from long experience of each other's business manners just what Waldo meant. He would speak, Peter would follow, but not add anything more. Knowing him as he did Peter was instantly aware that what was about to happen was a great deal more important than any business deal.

As Maria showed Kim into the room Waldo stood up, and went across to greet her with the most relaxed expression possible, a remarkable piece of acting, considering how he actually felt.

'Ah, there you are, Kim. Come in, sit down.'

'Good afternoon, Mr Astley, good afternoon, Mr Sykes.'

Despite having known them all her life, Waldo and Peter could see that Kim of all people was reluctant to look either of them in the face as she hurriedly shook their hands before taking a place by the fire.

As soon as he saw how soaked she was from the rain Waldo turned to Maria.

'Hot chocolate I think, don't you, Maria?' As Maria hurried off, Waldo went on, 'Take off your shoes, why don't you, Kim? Go on, wiggle your toes in front of the fire. I can see your shoes are soaked through.'

'It's all right, thank you. I'm fine.' Kim stared into the fire rather than look at either of the men seated near her. 'Really, I'm fine.'

Waldo said nothing, but for the second time that week his heart sank. He could see that the young, energetic, life-loving Kim that he and Peter had always taken for granted had all but disappeared, and if that wasn't enough he could hear from her toneless voice just how deeply her depression must have taken hold.

'I had a letter from Tam yesterday, Kim. He sends his love to you, and hopes you're getting along fine.'

This was a complete lie, of course. Since Tam had gone to America the only way his family could, or did, hear from him was if they telephoned to him. Tam was not a letter writer, and Peter knew it. What he didn't know was why Waldo was finding it necessary to lie about such a thing.

Maria had returned with a cup of hot chocolate, and it looked so delicious that Waldo knew that, no matter how depressed she felt, Kim would surely have to drink it, for what with its creamy frothy texture, and the sprinkling of chocolate on the top, it was irresistible. As she sipped it cautiously he continued talking to her.

'Actually, Tam's not quite the thing, yet. America is so different from Bexham. He's having a lot of problems settling down, you know?'

At that Kim looked round at Waldo and for the first time their eyes met, and Waldo was shocked to see how dulled was the look in her large blue eyes. She had the eyes of a prisoner, worn down by the badness of things, or maybe just the attitudes of everyone around her.

'How do you mean?'

'It's not just that everything's so different in America, but *he's* so different. He misses Bexham like crazy, as you can imagine. Misses his family, Flavia, everything, misses that sort of normality that we all take so much for granted, that everyday jam-along thing that we like to call *home*.'

'Misses you, too, Kim,' Peter put in.

After that Waldo allowed a silence to elapse as the fire spat and hissed, and Kim sipped her hot chocolate, not breaking the silence until he felt quite sure that Kim was a little more relaxed.

'Why I called you up to Cucklington, Kim, is a lot to do with what has happened recently. I need your help, and so does Peter. I wonder, at least *we* wondered, if you'd mind going round to Peter's house on Sunday and, when the family calls Tam up, having a word with him? It would mean so much for him to hear you, I know it would. It was Peter's idea, and I really think it's a good one.'

Kim looked round at Peter, her face registering surprise, and as Peter looked back at her he made sure to look calmly innocent. His commanding officer in the war had always instructed them that whenever they met with suffering, whatever else they did, to keep an even look to the eyes.

'How will I get there? How would I get to Churchester, to your house?' Kim's tone was still listless, but the very fact that she was asking such a thing must surely be, Waldo hoped, a small step in the right direction.

'Flavia and I will come and pick you up. You can stay to lunch, maybe? I mean, I know Flave would

130

like it, that is, if you wouldn't find it too dull, and all that?'

The idea of not having to have lunch in company with her father was all at once so heavenly that, without her realising it, the expression on Kim's face was already much brighter.

'No, no, it wouldn't be dull at all. In fact I'd – I'd like that.'

'Well, that's settled then.' Waldo beamed. 'Peter and Flavia will pick you up on Sunday, and you will stay the day and cheer up Tam when he rings at five o'clock our time. Very kind of you, I think that is, young Kim.'

'Don't be silly,' Kim muttered. 'I know how Tam feels, except I'm not in America, worse luck.'

Waldo had been careful not to look at Peter during the whole interview, but now he risked a 'we may be home and dry' glance.

'Now, if that's all right, Geraldo will pop you back home, and so long as your mother and father don't have an objection, you'll be picked up by Peter and Flavia on Sunday.'

Kim stood up quickly. 'No need for anyone to drive me, really. I'd actually rather walk.'

'It's all right.' Waldo looked at her. 'He'll just drop you at the end of the lane. It's still pouring down. Don't want to waste all your good work on those toes of yours now they're dry, do we?'

Some few minutes later Kim left the two men, and was duly driven home by Maria's husband. As soon as he heard the front door close Waldo went to the drinks tray and immediately poured Peter and himself a Scotch.

'What was all *that* about, Waldo?'

Peter drank his Scotch gratefully and stared at Waldo. He'd known from the first that something pretty serious was going on, but even while Kim was with them and he'd been following the conversation he couldn't have said precisely what it was, only that he was needed.

'That, my dear Peter, was all about Miss Kim Tate, who, it seemed, was contemplating ending it all – and by that I mean her life, Peter.'

Peter stared at Waldo. 'Young Kim? Young people don't commit suicide, Waldo.'

'Unfortunately young people commit suicide all the time, Peter, and that is precisely what she'd told her brother that she intended doing before the end of the holidays, before she was sent back to school. She couldn't stand the isolation any more. School's been hell, no one speaking to her, all that. She was apparently planning to throw herself over the railway bridge in front of the London train.'

'Teenagers. They're always threatening things, but they never do them,' Peter protested, but his face lost colour as he thought of Tam and his loneliness, the distance between them.

'Wrong again, Peter. They do it all the time, believe me. Don't worry, I think we've saved the day. I doubt that she'll do anything now. You see, in order to take her life she would have to be

132

concentrating on her own mental state. I therefore fixed on a simple strategy. I attracted her attention away from herself and towards someone else, i.e. Tam, who is not suicidal, but, as I understood it from you, naturally enough, very homesick. So now they can talk to each other on Sunday. That's why I needed you here. To distract her from her own troubles, tell her about Tam.'

'He sounds all right, when I phone him, he sounds fine.'

'He's sure to be homesick as hell, Peter, believe me. Do me a favour, get the two of them talking again, and leave the rest to me.'

'What's the rest, Waldo?'

'The rest is getting Kim's mother to see sense, take Kim away from school, and let her loose in some other place, well away from Bexham.'

'No one knows I'm here. I came round the back lane.'

'Everyone knows you're here. This is Bexham, after all.'

Waldo laughed, but Judy found she could hardly smile. She felt guilty enough coming round to talk to Waldo, rather than Walter, about their poor daughter, but what could she do? The mere mention of Kim's name nowadays seemed to make Walter instantly angry, although Judy sensed that in part he was angry at himself, but helpless to actually do anything.

'Stay right where you are. I'm going to make you a martini, just how you like it.'

As Waldo went to mix the drinks Judy found her eyes turning to the portrait of her old friend over the mantelpiece. It was a brilliant painting of Meggie. As she stared up at it she couldn't help herself envying beautiful enchanting Meggie for being Waldo's great love, the girl whom he still mourned, his wife of only a few days. Lucky Meggie for dying, lucky Meggie for staying beautiful and not growing older, lucky Meggie for staying as everyone would always remember her, loving life, while laughing at it, defying the fates, brave and loyal, not as Judy felt now, got down, helpless, not knowing which way to turn.

'They shall not grow old as we grow old . . .' she murmured as Waldo handed her the perfectly made drink, and then as she sipped it she couldn't help thinking how Waldo made drinks better than anyone she'd ever met. Waldo's drinks were not the sock-you-in-the-taste-buds drinks of the older military and naval men of Bexham. Waldo's drinks took into account that women didn't always like drinks that would make them end up, as Meggie used to put it, 'pulling your nightdress on over your ballgown before trying to comb your hair with your toothbrush'.

'How do you think I look?' Waldo eyed Judy from the looking glass over the mantelpiece as he went back to trying to finish tying his fashionably large bow tie.

'You repay dressing, Mr Astley. Très elegant, if I may say so.'

'To play cards well, it pays to dress well. Cheers.' Waldo picked up his own martini.

'So, you wanted to see me?'

'Don't I always?' He looked across at her with his sudden intense gaze, and suddenly the space between their two sofas, which was covered by a beautiful eighteenth-century style rug, seemed to Judy to be very much smaller, perhaps only the size of a small hand towel.

'Not always, no, you don't always want to see me,' Judy stated factually, quickly trying to replace their relationship in the file marked 'friendship' while she lit a cigarette which she had taken from the silver box beside her sofa.

'That's true. I stand corrected, I don't always want to see you, nor you me, but now there is a matter of some urgency, Judy.' Waldo cleared his throat. 'It's Kim.'

'I thought you were going to say that,' Judy said, quickly, which wasn't actually true. 'Kim is my business, or rather our business, Walter's and mine, really she is, and believe me, we have her best interests at heart, Waldo.'

There was a short pause while Waldo examined this put-down intently from every angle, shrugged it off, and then decided to return to the fray.

'Quite so, of course Kim is your business, Judy, but please remember that without my help there would be no Kim.'

Judy blushed instantly, remembering.

'That's all a long, long time ago, Waldo, and you know it,' she protested.

Immediately seizing his advantage, Waldo jabbed a teasing finger towards her, relishing the moment.

'If it hadn't been for me I dare say you would never, ever have had Kim, or Hubert. Remember it was I, Waldo Astley, who helped you make Walter jealous, and risked life and limb to do so, if you remember; and look what happened as a result? I'm proud to say what happened was – Kim. So, sorry, Mrs Tate – Kim *is* my business, because of me she is here, on this earth. And I have now proved it, and you can't deny it, not for all the fish in the harbour.'

'All right.' Judy started to laugh. 'Very well, I give in, this is absolutely true. Kim would probably not be here if it wasn't for you, and neither would Hubert. So what exactly do you want to say about *your* Kim?'

'She needs to get out of Bexham.'

'She does get out of Bexham. She goes to school.'

'In that case she needs to leave her school, and Bexham. She has to have some kind of radical change.'

'She's just a bit run down. She has developed a rather painful eczema, inherited from her grandmother. She's just a bit run down. Lost weight, a bit listless.'

'No, Judy.' Waldo's voice was very firm. 'Not a

bit run down, she's literally a shred of what she was.' For some reason his eyes strayed towards Meggie's portrait, and then back to Judy. 'Sometimes, you know, you have to be away from someone to see what everyone else can see, sometimes it takes someone from the outside to point out what you can't see, because you're too close up. Believe me, Judy, Kim has to go – away.'

He had allowed his voice to take on an urgency which startled Judy, as it was meant to do.

'I know, Waldo, I know.' Judy looked across at him, giving in suddenly, while feeling both helpless and hopeless at the same time. 'But where? And anyway, Walter will never hear of anyone giving up school. She's miserable, I can see that, but what can I do?'

'Do what we all have to do, do what you think is right.'

Judy thought of all this now as she struggled to serve up Sunday lunch for herself and Walter, and wondered when she could introduce Waldo's plan.

Walter really liked Waldo, which was a good thing, but Judy knew that Waldo might be a paragon of virtue, the saviour of England, King Arthur and his knights rolled into one, and it would mean nothing to Walter when it came to his family. No one ever told Walter Tate what to do about his family, not even Judy. As far as his family went when Walter spoke the waves parted, and they all had to kneel before his advancing paternal figure.

'I think we should have a little talk after lunch, Walter,' she began as she sat down, and they both started to eat the delicious roast beef, roast potatoes and fresh vegetables with an eagerness belied by the atmosphere in the dining room, which was about as cosy as damp sheets.

'Judy. I will not speak about this. Do you understand? I will not speak about it. I am fed up with people talking about Kim, to Kim, and all the rest of it. Very well she has a little bit of eczema, it's a nervous disease, not a death sentence; very well she's lost weight, and her headmistress is worried about her, but quite frankly, at the moment what's making me bloody nervous is I have a murderer to defend tomorrow, and I can't do that effectively while listening to you moaning about Kim.'

Judy put down her knife and fork quite carefully, and having taken a sip of wine to give herself courage she breathed in and out and began again.

'Yes, of course, Walter, and I do understand, and I hope you win, really I do. But you see, tomorrow you will be in London, and I can't really discuss this sort of thing on the phone with you, and yet I feel I must. I am, after all, Kim's mother, and quite frankly I am so worried about her, Walter. She looks terrible. It can't go on. Kim has to start again, or something dreadful will happen to her. I know this, don't ask me how I know it, but I do.'

'Kim has to stop being such a thorn in our sides, Judy. Kim has to go back to school, settle down, and generally resign herself to being a proper

138

person again, Judy, that's what Kim has to do. She is not a nice person to have around the house any more, she drips sorry-for-little-me attitudes, and it's time she stopped. We fought a war, Judy, our generation fought a war, lost our friends and family to defeat the Nazis. Kim isn't fighting a war now, she's being asked to become a civilised human being, and frankly I don't find that's too much to ask of someone.'

'It's no good *lecturing* me, Walter. I can see how you feel, we all can.'

Walter put down his knife and fork.

'What do you mean by "we all"?' he asked ominously.

'Nothing really, it was a way of speaking, that's all.'

'Judy.' Walter stared down the table at his wife prior to picking up his knife and fork again and continuing with his lunch. 'If you want us to be happy, just don't mention our daughter any more, if you don't mind.'

'Kim, you mean? And I think I probably will, Walter, although not, for your sake, this afternoon.'

After that Walter just went on eating, while Judy pushed her plate away and stared out of the window behind his head. She knew that Walter had a big case coming up that week, many things to read and attend to after lunch, which meant that she would be able to go for a walk on her own, really think things out for herself, thank God.

'Where are you going?'

'To wash up.'

'We haven't had coffee.'

'I'll bring it through to you in your study.'

Walter put his napkin down and stood up. It was always Kim, always, always Kim that made the trouble between them. They were as happy as it was perfectly possible to be, until Kim came into view, and then, inevitably, they fell out.

'What are you going to do now?'

Judy could almost see Walter with his wig on frowning round the court in his new dark-framed glasses as she set the coffee beside him on his desk.

'I don't know, really. Read the papers, that kind of thing.'

She'd hardly finished speaking when he returned to his own legal papers, already preoccupied by his work for the next day. She went out closing the door quietly behind her.

In the event she did go for a walk, out of the village, up the familiar road to Cucklington House once more. She knew exactly how it would be at Waldo's house, she would disturb him at work on his many charitable projects, but she also knew that, unlike Walter, he wouldn't mind, that he would spring up to greet her as if he'd been expecting her all the time, which was exactly what happened. He pointed towards the tea table.

'I knew you'd call round and help me out with this cornucopia of teatime delight – cucumber sandwiches, cucumbers from our own greenhouse,

140

home-made scones, chocolate sponge cake fresh from Maria's oven, what more can one ask?'

'Speaking personally? I would like to have Walter at least listen to me – even if he does end up disagreeing.'

Waldo placed a cup of tea beside his guest, and hurried back to heap up a plate with cucumber sandwiches for her.

'You're not like that, Waldo, and you never have been.'

'If I was Walter I would be exactly like that, but I'm not. I'm a widower who lives only for his hobbies. If I had a family I'm sure I'd be different. More stubborn and more intransigent than you could possibly imagine.'

'What shall I do, Waldo?' Judy's voice, even to her own ears, sounded desperate.

'I think what you should do is what you think you ought to do, that's the first thing. And then I think you should tell Walter what you've done, and hope for the best. At this moment, and I've thought about it a great deal – more than you might imagine – I think you really have to put Kim before Walter. It's hard, but I don't see that you can do anything else, that you have any alternative. It's just how it is.'

'Yes, but having done so – what exactly should I do for Kim?'

'Send her to a place I know in Ireland, a healing place.'

'Walter will have a fit.'

'No, he won't.'

'Why not?'

'Because I won't let him.'

'Her grandfather will, too. Hugh will have a fit. They both believe in boarding school the way the vicar believes in God.'

'Well now, Loughnalaire is, as the Irish say, a kind of a sort of a species of school, and yet it's not a school at all. There will be other children there, all of different ages. Some of them are orphans, some of them have had problems at home, but they're all happy, really happy.'

'How do you know?'

Waldo smiled his brilliant smile. 'Let's just say – I do.'

Chapter Four

Much as Judy would have liked to have taken Waldo's advice about Kim and stood up to Walter, she didn't quite dare, always putting off the moment until another weekend. It was not until the headmistress of Kim's school rang up and suggested that should things continue as they were she would have to ask Mrs Tate to take Kim away from the school, that the penny finally dropped with Walter.

Naturally he took the news very badly. As a matter of fact Judy had rarely seen him so cross.

'They shouldn't be running a school if they can't deal with a troublesome teenager.'

'She's not been expelled, Kim's not been expelled, Walter. We're being asked to take her away. Because she is ill. Very ill—'

'Eczema—'

'No, she's not eating, and she rarely even speaks now. She has regressed right back into something I can't recognise, she's just not our Kim any more. She's – well, she's gone into herself, it makes her

143

seem sullen. It's as if – as if she's downed tools and given up on life. I thought we might be getting a bit of the old Kim back, after she went to lunch that day with the Sykeses—'

'She *what*?'

'She went to lunch with the Sykeses, Walter. She spoke to Tam on the transatlantic telephone, because he was feeling homesick.'

'Now I've heard everything.' Walter sat down, shaking his head.

'Doubtless,' Judy agreed, not understanding why her voice sounded so icy, so unlike her own.

'If my father and mother get to hear of this . . .'

'Walter.' Judy faced him across the room, standing by the door, as if she needed to know the whereabouts of the exit. 'Whether you like it or not, whether your father or mother like it, I'm taking Kim away from her school. I'm asserting my right as her mother to do as I wish with a child of mine.'

Judy had never spoken so furiously to her husband, and she didn't know why but she found herself placing her hand on her chest as she finished speaking, looking angrier than Walter had ever seen her.

Walter breathed in and out. 'You must understand, this is not what I want for *my* daughter, Judy.'

'If you were a woman, if you'd actually given birth you'd feel differently—'

'Oh, not women and childbirth raising its ugly head again.'

144

'No – male indifference.'

Walter stopped as if he'd been shot and for once he was quite silenced.

'Miss Tufnell, the headmistress—'

'I know who the headmistress is, thank you.'

'Miss Tufnell has been told that I will collect her from the school tomorrow.'

Judy put her hand to the handle on the door and started to turn it, because as far as she was concerned that was an end to the matter.

'This is not what I want, Judy,' Walter repeated, using his most ominous tone, and for no reason she could name Judy thought back to the war years that Walter spent in Norway, years when he had had to do terrible things in order to just survive, years which had hardened him, in the same way that her dear friend Meggie had been changed so terribly by the war, by the things she'd had to do.

Judy turned from the door, advancing back .. slightly into the room.

'I know it's not what you want, Walter, and I'm very sorry, but things have gone too far already, really they have. Quite frankly I had rather take Kim away from her school than be facing her funeral.'

'What nonsense—' Walter started to say, but then stopped, looking less certain about everything, less of a patriarch, and more of a human being.

Judy turned back to the door.

'It's all gone so wrong, everything's gone so wrong since the accident,' she muttered, and was gone before Walter could think of anything else to say.

Kim was home within twenty-four hours, not entirely sure of what was going on. Once she was home Judy did her best to help her with her medical problems, taking her to see Dr Farnsworth, but the doctor was unable to prescribe much except emollients, and a better diet, with plenty of fresh air.

'Perhaps when the young lady comes back from her new school, we shall find a vast improvement. I'm sure we will,' he added, giving Kim an avuncular smile, but Kim, as was her permanent habit nowadays, didn't even seem to notice it, her eyes being fixed somewhere between the doctor and the floor. 'Personally I'm a great believer in a change of scenery for these kinds of conditions,' he went on, having received no encouragement from his young patient. 'Now, Kim, I want a word with your mother, if you wouldn't mind sitting outside for a few minutes?'

Kim having taken herself back to the waiting room the doctor faced Judy alone, and took from Kim's file a letter whose heading rang more than a bell with Judy, as it should, since it was a letter written on Walter's town writing paper, and in his own hand.

'Kim's father has written to me, in his absence, voicing his concern about his daughter, and I have to say that I take a great deal of what he says quite

146

seriously. In his opinion, the current manifest
ations we are witnessing with Kim – loss of weight,
inability to communicate properly, the eczema on
her arms and legs, and so on – are just the result of
some sort of shock after the appalling accident that
happened to her cousin. He may, of course, be
right, her father may well be right, that Kim is
merely suffering from some long-term shock.'

'Then I have no more to say on the matter to you,
Dr Farnsworth, because I don't happen to agree
with my husband.'

The doctor nodded as if Judy hadn't spoken, a
male habit which Judy always found peculiarly
irritating.

'On the other hand he may well be wrong.' The
doctor stood up and walked to the window. 'I
myself think that Kim may actually be having quite
a serious breakdown. You see, when we say
"breakdown" we mean just that. Her mental and
physical health has broken down under the stress
of seeing the awful result of the prank that resulted
in her cousin's accident. The mind has a huge influence on the body, as we are all increasingly aware.
It is not a myth, people, and animals, do die of
broken hearts.' He turned to face Judy. 'Your
husband doesn't think she should be sent away, but
after giving it some good deal of thought, I think
you're right, I think she should go away, to somewhere quite other, somewhere where she could run
about and not be "Kim Tate" any more. I think that
might just pull her back from the brink, you know?'

'Is she that bad?'

Judy found herself standing up, her hand again on her chest, and as always at times of panic hardly able to swallow, let alone breathe.

'She's very bad, Mrs Tate, you and I can see that. Always provided that you place her in safe, re-assuring, above all happy hands, I think we can win this one. But believe me, you have stepped in just in time, and only just in time too. Nevertheless, we are in time. And that, after all, is all that really matters.' He smiled reassuringly at Judy. 'Take heart, Mrs Tate, you'll win, I know you will.'

As they walked back home with Kim silent by her mother's side, her eyes on the ground, the doctor's words came as a great comfort to Judy, and she found herself trying to memorise some of the phrases he'd used so that she could repeat them to Walter, but then, remembering that Walter had written to the doctor to try in some way to persuade him that Kim didn't need to be sent away, she resolved just to make all the necessary arrange-ments to book their passage to Ireland, and on to the place recommended by Waldo, whatever it was called – Loughnalaire.

Kim didn't know it, but the moment she stepped on to the boat and, turning, waved to Hugh and Loopy who were standing on the quay, she could feel Ireland stretching out its arms to her. She could feel its wild, assertive spirit, its gentle, moody humour, its air of being cut off from the rest of Europe, of being its own person, always sweetly summed up by its friends in the words *ah – Ireland*.

How it was that she had at one moment been summoned to the headmistress's study, and the next discovered her mother throwing out her school uniform, replacing the wretched grey garments with Kim's own home clothes, Kim would not find out for many years. That it had happened was undisputed, that it was due to Mr Waldo Astley she didn't know, but whatever the reasons, whatever the decisions, the very idea that she wasn't returning to school seemed so un-believable that even kissing Hugh and Loopy goodbye was only sad once she saw how small they were growing on the harbourside. Tiny figures reminding her of the tiny figures that Hubert used to place on the station platforms of his toy train set when he was little, and their black Scottie dog Hamish used to take such a personal pride in swallowing.

''Bye, Granny, 'bye, Grandpa!' she called suddenly.

Seeing her waving one of the other passengers turned and smiled at Judy. 'You'll be returning to Ireland, will you, then?'

Judy shook her head.

'No, I'm taking my daughter there.' She indi-cated Kim who was still staring back to where the shore had once been. 'To school.'

'To school is it, in Ireland? It's usually the other way, we usually get taken to school in *England*.'

Judy laughed. 'I'm taking her to Loughnalaire.'

'Loughnalaire?' The tall, thin lady in the immaculately cut tweed suit stared at Judy for a few seconds, obviously lost for words. 'Loughnalaire. I see. Have you been to the place, yet?'

'No, but I've seen photographs of it. And a family friend recommended me to it. It seems he knows it very well.'

The woman glanced secretively towards Kim and then looked back at Judy.

'I don't know whether she'll like it. It's very – unconventional. I just hope she'll like it, poor child.'

She left them to go below to the bar, while Judy and Kim remained on deck, Judy staring back at the widening sea behind them and wondering what on earth she was doing taking Kim across the sea to a strange place merely on Waldo Astley's say-so. After all, what would he know, for heaven's sake? He didn't even have children. What if Walter turned out to be right, and it was just the wrong thing for Kim?

Finally she said·in over-bright tones to Kim, 'Come along, young lady, time for some lunch, methinks.'

There was nothing Kim felt less like doing at that moment than eating lunch, but seeing that the sea was roughening she followed her mother down below.

'I know the last thing you want is lunch, darling,' Judy said, guessing at her thoughts. 'But the truth is you have more chance of surviving crossing the Irish Sea if you eat than if you sit about watching the waves and the winds, believe me.'

Kim didn't know it but her pale young face with its dark hair and dark eyes peering out from under her black astrakhan hat, with its matching black astrakhan collar, was a touching sight. All she knew was that her mother was ordering lunch, and she was meant to eat it. She stared unhappily about her, and was relieved to see the woman who had first spoken to her mother coming across at Judy's invitation to join them at the lunch table. It would take Judy's mind off how much Kim wasn't eating.

'It would be your first trip abroad, doubtless,' she said comfortably to Kim, pushing a cigarette into a long black holder and placing it to the side of her red-lipsticked mouth, the way a sea captain might place his pipe while intent on steering a boat.

Kim quickly realised that the placing of the holder was most strategic, for it enabled Cicely Smythe to smoke and talk while carefully avoiding the smoke drifting past her eyes. In some awe she wondered whether Miss Smythe would keep the holder there while raising her gin and tonic to her lips. She was almost disappointed when she found that the holder was carefully placed against an ashtray and Miss Cicely Smythe drank her gin in the normal way. She and Judy chatted and drank, ate and reminisced about the war for the whole journey, so that Kim was able to avoid doing anything at all except pick at her food, and stare out of the window at the wind and the rain, at the tops of the waves that seemed to be determined to hurl themselves forward against the windows of the ship, as if infuriated by the disturbance the vessel was causing as it ploughed through the rough seas.

As Ireland approached, and despite the gale, they finally went to the windows and pressing their noses against the glass saw the wonder of Cobh, and the approaching shore. As she watched it, silent as always, seeing its wild, strange outlines, without quite realising it Kim was already putting Bexham behind her.

Once they were through customs and reunited with their luggage, Cicely Smythe shook Judy and Kim by the hand.

'I'll keep in touch with the young lady here, if you'd like that, Mrs Tate, once you've returned. Just keep a weather eye on her. Meanwhile, if you want to prolong the journey, why not take the jaunting car? Kim will enjoy that, and it'll drop you right at Loughnalaire's doors.'

She nodded briskly at Kim.

'Pat the pony for me,' she ordered. 'He's quite a friend of mine.'

Kim hesitated, hearing Cicely's words but not meeting her eyes, her own as always fixed somewhere near to the ground. Nevertheless she went to the pony's head and patted it, and the pony, knowing that she was a stranger, picked up his head from its sleepy position in the shafts and stared at her. For the first time since the accident Kim found herself really looking into another pair of eyes, eyes that were somehow so shamingly honest that instead of turning away from him she stayed at his head, talking to him in a low voice.

'He likes that, does Josephat.'

The driver, a tall man, red-faced, large-handed, with a nose that spoke of having been boxed at a great deal when he, and it, were much younger, nodded at Kim and the pony.

'Ladies.' He touched his cap. 'I'm Phelim O'Brien and I gather I'm to take you to Loughnalaire where one of you will be stopping for the nonce, is that right?'

'And then it'll be your brother over there who will be taking me to Tarkington House, young man, is that right?'

'So it is, ma'am, so it is.' Phelim scratched his head, and replaced his cap, before opening the passenger doors one by one.

'And how far would Loughnalaire be from Tarkington House?' Judy asked him as she stepped in.

'As the crow flies it'll be about fifty, I'd say.'

Kim looked round at that. She'd heard Cicely telling Judy that she lived 'nearby' and would keep an eye on Kim. Now it seemed she lived far away, miles away, and would no more be keeping an eye on Kim than she would be giving up smoking.

'Do you think, like,' Phelim asked them, shouting over the sound of the weather, while swerving to avoid a clutch of horse-drawn caravans with donkeys tied behind, 'do you think, like, that you deserve to be sent to Loughnalaire, miss?'

'How do you mean?'

'Well, like Loughnalaire, you know, it's a kind of a class of a strange place, full of hopeless cases and that's just the teachers!'

Kim's grip on her new handbag tightened and for the first time in a long time she looked directly at her mother. First Miss Smythe's house being miles away and not nearby at all, and now the driver making jokes about her new school – what on earth would this place Loughnalaire actually be like?

However, she was soon distracted by Phelim who, having a corner in good stories, kept Judy and Kim so entertained on the short journey. It was only when the red-painted cart finally left the road to make its way up a stony track towards no visible house, that Kim's nerves returned with a vengeance.

The drive was up a steep hill, reducing the pony to a slow walk, and as she looked back behind them Kim realised that it must be well over a mile long, reaching back to the road, and, in her mind's eye, to freedom. She imagined that she could always run away, although she thought she would not run back to Bexham. She would run far away where nobody knew her, where the haunting thought of Jenny and her scars, of the pain she must have suffered, must still be suffering, was put so far

154

behind her cousin that it would eventually fade away, never to return.

Finally and at last the crest of the hill was reached, and down below them they could see a colony of whitewashed thatched cottages built round a square house with long elegant floor-length windows, the whole surrounded by semi-tropical plants and palms leading down to a strand of fine white sand, and a blue sea that sparkled under a sunny March sky.

Phelim pulled up beside the largest of the cottages. It boasted a dark green door set about with fishing nets and buckets which when Kim stared into them held everything from fish to crabs.

'This is it, this is Loughnalaire?'

'It is so, ma'am. It is that.' He jumped down from his seat, removed Kim's large suitcase and two smaller ones from the boot of the jaunting car and placed them beside the buckets and fishing nets. 'You'll be thinking like you've arrived in some kind of madhouse, but you'll find good understanding here, and that's the truth.'

'So this is Loughnalaire?' Judy said again.

'It is so, ma'am, and has been for some years now,' Phelim said, climbing back into the jaunting car and flicking a fly from his pony's rump. 'The gint what owns her had the cottages all knocked down where they were, and then again around the house, which has been here a little longer, as you can see from her height. And hasn't each of the cottages been *modrenised*, as we say in Ireland, d'you see, so that they no more resemble the things they all once was, any more than I do them Beatles now, if you get my meaning? And haven't they all been installed with not just running water but hot and cold running water and comprehensible radiators too, the shibeens that is, not the Beatles. And now here's Mrs Hackett come to welcome you, and with some luck she'll have a mind to make some tea.'

Phelim hopped off his driver's seat again, dropping the reins on his pony's back so that the animal immediately walked off to find a bite of grass, taking the startled Judy and Kim along with him, while Phelim took off his cap and blushed scarlet as he greeted the tall and beautiful figure of Mrs Atlanta Hackett. Mrs Hackett, a widow for some years as Phelim had explained to his passengers, and dressed in a long gown made of a vivid red velvet embroidered with a large gold Celtic A on its bodice, was sweeping majestically down the steps at the front of the lovely stone Georgian house.

Unable to find the exact patch of grass for which it was searching, the jug-eared pony continued his ambulation further and further from the house, until he pulled himself to a stop on a circle of emerald green in front of a group of whitewashed cottages.

'Get lost, Josephat!' a cheerful voice came from within the nearest of the cottages. 'Hasn't the Widow told you off enough about eating her precious herbs?'

156

A young, dark-haired girl who looked to be about Kim's age appeared in the doorway dressed in an Aran fisherman's sweater, black wool trousers and wellington boots. Although winter was barely over, her skin looked brown, perhaps tanned by salt sea winds and early spring sunshine.

'You must be the new guests,' she called up to the jaunting car, and wandered up unhurriedly towards the trap to pick up the pony's reins and lead it round to its proper position nearer the house. 'I'm Dorothy, and if you're quick and change, you'll be just in time to come and sea weed.'

For the first time for heaven only knew how long Kim's eyes met Judy's, before she turned to the girl.

'There isn't a verb to sea weed,' she said, at her most prim. 'So I don't know what you mean.'

'There is too, at Loughnalaire.' Dorothy laughed. 'Oh, there's a verb to sea weed all right, as you'll discover soon enough.'

By now Judy and Kim were preparing to step down from the jaunting car, which had been duly returned to Phelim. He rolled up his cap and pretended to threaten Josephat with it, then carefully spat on his hand and wiped his cap over it before handing Judy and Kim down with solemn courtesy.

'I keep telling Josephat he'll have someone over the cliffs one of these days, the great eejity moke,' he sighed. 'I'm just praying it won't be someone notorious.'

The small party's attentions now turned to their hostess.

'Mrs Lyle,' Mrs Hackett boomed in a quite wonderful baritone. 'Miss Lyle. I trust you had a pleasing journey, and have indeed and duly arrived safely on the shores of Erin?'

'Tate,' said Judy. 'Actually. Tate. Not Lyle. An easy mistake. And we had a good journey, for the time of year.'

'Ah yes. Do you know, I kept saying "sugar, sugar" to remind myself when I heard the jaunting car at the door bringing you to us, but it's difficult when you don't take it yourself, don't you find? Now come in, why don't you? There's tea made and plenty of it laid, as I am convinced you'll be starving after your epic passage.' She turned to stare at Phelim's feet before pushing open the tall, elegant door that led into the tall and elegant hall of her house. 'Phelim, you will do me a blessed favour and remove those boots of yours before you set one foot in my house, and pray to God that one day we will indeed see you finally change your stockings.'

'Ah me, the Widow Hackett's had it in for me socks these two years,' Phelim sighed, but he removed his shoes, revealing a sock so thick that it might have been made of chain mail.

'Follow me, now, ladies, follow me,' Mrs Hackett called. 'Kim, isn't it? She'll be wanting some tea, and then off to sea weed I dare say, as they all do.'

'I think Kim's wondering,' Judy began, 'I think

Kim's wondering what sea weeding is, Mrs Hackett.'

Kim was wondering what sea weeding was, but since she was also feeling a little lost for words she nodded in agreement with her mother, her eyes sliding round the house, taking in the old furnishings, the silks and the brocades of bright but faded nature, the sculptures of horses long gone to their makers, the velvet cushions that had received so many visitors that they were now as thin as tissue paper.

'Ah, Mrs Sugar – no, no, it's Mrs *Tate* – sea weeding is the main and wonderful occupation of everyone at Loughnalaire.'

'Yes, but what *is* it?' Kim spoke up for herself at last.

Mrs Hackett stared at Kim for a few seconds, one hand placed nobly on her gold embroidery, the other still held in a welcoming gesture.

'Well, now,' she began. 'How shall we explain sea weeding? If I said to you now – Kim – we are now all of us going sea weeding, what would you expect to experience? What is it now that you would be thinking?'

Kim's eyes returned to the floor once more.

'Well,' she said, addressing her feet. 'I'd say it would sound as if we were expected to weed the sea.'

'And you'd be right, for that's what we do here, morning, noon and night. We weed the sea, thanking God for its abundancy as we do so. The weed, you see, is good for everything from medicines to frying with your breakfast bacon – that's the thin one, mind, not the thick old leathery stuff.' She clapped her hands as they walked into the conservatory, calling back to Phelim. 'Hurry along with Miss Tate's portmanteaux, would you, Phelim. Or there'll be no tea for you, and that's the truth. Ah, now here's young Dorothy again. She'll take you off to your shibeen while Phelim follows with the cases. Mind, not a crumb of tea, Phelim, and never mind you've no teeth to your head, until that pony's tied up as it should be. Off you go now, all of you, while I give tea to Mrs Tate here in the orangery. Off, off, off!'

For a moment, as Kim looked back at her mother, while dutifully following Dorothy and Phelim, she was once again a small child being left at Bexham kindergarten, but then, thankfully in a way, Judy saw the distant, seemingly uncaring look come back into her eyes, and she followed the others out of the orangery, tossing her dark hair back in a manner that told her mother that really, she did not care who she was with, or where she was left.

Mrs Hackett went to the tea table, which was both welcoming and laden.

'You will of course concern yourself no end at having to leave your daughter with us, Mrs Tate,' she said, in a matter of fact voice, as Judy, now feeling quite as lost as Kim, stared round the fine old glasshouse filled with orange trees, and jasmine, with clusters of plumbago and strange tall nodding purple trumpet flowers, not to mention a mass of prickle-branched bougainvillaea climbing unchecked through many of its immediate neighbours. The profusion of growth and flower was helped partly by the vast expanse of thick Victorian glass, but in the main by a huge cast iron stove that stood in the corner of the room and centrally heated the domed glasshouse through a complex of matching heavy iron pipework.

To one side of it in an old deck chair a very large red-bearded man in a collarless grey flannel shirt, brown cord trousers held up with a length of clothes line, and large hobnailed boots with no laces had collapsed. He was fast asleep, the top half of his face shielded from the remains of the daylight by an open copy of Dante's *Inferno*.

'It would be better, on the whole, if you take no notice of Mad Rufus there,' Mrs Hackett advised Judy, seeing her guest's eyes straying to the recumbent figure. 'He's the odd-jobber, and sure if ever there was a depiction of a trade that fitted the subject quite properly, there you have it. He's as lazy as a Sunday in July, and if he can do something wronger than either you or I he will take it upon himself so to do it. A fence needs mending, Mad Rufus will mend it so it falls down quicker. A gate needs painting, he will paint it so that it peels the faster. A door needs a handle, be sure that the next time you make to turn it the wretched thing will come away in your hand. He's only good for reading, and even then.' She shook her head, and poured a cup of tea while nodding to the milk and sugar. 'It's all there. Please help yourself, especially to the dropped scones, for if ever there was a product that deserves its name Loughnalaire's dropped scones do exactly that, and then let us sit down and set to and realise what the full extent of what you're committing Kim to exactly is, or something like.'

Mrs Hackett sat down opposite Judy, and her handsome head inclined towards her guest with a serious sense of purpose.

'I will proceed now – if you won't be upset – to try to commit to you our sense of purpose here. To begin with there are no rules. There are no punishments. The young adults, as they are always referred to – thus setting in their own minds that they are no longer children by any stretch of the imagination – are allowed to do what they want, which means they go where they want and how they want, from their own shibeens. If that sounds alarming, believe me, you find that young adults, after the initial surprise, soon turn out a great deal more sensible than older adults ever give them credit for. That's to begin with. Next we find that talk is of no use whatsoever – the young people who come here have often been wounded by too much talk, too much time spent dealing with them when what they really need is to be turned loose, like the horses in spring, and let gallop about a bit, so that their spirits, which are often in a dark mood when they first arrive, are changed by the feeling of freedom and unity that nature brings to us all, if we would but stop and listen.'

As she listened to Widow Hackett Judy found a feeling of peace gradually settling round her. Perhaps it was the tea, the sound of snoring from the corner, the warmth of the room, the flowers and plants, but she found herself wishing that she could stay behind with Kim and enjoy just such benefits as Mrs Hackett was describing.

'So, as I'm saying, Mrs Tate, the discipline of Loughnalaire lies within us, not within a rule book. We have no particular order to the day, no set times for set lessons, not at any rate that we give out. What happens is that teachers arrive at certain times to give lectures, and as at university those interested turn up. Curiosity d'you see, Mrs Tate, is one of the best teachers in the world, in fact the best, as far as I can see. If you become curious about the history of such a place as Loughnalaire, then your curiosity can lead you to the history of Ireland, the history of the English in Ireland, ancient Ireland, the invading Danes, mythology, and heaven only knows what other subjects. Equally, if you become interested in fly-fishing, which Phelim takes – in a moment you might well find you're interested in the habits of fish, their feeding and their breeding. From the fish can come an interest in the lakes, and in the sea. And so we come perhaps to the Irish Sea, the coracles in which our ancestors set out across the water, the monasteries where they wrote and illuminated the scriptures, the gardens they tended, for food and flowers. And from there to the deities, to the mysticism upon which we can base belief, to belief itself, and the nature of love. More tea, Mrs Tate?'

Judy nodded and held out her cup, a magnificent affair of faded flowers and gold edging, the saucer of which had been much mended.

'I wish I'd been sent here, Mrs Hackett,' she said simply. 'I don't suppose you have exams, do you? It might be difficult, I would have thought, with such a – such an unusual way of learning.'

Mrs Hackett placed the cup beside her and sighed before returning to her own place.

'We would have exams if we wanted to know how well or badly all the members of our family, as we call them, knew every subject, but it's really of very little interest. We look at the whole person, not just a narrow piece of knowledge. Now as soon as you've finished that piece of tea, we'll be on our way round the grounds and I'll show you more, and you can ask more, and make up your own mind if this is the place for Kim. Although whether she wants to remain Kim we won't know until she's been here a few days, sometimes weeks.'

'How do you mean?' Judy leaned forward, not understanding.

'Well, see how it is, Mrs Tate. We find that when they first come to us, they often decide to change their names. It helps them forget their sorrows. At present we have, now let me see – yes, we have Bat Masterson, King Arthur and Cleopatra, not to mention any number of film stars – and all of them, at this moment, I sincerely hope, are in the middle of making us some excellent continental pastries for supper.'

The Widow smiled suddenly, a wide smile that was soaked in humour, as if she knew just how mad she must sound to Judy, but it was also a confident smile.

As Judy was shown round the small estate it occurred to her that such a place as Loughnalaire was more special than it was possible to imagine. It wasn't just the proximity to the sea, with its wonderful early spring colour, and the coastal paths that ran from the gardens to a great expanse of water which was whipped daily by the wind, reflecting every nuance of the weather like some vast obliging mirror, but the cottages themselves, grouped as they were near, but not cheek by jowl with, the elegant old house. Here each young adult was given their own 'shibeen'. Generous enough in size they were also simple to the point of being Spartan. Whitewashed walls, rough hewn, a simple desk and chair, a plain iron bed, a bathroom, and galley kitchen made up the whole.

'They eat alone, or they eat with us. Most eat with us, you'll find, not just to get out of cooking for themselves but because they all turn to cooking. A bit of competition in the kitchen does no harm, we find. Plus of course there's a great deal of music played after supper and lunch too, sometimes.'

Mrs Hackett gave a sudden, warm laugh, as she opened the door of yet another of the cottages. 'This is reserved for young Kim. Ah yes, I see Phelim has put her bags in there, good, good. Now time for you to say goodbye. If you would oblige by not making too much of a fuss. It does help with the first few days if the parent or guardian does the quick peck on the cheek, turns on her heel and goes off with an attempt at cheeriness. It's to do with not making them feel as if they're being left with the gargoyles and the ogres, not to mention the banshee.'

Hearing footsteps behind them on the stony path and a whistle that she thought she recognised Judy turned to see Kim approaching them from the beach, but before she could hurry forward she felt a restraining hand on her arm.

'Remember not to show your anxiety now, Mrs Tate. For isn't it just like the rider's seat on a horse? Show your anxiety and it conveys itself.'

Behind Kim, and indeed below her, talking and laughing, wandering along the shore in great groups came an army of weeders. Boys and girls, tanned and healthy from being outdoors, in fisherman's sweaters and sturdy shoes, carrying buckets of the precious thin seaweed – all were climbing up towards them reminding Judy of some kind of young, heavenly choir. Indeed such was their outward serenity, their sense of being at one, that had they been carrying palms they might have been early Christians.

After an anxious look back to Mrs Hackett, Judy called to Kim, 'And how much weed did you pull, young lady?'

Kim thrust her bucket towards her mother.

'Quite good,' she said, 'considering it's my first time.'

'Well done, darling.' Judy swallowed something near to a lump in her throat away, before patting Kim lightly on her arm. 'I'd best be off now or I'll miss the evening boat. Phelim's taking me back,' she added, as if it was something he always did. 'And then I'll be home, at Bexham, in a trice.'

Kim looked away down at the advancing crowd below.

'Dorothy said you'd be going soon.' She nodded back down to the dark-haired girl, who waved cheerily in reply. 'I'm going to have tea with her, in the shibeen. 'Bye.'

She kissed Judy perfunctorily, and as she did so Judy realised that she was being given her marching orders, and so she turned quickly, leaving Kim to walk back down to her new friend.

Phelim drove Judy back to the boat, which she duly caught feeling oddly light without Kim and her luggage, and although she sat on her own for the whole journey, gazing out to the darkening sky and the sea stretching behind the boat in a dark, ever widening sheet, she felt at peace.

Kim didn't watch her mother leave. Instead she followed Dorothy back down to the beach where Dorothy had left her spade.

'See?' Dorothy picked up her spade, and then, turning once more to the path, she went on in approving tones. 'See how much easier it is for them, if you let them just go off, don't make a fuss? That way they don't feel as if they've thrown you to the wolves. It's much easier for the poor things if you let them go quickly and quietly.'

Kim nodded. It was true. It was much easier, but it was also odd, because suddenly Judy didn't seem quite like her mother any more, more like a friend of whom she had to take great care.

'Come on . . .' Dorothy turned. 'Oh, and by the way, what do you like to be called?'

Kim thought for a second.

'Jenny.'

If she was honest with herself Mattie had been both dreading and looking forward to Jenny's coming home. The night before she hardly slept, lying staring into the light that filtered down from the attic into the main bedroom wondering how she would cope, hoping against hope that she wouldn't panic at the sight of her daughter's bandaged face in familiar surroundings once more.

'Darling, I can't tell you how wonderful it is to see you home.'

Jenny lay back against the familiar faded brocade of the old family sofa.

'It's wonderful to be home, Mummy,' she lied.

In actual fact it was terrible. As the ambulance men had helped her through the door she'd wanted to turn and follow them, go back to the hospital, to the kind nurses and concerned doctors, for the truth was that being home was almost worse than anything that had yet happened to her, because it was only now that the extent of her injuries became totally apparent to her, only now that she realised that she, Jenny Tate, was truly scarred for life. In the hospital there had been so many other people, of all ages, much worse off than herself that she'd felt practically normal, but once home, just one foot over the threshold, she sensed at once how odd she had become, and how normal everyone else was. The moment the ambulance men said goodbye to her, and carefully closed the front door behind them, Jenny knew that everyone else in the world was going to be like her mother who was now bending over her smelling vaguely of Chanel No. 5, straightening the cushions behind her, putting on the television for her. Everyone else, apart from Jenny, was going to be perfect.

'I'll bring you tea on a tray, shall I?'

'No, I can come and get it . . .'

'Darling, don't be silly, we'll have it together.'

Mattie hurried off to the kitchen where she half shut the door and then leaned against it, her hand on her chest, breathing in and out, as slowly and evenly as possible. She must not panic, she must not show her distress. She knew from everything she had read on the subject that the first thing nurses were taught was not to show fear or concern for their patients in their eyes. Already she felt she

169

had failed, fussed too much. John would be home soon. John would know just how to be, he always did. John was so patient with anyone ill or injured, the old and the sick, with children, with people in the village who were down on their luck. The thought comforted her, calmed her, made her able to start to lay the tea tray, putting out all Jenny's favourite teatime foods: scones, coffee cake, chocolate fingers, everything she could think of she had made or bought for her home-coming.

'I am hoping Daddy will be back soon,' she said conversationally to Jenny, while the kettle on the hob appeared to be taking an hour to boil, and she plumped up yet more cushions on the sofa. 'Before he left for work this morning he said he's going to take us out tomorrow, round the Point, that sort of thing. That will be nice, won't it?'

Jenny nodded, wishing that nowadays her mother wouldn't use a special voice to her, wouldn't talk to her as if since being in hospital Jenny'd become someone else entirely, as if the accident had left her not injured, but brainless. She stared through her bandages at the small black and white television in the corner of the room trying to make out what was on the screen, and realising it was children's television she quickly closed her eyes. If her father too started to talk to her in a special voice she thought she might scream and run back to the bright white room in the hospital that had become her womb, her place of safety where there were no perfect people, no people without scars, fussing and using special voices, and plumping up cushions too often.

'Well, now, young Jenny, back home at last.'

She must have fallen asleep momentarily, or at least retreated into another world, because it seemed to her that she was only woken by the sheer weight of John Tate sitting down on the sofa.

'Hallo, Daddy.'

Jenny tried to smile at her father through her bandages, while her mother chattered inconsequentially in the background, pouring tea, and handing out small scones with cream and jam on them.

'Glad to be home, I expect.'

John bit into his scone and smiled as if he knew that the answer would be sure to be in the affirmative.

'Not really, no.'

John put his scone down on his plate, turned to where he could hear Mattie busying herself in the kitchen, and then back to Jenny once again.

'What do you mean, Jenny?'

'I feel worse here, actually. I want to go back to the hospital.'

'But we've been so looking forward to this—'

Jenny stared at her father, realising at once that he really, really didn't understand. She didn't want to have to lie to her parents, she didn't want to have to lie to make them feel better about how she felt. Lies were for people who were going to go through life without scars, lies were for people who hadn't

171

been in a dreadful accident, lies were for the rest of the perfect world, not Jenny's imperfect one.

Her father put a hand out and laid it over one of her bandaged ones. 'You'll soon start to feel yourself again.'

'More tea coming up!'

Mattie's voice came floating towards the pair of them on the sofa sounding more relaxed. Jenny looked ahead of her. Oh well, so long as they felt better about everything, now that she was home, what did she matter?

Later, as she lay in the confines of her familiar room, with its pictures from a childhood that now seemed to belong to someone else, its photographs of herself and Sholto, sailing, playing on the beach, walking the Downs with their parents, the person in the photos definitely seemed to be another girl, another Jenny Tate, someone she had once known but did not now even recognise. Night time was the worst, staring into the darkness wondering if morning would ever come, staring at a future that seemed too bleak to even imagine.

When morning came she watched the light filtering through the pale lemon chintz curtains and thought she saw sunshine which she now realised she dreaded, thought she heard voices outside raised in happy laughter in which she now believed she would never join, thought she could smell frying bacon which she would never again look forward to eating. She heard her father's calm, clear and mellifluous voice calling goodbye to her mother, and she hated both them and their joy, and more than that she hated their happiness and their love for each other. Most of all, she hated herself.

'I don't want to get up today, if you don't mind.'

'No, of course, if you don't want to, darling. What would you like?'

'Just to stay here – no, don't draw the curtains.'

'Daddy's hoping to come by and take us for a spin this afternoon. He thought if I sat in the back with you, he could drive us to Ditchling for tea.'

'Not today, Mummy, if you don't mind. I don't want to go out today.'

Jenny didn't add *or any day*, because it was really quite obvious from her voice.

Loopy called round a few days later and hearing that Jenny was refusing to come downstairs just nodded her head as if she hadn't expected anything different.

'She's bound to hate the idea of being seen in public. I would.'

'Doesn't want to go in a car. Yesterday when John tried to coax her downstairs to go out for a spin, she burst into tears.' Mattie looked at her mother-in-law, despair in her eyes. 'I know I'm failing her, Loopy, and I can't stop myself. I fuss too much, or too little. I'm either coming over too harsh, or too smothering. I've completely lost my balance. I can't sleep. I keep listening out for her. I keep thinking of myself, when I should be thinking

173

only of her. I really thought, after the war, after all everyone's all been through, that I might be better than this, but the truth is – I'm not.'

'Rein back, Mattie. Try to take each day hour by hour, even minute by minute, it's the only way, believe me. Tick off your achievements, and not your failures—'

'I'm all failure at the moment.'

'Not in my eyes.' Loopy gave her daughter-in-law a firm look. 'In my eyes you're coping quite splendidly. You haven't taken to the bottle, you haven't fallen to pieces and left everything to some nursing agency, you haven't become hysterical, which so many women would.'

'Oh, I have, I've become quite hysterical. Yesterday when Jenny was asleep, I walked out to the Point and yelled blue murder, all on my own.'

'Good, well if that's what's wanted, that's what's wanted. Put it down in your credit column. You did something practical to relieve your feelings. Now can I go and see my granddaughter and take her off your hands for a few days?'

'Of course.'

Mattie watched Loopy's elegant figure climbing up the stairs with an easy swinging gait that far belied her seventy-odd years. At that moment she seemed to Mattie to be stronger than she herself could ever be.

'Jenny? It's Grandy, darling, can I come in?'

Jenny had known all day that her grandmother was coming to visit her, and had been dreading it, but as soon as she saw her she felt quite differently. As if determined to look reassuring, her grandmother was wearing Jenny's favourite blue dress with the embroidered collar and cuffs, and she was just as she always was, slim, tall, American, with a husky voice and an easy manner.

'OK, so it's time for a change,' Loopy told Jenny without any preamble, having greeted her with a kiss.

Jenny stared at her. Perhaps because Loopy was an older woman, Jenny felt less imperfect in front of her grandmother than she did in front of Mattie. It was as if the older woman had scars that Jenny couldn't see, scars which were as real as Jenny's own none the less.

'How do you mean, time for a change?'

'I mean just that, it's time for a change, darling. Change of bedroom, change of view. So boring to stay in one place. So, you're coming to me at Shelborne, OK?'

'How do you mean?' Jenny's voice was still so listless it was hardly audible.

'You're coming to me, to my house, to stay with me, and I'll tell you why, because I need you to help me with my painting. See these?' She held up one of her hands and waggled her fingers at Jenny. 'They're giving me gip this damp old winter. I need someone to squeeze the tubes for me, or I will never finish what I have to do in time for my next exhibition. Waldo will drop me from his list, and I will then be out of a job, and getting in everyone's way.

175

So what do you say, will you come and help?'

Because she couldn't think of what to say, Jenny found herself nodding in agreement.

'Good oh. Then put your outdoor things on, and follow me. Mummy and Daddy will bring your suitcase round to Shelborne later.'

For Mattie, seeing Loopy coming downstairs with Jenny on her arm was a more than difficult moment, it was a shocking moment. The realisation that her mother-in-law had succeeded where Mattie had failed was devastating, and yet when Jenny suddenly stopped at the front door, reluctant to go any further, Mattie's heart stopped with her.

'People will stare, I hate people staring.' Jenny turned to her grandmother, the expression on her face one of outright panic.

'No, they won't, we won't let them.'

'People stared terribly in the hospital when I was leaving.'

'Then we'll stare right back. Now come on, Gwen's made tea, and you know what that's like, if anyone's more than two minutes late she moans terribly that we're keeping her from her telly. Besides, I have to get back to finish off a piece of the sky.'

Having packed a case for Jenny, Mattie watched as the two of them walked slowly down the front garden to the gate, then she went immediately to her small desk in the corner of the sitting room and sat down to write to Sholto at his boarding school.

Darling Sholto, I do hope you're not too worried about

Jenny, because if you are, don't be. She's come home from the hospital, and is staying with Grandy and Grandpa. We're all very thrilled to have her back, as you can imagine, Grandy most of all because Jenny is helping her with her paints on account of her fingers being a bit stiff at the moment. All the animals send their love, specially old Tousle. He misses you dreadfully, as I expect you miss him. It was a bit windy today, but the boats still went out, and I saw two yachts sailing round the Point so fast it was amazing. Do try hard with your Latin even though you hate it. Lots and lots of love, Mummy xxxxxxxxx

Mattie licked the envelope, licked the stamp, and then put the letter on the table beside her, wishing that it was the holidays and that Sholto was at home to play Scrabble with her. She glanced up at the clock. At least John would be home soon and he would help her pack up Jenny's things, and take them round to Shelborne, but whatever anyone said, relieved though Mattie was that Jenny had at last taken it into her head to go out and about, the fact was it was Loopy who'd wrought the miracle with Jenny, not Mattie, and that made Mattie feel not just wanting, but a complete failure.

Jenny settled contentedly into Shelborne in a way that continued to hurt her mother and, not unnaturally, delighted Loopy. She knew that Mattie must be hurt by her daughter's choice, but sometimes, as Loopy knew only too well, hurt maternal feelings had to be put aside for the good of something

177

much more important – in this case, Jenny.

Besides, Loopy thought, perhaps wrongly, that she knew a little bit more about depression and its physical effects than Mattie did, or ever would, she devoutly hoped. The months and years when her middle son, Walter, was missing presumed killed had taught Jenny's grandmother more about that particular form of continuing despair than she ever wished to learn. She knew what it was like to wake to darkness twenty-four hours a day. She knew what it was like not even to want to see those you loved, to care where they were, to mind about how much they cared for you. She knew what it was like when your pillow turned to stone, the floor beneath your feet to marshmallow, when every substance on earth, even earth itself, presented itself in a different, nightmarish form.

But despite Loopy's understanding, despite the fact that Jenny actually allowed her grandmother and grandfather to drive her about – as long as she was able to sit in the back seat, in the no man's land between the windscreen and the oval back window of Hugh's Rover 14 – it was Dauncy, her youngest son, back from the States with his lovely young wife Letty and their twin sons, who precipitated the necessary breakthrough.

With relatives running all over the house, and the consequent loss of privacy, Loopy was sure that Jenny would hightail it back to her parents' home. Jenny after all had a horror of anyone seeing her face. She did hightail it out of sight, which was perfectly understandable, but not back to her parents' house. She hightailed it up to Loopy's studio.

With Loopy out of the way seeing to her visitors, Jenny found herself at a loose end. Unable to just sit about staring at the view of the harbour and the water that the first-floor studio enjoyed, and in her grandmother's absence unable to occupy herself in squeezing tubes and handing them to Loopy, Jenny found herself drawing the view, and then painting it.

Except she didn't draw it once, she drew it over and over again, just as she painted it over and over again, never happy with the result, rubbing off the paint from the small canvas, only to re-apply it in tiny strokes. Time had seemed to cut itself into wedges like a too-heavy sponge cake made by some doting relative, and as with an unappetising cake time had to be got through, had to be swallowed, appreciated, only because it was there. Now, while she painted, perfected, groaned at her ineptitude, started again, over and over, until at last, as Dauncy and his family departed to complete their tour of England, the painting was finished, Jenny looked round and found to her astonishment that a week had flown by.

'You don't want to see it.'

'No, of course I don't.' Loopy looked calmly across at her granddaughter.

'I don't want to show it to you.' Jenny walked

179

over to the window, staring out at the scene below, which she knew had eluded her. 'I don't want to show it to you because I know it's no good.'

'And I don't want to see it because I know it's going to be better than anything I could do, so that's all right, neither of us wants me to see it.'

Jenny looked back at Loopy, at the same time turning the painting towards her grandmother. There was a small silence, and then Loopy patted her granddaughter lightly on the shoulder.

'This is good.' She gave Jenny a shrewd look. 'This is a good painting, and I will tell you why, because you have not depicted, you have painted. You have made a painting, not just a pale imitation. The waves, the boats, everything you have seen you have translated into a proper painting. That is what artistry is all about. Well done. It has a wonderful passion to it, this painting of yours. I wish I'd started younger, I'd have more vigour, the way you have, you lucky girl.'

'You paint wonderfully, Grandy, you know you do.'

'No, I don't. I paint adequately. I started too late. I'm simply not good enough. I sell because people share my vision of life, and they like what they see. Painting, for all that people intellectualise it, is, at the end of the day, Jenny, only entertainment on walls. Because it's sometimes a very painful process we try to make more of it than we should. Of course it's difficult, but then so is being a surgeon, so is being a general in an army. Doing anything properly is difficult. We mustn't make art into a special case; to do so is, in many ways, to demean it. It is a necessary and vital part of life, but it isn't, if you will forgive the analogy, the whole picture!'

Loopy laughed lightly. She wasn't given to making speeches, but, knowing Jenny as she did, she knew that while she might be pushing the verbal boat out a little too far, Jenny would be listening. Of all their grandchildren she was the one to whom Hugh and Loopy most related. Not that they didn't love them all, but Jenny had always seemed, quite naturally, to be closer to them in type, loving to play duets on the piano with Hugh, always sitting quite quietly, from a very young age, while Loopy painted, before the arthritis in her fingers and wrists made it less easy to do just what she wanted when she wanted.

Now the arthritis, because it meant she needed help, was helping Jenny, so, as Loopy always believed, some good was coming out of bad, something positive out of her pain.

But it wasn't just Dauncy visiting with his family that brought Jenny to begin to realise her artistry. Sometimes when the house was empty, Hugh having taken himself off to the Three Tuns, or to visit old friends down at the Yacht Club, Jenny would slip downstairs and play her grandfather's piano. Loopy would be painting busily but unable to help noticing the sound drifting upstairs, or that it was a quite different sound from Hugh's, that there was a deeper, more plangent quality to her granddaughter's playing. And as she listened, it seemed to Loopy that here too Jenny could find some sort of relief from the pain of what had happened to her, some kind of escape from her all too visible scars, from the realisation that she might never even be considered pretty again.

Nothing was said, not only because that was not Loopy's way, but because age had brought her to the knowledge that to comment on something was, all too often, to kill it stone dead. Artistic achievement was come upon in silence, as was healing.

Loopy had therefore said nothing to Hugh about Jenny, neither her paintings nor her piano playing, she had simply let it be. She pretended not to miss her tube squeezer, but merely arranged for Jenny to put the paints in squeezing order, and she herself got on with her work.

It was therefore only when Hugh returned early one day from his walk, the weather having suddenly turned, catching him unprepared in a heavy shower, so that he had hurried home to the warmth and comfort of his house, that he heard Jenny playing his beloved Blüthner. He knew it was his Blüthner, the way he would know the footsteps of his owner if he was a dog. He hurried through the gardens from the towpath along which he always returned, and started to let himself quietly into the drawing room, through the French windows, only to be hauled away by Loopy who'd seen him hurrying up to the back of the house from her studio window.

'Shsh!' Loopy put her finger to her lips, and beckoned to Hugh to follow her round to the back door.

'What's the matter?' Hugh asked, a little too loudly, as he always did when he was interrupted or put off course in any way.

'Nothing's the *matter*, Hugh,' Loopy told him, trying to keep the impatience out of her voice. 'Far from it, everything's fine and dandy. No, what *isn't* the matter is Jenny.' She put her finger to her lips again. 'Listen.'

Hugh listened. His granddaughter was playing a piece of Mozart. It was definitely Mozart, a piece he couldn't quite identify, but she was playing it quite beautifully. He stood listening, recognising the new, deeper tone that Loopy had been privileged to hear developing over the past weeks.

'She's playing just like my mother,' Hugh said, turning to Loopy, astonished. 'My mother played the piano just like that, after she lost her first baby, the baby before me. The power – it's not like a woman playing at all, more like a man. Such power – you'd never know it was a sixteen-year-old girl playing, would you?'

Loopy shook her head. Darling Hugh was so silly. Even though he loved women, he couldn't help making ridiculous comments, but that mattered not a whit. What mattered was that she knew from looking at his face that she'd been right – Jenny's talent was becoming exceptional.

Hugh turned to Loopy.

'We must help that,' he said, factually. 'Not to help that would be criminal.'

'Yes, it's what she needs to rebuild her confidence, I agree – always remembering, though, that since the accident the last thing that Jenny will ever do is appear in public.'

It was a challenge to Hugh, as much as to Jenny, and Loopy knew it. He turned away, his expression one of grim determination. Loopy knew that expression. It was one that had helped them all through the war. No matter what, now, as far as Hugh was concerned, his granddaughter Jenny was going to appear in public, playing the piano and dressed in a beautiful gown, that is if her grandfather had anything to do with it.

Long before he collapsed while walking home with Waldo Astley, Lionel had suspected that there might be something wrong with his health. He was too sensible not to notice that he kept feeling giddy at odd times, but he was also determined not to let it worry him. In his opinion, as he'd told young Max, to start worrying about your health when you were older was the thin end of the wedge, and meant you'd be in the croaker's parlour every five minutes plucking prescriptions out of his hand, and swallowing pills by the bucketful. No, as far as he was concerned, he was going to go out the way he wanted, playing bridge, or after finishing off a perfect gin and tonic in the Three Tuns.

Of course Waldo had known all this without

being told, and as soon as he could had Lionel facing Gloria and her new escort, one Mr Derek Burt, across the Bexham bridge table, which was an excellent dry run for the real match, to which they were to drive, it now seemed, in Waldo's spanking new Aston Martin DB4 convertible.

Lionel walked round the car, first this way, and then that, admiring it in silence. Finally he spoke.

'Pity you got rid of the Jag, though. I was very fond of that car.'

Waldo smiled, at the same time opening the passenger door for the older man. He knew this was in the way of being a rebuke for his extravagance, and couldn't have cared less.

'Haven't got rid of it, Lionel. No, I've mothballed the Jag for young Max, for his twenty-fifth birthday, if he can afford it. Told him so too, thought it might make him work harder at not being out of work.'

'You spoil that boy,' Lionel grumbled, but he smiled and touched his white moustache lightly before settling back in his seat. Waldo's having no children of his own was a great advantage, and Lionel would be a fool not to know it.

They sped along the long country road that was taking them to their game, feeling pleasantly nervous, and pleasantly excited at the same time. The challenge match was to take place at a large Regency house owned by a certain Philip Basnett, and when Lionel saw how elegant it was, and how perfectly set out the gardens and grounds, how the door was opened to them by a liveried servant, he found himself feeling distinctly pleased that they had driven up to the place in such a dazzling motor car. It then occurred to him that such was Waldo's pride in their partnership, and knowing him as he did now, he would not have put it past him to have bought the car for no better reason than to give them both the sort of confidence necessary to drive up to such a spread, with victory very much in mind.

Philip Basnett was a short, stocky man in his early forties. The fact that he was nominally patrician was in no way evident in his demeanour, which was full of the swagger and indifference to others which comes from inheriting a large fortune, too young. It seemed that Basnett had inherited steel much as some people inherit money, and now played with the vast income that it had afforded him, investing in everything from antiquities to fine art, and acquiring houses in the same way that other people bought clothes. He also loved to gamble.

Most unfortunately for all those who disliked him to about the same extent that he adored himself, he was instantly successful in everything he did. He had developed winning systems at the baize tables, and on the racecourse, so that while his investments went to fuel his indulgences, his indulgences also proved more than lucrative. Had he had even a half acceptable personality to go with these gifts he would have been one of the toasts of the town, but the man with everything also lacked everything. As far as good looks or good manners, or even social graces, went, from the moment that Philip Basnett introduced himself it became abundantly evident that he made up for everything he owned by lacking everything that everyone else would wish for him.

'Good evening, good evening.'

He smiled thinly at Waldo and Lionel who'd been ushered into the drawing room while a servant offered them both a choice of drinks from silver tray.

'Have you seen my Canalettos?'

Waldo looked momentarily taken aback, knowing that this was not the English way. The English hated anyone to mention their possessions, and would never dream of drawing attention to them. It was a rule.

'I have,' Lionel chipped in to Waldo's amusement as Basnett stared at him, frowning. 'In my book on Canaletto. Seen them all, so not to worry showing us, eh? Good stuff, of course, but we're here to play, aren't we?' he ended, looking at Waldo, all innocence.

'Yes, as my partner says, we're here to play,' Waldo agreed.

Basnett looked momentarily affronted, but within a few seconds had regathered his odious personality.

'Quite so, quite so,' he said, after a short pause. 'Your reputation precedes you, Mr Astley,' he

187

droned in his carefully constructed voice. 'One hears you are considered to be quite simply the tops.'

'All depends on who's doing the considering, Mr Basnett.'

'Let us find out the truth in the rumour, shall we? If I have a target in my sights, I like to shoot.' He smiled round at various of his other guests who were within earshot, and reassured by their polite smiles he pulled at his bow tie, tightening it in such a way as to make him look over-groomed. 'Yes, I like to shoot, all right,' he said again.

'Just what my friend Mr Hemingway always said.' Waldo smiled.

'You shot big game with Ernest Hemingway?' For a second Basnett was visibly impressed.

'No, sir. Just crap.'

At last, giving up on the lack of seriousness of the company, Basnett led the way through the drawing room to the card tables. He indicated that he was to be in the North seat and his partner, the enviably beautiful Marcia Farrow, in the South. Despite having met her and played against her before Waldo took time out to breathe in her magnificent beauty. Her fine sculptured face was, it had to be admitted, quite breathtaking. The almond eyes, the doeskin complexion, the sensual mouth, the air of haughty insouciance, it all had to be carefully noted before facing the cards. No, he must not be distracted by the stunning looks of South.

Having firmly put aside the image of Marcia's

beauty, turning it into something quite ordinary, and not at all distracting, Waldo found himself picking up the first hand of the night, an interestingly distributed hand, with long lines of clubs and diamonds, a singleton heart and a void in spades, but without enough points to open. If Lionel held cards strong enough to put them in the game, it could be a most interesting hand, a promise that looked even more like being fulfilled when Basnett and Waldo, not to mention Marcia, passed, leaving any bid to be made up to Lionel seated at West. Waldo waited. As the pause for Lionel became longer than usual he continued to stare at his cards while beginning to feel vaguely worried. After another fifteen seconds and still no bid, his anxiety accelerated. After all, a great deal was running on the game that night.

'What a – what a . . . Ruddy Yarborough. Got a ruddy Yarborough.'

Waldo kept his eyes on his cards while his heart sank, and he waited for the referee.

'West?' the referee began, only to be interrupted by Lionel.

'It's going to be this sort of evening,' Lionel continued as if nothing had happened. 'First hand and I get dealt a ruddy Yarborough. Although why it was ever called such, I shall never know.'

'West?' commanded the referee, his tone expecting silence.

'Some earl apparently called every hand with nothing over nine after himself. He was so

189

determined to be famous. And damn it, he is.' He stared at his cards more intently. 'Nothing over nine! Not a ruddy card.'

The silence around him had grown leaden with astonishment, a major contribution coming from various spectators who had drifted into the room from other parts of the house. Everyone was looking at Lionel, including Waldo, who like Basnett and Marcia had placed his cards face down on the table.

'Something wrong?' Lionel demanded. 'Chatty bridge, is it? Any round with no bid over one thrown in and play again, no shuffle? That's the ticket?'

'Ladies and gentlemen,' the referee intoned. 'I declare a misdeal.'

'I have never witnessed anything like it,' Basnett muttered. 'Never.'

Waldo summoned the referee. Nodding at Lionel, he said, 'Case of nerves, I'm afraid. Most unusual. If you will just give us a minute. He's on pills, might have affected him, you know. Shan't be long.'

He stood up and taking Lionel by the arm directed him into the next door room while Basnett and Marcia sat back sighing and lifting eyebrows at each other.

'Look – Lionel?'

Lionel looked at Waldo, a pathetic helpless look, as if he didn't know what was happening and needed Waldo to tell him.

'Look, Lionel,' Waldo began again, and then,

realising that if he told Lionel that he had just committed a major blunder it might lower his self-esteem even more, he changed his mind, and contented himself by saying, 'Look, concentrate on the cards, old boy. Just try to concentrate. You had a little lapse, that's all, so you need to concentrate even harder now, do you understand?'

'Extra hard. Of course. I understand.'

They returned to the card room only to be confronted by Basnett once more on his high horse.

'We can't have this kind of fiddle-faddle,' he burst out. 'This game is meant to be conducted on the highest playing level. I therefore demand that we set a bond in place. Five thousand pounds, we are all witness to this, five thousand pounds paid by anyone who further breaches the rules of the game.'

'Very well.'

Waldo reached into his breast pocket for his cheque book and quickly signed the security, handing it over to the referee without a sign of emotion. If it was money that Basnett wanted, he would give him money, and then he would thrash him leaving him scarred for any other game, in the same way that in the old days he would have left him with a duelling scar.

'Play,' the referee commanded, presenting North with a new pack of cards. Basnett dealt, and the game was on.

They seemed to have hardly begun when the small crowd that had gathered to watch swelled with the intensity of the play. As Waldo well knew Marcia Farrow was famous for her seemingly rash play, play that actually hid a cool head and a pragmatic heart. Throughout the subsequent game it was apparent to Waldo that Marcia, as always, had worked out the percentages, the distribution and the possible displacement of the cards with the precision of the Ice Queen that he knew her to be. But then with the thrust of the bidding, the to and fro of the play, it became gradually apparent to her opponents that Marcia might, just might, be still judging the elderly gentleman on her left to be as feeble-minded as he had first appeared to be.

Waldo stared at his cards. Bound by the rules of competition bridge he was unable to glance at Marcia. If he had been able to he might have sensed her dilemma, that she was hoping that her partner's singleton diamond would prove to be the ace which would without doubt give her a slam, a small one, but nevertheless a slam, and would effectively block her opponents' chances of going to Seven Diamonds. Both couples were vulnerable and therefore liable to draconian penalties for over-bidding. But. The eternal but that changes the nature of play – her partner had doubled, and if their opponents were bidding diamonds up to slam level that double had to mean something – that her partner had the required ace of diamonds. Banking on her hunch, Marcia called, taking the gamble for two reasons.

Firstly, the old gent was clearly only half there, it

would explain the oddness of his opening bid, and secondly the thing Marcia Farrow was most famous for at the bridge table was her cunning mixed with dash, her apparent ability to throw her hat into the ring before plunging into an unjustifiable contract. So now it was that seeing the winning post well in sight Marcia took the plunge and bid Six Spades.

'Double.' The spectators all stared at the old gentleman, knowing that he was possibly the least reliable of the four.

'Redouble,' came from a Basnett who suddenly did not care that he was out of control, so great was his impatience. He then repeated his bid, to be quelled by a look from the referee.

Since there were no other bids forthcoming, the auction was closed and the contract stood at Six Spades by South, doubled and redoubled.

The atmosphere intensified as Lionel led his ace of hearts on which Waldo discarded the five of clubs, having no hearts, just as Lionel had hoped. Lionel at once led another heart, which North, having hearts, had to cover, only for Waldo to trump it with a low spade, gambling on the fact that South must have high hearts in order to make up her points. He was proved right and the contract failed from that fell card alone. As it happened, and as Waldo and Lionel had sensed, they won another trick at the eleventh round when South's attempt to draw trumps without losing any foundered against Lionel's void in spades and Waldo's five spades to the ten. Distribution had won the day, but would not have done so had it not been for the astuteness of Lionel's read of the cards and his subsequent boldness in bidding.

Severely rattled now, as well as penalised 1000 points, Basnett and Farrow fell meekly and with hardly a blow struck in their defence in the next hands. When Waldo and Lionel got up from the table to enthusiastic applause they felt that not only had luck gone their way, but a little bit of good play had been rewarded too.

As they drove home, Waldo having torn up his bond – in the absence of Lionel who had marched off to pay nature a well earned visit – Lionel began to laugh.

'OK, so share the joke, you old rascal.'

Lionel put on a feeble face and assumed an old shaking voice. 'First hand I get dealt a ruddy Yarborough. Wonder how it ever got its name. Yarborough. Something to do with some earl, I believe.'

Waldo stared at him briefly before forcing his eyes to return to the road. 'You played the old fool up to the hilt!'

'Touch and go. I thought that miserable prune Basnett was going to call it a day, and then we'd have been done for, and that's the truth.'

'You fooled me, and you fooled them, and I can tell you at a pound a point I'm very glad you did – even if you didn't bargain on my having to stump up the bond.'

It was Lionel's turn to stare at Waldo.

'A pound a point? A *pound* a point? My God, Waldo – that means I've won – we've won – I've won . . .'

'Two thousand pounds, old *boy*.'

'In that case that's my swan song, Waldo old thing.' Lionel stared ahead of him, smiling, and paying no heed to the newness of the car he placed his feet up on the dashboard and closed his eyes contentedly. 'What a way to go, thrashing someone like Basnett, it's the stuff of dreams, really it is.'

'Come, come, you can't retire.'

'No, no, I shan't retire, I just won't play any more. But we certainly have had some sport, you and I. Great days.'

And he fell to silence, staring once more at the road in front of him lit by the Aston's headlights, by the moon overhead, by the memory of his last great evening at cards.

Chapter Five

Four thousand miles away Tam was not having such a happy experience. His first impression of the vast ranch on which he found himself in the hinterland of Texas was one of terrifying size, since it seemed to him that the whole spread must be as big, if not bigger, than his native Sussex.

'It's beef mostly, boy,' R.J. Dysart the owner told him, driving his huge red Dodge truck one-handed while smoking the longest King Size cigarette that Tam had ever seen with the other fist. 'We have ten thousand head of beef, and we do a bit of wheat and corn too, as well as forage for the stock, course.'

'How many acres do you farm altogether, sir?' Tam wondered, watching a herd of wild mustangs gallop across the track in front of them only to disappear in a cloud of dust over the nearest rise.

'I'll be rounding you scoundrels up later,' R.J. murmured as he too watched them, before stubbing the end of his half-smoked cigarette out between thumb and forefinger and dropping it out of the truck window. 'And if you're going to smoke here, boy, don't ever let us catch you throwing a lit butt out of no window, d'you hear?'

'Yes, sir.'

'Do you ride, boy?'

'No, sir, no, not really, just a bit. I imagine that's one of the things that I'm going to learn out here?'

'Sure is.' A deeply bronzed and craggy face turned to study Tam as he continued to drive without watching the track ahead. 'It sure is. And you wanted to know much land we farm, that right? Is that what you asked? How much land we farm?'

'Yes, sir. I did,' Tam replied, anxiously watching the road ahead, as if he might be able to do something should another herd of mustangs gallop across their path stampeding towards the hills.

'Don't you worry 'bout my driving, boy. I know every inch of this land better than I know Mrs Dysart. And I tell you, in these parts, if you know how much land you have, you ain't a real Texan.'

R.J. roared with sudden laughter, and shook his head a few times, still appreciating his own humour as he returned his eyes to the road.

'No, sir,' he repeated. 'You certainly ain't a real Texan.'

'Mr Astley told me you two had known each other for quite a time,' Tam said, still stunned at finding himself abandoned in the vast and daunting state whose symbol was a yellow rose.

'Waldo?' R.J. stated with a dramatic raise of his eyebrows. 'Hey, listen here, I would not be here, boy, if it were not for Waldo Astley. Waldo Astley,

197

if you'll pardon me for so saying, saved my ass. But then as you must know Waldo Astley has made a bit of a lifetime's vocation of saving people's asses, if you'll twice pardon me, boy.'

Again the large Texan shook his head of shock-white hair and threw back his head and roared with laughter, reminding Tam of some great giant in a children's story. Shaking out a fresh King Size from a crumpled pack of Pall Mall which he'd fished from his shirt pocket, he caught it with alarming accuracy between his huge white teeth, and rolled it around his mouth before lighting it with a large steel lighter with THE BIG U engraved upon it in no uncertain letters. Finally they drew up in a cloud of dust in front of the ranch house, a collection of buildings in front of which there seemed to be ceaseless activity.

'Now we'll get you hunkered down, so you'll be ready for your first day on the Big U.' R.J. turned and glanced at Tam, perhaps seeing him for the first time. As he eyed him Tam began to feel uneasy, as if R.J. was measuring him for something really rather unpleasant. 'You're going to need to muscle up some, boy, before you'll be much use to the Big U. Yes, sir, muscle up and fill out, like a young bull, but then I dare say that won't take too long neither.'

He leaned across Tam, smelling of everything from cigarettes to cattle feed, and flung open the truck door.

'Out you go, and the boys' dormitory is straight

198

in front of you. Take your bag from the back and
I'll see you in the house for an egg and steak. I dare
say you'll be needing it.'

Tam did as he was told, and the truck drove off
leaving him to walk up to the boys' dormitory, his
heart sinking as he heard the sound of music and
laughter from within. He was English, he had no
muscle, and no head for drink, and what was more
and what was worse, he couldn't really ride.
He thought of Bexham and his grandfather, he
thought of their sailing days together, and deep
down inside he sighed for the blue, blue days of his
boyhood. He'd spoken to his family, and to Kim,
before taking the train down from the East, that had
been nice, but now – now was not nice. He opened
the wooden door. A boy's face grinned down at
him from a bunk as he walked further into the
room, which was swirling with smoke and shaking
to the sound of a loud and local radio station.

'Hey! Hank? The new Blue's arrived.' He turned
on his side and stared down at Tam once again.
'Out here on the Big U we always call all English
boys *Blue*, on account their letters when they arrive
are always blue.'

He waved an airmail letter at Tam before
throwing it at him. Tam leaned down to pick it up,
immediately recognising his mother's writing, and
just as quickly feeling a lump coming into his
throat. His mother's writing on letters, on shopping lists, little notes left to him in his school satchel
to urge him on to better things at school.

'I dare say you'll be gettin' a ton of these before too long – *Blue!*'

Besides his genial but obviously tough host, no one else took much, if any, notice of the new arrival from England. Sue Sue, R.J.'s third wife, usually treated Tam as if he was invisible, being much more interested in staring into the many mirrors that adorned the main part of the ranch house.

However, as Tam appreciated whenever he caught sight of her, Sue Sue's looks warranted taking care of, of that there was no doubt. Tall, even for Texas, she was, as she frequently stated, 'just under six feet in my stockings', sporting blond if over-stiff hair, and a figure whose measurements would have made any movie star, anywhere, very proud.

A large staff was in permanent residence at the ranch house, which meant that Sue Sue had no need to concern herself with anything other than such vital matters as painting her toe and finger nails, and going into town to spend hours in the beauty salon. Passing Tam now and then she would wave to him, either from her personalised purple ragtop, or from horseback. That she did this was probably, Tam realised, because he was English, and so, different from the other hands.

Not that the other hands took much notice of him either, unless it was to get a cheap laugh from mocking his odd way of talking, or to try to rile him because of what they considered to be his puny physique. Tam didn't mind. Before setting foot in Texas he thought he'd come to understand exactly why Mr Astley and his parents had decided to send him out to America to work on a ranch. It was to make him suffer. Every time he tripped and fell into yet another dung heap or water barrel, or backwards off his horse, it was to the sound of Texan laughter. Tam felt like writing to tell everyone back at Bexham that he hoped they'd be glad to hear he was suffering all right. He was black and blue, and lonely.

At night as he heard the wildlife hooting or calling outside the wooden structure of the boys' dormitory, as he heard the cows bellowing for the calves taken from them in such arbitrary fashion, or the far distant sounds of a car filled with drunken hands driving down some dirt track somewhere, it seemed to him that it mattered little if he lived or died, because he was certain no one else seemed to mind. Bitten by mosquitoes, his hands red-raw from the work, the only thing he lacked to make his life totally intolerable was a slave-driver with a bull-whip; although even that, he knew, could come at any moment; and that too finally presented itself to him, albeit in an unexpected form.

Her name was Tammy, and she was R.J.'s daughter by his second wife, and it was quite obvious from the start that she loathed Tam, and for one reason, and one reason alone.

'You're not going round with my name, boy,

leastways not if I have anything to do with it. You're going to have to change that for a flying start, and that's the truth.'

'Why not just call me Blue like everyone else,' Tam suggested carefully.

Tammy looked at him, and then round at her three brothers who'd joined them in the yard staring at the new boy who'd dared to sport their sister's name.

'Blue, you say? No, hold on – surely *Yellow*'d be better, because from what I hear tell you're a funk, English boy, isn't that so?'

This was followed by general laughter.

'No one calls me a funk and gets away with it.' The words burst out of Tam, shattering the heart-felt resolution he'd made after the accident to stay clear of trouble all his days, that no matter what, he would not involve himself.

'Oh, but they do get away with it, *Yellow*, they surely do, and I just have.'

Tammy stepped forward and smiled, almost politely. There must be something about the air or the food at the Big U because of a sudden it seemed to Tam that Tammy must be as tall as her step-mother, Sue Sue, but a whole lot better muscled.

'You don't want to truck with Tammy,' one of her brothers begged Tam. 'It's like fighting a rattlesnake, you're bitten before you know it. She fights dirty, and she fights tough, and you will be left scarred. Run, boy, run before she starts in on you.'

But it was too late. She had already charged at the amazed Tam, head-butting him with such force that it knocked him off his feet, and against a less than friendly wall. He reckoned he must have swallowed a bagful of dirt before he finally gave up his struggle and lost consciousness.

He came round what he imagined might be a few minutes later with R.J. and Sue Sue standing over him. He tried to struggle to his feet, but feeling more dizzy than he would have thought possible sank back once more against the large cushioned sofa on which he'd been laid.

'Oh, I say, I am sorry.' He stared dazedly up at R.J. and Sue Sue.

'No need to be, boy, that daughter of mine scares the living daylights out of every man within a hundred miles. No shame in Tammy whopping you.'

Sue Sue flicked back her blond hair, and for once looked mildly interested in what was going on.

'I should have warned you, English boy. No one trucks with Tammy on account her father here clean forgot he was meant to be bringing up a lady. Never had a daughter before she came along, and so he didn't know any better than to teach her the same old things he'd gone and taught her brothers. Only trouble was Tammy learned 'em better, and she's learned 'em good. She thinks she can stop bullets at a hundred yards, I swear it.'

'Now, Sue Sue, you're going sadly wrong here,

darlin'. Tammy only fights dirty, she don't fight like a man. Be fair, honey, she don't fight like a man, no sir.'

Sue Sue flicked back her hair once more and turned to make her way to the bar.

'I'm going to get poor English boy a drink.'

R.J. grinned. 'And to make up for your whopping, English boy, I'm going to lend you my Mustang.' He took a key ring from one of the side tables and threw it over to where Tam was now sitting up, holding the ice that Sue Sue had given him to his throbbing face. 'You take that car and you drive where you want, on me. Make up for your beatin', boy, make up to you good. You don't have to come back for a week. Meanwhile I'll warn that daughter of mine she can't go round whoppin' the daylights out of everyone who shares her name – hell, if you're called Mary, or Susan like Sue Sue here – hell, you're going to be in a fight every day of your life.'

R.J. gave a great laugh, lit one of his extra long cigarettes and sauntered off, leaving Tam to Sue Sue's ministrations. Outside Tam could hear him calling for his daughter. Sue Sue watched him from the window.

'I know Tammy, she'll be gone for days now, losing herself all over the ranch, or goin' into town when she's not meant to, that's my stepdaughter.'

She removed the lid of a large silver ice bucket, and came back to Tam.

'There, boy, there.' She held the fresh ice cubes

tenderly over the bruising. 'You stay right there and let me look after you.' She handed Tam a couple of tablets and a glass of water. 'Take these, for the pain. That Tammy, really.' She sighed. 'She gave me a whoppin' once when I first came here and I was in bed for a week. R.J. he had to step in and tell her off good and proper. But I learned my lesson good, never spoke to her since, not if I could help it, not even on Christmas.' She sat down on the end of the sofa, and smiling at Tam she put her hand on one of his stretched-out bared legs. 'You English boys, you have such soft skin, like a doe. We don't get that out here.'

Happily for Tam he had other things on his mind than his soft skin, what with his cut mouth, and his bruised face. Happily too the tablets soon started to take effect, and not much later he found he'd drifted off into a doze, which was all the more comforting for the fact that he was convinced that Sue Sue had left him.

Rusty looked over to Peter.

'We haven't heard from him for weeks.' She stared miserably at the pile of letters on the hall table.

'That's because he's too busy,' Peter stated for what seemed to him to be the hundredth time. 'If you haven't heard from Tam he must be settling in, no time to write. It was the same in the army, so busy you never had time to sit down and write. I know I never did. I did write to you before I was posted, mind you, I just never had a reply.'

Rusty stopped by the staircase, her hand on the newel post. It all seemed so long ago. Peter and she had made love and then he'd gone, back to his regiment, and she'd been left pregnant. It might have been thought a disgrace by her family, but when Rusty looked back, those months alone with Tam when he was a baby, and then a toddler, now seemed blissfully carefree.

'Peter . . .'

But Peter had already moved away, heading towards the front door, where he turned. 'Yes?'

'Nothing.'

'Oh no, not nothing again. That's all you seem to say nowadays.'

Rusty nodded. It wasn't quite accurate, but it was fairly true none the less.

'Very well.' She looked across at him. 'You know, since Tam left, I've become – bored.'

Peter had half opened the front door and now he shut it again.

'What? You've become what?'

'Bored, Peter. I feel cooped up, here, with you and Flavia. I can't stand another minute of entertaining those women from the League, and being nice to townspeople, and members of clubs, and all the other song and dance.' She sat down suddenly on the bottom step of the staircase and stared into space, not looking at her husband. 'I'm just not like these people you've thrown me among, Peter. I grew up in Bexham, I went sailing, I went fishing,

206

I had my brothers, never a dull moment. Now you've put me in this large house with a wardrobe of clothes—'

'And everything you could ever want. A modern Formica kitchen, matching table and chairs, a car of your own, clothes, furnishings, what more could you want?' he repeated.

'Nothing more, no more. No.' Rusty looked helplessly round. 'No, I want nothing more. In fact I want much less. I feel weighed down with all this.'

'Just thank your lucky stars for what you *have* got, Rusty, because believe me, it could all go tomorrow.'

Rusty nodded. She'd thought he'd say that. The door closed behind him and she heard him going out into the drive, and eventually driving off in his new Bentley. Peter had changed since Tam went. She'd changed since Tam went. Only Flavia was still the same.

She stood up, hearing her upstairs, not wanting her daughter to find her looking miserable. She'd go for a walk. She'd walk to Bexham and back. A good walk, the wind blowing her hair, the dog beside her, it would all make her feel better, because she certainly needed to feel better. For a second she didn't know when she'd felt worse, and then remembering when she'd felt a lot worse after the loss of her second baby, how close she had been to madness, if only for a few months, she pulled herself together and set out to walk to the seaside village where she was born.

At that moment, without realising it, Tam was driving too fast. Driving away from the humiliation of what had happened to him at the hands of R.J.'s daughter. Never mind his face and head still hurt – he couldn't care less. As he drove along the straight open roads that led away from the Big U he failed to appreciate the unspoilt wild beauty of the scenery, the other ranches that he passed. All he could see were the concealed smiles of the other hands, and their laughter as he walked out of the ranch house, released from the all too caring hands of Sue Sue. Rather than spend another moment living with the other boys' derision, he'd headed straight for the Mustang loaned to him by R.J. and driven off, not knowing where just so long as it took him away from the ranch house at the Big U.

As his mother walked away from Churchester towards Bexham, Tam drove further and further away from anything or anybody that was remotely familiar until he'd clocked up more miles than he cared to think. As he did so he found himself struggling with overwhelming feelings of loneliness and despair. He felt desperate. He couldn't go home to Bexham, and he didn't want to go back to the Big U. At times he saw himself from far above, a lone figure in a large car, not knowing where he was going, and caring less, yet needing to know where he was going, needing to care. Once or twice he stopped the car in the middle of some lonely road and putting his head on the wheel cried his eyes out. He cried in pity for himself, and he cried in pity for his family whom he knew he'd disgraced. Eventually he grew tired of feeling sorry for himself, and started to look around him as he drove, started to appreciate the scenery, the mountains, the emptiness stretching everywhere, challenging him to feel lonely when it was there to be his friend. Stopping in small towns along the way he ate at diners that were cheap and clean and served him with waffles and maple syrup, with steaks and chips, with chicken fritters and blueberry pie, not to mention gritty black coffee and ice cold drinks pumped into frosted glasses placed on thick white paper coasters.

He spoke to no one except to point to his order, not wanting to be identified as a stranger, or to attract attention to himself, but speaking little he listened a lot. He listened to the cadences of the cowpokes and men from the ranches who sat about the diners. He listened to the waitresses and the barmen, until after a few days he started to risk speaking to them in what he hoped was their language.

'You out here to work, boy?' a great white-bearded hand turned and asked him one night.

'Dumped out here, more like, friend!'

The older man laughed. 'Well, that's what happens, boy. You misbehave, you gotta expect to get dumped. I got dumped for beatin' up my step-daddy, and now my ma wouldn't know me if I fetched up on her doorstep and called her by name.' He laughed again, and spat, drank his beer and left.

After that short exchange, the homesickness threatened to return. Tam instantly imagined himself, like the old man, fetching up in Bexham, and Rusty not knowing him.

And so he upped and left and headed back for Reedsville and the Big U, driving fast and furiously through the night, as if he was afraid that any moment his hair too would turn white, his eyes grow misty.

Reedsville being the town nearest to the Big U it was the place towards which the other ranch hands gravitated in search of excitement and, on occasion, night life in the form of music or, equally occasionally, dancing, although neither of the last two were of much interest to men who worked all day in wide open spaces, beer and fights being more to their taste.

The main saloon in Reedsville was Charley's Bar. As Tam drove in on the Saturday night that marked the end of his week's break, the crowd from inside Charley's was spilling out through the doors into the car park, such was its popularity. Tam managed to make his way to the bar without either drawing attention to the fact that he was queue-jumping or upsetting any of the many drunks who were propping each other up. It was at times like these that he was grateful for his slender physique, being able to weave in and out of larger men as a prairie fox might weave among the tall summer grasses that

210

swayed and sang in unison outside the town.

Finding himself at the end of the long, polished mahogany counter, he waited to catch the bartender's eye. It threatened to be a long wait, so flicking a Lucky Strike out of a freshly purchased pack he stuck it in the corner of his mouth and lit it with a shiny Zippo lighter, nicking the top open and the flame alight with a downward and upward rub on his Levi's, as he'd been practising alone in dark corners of diners over the past few days.

'Beer?' At last the barman stood in front of him.

Tam tipped his hat back a little and nodded, letting his cigarette roll in the appropriate manner between his teeth. But that was all he did do – nod. He'd learned that on the road, a nod was big conversation in Texas. Still rolling his cigarette round his mouth he pulled out the appropriate money, and nodded again. The second nod meant 'keep the change'.

'Thank you, sir!' The barman was gone down the other end in a flash. Tam drained his beer in one. He was, after all, a man.

Rusty paused at the top of the hill looking down at Bexham – its church, its harbour, the Three Tuns, the estuary with the boats bobbing – as if at an old friend she hadn't seen in a long time. She'd hated leaving Bexham for the grander ways and bigger house where they now lived in Churchester, missed seeing people passing by on the green, missed the silly gossip. She knew, of course, that she should go and visit her father who would be alone in his cottage, probably staring into the fire, missing Tam every day. Tam had always been Mr Todd's ewe lamb, his favourite grandchild, Flavia never getting a look in, not even now when her brother was so far away, possibly even less now. For with Tam gone Mr Todd would only see Flavia as a very poor substitute for what he would consider the real thing – his one and only grandson. Tam had been Mr Todd's hope for the future, his substitute for his long-lost elder boy killed at Dunkirk.

Rusty stopped suddenly, knowing that she had no intention of visiting her father, who after all was coming to have Sunday lunch with them in a few days' time. Her eye was attracted by a For Sale sign which was standing in the front garden of Laurel Cottage, one half of a pair of Edwardian cottages which had been built only a hundred yards from Post Office Cottage.

Rusty would always be grateful to Peter for sounding so indignant, so almost outraged at her inability to be content with her large house and her Formica kitchen, not to mention her own car, for the truth was she could still hear his voice ringing in her ears when she found herself going in to find out from the new owners of the post office the asking price for Laurel Cottage.

It was, naturally, more than she could afford, but less than she had thought, so all at once it became highly desirable. Again she could hear Peter's voice ringing in her ears. *What do you want a cottage of all things for?*

As she came out of the post office she saw her father coming towards it clutching a thin blue airmail letter which she knew must be for Tam.

'Dad, the very man I've come to see,' she lied, hugging him lightly, all of a sudden realising just how frail he'd become.

'Rusty Sykes.' Her father stared at her, smiling. 'I'd have known you anywhere,' he teased her. 'That's a strapping good idea, to come to tea, because Gwen up at Shelborne's just been by, and dropped me in some seed cake, and we can toast some crumpets on the fire.' He posted his letter and then turned and looked at Rusty. 'So, now that's done, and you're coming,' he turned to walk back across the green, 'tell me why you're really here?'

Rusty nodded back at the For Sale sign on the cottage beside the post office.

'I want to buy that cottage, Dad. Daft, isn't it? I want to buy that cottage, and start a boutique, like they have in London.'

Mr Todd stared from the cottage front to Rusty and back again.

'But have you got the money, Rusty Sykes? Money's hard to come by if you're married to a man as rich as Peter.'

Rusty laughed. Her dad was such a shrewd old tar.

'Oh, I've everything I want, except what I want, which is a business.'

213

Mr Todd stopped. 'I'll give you the money for your business, Rusty. I've got savings in the Post Office, and they're doing nothing since I sold the boatyard, and since Mickey's set up on his own I've nothing to spend my money on, except writing to poor Tam.' The expression on his face became sad and thoughtful. 'Poor Tam.'

'Tam's all right, Dad,' Rusty said brusquely. 'Really, he's doing something we should all do – getting stuck in. That's why I want a business, I want something where I can get stuck in. If I have to give lunch to the Ladies' League one more time I think I'll be sick on my shoes.'

Mr Todd put his key in the lock of his old oak front door and pushed it open.

'Peter won't like you havin' a business, girl,' he said with some relish. 'You know young men, they don't like women having anything of their own. You'd better go and tell him before I give you the money to buy it, or there'll be hell to pay.' He went on down the small dark passage of his cottage, Rusty following him. 'Yes, I'd say you'd better tell him all right.'

That evening Rusty did as her father had advised, waiting until Peter had downed his first drink of the evening, but not finding quite the right words she came out with it as a bald statement, which she realised too late might have been quite a big mistake.

'Peter. I'm going to open a boutique.'

Peter turned and stared at her. 'What did you say?'

'I'm going to open a boutique, to sell modern clothes, things we'd all like to be able to buy in the shops, but – I don't know why – just can't find. I want to find and sell clothes that aren't . . .' she paused, before finally saying, 'dowdy.'

'*Dowdy*? You don't look dowdy.' Peter stared at Rusty's three-quarter-length tweed skirt and Shetland wool twinset, tan-coloured stockings and brown court shoes. 'You look very nice.'

'But that's just it! I don't *want* to look nice, Peter, that's the point. And I don't think many people do, not any more. That's why I want to open a boutique, to stop looking nice and start looking – zippy.'

The expression on Peter's face registered one word, and one word alone: *Women!*

'I don't understand you, really I don't. Why should a woman your age, with everything you have, want to look *zippy*? It's a little ridiculous, if you don't mind me saying so.'

Rusty stared at her husband's back as he poured himself another drink, thinking that it was at least something to have got him to speak his feelings, which was not something at which Peter exactly excelled.

'You always say you don't understand me when I've upset you.'

'Well I don't – you've got everything you want, but that's not enough.'

215

'No, Peter, I've got everything *you* want me to have, not what I necessarily want for *myself*.'

Peter sat down again. 'And now I suppose you want to borrow the money from me?'

'No, actually, I don't.'

He stared at her.

'No, as a matter of fact – I've already borrowed it.'

'Not from Waldo. I won't have you borrowing from someone I'm in business with, Rusty. That's right against the rules, and you know it. I won't have it.'

Rusty, suppressing the anger building up in her, paused for a moment.

'No, Peter, I've borrowed it from my father. As a matter of fact he volunteered to lend it to me. You see I think he sees the boutique as a way of seeing me more often, and Flavia, of course, because she can help me in the boutique, sitting behind the counter totting up things. With Tam gone, and my brother Mickey permanently up north, it'll be a bit of a distraction for him.'

Rusty thought back to earlier in the afternoon when she'd been shamed into going to have tea with her father, after she bumped into him outside the post office. His pleasure at seeing his only daughter was so apparent that it'd brought tears to her eyes, although she'd been at pains not to let him see. Rusty knew that her dad missed Tam, every day, hardly an hour going by when he didn't think of him.

216

'The lad's gone, but he writes to his old granddad,' was all he said, as Rusty noted that all Tam's airmail letters were propped up behind the photograph of her poor dead young brother, killed at Dunkirk.

She turned away, feeling her insides turning over as she realised that Tam might be writing to her dad, but not to his own parents, or even to Flavia. That must mean that Tam blamed his immediate family, Peter and herself, for being cast out of Bexham, and sent so far away from everything he knew and loved.

'Well,' Peter volunteered after a pause that was so long it had become ominous. 'What time's supper? Or do we get it ourselves?'

At this hint Rusty went obediently through to her Formica kitchen with its Formica-topped table, and its chairs covered in easy-wipe plastic. The subject was obviously now closed, which meant that Peter, as always, had accepted what she wanted without argument, because that was Peter's way. He would never put up a fight, considering himself too much of a gentleman for that, but he would be watching her none the less, waiting to pounce the moment her armour showed a chink. Rusty pulled open the oven door. Thank God it was chicken pie, Peter's favourite; that at least was something.

That night before she fell asleep, Rusty said her prayers, as she always did, first and foremost for the safety of her children, next for the safety of the world, thirdly for her own special intention.

Tonight, as she found herself praying for the third item, she couldn't help hoping that God was as shallow as herself, because she knew that for her, making Laurel Cottage Creations into a flying success meant more than she cared to admit even to herself, although what it meant to God was quite another thing.

The moment Tam heard the scream he knew that it was up to him to do something about it. First of all it was not a woman's involuntary scream, not the scream of fright at seeing a spider or some such, but a girl's terrified, insistent scream. Forgetting his resolution never to become involved in an incident, he pushed his way out of the men's room. Throwing his cigarette butt on to the tarmac of the parking lot, he realised that the screams, now continuous, were coming from one of the parked cars over by the road. Weaving his way between pickup trucks and clapped-out Fords, he made his way to a Ford Woody, new-looking, shiny and multi-chromed with flash lights, the sort of vehicle favoured by cowpunchers who lived in the fast lane, a heavy-duty four-wheel drive that could not only shift loads but also shift miles with the speedo needle flicking around the ton, and guzzling gas as fast as the owner probably guzzled beer.

By the time Tam reached it the pickup was about to move off, but that wasn't going to stop Tam, now in full heroic mood. He after all was not just a Sykes, he was a Todd, and Todds sailed to Dunkirk and lost their lives or – like his mother – came back and refused to talk about it, ever again. He ran fast and he ran hard until he found himself level pegging with the vehicle out of which a peculiarly feminine boot was sticking. He remembered those yellow boots. He'd had just enough time to take them in before he passed out, the day Tammy had floored him. Without another thought he wrenched open the door of the big Ford, and thrusting his hands inside he pulled the driver towards him by the thick black cotton of his much-studded shirt, yanking him out of the cab while the driver grabbed the handbrake.

'What in hell—'

Before he could say more Tam turned to see Tammy's face, her eyes huge, her lips trembling with fright, her clothes everywhere except where they should be, a streak of blood across her mouth. But she was still Tammy.

'Ah bit him!' A momentary look of triumph came into her eyes. 'Ah bit him, good and hard.'

'Not enough to put him off, though, was it?' Tam yelled at her, still pulling at the driver, who once out of the cab proved to be a good three stone heavier than his assailant, not to mention a good six inches taller.

'Go at him!'

Tam obliged by swinging at the man, smacking him across the face with a closed fist. He fell against the door of his cab, his hand shooting up to his mouth and a look of astonished fury on his face.

Wiping the blood away he stared at his reddened hand with disbelief before launching himself at Tam.

Tam steadied himself, put his left foot forward and his right one back, raised his left hand in classic defence and cocked his right arm back in line with his shoulder, unleashing a killer punch. The big fellow felt it, but it wasn't enough to stop him coming after Tam, swinging at him so wildly that Tam was able to dodge his sledgehammer blows, the punches missing him by some way, thanks to nimble footwork. Tam had been taught by his uncle Mickey to jab quickly, jab, jab, jab, and then dodge, dodge, dodge, bang, bang, bang.

'Fighting's all footwork,' Mickey used to tell him before he went up north to marry a Yorkshire lass, leaving Bexham for good. 'Don't matter how strong someone is, if you can dodge 'em, you've got 'em.'

And Tam had got the big brute. A minute or so into the contest and a crowd, men and women, most holding glasses, all smoking, started to gather in the parking lot, word having spread there was a fight on, some even leaving their pool games to watch the haphazard contest.

By now the big man was bleeding profusely. He was staggering too, unsteady on his feet, but still red hot with bull-like rage, lunging at the taut figure in front of him, despite the blood dripping into his eyes, despite the pain that was beginning to make itself felt. He wanted to kill this boy who'd dared to interrupt his night.

Of course, seeing how unsteady he was becoming, Tam knew that he had him now. It was easy to dodge him, easy to avoid the wild, slow, drunken blows being aimed at him. Before he delivered his *coup de grâce* he wondered just for one quick moment why he was so engaged with the brute, and then remembering the state of Tammy's clothes, the fear in her eyes, he delivered a punch so quick that a murmur of satisfaction went up from the watching crowd, and they fell to something near to silence as the bruiser's square-jawed head went backwards and the huge man was lifted off his feet. And then they sighed with gratified awe as the blow finally felled him backwards, and he crashed on to the bonnet of a neighbouring shiny black Cadillac, his arms hanging uselessly at his sides, momentarily reminding Tam of one of Flavia's rag dolls.

Tam stood over his opponent's inert body and smiled as a roar of appreciation went up from the crowd. He nursed his aching fists, trying to rub the pain from them, before turning back to find Tammy standing behind him, also staring down at the large, inert body.

'You hadn't come along,' she drawled, 'I would have bitten his head right off, but seeing that you did, I guess you've been able to put in a bit of practice, Blue.'

Tam grinned at her bravura, still nursing his knuckles. The crowd was thinning out now, anxious to go back to the bars and the pool rooms to tell their mates of the David versus Goliath fight.

'You done good, boy.'

Another of the ranch hands who worked at the Big U now came forward, and staring first at the man on the ground and then at Tam he nodded appreciatively.

'Yah, you done good, Blue boy.'

Tam was just about to say 'Thank you, Ned, thank you, Tim' in a rather too Bexham way, when he remembered what he'd learnt on the road, and contented himself by merely nodding.

They all turned back towards the bars, beer being the only possible antidote to a fight. Tam felt as if he'd lost all the saliva from his mouth.

'By the way, boys.' Tammy spoke. 'You ain't seen nothin', you hear?'

They nodded. They knew. Tammy's father back at the Big U heard of this there wouldn't be a fight, there wouldn't be a battle – there'd be war.

Later, as Tam walked Tammy back to the Mustang, he found his second and third beer of the night had made him curious.

'You know him?'

Tammy shook her head. 'Course not.'

There was a long pause as Tammy stood by the old car waiting for Tam to open the passenger door for her while he waited for her to volunteer more.

'I don't rightly want to tell you, Blue.'

'Well then, I don't rightly want to take you home, girl.'

Tammy sighed and looked down at her feet.

'He sold me these 'ere boots a while back, that's what. Sent to tell me he had some more. Red. Red boots. I always did want red boots for myself. But then my money wasn't enough. He wanted me *and* the money.'

Tam nodded, still remembering to say as little as possible, the Texan way.

'Some people just don't know when too far is too far.'

'Good boots, though.'

Tammy stretched out her legs and stared ahead as Tam started to drive out of Reedsville towards the Big U. 'Yah, but I ain't giving myself to no one for a pair of boots.' She turned to look at Tam briefly, her green eyes seeming to glitter in the lights they were passing as they left town. 'Until now, that is. You saved me, Blue. Ah owe you for that.'

Tam shook his head.

'Yes, you did.'

Tam shook his head again.

'So what was that back there, then, Blue?'

'That,' Tam answered, luxuriating in thinking that he had at last conquered the Texan manner. 'That was just me having fun, girl. You didn't need me.' He looked sideways at Tammy before re-directing his gaze to the road ahead. 'One more yard and like you said, you'd have bitten his head off.'

There was a long silence as Tammy digested this thought.

'Ah would, wouldn't I?' she finally agreed, sighing with some satisfaction and propping her yellow boots up on the dashboard in front of her. They drove on in a new silence.

'Urrrrrrgh! Urrrrrrgh!' The sound came out of Max as if it had a life of its own. It must have been vaguely impressive because it caused his flatmate Tony Miles to open one bleary, beery eye to witness Max staring at the television screen while writhing over-dramatically on the other end of the sofa.

'Please, Max . . .'

But Max was determined to continue with the sound.

'Urrrrrgh! I can't believe it, I won't believe it, this is not acting, this is aaar-cting! Whatever happened to naturalism? What – ever – happened – to – naturalism,' he repeated, emphasising each word one by one in order to spell out his disgust more heavily. 'And whoever thought to cast John Deerham in that part should be *shot!*'

Tony having settled for taking in one minute of the said actor's performance promptly reclosed his eyes again. Nothing new going on there, nothing that had not been happening, over and over again, in their rented house by the river at Twickenham for the past heaven only knew – and only heaven did know – how many months. The fact was that the whole house was out of work, which meant that there was always someone either returning from the pub, or going to it, to drown their sorrows,

224

or sitting in front of the telly bemoaning the luck of other less talented actors who had been cast in parts that could have, *should have* been theirs.

At that point the telephone in the far end of the sitting room rang, and both actors leaped up from their variously prone positions to bolt towards it.

'It's for you. Your agent.' Tony handed the telephone to Max who, after a statutory few seconds, took it from him and assuming a deeply uninterested voice said, 'Yes, hallo, Barry.'

Tony, slouch-shouldered and drawing on his cigarette twice as hard as strictly necessary, wandered off back to the television and resumed his seat.

'Look at that untalented so-and-so,' he muttered, squinting at the black and white television, 'look at him! Can't act his way out of a paper bag.'

He continued muttering while at the same time trying to catch what Max was saying to his agent. Eventually, when Max strolled back to the sofa and sat back beside him, he turned and smiled at him.

'Good news?'

Max shrugged. 'The Royal want me for an audition. Well, no. They want to see me.'

'Hey, that's great.' Tony stubbed out his cigarette and turned and smiled at Max. 'You'll be making the bridge then? No more revue, on with the straight acting.'

'You do have to act to be in revues, Tony,' Max told him for the twentieth time, in a tired voice.

'So what's the part?'

225

'Puck.'

'Puck?'

There was a long silence as Tony considered this.

'Not your part, mate, sorry, just not your part.'

Max stared at him. 'They don't happen to think so. The powers that be that rule our destinies seem to think it's only a matter of seeing me, old love.'

He turned and looked at Tony, implacable, assured. He wasn't going to get talked out of Puck, not for all the pints of lager in Twickenham.

'No, mate. Puck's just not your part. You have many parts ahead of you, but not Puck, believe me. Besides, it will be taking a too big step for you at this time, after revue, too big a step.' He shook his head and resumed staring at the television.

'We'll see. I'd like to have a crack at it, I must say.' Max smiled happily. With any luck he would be in work in a matter of days. Wow, that was just such a *wowee* thought. Tony turned back to him and patted his shoulder.

'What you *don't* want, old love, is to get cast in a showy part like that, make a hash of it, and . . .' He drew a finger across his throat. 'And so endeth the career of Mr Max Eastcott, of number forty-three Victoria Villas, Twickenham.'

Max shrugged his shoulders. He would see. He looked at Tony lighting another cigarette. And he smiled at his profile as he watched the television, eaten up with jealousy for everyone who was on it. If Tony thought Max was that stupid, he would need to have another thought coming. He might be a *'middle-class so-and-so'* as dear, working-class Tony was always stating, but a *brainless* middle-class so-and-so he wasn't.

Judy was finding it impossible to write to Kim addressing her by her adopted name. She'd also held back from telling Walter that this was what Kim wanted.

'What is this?'

Walter, home for the weekend, was standing in the extension to Owl Cottage that made up his study, a small sitting room, and a new guest room with bathroom, and pointing, frowning, at a letter from Kim. Judy stared at the signature as if she'd never noticed it before, but, finding herself helpless in the face of the all too clearly signed 'Jenny' that Kim had written at the bottom of one of her rare letters home, she frowned and looked from it to Walter, who was still pointing accusingly at the signature, and back to the letter.

'I don't know why she puts that, Walter,' she said, in a vaguely puzzled voice. 'I think it must be all part of the therapy at Loughnalaire.'

'Therapy!'

The word burst from her husband's lips as if she had said 'Nazi' or 'Communist'.

'Loughnalaire does have its own built-in – er, therapy, Walter.' Judy paused. 'I did tell you all about it when I came back from Ireland.'

Walter turned away. 'The more you tell me about that place, the dafter it sounds.' He shrugged his shoulders. 'It sounds to me like a lot of fey Irish leprechauns running about letting a load of badly behaved teenagers do what they blasted well like.'

'It's not like that, Walter. You should go there for yourself, you should really, you should go there and see, and when you have, you'd be better for it, really you would.'

'Even if I had the time, it's the last thing I will be doing, Judy, believe me.'

Judy gave a small sigh. 'I understand. You do work so hard, Walter.' She stared at his back. He was still slim, still so good-looking, tanned and fit from sailing, even at this time of year. 'They're doing Kim a lot of good at Loughnalaire, Walter, really they are. Mrs—'

'They're taking you for a ride, Judy, that's what they're doing, but really – if that's what you think's right for your daughter, then that's what has to be. Hubert is different, thank God. Hubert is not going to give us that kind of trouble.' The meaning behind Walter's words was quite clear. Hubert wasn't going to be allowed to give trouble.

'Mrs Hackett wrote to tell us – you saw the letter, I think – that Kim's eczema is clearing up, that she is putting on a little weight, and that, best of all, she seems really happy. Made friends, everything.'

'So you keep saying.'

Walter moved off, yawning suddenly. Judy started to say something but then she too turned away. What in heaven was the point? In all honesty, there was none. The Walter that she loved was not

228

at home at that moment, he was somewhere else. 'Not at home' – the very phrase reminded her of the old happy days, playing Happy Families with her children in front of the fire.

Flavia was suffering. OK, if she was missing just Tam, but she was also missing Kim and Jenny. Moving to Churchester had been bad enough, but now it seemed as though everyone else had moved from Bexham too, and she had no excuse to go back, no one she could go and see, taking the bus, her hair arranged perfectly, her new clothes the same, staring out of the widow at the countryside they passed, imagining that instead of hedges and trees and cottages she saw shops and boutiques, cafés with chairs and tables set about and pretty people sipping coffee, not farmers with cows ambling along in front of them, or chickens in runs.

Staring out of the window was one occupation, but it had to be admitted that another occupation, and one she particularly preferred, was staring at herself, whenever possible. Staring at her own reflection as she passed shop windows, as she sat in the front seat of the bus, or passed a mirror in her own or someone else's house, for the fact was that Flavia was not just becoming beautiful, she was beautiful. The shop windows, the mirrors everywhere showed her a young woman with perfect features, tall and slim, with long shiny auburn hair and gratifyingly long legs. Besides the shop windows, the men she passed, and not just those working on building sites in Churchester, stared after her, whistled, or just generally showed their admiration in an equally gratifying way. So gratifying that it seemed to Kim, more and more, that the only way forward for her was stardom. And nowadays, in the way of the world, there was only one way to stardom, and that was to become a fashion model. Once you'd starred on the catwalk the world inevitably opened its arms to you, and you became not just rich and famous but, in time, invested with talent, for, as the whole world knew, modelling was only just a short step from the stars.

Following on these conclusions, Bexham became for her startlingly uninteresting. The fishing boats coming in and out in all weathers were no longer crewed by the brave, bonny men that she'd known when she was growing up, all of them friends with her grandfather, but by dull purveyors of fish, who smelt, and drank too much. The gulls, once a source of fascination as they sat posing on the sides of every available spare space, now seemed hysterical and hideous, their curved beaks cruel and greedy, their outlines against the sky as ordinary as wheels on a car. And as for the grown-ups among whom she had lived for so long – if one more adult intoned about the sacrifices that they had made during the war, about the lack of food, the loss of life, she thought she'd scream.

'But I don't particularly want you to be a model, it's such a brainless occupation,' Rusty had said, once

Flavia had confided in her. 'I'd like you to do something more exciting. Models are just clothes horses.'

Staring out from her Boots mascara, her lips shining with a translucent mauve-pink colour that made her eyes look even larger, Flavia pushed away her plate of carefully prepared steak and kidney pudding and stared out at her mother, realising that Rusty was at her most stubborn. But then Flavia was too, although she was careful not to say anything. She reverted her gaze to her plate. In retaliation for her mother's remark she made the lightning decision not to eat her steak and kidney pudding. She didn't care how much they'd all yearned for it during the war, she was not going to eat it. She wanted to look like an emaciated panda, and she certainly wouldn't achieve that goal if she was forever swallowing large chunks of suet. Instead of eating she returned to the main thrust of her argument.

'I know I can do well, Mum, at modelling, because I'm so tall, now. They want tall models in London. And if you're tall you're going to make the top jobs, and they're really well paid.'

'You're not old enough to go to London to model.'

'You'd be surprised how young some of these models really are.'

'Your father would have a fit.'

Rusty quickly cleared their plates, not saying anything about the leftovers, or how long she'd spent making the meal, not wanting to get into a food tussle. Never mind the woman-hours it had taken her to make their dinner, never mind that Peter hadn't even bothered to turn up for it, preferring to go out with Waldo for a few drinks and a game of snooker, never mind all that, she would give the wretched pudding to the dog, and go for an early night.

As she put the dishes in the sink her thoughts turned once more to Laurel Cottage Creations, and she sighed with sudden satisfaction. Her father's spare money having come from the sale of the boatyard, when Mickey married and went north, she was not going to risk his security, or her own. She had all to play for, and play for it she would.

Upstairs Flavia quietly locked her bedroom door, and going to her dressing table she removed a bumper pack of Peter Stuyvesant cigarettes from under a pile of immaculate white underwear. There were twenty-five in the flat cardboard box. She tiptoed over to her bedroom window and pushed it open. She had to smoke to get thinner. She would smoke and smoke until all appetite had left her. Not very long afterwards she quickly closed the window and hurrying to the hand basin in the corner of her room was quietly sick.

Max was facing what looked like a clutch of uninterested faces. In one of the first rows of the stalls, as he shaded his eyes against the working light of the stage, someone was actually asleep.

232

'Anyone out there? Director? Anyone?' he called boldly.

There was the sound of voices, and then eventually, as Max called out again, a single voice.

'I'm sorry "Sir" couldn't be here. He's been called away to – ah – a press conference . . .'

Max smiled and shook his head.

'No,' he said. 'Sorry.'

The triumvirate stared at him. They had at least called him, but then, he quickly realised since 'Sir' wasn't out front, it was obviously because they were the second team and had been put in to deal with the no-hopers.

'No,' Max said again to the startled faces he could just see if he peered down. 'I won't tell you what I have done, because if I do I will only end up . . .' He put his feet apart, placed an imaginary spear in his hand and stood motionless.

There was general laughter at this, as one and all, no matter their preliminary lack of interest, now had no trouble in recognising his imitation of the spear carriers so beloved of Shakespearean productions.

'I don't want to be carrying the old spear through seventy-two seasons.'

Max began his audition piece, which was from *Midsummer Night's Dream*, Puck being one of the parts for which he was being auditioned.

From the first he had them, not just because he'd made them laugh at the outset, but because he'd thought out a new angle to this well-loved character. Whether they agreed with it or not, whether it would fit in with the well-known director's reading of the play, no matter. He had them, and once you had 'em you were halfway to being cast.

Afterwards he flew home on the wings of confidence. They'd shaken his hand, violently, once if not twice, all of them. The man in the first row had woken up. It didn't matter now whether he was cast or not cast, all that mattered was that he hadn't failed that first crucial test. He lived again in his own eyes, and, after months of being out of work, that meant a lot.

As he turned his key in the lock of the front door he heard the telephone in the sitting room ringing. He ran to it, thinking naively that the caller might be his agent, and he might have heard already. But it wasn't his agent, it was Tony's.

'Tony there?'

Max gave a quick look round the sitting room. 'No.'

'Well, when he comes in, tell him the Royal will see him about Puck. Ten thirty tomorrow. Wish him luck, although after what I told them he won't have much need of it. He has a great new angle on the part, he really has, terrific new reading.'

'Yes, he has, hasn't he?' Max's heart was beating faster and faster.

'He told you, did he? Going to make him send up all the other fairies, not just make with the mischief. Rather good I thought.'

Max nodded at the telephone. 'Yes. I thought so too. Apparently he's going to bend the little finger, and go ever so dainty on the vowel sounds, and so on,' he said, lightly detailing the audition he himself had just given.

'Yah. Anyway, tell Tony from me, good luck. I'm off to New York, hear all about it when he gets back.'

As Max replaced the telephone his heart still seemed to be turning somersaults.

'You bastard, Tony. You bastard.' He turned away, making towards the kitchen and a glass of water which he drank sipping slowly as if he had a bad attack of hiccups. As he finished he dipped two fingers into the water and ran them across his head to calm himself. 'Right, Tony old love, now you've had it,' he murmured.

When Tony came in, much later, Max was watching television.

'Oh, by the way, mate, your agent phoned.'

Tony, half throttled from an evening in the pub, turned by the staircase and came back into the sitting room.

'Ian rang, did he? What did he say?'

'The job he put you up for . . .' Max feigned vaguely slurred speech. 'Yes, they can see you next week.' He picked up a telephone pad. 'They can see you next Wednesday. Yes, next Wednesday, at ten thirty.'

Tony took out his very small, dark blue, distinctly unglamorous diary.

'Wednesday next, yes, I can do that. Good.' He turned the pages of his blank diary. 'Yes, I think that will be fine.'

Max turned back to the television, acting casual.

'Do you know that – that untalented so-and-so John Deerham? He's only on both channels tonight, did you know that, mate? Both bloody channels,' he murmured, shaking his head.

'Untalented so-and-so. He'd sell his grand-mother for a part, he would,' Tony stated, once more heading for the stairs and his bed. 'They're all so-and-so's, untalented so-and-so's. We'll show them, we'll crack it, you'll see, mate. We'll be up there,' he turned and pointed up the stairs, 'and he'll be down there.' This time he pointed down at his feet. 'Yes, we're going to be up there, with the stars.'

Max watched him weaving his way up the stair-case.

'That's right, mate, you'll be up there with the stars.' He waited until he heard Tony's bedroom door slam, and then he murmured, 'But not if I've got anything to do with it, Tony love.'

Loopy stared across the estuary at the lights on the other side of the inlet. It was one of her favourite times of day, when the lights seemed to be appearing one by one, sometimes suddenly three or four at a time, but all as if by some unseen instruction. She turned to Jenny who was sitting beside her on the conservatory sofa, sipping a lemonade while Loopy sipped a glass of sherry. Since coming to her grandparents Jenny seemed to have improved in leaps and bounds. She no longer stayed upstairs in her room, but came down every day at the usual times, and in between developing her own paintings helped Loopy about the studio, washing up and tidying, while they chatted and talked about what mattered to them, what should matter to them, and what had mattered to them.

That she had no wish to return home to her parents was a sadness, but it was not a sadness that Loopy was prepared to indulge. *She* knew that Jenny must go home, and she knew that now, before she went in for another operation, was the perfect time. Mattie had been patient enough God knows, and John too, of course. They had spent hours transforming two of their rooms into a suite specially for Jenny, with a piano and paints and heavens only knew what else. For Jenny not to go home now would be quite wrong, no matter what Hugh had to say on the matter.

Hugh of course wanted her to stay, to play the piano, to go on painting and helping Loopy in the studio and generally being about the place for him to love and be concerned over, but Loopy knew that would not be right. Jenny was her parents' child, not theirs. She must go home to be with younger people, to face operations on her face, and come back and forth from her parents' home in the normal manner. For Hugh and Loopy to try to be more than her grandparents would be quite wrong, and finally even Hugh accepted this.

'Besides, she can come here whenever she wants. We are always here, at the moment, and she knows it.'

Their last evening together in the studio, before Jenny returned home, Loopy put her arm round her granddaughter, sensing her feelings of loss and unease, and hugged her.

'You'll be OK, sweetheart, you'll see.'

Jenny allowed herself to be hugged while her eyes still stared ahead to the water, and the lights. She was sure that Loopy was right, she would be OK, but how long would it be before she was more than that? How long before she was just like everyone else? She turned away from the thought, watching, always watching the lights, concentrating on them as if she thought she might never see them again.

Chapter Six

By the time the spring term ended and April turned the wind about, bringing sharp squalls of rain in off the sea, they'd finished fitting the shop out and painting the sign above the street window in a smart, deep red glossy paint, the sign writer adding the final touch:

LAUREL COTTAGE CRAFTS
Proprietor Rusty Sykes

Needless to say, as soon as it was painted in gold the proprietor was to be found standing outside looking up at the nameboard with a mixture of pride and panic. In the windows were a small selection of mugs on which she'd managed to persuade a local craftsman to paint scenes of Bexham Harbour with its boats, and the church spire in the background. Besides the mugs there were some hand-painted eggcups, by the same artist, a stock of Official Guide Books to Historic Bexham, and a quantity of tea towels die-stamped either with a map of Bexham and the surrounding countryside or, to give choice, a seagull on the side of a wooden rowing boat.

'I thought you said you were going in for fashion,' Peter said, when he picked her up the day before the opening. 'I thought that was what Laurel Cottage was all about.'

'I'm starting small,' was all Rusty would say, and she stared out of the window at the countryside thinking that whenever she left Bexham, even for the evening, she felt a pang.

On Opening Day, the ceremony was performed, most graciously, by Lady Melton.

'If you don't mind my saying so, I think you should also have some tea towels with the station on them,' she told Rusty after a preliminary polite inspection. 'After all, Bexham station has won Prettiest Sussex Station for *four* years running now.'

Despite knowing Lady Melton's weakness for the station, and not least her beloved trains, a weakness that had achieved something of a flowering when she and her old maid, Gardiner, had acted as stand-in ticket inspectors during the war, Rusty thought this a good idea, and quickly made a note to ask the artist in question. As she did so a flash bulb exploded and Lady Melton turned and smiled graciously towards the camera pointing at them.

'The *Churchester Chronicle* – if you could give me your names and ages.'

'The first but not the last,' Lady Melton told the photographer, quite firmly, still smiling.

For the remainder of the photographs they were joined by members of the Yacht Club. Since the editor of the *Chronicle* was a keen member of Bexham's exclusive yachting establishment, it was to be hoped that this tactfully ensured the item's being printed in a prominent position in the paper. Of course other village residents also came to the opening, but having duly exclaimed apparent appreciation of the all too limited stock they drifted away with vague smiles to escape out of the door and return to their television sets.

'That went quite well, didn't it, Flavia?'

Rusty tried to keep the anxiety out of her voice, while Flavia turned away, too embarrassed by her mother's tone to be able to say anything remotely encouraging.

During the first week of its existence, Laurel Cottage Crafts sold one hand-painted mug, and three tea towels. During its second week it sold two hand-painted mugs, and one tea towel. Week three saw the sale of three mugs and two eggcups, and a run of two copies of the Official Bexham Guide Book, but no tea towels. Trade was so slow that Rusty didn't even have to bother to ask Flavia to stand in for her, closing time inevitably finding her mother pulling down the blind after a day of reading paperback novels, dusting the already spotless mugs in the window, or making endless cups of tea in the tiny back room.

241

Rusty was heading for a flop, and she knew it. Her father might have lent her the money, but she still felt honour bound to pay him back, and at this rate that would take more years than he'd already been alive.

'You should stock up with fisherman's sweaters and yachting clothes,' Flavia kept telling her. 'They're really dolly, they are.'

'*Dolly*?' Rusty turned and stared at Flavia.

'Mmm, really, they are.'

Rusty ignored Flavia, until the day that rare sight, a customer, came into the shop and started to grumble about the sale of a fishing licence out of the harbour.

'That's disgusting,' she heard herself agreeing with Mrs Chimes, the stout and redoubtable matriarch of the Chimes family, one of those already affected by the loss of the licence.

'That's boat owners for you,' Mrs Chimes sat down on the one wobbly bentwood chair provided, while most regrettably not making any movement towards her worn handbag, or her purse. 'They sell the boat and the licence and in one fell swoop two families lose their way of living. It's more than disgusting, to my mind it's criminal.'

'So what are you going to do now?'

Mrs Chimes shook her head miserably. 'No idea, no idea at all. And he's only gone and sold to a foreigner, at that. First time it's ever happened in Bexham for someone to sell a licence outside the village. Never been known before, really, it hasn't.'

Since she herself came from one of the oldest families in Bexham, Rusty knew this to be true.

'We're just going to have to find something else we can do, that's all.'

Mrs Chimes, after a cup or two of tea, not to mention a Rich Tea biscuit, left without buying anything, and Rusty shut up shop. She'd absolutely no need to clear the till, since it had nothing in it.

It was only a few days later that, at Flavia's insistence, she went to call on a supplier of yachting clothing. As she drove towards her destination Rusty knew that she had to come to terms with the fact that she'd opened Laurel Cottage Crafts far too hastily, and without enough thought.

'I don't know why you're bothering, Mum, really I don't. It's not as if you haven't got enough bread – I mean Dad says you've everything most women want, and more, so why bother with a shop?'

Rusty stopped her brand new dark red Morris convertible with a jab of her foot on the brake, making Flavia jerk forward on to the dashboard.

'Mum!'

Rusty turned furiously to her daughter.

'I don't want to hear any more about what I have got, or what I haven't got – my bread, as you call it, I have earned with every fibre of my being.' She stopped, thinking that sounded rather pompous, and after a second started again at a lower pitch. 'I have helped your father build up his business. I have helped sell cars, advertise cars. I have held the hands of his staff. I cleaned for Waldo Astley, years ago, before you were born. There's nothing I haven't done to keep our ship afloat, but now is my time. It's *my* time, to do with what I want. And I want a business, of my own. So.' She started the car again. 'So that's what I'm doing, and whether or not it's a flop, or will be a flop, I don't know. All I know is that it's my time, and I'm going to keep it that way.'

She drove on to stunned silence from Flavia, most particularly since that was precisely how Flavia felt, but what she couldn't understand was how come her mother, of all people, a woman so much older than Flavia, could feel exactly the same as a sixteen-year-old. It simply didn't make sense.

The supplier of nautical clothing was housed in a premises on the outskirts of Churchester. There was a small showroom, and behind it a much larger stockroom piled high with clothing of every kind. Having inspected the oilskins, the navy blue, cream and brown sailing pullovers, and various other items on display in the showroom, Rusty turned to Flavia.

'Your idea, Flave – you tell me why we're here, or rather tell him.' She nodded towards a man approaching them from the stockroom beyond.

'Good morning, ladies. I'm Ted Austin. Can I help you?'

'Rusty and Flavia Sykes, and yes I think you can.'

244

There was a small pause during which Rusty nodded to Flavia, meaning, *You go ahead, since it was your idea that we came*.

'OK, so, Mr Austin.' Flavia cleared her throat. 'We – er, that is, Mrs Sykes here, and myself – I'm um Flavia Sykes – we are starting up a clothes shop in Bexham, and we would very much like to see some of your stock, with an eye to selling it in our Laurel Cottage Craft— catalogue.'

Rusty's eyes widened, just slightly. They had a catalogue? It was the first she'd heard of it, but now Flavia had mentioned it, it had to be said it seemed a more than sound idea.

'I see. Well, follow me, please. We have much more stock than we are able to put out here, so please. Come backstage, as we like to call it, and let's see if we can't find something to satisfy all tastes.'

They followed Mr Austin through to the stockroom where they once more perused the thickly knitted fisherman's pullovers, the oilskins, and the other seafaring kit.

'Do you have a changing room, Mr Austin?'

He did. Flavia immediately disappeared into it, only to re-emerge a few minutes later wearing one of his pullovers and a pair of slacks, over which she had thrown an oilskin.

'Looks to me as if you could win the Regatta dressed like that,' Rusty admitted as Flavia made her laugh by walking up and down the stockroom, hips thrust forward in an exaggerated manner as if she was already on a catwalk. After a couple of turns she threw off the oilskin and, taking a belt from her own clothes, tied it decoratively round the waist of the pullover, turning it in an instant from a nautical look to something more stylish and modern.

'But wait . . .'

She went back into the changing room, and this time reappeared wearing only the oilskin over her much hitched up skirt.

'Now don't tell me that's not *dolly*,' she insisted to her audience of two.

Rusty turned to Mr Austin.

'She's got hold of this word "dolly". Everything's dolly at the moment.' She shrugged her shoulders helplessly. 'I don't know what to say. What do you think, Mr Austin?'

Mr Austin stared at Flavia, tall, auburn-haired, stunning, the clothes making her look taller, and even more than stunning, like something out of a glossy magazine. But what was better was that she made the really very traditional clothes look modish, fashionable, new. At that moment an influx of store men coming back into the workroom from their lunch hour stopped as one person, staring in open admiration at the sight of a long-legged girl modelling what now looked like not a piece of fisherman's clothing against stormy weather, but a highly desirable fashion accessory.

One of the men whistled, long and low, and as

he did so Rusty felt as if she'd been punched in the back by the sound. Flavia was being wolf whistled. Flavia being whistled at? Suddenly, more than at any moment either before or after, it seemed that Flavia was no longer Rusty's daughter, but a glamour girl, a model, what you will, out there on the floor smiling serenely at the sound, no longer Rusty's daughter but an object of masculine admiration filled with that strange power that adolescence brings. It was as if Rusty'd never known her, and at the same time as if she'd always known her. Why should she be so surprised? Flave, the Beauty of Bexham, had after all always been obsessed with her looks, but this was different. Rusty stared at her, trying hard to understand what the difference was exactly, and then, realising it, she turned away. This was different, because for the first time she realised Flavia was in charge of them.

Mr Austin came up to Rusty's shoulder.

'I should get the clothes photographed like that, with Miss Sykes modelling them, Mrs Sykes, and put them in your catalogue straight away. We'll be sure to sell hundreds of them, modelled by her, I'm sure of it. She makes them look . . .' He paused, smiling, his eyes never moving from the sight in front of him. 'She makes them look so – modish.'

He beamed at Rusty who suddenly smiled at Flavia, who tossed her great mane of hair and went back to the changing room, triumphant.

*   *   *

247

Rusty was driving them back to Churchester, secretly thrilled with the events of the day while at pains not to show as much to Flavia.

'I don't know what your father will say, you modelling garments in a catalogue. Besides, it's so expensive, printing costs and so on. And there's still a paper shortage, someone said, still quite a paper shortage, although why I wouldn't know.'

'All old-fashioned nonsense.' Flavia snorted lightly, staring ahead of her, also well pleased with the way things had turned out. 'We'll do the photographs on cards, like postcards, only a bit bigger, and then we'll stick them in the shop window. You'll see, before the year is out we'll have shifted hundreds of them. Well, dozens anyway, Mum. We're going to be successful, I know it.'

Rusty frowned, still determined on pessimism, while her heart lifted at her daughter's words. It was difficult for her to admit that Flavia was right, that it was a really good idea, that they might indeed sell a great many pullovers and oilskins, if Flavia modelled them as she had just done, and they had them photographed and placed on cards in the windows of Laurel Cottage.

'Besides which, instead of just buying from Mr Austin, we should start getting people in the village to knit for us – you know, like poor old Mrs Chimes, and her family, and all those affected by the sale of the fishing licence. We should start up a proper cottage industry, and then no one in Bexham will

248

criticise us. Not even Dad. Think of that, Mum!'

Rusty turned and looked at her daughter. She was talking everything up, of course, Rusty knew that, and yet she had to admit all her ideas were not just good, they were verging on the brilliant. They *could* get people like the Chimeses to start knitting, and they *could* get Flavia modelling the results, and then photograph her, and it *would* be good for the village.

'I wonder if Mr Austin could make that oilskin material a bit thinner, less toughened? They'd mould into a more fashionable shape then, wouldn't they?'

'Oh, I dare say, if we ask him, of course. He'll do anything for us, you can see that. Anything.' Flavia tossed her hair back, and taking off her shoes placed her feet carefully on the dashboard in front of her. She'd won her mother over. Better than that, she'd won the day. From now on in, she thought exultantly, if she played her cards right, she would probably never have to go back to school – she could model. She'd won the day, and she knew it, most especially because her mother was not saying anything, and when Rusty was quite quiet Flavia always knew she'd won. She was on her way. Next stop London, no doubt of it, and after that, well, anything could happen. She stared out of the car window at the dreary-looking people passing slowly by, none of whom, in her opinion, had really lived their lives. She wanted to really live, and now, at last, she knew she was going to.

*   *   *

Relaxing in his favourite window seat in the Three Tuns, and for want of anything else to read, Waldo picked up a discarded copy of the *Churchester Chronicle*, and flicked idly through it. It was a fine May morning and the estuary filled with the sights and sounds that were most dear to those who lived by it: seagulls perched on the sides of rowing boats, sailing boats upturned, their bottoms being loyally scraped, water lapping against the harbour walls, and with it all weather warm enough to have the window beside him open. As he browsed lazily through the newspaper Waldo found himself more interested in the conversations of the fishermen seated on the black iron capstans below the window, than in items about the Mayor opening a new shopping complex.

As he listened to the gentle drift of their talk, which ranged from the weather to the tides, to their wives and, more importantly, the state of their lobster pots, Waldo found his eye travelling from them to the group of women further down the quays. Here stood a clutch of wives, their hairstyles as tightly coiffed as the nets their husbands used for fishing, their arms akimbo, their flowered aprons immaculate, and their attentions on a tall young girl wearing little more than a shortened oilskin, walking up and down beside the boats, a yachting cap set on her auburn hair, a stylish pair of wellington boots on her feet.

'The only thing young Flavia Sykes'll catch in

that is a cold, you mark my words.' Richards set down a midday drink beside Waldo and nodded towards Flavia.

'Do I know her?' Waldo stared at Richards, pretending ignorance.

Richards sighed and shook his head. 'Know her? I think you even changed her nappies once or twice, didn't you?'

They both laughed.

'Diapers in my country, Richards, not nappies. So what may I ask is young Flavia up to down there?'

'Modelling for her mother's shop, would you believe? She's modelling some clothes that they've taken it into their heads they can sell.' Richards sighed as Waldo smiled.

'The way Flavia's built I would think if she modelled dishcloths they would sell.' Waldo nodded appreciatively back to the sight outside the windows.

'Style, that's what's gone, know that, Mr Astley? Style. No style at all, these young people. I mean where the young Cécile *Sorels*, where the young Vivien *Leighs*, nowadays, tell me?'

'Well, I think Cécile Sorel is no longer with us, but Miss Leigh certainly is, Richards.'

'The young nowadays, I don't know. They think hitching up their skirts to their knees will make them stylish. Lampshades are more stylish than what *they're* all wearing.'

Richards sniffed his disapproval, after which he

251

retired to his own bar stool from where he liked to view the world with an increasing astonishment, verging on disdain. Waldo on the other hand went back to staring out of the window at the sight of Flavia modelling a fisherman's mackintosh and sou'wester.

'That,' said a voice from behind him, 'is one of the cutest sights I've seen for a very long time and anyone who says any different is a liar.'

Waldo turned, and, seeing Judy, immediately stood up. 'Isn't it just?'

They both laughed and turned back to the window, staring towards the harbourside as Flavia, with the photographer in close attendance, moved first this way and then that, her eyes blankly fixed on the horizon, her hand to her eyes, for all the world as if she was waiting for her ship to come in, rather than trying to sell mackintoshes for her mother's gift shop.

'Wonderful, isn't it?' Judy sat down, removing her gloves and shaking her head, at her most amused. The sun was shining outside, Flavia was modelling for Rusty's shop, her own daughter was getting better. There was very little reason not to feel relaxed that morning.

'Gin and tonic?' Waldo turned to her, still standing. Judy nodded.

'How did you guess?' she asked, still smiling.

'I don't know. Possibly because the sun's shining. By the way, may I say, you're looking very pretty in that suit.'

Judy looked down at her excellently cut spring suit. 'It's actually a Utility Suit, would you believe?'

'Well, it's beautifully tailored – Digby Morton at his best.'

'That's what Walter always says.' Judy laughed. 'And not just beautifully tailored, but built to last. And just as well.'

The expression in Waldo's eyes was non-committal, and he turned to go back to the bar. Judy watched his tall, slim figure for a second before turning back to the enjoyable sight at the harbour's edge. She couldn't help feeling nostalgic, remembering the day when Flavia was born, and now look at her – a beautiful, long-legged model. She lit a cigarette, and thought back to the war years. The things that had happened to her, like when she and Rusty had helped to deliver Max Eastcott, in the middle of one of the worst bombing raids; when, in the months before she was killed, their mutual friend Virginia had managed, to everyone's astonishment, to coax Rusty into actually starting to look like a girl rather than a tomboy. When women of all ages were frequently to be seen crossing the village green on their way to Virginia's hairdressing shop, carrying their towels, and their precious liquid soap, if they could find any.

'Three dollars for your thoughts.' Waldo placed their drinks on the table and sat down again.

'That's far too much for my thoughts, Waldo.' Judy laughed. 'I think three cents would be quite enough.'

'So? What were they – these three cents thoughts?'

Judy shrugged her shoulders, reluctant to seem nostalgic.

'No, come on.' Waldo pushed a sixpence across the table. 'Thoughts now paid for.'

'Well.' Judy took the sixpence and turned it round in her fingers, staring at it, before continuing. 'Well, if you really want to know I was just remembering when Max was born in the middle of a bombing raid, and all that kind of thing. You know, how Bexham was before your time. I was just remembering the war, all the things that happened. How Virginia who used to run the hairdressing shop – how she ran for the midwife when Max was arriving at the Eastcotts' house, only to be killed, poor lovely girl. And then I was remembering all kinds of other things that – well, I was just generally becoming nostalgic, really.' She sighed, and turned to look out of the window again. 'We were all *so* close in those days, and now look at us. Tam has a stupid driving accident and everyone's taken sides, and – well, we both know the rest.' She shrugged her shoulders. 'I sometimes think that peace is much, much more difficult than war, and then I remember just how awful the war was, and I think what tosh – *everything*'s difficult.' She placed the sixpence back next to Waldo's place. 'Not even worth sixpence, my thoughts aren't, Waldo, not even a penny, not even a ha'penny.'

They continued to talk, seated in front of their

drinks, the sunshine spreading over the harbour scene in front of the window, Judy's cheeks becoming a little flushed, Waldo lighting a cigar, which caused the nearby table to stare in disapproval and Judy to sniff the air appreciatively.

As they chatted on, their sandwiches arrived, which they duly ate while watching the photographer setting up at a different point in order to go on photographing Flavia, until Rusty arrived to supervise, and quite obviously directed the photographer to go back to his first vantage point. All of which made them both laugh, and commanded their conversation and attention in the most natural way, so that anyone coming upon them would have been able to appreciate that all they made was a perfectly charming couple. Two old friends can surely meet for a drink and talk, stare out into a well loved vista over the harbour to the other cottages, at the fishermen mending nets, at others seated in the old inn, turn and talk some more, order more drinks, without there being anything to suggest that there is any more to their meeting than just simple enjoyment?

Waldo, after all, was a well-loved figure in Bexham, despite the fact that Judy's in-laws were still rumoured to have distanced themselves from him for helping Tam, and even despite the fact that he had been generous to a fault towards all and sundry.

Miraculously, Waldo had somehow managed to avoid being disliked for his philanthropy, probably because he was always at pains, publicly, to send himself up, calling himself 'the Great Provider', and generally going about making it plain that he knew that he had to be forgiven for being so patronising as to help those in need.

But more than that, more than his ability to make fun of himself, to stimulate laughter whenever he appeared, at whatever gathering he graced, it was his great, constant and sustained love for a heroine of Bexham, his wife of a few days, Meggie Gore-Stewart, that had made him so beloved of her native harbourside village. The fact that he had never remarried, that since her death he was known never to have even taken out another woman, meant that he met with approval from the women, and respect from the men.

Judy suddenly subsided into laughter at something Waldo had just said, and despite her covering her mouth with her napkin several people turned round to stare.

'I'm sorry . . .' She shook her head, still laughing. 'I'm so sorry.'

Waldo too stared briefly, if humorously, at the over-interested, as Judy tried to control herself. His look said it all. There was nothing wrong with Mrs Walter Tate's laughing at one of his jokes in the Three Tuns. She was, after all, allowed to laugh publicly, and eat sandwiches with an old friend. There was no law against it, and no one in Bexham could or would criticise or gossip about such an occurrence. Just as, later, they would be seen to kiss each other on the cheek publicly and affectionately, in the car park, and part with much hand-waving and all the rest to drive back to their very different houses, without causing so much as an eyebrow to be raised.

And so it was.

No eyebrow was raised, no scandal caused by their having enjoyed drinks and sandwiches together, any more than by their open enjoyment in each other's company. It was all perfectly acceptable.

Except to the landlord of the Three Tuns.

Richards had been watching them from his usual corner by the bar. Not overtly, of course, because that was not his way. Nevertheless he had taken in every moment of their lunch together, as he took in every activity that took place under his roof in the old inn. After they'd left, he slipped off, making his way slowly to his flat above the main rooms on the old harbour side, and having chopped up some fresh fish for his Persian cat, Richards sat down, as he always did, to watch him eating it with his usual elegant feline delicacy.

'There's trouble brewing down there, Titan. Mark my words, my boy, there's going to be trouble all right, with Mr Astley and Mrs Sykes. And why do I know there's trouble, Titan?' He paused, staring from the cat to the view and back again. 'Because I'm a silly old man, that's why.'

'But there are good things too,' Max was saying, as he wandered around the small sitting room and bedroom suite that Mattie and John had made for a surprise for Jenny's eventual return home, while Jenny herself sat on the sofa, the newspaper open on her lap. 'I mean I think the very fact that Russia and America have agreed on having this so-called hot line between the Kremlin and the White House – I know there's something about it in here.'

He picked the newspaper up from his half-sister's knee and started searching the pages.

'It says if there's ever the sort of death dance there was over Cuba,' he continued, 'all they will do – that is Kennedy and Khrushchev – is pick up this phone, because the line will always be live, and they will sort it out.'

'I see.' Jenny looked up at Max, half admiring, half bored by her restless, fascinating half-brother.

Being with Max was so different from being with anyone else. For a start, which was pretty different after being in Bristol and spending so much time with other victims of road accidents – children with disfigurements, all of them recovering from oper-ations – refreshingly, Max had nothing wrong with him. He was whole, not in need of a nurse or a surgeon, not waiting to get better, or for yet another operation. Weeks and months spent in hospital had a greying, dampening effect. Weeks and months, when, as one child described it to Jenny, all you knew of time passing was that sometimes there were leaves on the trees outside your windows, and sometimes there were not.

And then too, because Max was an actor, he was

all too used to making faces look different. Noses bigger, eyes smaller, age added, hair bleached or blackened. Faces to Max, other people's faces, or his own, were just a series of make-ups, good or bad, and meant little to him. So from the first Jenny had sensed that, to Max, her face, such as it was, scars and all, was just another make-up, and one he expected everyone else to be well used to by now. More than that, it was one that quite obviously he expected Jenny to be used to too, feeling not pity for her, but quite normal and jam-along, which meant that Max's company was more than relaxing, it was a warm bath, it was a sunny day. It was like the days before she was hurt. He made her forget, he made her feel whole, and she loved him for it.

It was also why she forced herself to pretend to tolerate his overt interest in politics. Max was now shaking the paper.

'This will mean,' he went on, turning to Jenny and hitting the paper with his free hand to emphasise both his and the paper's point, 'this will mean that instead of just pushing the button blindly . . .' He turned the pages of the newspaper, muttering. 'Why can't I ever find anything?' Finally, 'Ah yes, here it is. They're also – Jenny, are you listening? They're also, which is greatly to be wished, going to sign some sort of Test Ban Treaty, they being America and us and Russia. So things really are looking up.'

'Oh. Well.' Jenny looked up at him, a little

sparely, feeling inadequate. 'That is – good, then.'

'It's all there.' Max handed her back the newspaper, tapping the relevant paragraphs for Jenny's particular attention with a solemn, pointed hand. 'All there, Jenny.'

While Jenny skim-read the news report Max had handed her without apparent enthusiasm, Max started to sort through the pile of books on the sofa beside her.

'Poetry, poetry, poetry. Robert Frost, Rupert Brooke, Emily Dickinson – Shakespeare's sonnets.' He sighed. 'Ah, *Silent Spring*. Good. Now how did you get on with that? Did you finish it?' he asked, interrupting Jenny's reading of the newspaper and tapping the book at the same time. 'I didn't think I would ever have a good night's sleep after that. What *about* all that stuff about DDT, and all that gloomy forecasting about our wildlife? I mean *what* about that? Brilliant, brilliant book, but if she's right, what are we losing in the way of wildlife?'

Jenny smiled at Max's concerned face as he walked up and down her little sitting room, part of the new suite that her parents had gone to such trouble to make for her, in between operations, but which Max's presence somehow made seem too small. Perhaps it was because she was seated, but Max's head seemed to reach the ceiling, his body disproportionately large.

'Oh, Max, you're such a doom-monger.'

Max stopped pacing.

'I'm not a doom-monger,' he protested.

'Yes, you are! I'm going to rename you Max the Baptist.'

'You can laugh, Jenny Tate, but I tell you one thing, if it wasn't for JFK I don't know where we'd be, I don't honestly. What would have happened last October if Kennedy had pressed the button? I mean, what?'

'But you hated him when he was elected. I remember you saying he was just a girl-mad spoilt rich boy, and now he's saved the world, it seems.'

Max turned and looked at Jenny and, knowing that it was time for her to wise up and face the facts, he sat down opposite her.

'Look, I know I'm a so-called doom-monger, and I know that it's part and parcel of the fact that I'm the odd one out at home, and all that, and everyone in Bexham thinks I'm just a stupid left-wing son of a you-know-what – but.' He stopped. 'But, if you'd been there when I was there, maybe you would be too?'

'Where, Max?'

'In the hall when Canon Collins spoke to every-one about the effects of nuclear war.' He paused. 'There was no publicity, nothing, just this clergy-man and his determination to channel how he knew we all felt about a nuclear war, and yet without any advertising five thousand people turned up that day. Five thousand of us, all feeling the same. I was only sixteen, but I went, because, as you say, I'm a doom-monger. All he really told us about that day were the horrific effects of the hydrogen bomb. Well, you can imagine, there was an appalled silence. Quite terrible. But, look, weren't us doom-mongers that day really rather right? Aren't we all, in a way, pacifists? All not wanting to end the world, but make it grow into something even more beautiful? Isn't the world worth saving – even Bexham,' he ended, jokingly.

'Mmm, yes, of course, but I can't be a pacifist.'

'Why not?'

'Because, Max, I'm a fighter. Look at me.' She turned her face up to him. 'I have to be, don't I?'

Max turned away, for once defeated. Jenny smiled at his back, feeling sorry for making her beloved half-brother feel awkward, and at the same time also feeling that he must understand that at that moment politics, important as they were, weren't her first consideration.

'Did you know that January and February this year of Our Lord 1963 were the coldest on record since records have been kept – ber-boom?'

'Yes, actually.' Jenny held up the newspaper and pointed. 'It says it here!'

'Well, I don't need to read about it, as a matter of fact, because there's a hole in the roof in the theatre, and it was so cold in February we had to wear sweaters under our shirts. One night snow even fell on the stage, and it got a round.'

'A round?'

'The audience clapped – thought it was part of the show.'

Jenny nodded, impressed. She liked stories of hardship, except from their elders and betters about the war, which were getting a bit boring now.

'Have you heard about Flave?'

'Flah-viah, you mean? About her wanting to be a model? Yup. Not very surprising, really.' Max sat down, stretching his long legs out in front of him, admiring his new suede half-boots.

'She had her picture in the *Chronicle* . . .'

'Yes, Mum showed me. She was wearing only a fisherman's mac and a sailor's hat.' Max crossed his arms akimbo like a village lady, and pursed his lips. '*Whatever next*, love?'

'And a pair of fisherman's knit stockings, knitted by Mrs Chimes whose husband got the push when the licence was sold. They think they're going to be quite big.'

'I never knew *fishermen* wore stockings,' Max mused. 'It brings a whole new dimension to stockings and fishing. And as for Mrs Chimes, as I remember her, she's quite as big as her stockings, isn't she?'

Jenny started to laugh. 'I heard Mum saying that Flave's been on television on an afternoon programme – just, you know, a women's one, but she's already got orders for the stockings because of it.'

'Flah-viah's face-for-the-world-to-see, on every knitting pattern. There'll be fishermen everywhere parading their legs, all over Bexham harbour. It doesn't bear thinking about, really it doesn't.'

'I think she's going to be terribly, terribly famous, Max, I do really.'

A dreamy look came into Jenny's eyes, before they eventually clouded over as she remembered the old days when she and Flavia and Kim had used to talk all the time about fashion, and film stars, and who they thought was really pretty, and who they thought might become famous, and all that.

Max, sensing suddenly from the long silence, which was something for him, that he had well and truly put his foot in it, floundered.

'Listen. Listen, how would it be – I mean how – I mean, look, Jenny. Would you come to London with me, one day soon? Mum and John would let you, wouldn't they? I could take you to see this new film about the bomb – *Dr Strangelove*. It's a comedy.'

'How can you make a comedy about the *bomb*, Max?'

'It's a satire, meant to be fantastic. Do you think you'd be allowed?'

'If you really want to know I should think they couldn't wait for me to go, Max. I heard them saying they were never alone nowadays, only the other day.' Jenny looked bleak, staring suddenly at something that Max couldn't see, some great lump of misery that wouldn't go away. 'No, they'd love it, actually, if I went to London for a bit.' She looked up at Max. 'It's just me that wouldn't.'

'Jenny . . .'

'Sorry. But no, Max. I know I should go. But. I just can't.' She picked up the newspaper again, and Max sensing defeat let the subject drop.

Later, as he was leaving, Mattie slipped out of the house behind him.

'How do you think she is, Max?'

'Oh, much better.' Max picked up his overnight bag, preparatory to driving himself back to London. 'Don't you think so, Mum? Doesn't John?'

'It's difficult for us to tell. She's not the same to us, not as she would be to you, as she would be with you, rather. I mean I heard her laughing just now. She never laughs with us.'

'I hear she's going back for more surgery.' Max was trying his hardest to be helpful, but they both knew he couldn't wait to get back to London.

'The surgeons think they're really winning, you know, that soon you won't really be able to tell what's happened to her.'

Mattie opened the front door for her son, as always ready to help her children leave home, knowing it was best for them. Max kissed her fondly, and then backed off down the garden. He didn't know why but he couldn't – no, didn't want to – talk to his mother about Jenny. It seemed like some sort of betrayal. Of course it wasn't, but it felt like it.

'I'll come and see Jenny when she's in hospital,' he called back to Mattie. 'If she'll let me.'

'Yes, do, darling. She'd like that.'

But of course they both knew Jenny would hate

265

it. That it would be the last thing that she would want, that she would never forgive Mattie for allowing it. Nevertheless Mattie waved to Max, kissed her fingertip to him several times, and then shut the front door.

Tam, now known even to himself as 'Blue', had become everyone's favourite cowhand. Of course he was well aware that this was entirely due to rescuing Tammy, but it couldn't matter less for the end result was that, without exactly realising it, he had grown in confidence. Didn't matter that everyone at the Big U went on tipping him into the dung heaps, or throwing him into the water troughs, and never mind that they made fun of his being English – they'd accepted him, and that meant more than a great deal to him – it meant just about everything, and what's more his nightmares had stopped.

Nightmares where Jenny lay bloodstained and dead in his arms, where cars blew up before he could reach them, where he was running through fire and never reaching victims – they all began to stop without his even realising it. It was then that he began to think about Jenny again, not consciously, because he was far too busy to sit down and think consciously about anyone or anything except the business in hand, but when he was out riding, relishing the vast acres that made up the ranch, or lying in his bunk at night, staring out at the moon, which like everything round the Big U seemed to be bigger than it was anywhere else. He found himself wondering if he should, or could, write to Jenny, and then realising that the very notion of writing to apologise to someone whose life you'd ruined was more than pathetic, it was insulting.

It was when a letter from Flavia arrived telling him all the news from home, including the fact that Jenny had now been told that her face not only could be mended, but would be mended, soon, and there would be no visible scarring, that he gave in to his all too suppressed feelings of guilt, and got riotously drunk.

'Mah heavens, Blue boy, but you got more than burned last night, you got scalped!'

Tammy ranged up beside her hero, and laughed at him appreciatively. He might be on the thin side, but he'd certainly proved he could drink.

'Tell me something new, Tammy, tell me something new.'

Tam looked across the short divide between himself and the ranch owner's daughter, his head throbbing as if it had seven hammers working hard in it, and wondered why it was that when he really would like someone to throw him into the horse trough, no one would?

Perhaps sensing his state of ultra-sensitivity Tammy moved closer to him, her green eyes running over his body with a great deal more interest than she had hitherto shown in him.

'I *will* tell you something new, Blue. I will tell you

that up there, above our 'ere heads, there's a great pile of sweet new hay, and I have a mind to go there with you. Do you have a mind to come there with me, Blue boy?'

'Blue' looked at her. He could hardly see out of his eyes. He could hardly hear her sweet suggestion, but he didn't care. He knew that he was still drunk from the night before, that he was liable to be thrown out on his ear for fornicating with the boss's daughter, but alcohol had empowered him, and he quickly followed Tammy's long legs up the rickety ladder to the hay loft. And when the usual ritual of lovemaking had taken place, Tam fell asleep caring less, and only wanting more.

'Only one thing you have to understand if you're dating mah daughter, boy,' R.J. was heard to say to Tam when the news reached him. 'No heavy stuff, d'you hear? You try anything on with Tammy and the next thing you'll feel is mah shotgun up your rear.'

There was little point in telling Tammy to behave herself, since she was so used to misbehaving herself she wouldn't have known how to do otherwise. Nevertheless, once sober, and more or less in his right mind, Tam took the warning to heart, and no matter what tricks Tammy tried to play with him he was never again tempted to go up to the hay loft, happy to keep the swirling, whirling, blissful recollection tucked up and put away in his bank of better memories.

'Blue's coming to the gig with me, d'you hear, boys?' Tammy announced, ahead of herself with the news as usual.

Although it was the first Tam had heard of any gig he managed to look creditably pleased, while at the same time feeling a sense of excitement, because he knew that Tammy's brothers had formed a group called, unsurprisingly, The Bros.

The night of the gig one of the band, a cousin not a brother, was poleaxed with pneumonia, leaving The Bros without a bass guitarist. About to hit the panic button they started to phone round friends who they knew could play guitar, at the very least.

'How about Blue here, boys?'

Once again Tammy was ahead of the game. Her brothers stared at her.

'Sure, but he don't play electric, Tammy. Blue only plays that damned old six-string of his. Even if he could lay it down he's not going to be heard.'

'We could mike him up,' Lee the youngest brother suggested, licking down a hand-rolled smoke. 'Shove a microphone in his soundbox.'

'Or you could ask him if he plays bass, couldn't you, you dumb ox?'

All the brothers stared at their sister, the penny finally dropping.

'Well?' They turned as one on Blue. Tam immediately assumed an over-modest expression.

'Ah have, just a little,' he confessed.

'Do you read, man?'

'Yup.'

'Now where you boys would be without your little sister Ah don't know.'

'We ain't heard him play yet, only folk song crap.' Brewster the eldest brother looked round the rest, nodding.

So Tam, having familiarised himself with the borrowed bass guitar, auditioned for The Bros, ending with extemporising for them through a couple of his favourite Buddy Holly and Elvis Presley numbers.

The Bros stared at him, then at each other, as he finished.

Tammy stared at them. 'He's going to blow you away, boys!'

Of course this wasn't true, and Tam knew it. Bass guitarists didn't hog the act, they just kept their head down and left all the showing off to the singer and the fender boys. The bass guitarist, if good and knowing his job, laid down the beat, giving a good solid bass line, which, when confident, he could improve on. This was what Tam did at the gig, which ended, unpredictably, in a riot.

'Cool, man,' Lee told him, through his home-rolled. 'And I thought you were just some blue dude. Cool, man.'

Tam was still holding his borrowed guitar when Tammy kissed him.

'Tammy, much as you're the cat's pyjamas, I have to tell you I treasure my backside more than your kisses.'

He stood away from her, holding the bass guitar,

now in its case, between himself and her all too desirable body.

'Big Daddy's no way of finding out, Blue boy.'

'Maybe not, but it's not something I want to risk.'

He backed off, and only just in time. Seconds later, Big Daddy, otherwise known as R.J., appeared on the scene, and Tam only thanked God, his lucky stars, and anything else that came to mind that he'd jumped backwards from Tammy, and not forwards to her all too luscious lips.

A few days later Tammy left for a long holiday in Northern California, while Tam took himself off to Reedsville to buy a bass guitar. Not a new one – he'd not enough money for that – but the instrument was good, and hardly used, and it soon supplied him with enough upon which he could concentrate to enable him to forget Tammy's kisses, at least until he received a postcard from her.

Dear Blue, I have met the most handsome life guard you have ever seen. He is teaching me to dive. Take care of yourself – Wild Thing.

Tam stared at the message. Wild Thing. That's what Tammy had called herself in the hay. He went back to his guitar. Might make a good song. '*Wild thing, may you never be tame.*' He smiled. That would be his wish for Tammy.

Flavia awoke to an unusual sound. She sat up, frowning, still sleepy, but the sound continued and she soon recognised it. It was the sound of her parents quarrelling. She lay down again. No need to ask over what they might be arguing so vociferously. It was bound to be Flavia herself, and her modelling career. She pulled a pillow over her head, trying to drown the sound out, trying not to feel both frustrated and furious that such a small thing as her wish to become a model should bring her parents' marriage to a state of near divorce.

The next morning she crept downstairs hoping against hope to see neither of them, only to bump into her mother standing in the kitchen beside the percolating coffee pot.

'I talked him round,' she told the astonished Flavia in a weary voice. She handed Flavia her schoolbooks in her school bag. 'There are conditions, mind. No professional work, nothing like that. You can only model for the shop, for Laurel Cottage, nothing else.'

'Oh, but that's useless.' Flavia threw the strap of the bag over her shoulder and shook her head in despair while at the same time unscrewing a jar of marmalade, eating a spoonful, putting back the lid, and turning to go, well satisfied with her breakfast.

'It might be useless, Flave, but it's at least something. Oh, and one other thing.'

Flavia turned to look at her mother.

'You have to have at least five O-levels before you leave school.'

'Five O-levels. For modelling?'

'I know, I know, but he's right in that. Even models do their job better if they're intelligent.'

272

Rusty waved goodbye at the door, watching Flavia, her skirt hitched five inches higher than it should be, striding off to the bus stop and school.

' 'Bye, Mum.'

' 'Bye.'

Rusty shut the front door and leaned against it. What she hadn't told Flavia was how Peter had taken the news of Laurel Cottage.

'You're doing what you want to do now, Rusty, so I got to thinking of all the things I haven't done, and I realised that you're right, we should each do our thing, as they say nowadays. So one of these days, when I'm quite sure of everything, I'm going to take myself off for a bit travelling. Derek – you know, Derek Woods – he's a mind to do the same, once his children have finished school, so that's what we thought we'd do. Take off somewhere, Australia, the West Indies, places we haven't seen.'

For no reason that she could think Rusty had been left feeling winded by this announcement, most particularly since, having talked and shouted Peter down about Flavia, she couldn't find one reason why Peter shouldn't also, like the women in his family, strike out on his own whenever he wanted.

Now, however, in the morning, it all seemed so different, and listening to the ticking of the kitchen clock, the silent house, the odd car passing by, the radio still on in their bedroom, it seemed to Rusty that she'd somehow been bested by Peter.

But the truth was that he had only stated the

truth. She was striking out on her own account, and therefore there was no reason why he shouldn't do the same. So why did she have the feeling that somehow or another, by announcing his plans to travel, he was revenging himself on her for starting up Laurel Cottage Designs?

She sighed, and started to clear the breakfast things. Not that it mattered, not in the grand scheme of things, for if going to Dunkirk with Mr Kinnersley to rescue stranded British soldiers had taught her one thing and one thing alone, it was to concentrate only on the bigger issues in life. All that mattered now was that she made a success of what she was about to do. She stared at the dishes she had just placed in the sink. For what she and Laurel Cottage Designs were about to do, may the Lord make her, and Flavia, truly thankful. Amen.

Chapter Seven

Kim had just begun to get through what the Widow Hackett always called 'the caterpillar phase' when her mother suggested that she came home for a break. Kim refused. Judy was hurt. The Widow was forced to write and explain.

What we at Loughnalaire have observed with our family here is that when they arrive they are as it were only eggs, or perhaps larva. This, you will not be so surprised to hear, is the dullest and most awkward stage. The new arrivals retreat into themselves. Just as our caterpillars here do, they hang around on branches, waiting, as it were, to arrive at the next stage, but never quite knowing themselves when it might happen. It is at this stage that it is often found helpful to adopt another name – in Kim's case, Jenny. Assuming the name of someone she imagines she has to take responsibility for injuring.

The next stage is only reached when the alien name, and with it the assumption of unbearable

275

guilt, is set aside. Kim is now at that stage. She is once again called 'Kim', and so she has become a pupa (chrysalis), but not a butterfly. That is why she is refusing to come home. She cannot risk not becoming a butterfly. This has nothing to do with her love for you and her home but everything to do with her progress. Please do not feel upset, either you or your husband. When you next see her I am sure, whenever it is, and it will assuredly be in God's good time, she will be a butterfly. Much changed, of course, but a butterfly none the less.

Yours truly,
Atlanta Hackett

Whatever she might write in a letter to Mrs Walter Tate, there was no doubt that the Widow Hackett was all too aware of the problems that came about if the butterfly stage was actually never reached.

A part of her often wondered whether the atmosphere at Loughnalaire worked against its finally happening, whether once the caterpillars were making good progress, feeding off the atmosphere, finding themselves in a way of life that was reassuring, they didn't refuse to even become pupae, solely because the atmosphere had been too cosseting.

It was a problem that she confided to no one except her handyman, the inimitable Mad Rufus.

'I sometimes think that some of them will never

leave us, and that's the truth, that they'll still be here when they reach their first centenary and you and I are either up there, or down there. But leave us they have to.'

Mad Rufus, who was busy staring into the fire, before proceeding to pretend to paint the back larder, shook his head.

'And haven't I always told you so, Widow Hackett? In your success at mending the crocks that turn up here, saving your presence of course, you have created for yourself a problem of *tenantry*. We have to face it, if you weren't a native of these shores they'd be accusing you of being part of the old Ascendancy, you've that many housed here.'

'We're a charity, Rufus, a charity, nothing less and nothing more, thanks be.'

'Exactly so.' Mad Rufus sighed. 'So who is it,' he asked in a kindly tone, 'that we have to send on their way this week?'

'Napoleon.'

'Ah, yes, old Boney. Well now, he's going to be a bit difficult to chase off. You'll be needing a Wellington for that, doubtless.'

The Widow nodded. She would. 'Or my six guns.'

She sighed. Sometimes she had only to take the guns out and lay them on the table. Sometimes she would have to draw; rarely, she had to shoot. Today, this morning, she had a bad feeling that she might have to shoot. She stretched out her hand and patted her dog's head.

'Will you want me to stay with you, then?' Mad Rufus towered over the Widow from the other side of the desk, while slipping a copy of her favourite Yeats into the front of his dungarees.

'No, don't stay, just hover.'

'I'll show him in, so.'

The Widow nodded. She was sure it was going to be a shooting job, but it had to be done. Napoleon had long ago progressed to the butterfly stage, and he had to go to make room for others with greater need. The fact that he was refusing to admit that he was now a butterfly was no one's fault, but Loughnalaire was not a housing scheme, nor was it a holiday home, it was a place of restoration, and once restored the inmates had to fly.

Mad Rufus was even now ushering a reluctant Napoleon through the door, and clearing his throat loudly as he did so, at the same time pulling a face behind the poor man's back. The face, and Mad Rufus's motion of drawing two hipster guns from his overall side pockets while bending his knees told the Widow everything. Napoleon was intent on making a fight of it. She straightened her back, said a prayer to her favourite saint, and began her message of farewell in her wonderful, impressive baritone voice, the red velvet sleeve of her embroidered jacket catching the sunlight from the window as she gestured towards the great wide world that would soon, if she had anything to do with it, be awaiting Napoleon.

*   *   *

Nearing the end of Kim's first term at Loughnalaire, as summer was about to cool, shed its greenery, and paint itself into russet and brown, Kim started to emerge into her last stage.

It was one of those days when the air is both warm and clear and the hint of winter is to be sensed but not felt. Kim and Dorothy were out with Phelim following Kim's now favourite occupation, namely fishing. Amidst many squeals of delight Dorothy had caught a conger eel, and Kim and Phelim had drawn a fine haul of mackerel. On their way back to the harbour the seas calmed and they drew near to another craft travelling considerably slower, but weighed down by what seemed to be a large fish in a large net.

'What d'ye have there now?' Phelim shouted, chapped hand cupped to his mouth. 'Looks like a bit of a shark or the likes! Or a marlin be'haps!'

'Not at all, and aren't you wrong on all counts? What I have here, Phelim O'Brien, is nothing less than a purpuss! Some foreen scallion had him caught up in his net and wasn't he tryin' his best to martyr the poor creachur?'

'Is he alive, so?'

'He is that! There or thereabouts anyways. But didn't I have to pay money to save him, God bless my wife. She'll be after killing me when she gets to hear.'

The two smacks were alongside now in the calmer waters, nearing the harbour. From her position in the prow Kim could see the big creature in the net, lying semi-dormant in waters that were colouring a beastly red around it.

'Is he sure he's not dead?' she asked Phelim anxiously. 'He looks ever so badly hurt, doesn't he?'

'No,' Phelim reassured her as he leaned towards the victim. 'He's not dead at all, no, he's conserving his strength that's all. They've more sense in their one fin, have fish, than we have in our whole bodies. Now see here, Kim, you take the helm while I help Tomas O'Flanagan bring the poor fellow in, and by that I mean the purpuss, not Tomas. He'll probably die on us, and by that I mean the purpuss, not Tomas, but at least he'll not end up on the table, and by that I mean—'

'The porpoise, not Tomas!' Kim and Dorothy finished for him.

'It's actually a dolphin, I think you'll find,' Kim told Phelim primly.

'Call it what you will, it's one of the Mer folk, and we have to save him from the foreeners. Mer folk has always to be saved, for they bring bad luck, else.'

'Do you mean mermaids?' Dorothy wanted to know.

'Mermaids, or Mermen, Mer folk must be protected.'

By now the other smack was alongside the jetty and was tying up. The net containing the injured creature was at the far side of the boat. Kim leaned over in order to get a better view. As with the pony

280

in the shafts when she had first arrived at Cobh, she was met with a gaze of such intelligence that it pierced her heart. Two small eyes searched hers, wondering, always wondering, why man was as he was? Blood was coming from the dolphin's netted body, from his shiny bottlenose. Kim found herself praying that the netted creature was not wounded internally, for if he was there would surely be no way of saving him.

'How much did you have to pay for him?' she asked Tomas in her Alice in Wonderland voice. 'Whatever you had to pay I will reimburse you for your efforts.'

'You'll do better than that, miss,' the fisherman replied huffily, struggling with his heavy ropes. 'Ye want the purpuss ye'll be paying me exactly what I paid for him, and that'll be ten bub.'

Kim put her hand into her jacket pocket and fished out a ten shilling note, but before she could hand it over Phelim had reached across and tapped her lightly on her arm.

'And where will you be thinkin' of taking the creachur? Sure he'll not fit into one of Widow Hackett's baths, any more than he will fit into one of our boats.'

'Phelim, all we have to do is keep his skin wet, and find out what's wrong with him. I've read all about it in one of Widow Hackett's American magazines. More and more people are taking in sea creatures off the coast of California, to heal them and then return them to the sea.'

'Yes, and we can put him in Widow Hackett's swimming pool,' Dorothy enthused. 'It will be quite big enough for a dolphin, and we can make him better. The pool's empty just now, but it will hold water enough, and we can keep him there while he recovers.'

'Always provided that he has no internal injuries.'

As this conversation neared its end, Phelim took the ten shilling note out of Kim's hand, and put it back into the pocket from which it had come.

'You'll charge this poor gel the going rate. You're a hard man, Tomas, to be robbin' a poor girl from Loughnalaire.'

'A man has to live, now, Phelim,' Tomas moaned, and he shook his head, an expression of such tragedy on his face that with the disappearance of the ten shilling note it looked as if he had lost a dearly loved relative.

'A man has to live, but not by bread alone, Tomas, not by bread alone. And not by cheatin' neither. Five bub is what you'd have paid, and five bub is what you'll be getting, and not a penny more.'

'He can have his five other bob if he recovers,' Kim hissed at Phelim.

'Fair enough, girl.' Phelim nodded his handsome head. 'Fair enough. And as for you, Tomas O'Flanagan, ye'll take the going rate for purpuss rescue, or ye'll take nothing at all.' He took five shillings from Kim's hand and offered it to his fellow fisherman.

'Man has to live, Phelim, man has to live,' Tomas moaned.

'A man has to live be rights, but not be cheatin'. Now don't forget to keep that for your poor auld mither, and not hand it to that rascally barman brother of yours for pints, now.'

Leaving the two men to argue and josh each other, Kim and Dorothy hurried back to Loughnalaire to prepare the rescue operations for the purpuss – or Mer person, as Kim thought of the dolphin now – hoping that none of its wounds were internal.

'Or,' as Kim remarked sagely, 'it will turn out to have been a waste of five whole shillings.'

Waldo was worried. He hadn't heard from Lionel for some few days, which was very un-Eastcott-like. Normally they would be on what Lionel still called 'the blower' at least once every few days, exchanging views, making plans, passing the time of day.

'My fault, I haven't called you. Been dashing about a bit,' Waldo explained, relieved to hear the older man's voice.

'Chundering along, chundering along,' Lionel told him, speaking a little too far away from the phone which made him sound suddenly a great deal older.

'I'll call round later, if I may, Lionel. Got to go to the Three Tuns first.'

'Ah, good man. Getting a few under your belt

before you come round, eh?' Lionel's voice was clearer now, a firmer tone to it.

'Yes, sir. That and having to consult the oracle of Bexham, otherwise known as Richards, about a certain little matter.'

'Tell me all, concealing nothing, when you get here.'

'I certainly will, Lionel.'

So it was that Waldo, still feeling a little uneasy about his old friend, but intent on the business of the day, drove into the car park of the Three Tuns and, having parked the Aston Martin with due care and attention, strolled up to the old inn doors, determined on finding out the truth behind the rumours.

'I'm afraid there is a great deal of truth in the rumours, sir. A great deal,' Richards told him in his saddest, on-the-eve-of-war voice. 'In fact there is all too much truth. Dreaded vested interest at work, not to mention dirty work at the crossroads, and all stations south.'

Waldo, who had grown used to the English way of putting things, kept an admirably straight face, gathering from what Richards had just said, as he pulled Waldo a pint of his best, that everything he had recently heard about the designs on the village by a certain person were actually true.

'But, Richards, come on – the Yacht Club. How can that be? Surely there must be some sort of safe-guard on a place like that, some embargo that will prevent any kind of building or expansion, surely?'

Richards moved out from behind the bar, and sat himself down beside Waldo on a bar stool, climbing up, despite his age, with surprising dexterity.

'They would have to get the consent of the membership, but don't forget that takes very little in these parlous times.' Richards sighed. 'A little extra lining to the pocket here, a little there, and alas, in a trice, the Yacht Club will have gone and we will be contemplating a hideous line of buildings overlooking the harbour. Don't forget it is a prime site, Mr A. – a prime site.' Richards shook his head mournfully.

'But the shares that are held,' Waldo remembered suddenly. 'The shares that are held are not held by the members, they're held by the board, so it won't be as easy as that, surely?'

'It will be quite as easy, sir, if you don't mind my correcting you, if you remember what boards get up to, even in England. They believe in what's best for them, particularly if they don't happen to live on or near the harbour. In my opinion it will be the end of Bexham.' Richards raised his eyes to heaven, and then dropped them to stare sadly at Waldo over the top of his half-moon glasses.

'Well, let's see now, Richards.' Waldo paused, marking off each board member on his long, elegant fingers. 'They'd have to get rid of Lord Rule, first, the Chairman. And he's also their patron. Then there is Hugh Tate, and Jeremy Lonsdale. My, I could name a dozen others who would be very unlikely to roll over, really they would. So, don't let's be too pessimistic, shall we?'

'We shall see,' Richards said evenly. 'The strangest things happen when there is vested interest at the heart of it.'

'I can't see Bexham letting it happen. Bexham would simply not be Bexham without its Yacht Club. They won't sell, I'm sure.'

'There are rumours about old Todd's boatyard too.' Richards climbed carefully down off the stool, and went behind the bar once more, this time to fill a glass from the whisky optic and place it in front of Waldo. 'You've possibly heard, have you?'

'What next? I must have my ears so close to the ground that I can't hear anything for listening. Either that or I've been too busy minding my own business.'

'That they've retired is old news indeed.' Richards picked off the proper money for Waldo's drinks from a pile of silver that Waldo was in the habit of placing in front of him when drinking at the bar. 'But we were all under the impression that it was at least going to stay a boatyard. I say "we were", but no longer.'

'Oh, my, my.'

'Indeed, you may well say "my, my", because we all imagined that boats would be going to go on being made at the boatyard, not that the new owners would have quite different plans. Not for building boats do they want the boatyard, no, not for supplying boats for the Yacht Club, which in

our simplicity we might have thought was goir
to be the case, oh no. No, the boatyard is going tc
become a *bistro*.'

The word bistro spun across the wooden surface
of the bar, passing Waldo's whisky glass, passing
other customers, until, gathering momentum, it
seemed to roll round the room causing those that
had overheard a satisfactorily shocking moment.

'A bistro? Opposite here? A bistro?'

'It's going to be lovely for us, isn't it? Competition of the worst kind right beside us.'

'By us, you mean – you?'

'Naturally.' Richards leaned across the bar again.
'You know what's going to happen?' he asked, his
voice lowered now. 'They're going to be serving
not decent English food, but imported foreign
food. There's going to be candles stuck in bottles,
and checked tablecloths, and fishermen's nets not
trailing in the water but hung overhead, and, to
sum up, I shall be ruined.'

He moved away to serve some other customers,
leaving Waldo to the contemplation of a ruined
Bexham, of a village without boats or club, with
only a hideous bistro and very little else to recommend it, excepting the church and the old houses.
Doubtless, if things went on as they were, even the
church would be turned to some other use,
possibly into a nightclub, or a private house.

He moved over to his favourite seat in the window of the old inn, intent on thinking over the
latest news, and equally intent on doing something

bout it. He could not stand idly by and watch his darling Meggie's beloved Bexham being ruined. What the Nazis had failed to do it now seemed the members of the Yacht Club, or rather its board, and certain individuals, were quite prepared to do instead.

Everything about Bexham was pretty. The church, the main street, the old houses, some of them dating from as early as the seventeenth century. The harbour was a hub for boating activity, the focus of old customs, themselves dating back into a past which everyone had quite forgotten. People had been setting sail from Bexham from the earliest times, since before the Roman invasion of Britain, since the days when the Irish were setting out in coracles to find the other side of the world that they devoutly believed to be flat. Places as perfect as Bexham should be immune from change.

Waldo thought of Meggie, and her childhood friends, all of them setting off from Bexham to rescue the British army from the French beaches. He thought of how Meggie had sacrificed, if not her life, certainly her health, by living as a British agent in Germany. When he had remembered everything there was to remember, his determination hardened. He would stop whoever was planning to ruin their little corner of heaven. It might be only a small Sussex village, but it was everything to him at that moment, and if he had to stand alone, well and good; but as he looked round the bar and heard the same conversation he'd been having with Richard; it seemed to Waldo that he would certainly not be alone in going to defend Bexham.

'What do you think of these Beatle chaps?' Lionel asked Waldo when he called round a little later that day. 'They're enjoying a huge success, but I can't see it myself. I mean, *is* it music, do you think?'

'I think so, most definitely. There's originality, certainly. Yes, I would say they're definitely a talented bunch of mopheads.'

'You surely don't think so?'

'I surely do. What's more, whoever's backing them is going to end up one helluva rich guy, mark my words, as you would say, Lionel old chap.'

'I can't see it myself.'

Lionel shook his head, and helped himself to another spoonful of sugar. He never could get over being able to have as much sugar as he wished, not after all the deprivations of the war. He still had a cellar full of sugar, and marmalade. Maude, his late wife, long before war had been declared, and much against his wishes, had started to hoard marmalade and sugar, and now it was his turn. Strange how the very things that irritated you about someone you loved turned out to be the same things that you now treasured. Maude. His late and lovely Maude who so loved to dance. Maude whom he'd never really treasured, until she'd gone.

'These Bobbysoxers, they're a bit of a nuisance,

.ren't they?' he began again, looking across at Waldo.

Waldo laughed. 'Not Bobbysoxers any more, Lionel, old thing. By no means. No, now it's fans, or *groupies*. Bobbysoxers went out with the New Look!'

'Groupies, did you say? What an awful word.' Lionel shook his head. 'Dreadful, dreadful word. No, but Waldo, must tell you, tell you who I've thought better of, and that's that chap Kennedy. I never did like him – his father, you know, no friend to Britain before the war, and not much of one after, but now – well, I've taken to the chap, really I have.'

'Good man. Ever since he stood up to Khrushchev, eh?'

They'd had this conversation many times before, but they both still enjoyed it. It seemed to Waldo that it was like taking a much-loved drive in your motor car. You knew where all the good turns in the road were coming, all the splendid views, all the places to stop, and its very familiarity only made it the more pleasurable.

'Now, have you heard about the possible sale of the Yacht Club?'

Lionel replaced his teaspoon on his saucer and, putting down his cup in the same place, stared at Waldo. 'What did you say?'

'There's a rumour that the Yacht Club is coming up for sale, and that it's going to be bought by a property developer, and that the children of the people to whom old Todd sold his boatyard don't want to run a boatyard any more, they want to turn it into a bistro. Richards is hopping mad, and so is most of his clientele.'

Lionel stood up. He hadn't been so shocked by anything since war was declared, or poor darling Maude was killed. If Waldo was right this would mean the end of Bexham. The end of everything that they'd fought for, their life the way they thought it should be lived.

'But Bexham is the Club, Waldo, you know that, I know that. The Yacht Club – the Club *is* Bexham. There must be rules governing it. Things like that can't just happen. Although saying that, since 1945 all too many things like that have happened. Look at East Weathering, ruined completely by insensitive building, becoming uglier by the minute, nothing but fish and chip shops and Kiss Me Quick hats.'

Lionel was pacing up and down looking more than agitated, he was looking both pale and flushed at the same time, as if he had lost colour at the news, and then it had heightened at the realisation of what such a change could do to the village in which he had grown up and lived all his life.

'We'll fight it, Lionel, you'll see,' Waldo tried to say, but his murmurings were brushed impatiently aside.

'You can't fight a voting board, Waldo. I know, my father was in the city, I know, believe me. Any more than you can fight an army board, or any other kind of board. The truth is that the entire world can't fight a board, not even the monarch. A board is a board is a board, and that, Mr Astley, is the truth.'

'Put it this way, then. I give you my word as a southern gentleman, sir, that I will, hand on heart, personally take on the powers-that-be to fight this on behalf of old Bexham, new Bexham, but most of all Meggie.'

Lionel stopped his pacing and stared at Waldo for a few seconds. Waldo never would get over his loss. Lionel knew it, Waldo knew it, possibly the whole world knew it.

'Meggie loved this place. She came here, sick and ill, and it put her to rights. She grew up with her childhood sweetheart Davey Kinnersley, and it was from here that he sailed to Dunkirk – eventually to pay the ultimate sacrifice – what greater reasons do I need to fight this asinine idea of selling off the Yacht Club. There Lionel, old friend? What greater reason?'

Lionel nodded. It had never occurred to him before that moment that Waldo and he had so much in common, not just their love of bridge, but their deep and lasting regrets, their feelings of loss for their wives, gathered too soon, leaving them to mourn them every day that passed. He decided to change the subject.

'I say, old chap, I was remembering this morning that game we had with the Egyptian fellow. Do you remember? That *was* something, wasn't it?'

'You set him up – you were brilliant. As a matter

of fact he was brilliant, but you won, and that was what was important.'

Lionel chuckled, remembering.

'I set the whole hand up again for John and Mattie the other night, and it still made the hair on my head, what's left of it, stand up on end! How much was it that we won that night? Four thousand quid?'

'It sure was, young sir, four thousand lovely pounds. And that was in 1947 when four thousand pounds was worth more than today, say what you will.'

Lionel shook his head, still smiling, still unable to quite believe what had happened all that time ago, the fun they'd had, the money they'd won.

'That was quite a night.' He picked up his newspaper and waved it at Waldo, still intent on distracting him. 'What do you think about all this then?' He pointed to the headlines.

'Not too much.' Waldo sighed. 'I'm never too sure of foreign policy, anyone's foreign policies, not just ours, not just America's, anyone's. I gather at this moment hardly anyone in the States knows quite where Vietnam actually is, not even the Senate!'

'I'm sure I don't.'

Lionel put the newspaper down again.

'I think I need a cup of tea, old thing,' he murmured, suddenly sitting down and staring into the fire. 'Do you mind getting me one? I feel a bit sleepy, I think that's what it is. Sleepy is what I feel.'

Waldo stared at him for a second, not wanting to tell him that he'd just had tea, and merely nodded.

'Yes, of course, I'll get you one, old chap.'

He went into the kitchen to make a fresh pot, hoping against hope that Lionel wouldn't have noticed him exiting with the tea tray.

Once in the kitchen he stared round in some surprise. Everything in Lionel's bachelor kitchen was immaculate. Everything labelled, everything cleaned and polished. It was more like a kitchen belonging to some exclusive gentlemen's club. Waldo knew that his old friend had long ago done away with hiring anyone to help him, insisting instead that he found it more interesting to look after himself and his dog, rather than have someone come in and pretend to do it. More than that, Waldo knew that Lionel had, for a short few years, conducted a discreet affair with a wealthy South African bridge-playing lady, and in order to keep it just that way, namely discreet, it had been necessary not to have anyone else around – Bexham being Bexham.

Waldo was in no hurry to leave, but when on taking the fresh pot of tea back into the sitting room he found Lionel asleep with his dog at his feet he retreated once more to the kitchen with the tray, and quietly let himself out of the house.

He walked along the side of the green from Lionel's house with his hat pulled down, not really wanting to meet anyone, not really wanting to talk to anyone. The autumn afternoon, although still bright and sunny, already had an early sense of darkness about it, so that as he passed the gardens and homes set about the green a sudden gust of rising wind startled the trees, swishing more dying leaves off their great branches to curl and spin down to lawns which were themselves already losing their vitality and growth. A thrush hopped out of a shrub to stand in hope above a series of worm casts, while smoke from an early bonfire drifted past the windows of the houses and cottages, obscuring the now tidied gardens. But other than the slight sigh of the wind it seemed to Waldo there was nothing but silence, as if summer had all at once stolen away to hide somewhere on the other side of the world, until once again it was time for the earth to shift its axis and for the sun to warm the buds of a new spring into life. At least, that was the hope, and despite everything that the politicians could throw at the world that would remain the hope.

They were odd days, not just the week that passed after Waldo's revelation to Lionel about the Yacht Club, but every day that passed something seemed to be changing, as if the loveliness of autumn was doomed to be only a challenge to the unsightly doings of man. Scandals in government followed upon each other with such speed that even the locals at the Three Tuns were left stunned as day succeeded day and still the revelations, the political scandals, continued.

'It was that Labour bloke Wilson who got 'im,' Charley, one of the older fishermen in the bar volunteered to Richards.

'*What* got 'im,' Richards murmured.

'If you say so,' Charley acquiesced, shaking out his *Daily Mirror*, and drawing on his old pipe. 'Prostitutes, lies in parliament, so what's new my wife wants to know! But still, I say it's that Wilson what got 'im. Wouldn't leave ole Macmillan alone, he wouldn't, snap, snap, snap at his heels like my Jack Russell here. No, he got 'im all right.'

Richards lifted a glass he was busy polishing to the light, as was his custom, and put it down before taking up the challenge.

'You're right, of course, Charley, it was Wilson what got 'im. Charging him with *indolent nonchalance*. Although I'm afraid I rather care for that. I think I shall use it about some of my staff – if some of us are not *very* careful.'

Richards cast a telling glance at one of his pot-boys who was leaning on the bar smoking and reading yet another copy of the *Daily Mirror*.

'He said that the Tories are entirely unfit to govern, and you know, as an adopted Englishman, I rather agree.' Waldo lowered his copy of *The Times*, and gazed back into the bar room from his window seat.

'Well, never mind, eh?' Charley continued, looking round for agreement. 'Wilson's broken his spirit entirely.'

'The Prime Minister's not been exactly helpful to

himself,' Waldo remarked drily, joining in at last. 'Surely he could have come to some sort of conclusion that an impropriety was in the offing when the letter from Profumo to Christine Keeler beginning *Darling* was produced. I mean to say, not exactly the kind of endearment an Englishman would use to someone he hardly knew, is it?'

There was general laughter at that, and Waldo sat back and lit a cigar, preparing to go on, but Richards waved a hand.

'I was brought up to vote Conservative,' he said, claiming the right of the landlord to interrupt. 'But there is no doubt about it, the writing is on the wall, and this time it will take a very large dose of washing powder to scrub it off.'

'You have your political scandals in America, Waldo,' Charley reminded him.

Waldo lowered *The Times* once more.

'Sure, but it's different in America. We're more open in our style of government. What you see is what you get, although sometimes one can't help wishing that one didn't have to see *quite* so much!'

Waldo always enjoyed the democratic process's being torn apart in the Three Tuns. It was part of the English way of life, and besides, it was in the Three Tuns that he had first noticed Meggie wearing a red dress, her hair all caught up, everything a little awry, making her seem more than beautiful, more than desirable: totally alluring.

'Did you know that the Almanack – to which as you know I am devoted – did you know that it is forecasting a shock of global proportions before the year is out?'

'Ah, you and your Almanack,' Charley said, shaking his head and returning to the *Daily Mirror*. 'You might as well consult the Bible, really you might, and look what people find there, every prediction except the right one, eh?'

'No, it *has*, it has predicted a global shock.'

Charley sighed. 'Not another tanner on baccy? Now *that* would be a disaster.'

As Waldo rose from the window seat at the Three Tuns, Tam was breakfasting off eggs, sunny side up, muffins and bacon and on the point of sitting back well satisfied when R.J. strolled into the bunkhouse kitchen, lighting up a fresh King Size Pall Mall, untipped.

'There you are, boy,' he said, eyeing Tam. 'Ah been meaning to find you. Reckon both you and I are due for a break after that roundup, so how's about accompanying Sue Sue and myself to Dallas for a bit of a hooley? Sue Sue hasn't done any proper shopping at Neiman Marcus since – well – since last month, and she's gettin' kinda restless. So how's about it, boy?'

Tam wiped his mouth on his red checked napkin.

'I should enjoy that, sir.' He nodded, careful not to seem too enthusiastic.

R.J. took a deep draw of his smoke and strolling over to the bunkhouse range he poured himself a large mug of black coffee in an unhurried manner. This was something that Tam particularly admired in R.J. – his sublime ability to be able to do everything, even rounding up steers, in a manner that was as unhurried as an eighteenth-century aristocrat. At that moment he was tasting the coffee as he strolled back to Tam's table.

'So you wouldn't mind tagging along, boy?'

'I would be honoured to be asked, sir.'

R.J. nodded. He knew that his wife fancied the English boy, he knew that his daughter had fancied the English boy, and he now knew that the English boy, having not fancied either of them, now fancied the daughter of his neighbour, one Dainty Swallowfield.

'Yes, boy, you can come with us. You can come shoppin' with Sue Sue or you can join the rest of us and wave at Mr Kennedy's motorcade as it goes through. Either way I dare say you'll have yourself a good time.'

At the mention of shopping Tam had, as R.J. had imagined, immediately thought of Dainty Swallowfield. He could buy her something really pretty, and Sue Sue Dysart could help him. Dainty was tall, blond, a great Country and Western fanatic, and had brought Tam's amatory techniques well into the second half of the twentieth century. Even better, although she liked to make love, she never pretended that her heart was involved, which of course made her a great deal more fascinating.

'I think I might fancy some shopping with Mrs Dysart. I don't rightly know much about Mr Kennedy, sir.'

'No, boy, I don't suppose you rightly do. I have to tell you he's not that popular in Texas, which is why he's paying us the courtesy of a call, I guess.'

It was a three hundred odd mile flight from where the Big U ranch lay, fifty miles to the north of Austin. They flew in the Dysart family plane, a twin engine Lockheed bought from the military and converted into a small luxury passenger plane. The weather was for the most part good and the visibility clear, so that Tam, sitting up in the cockpit with the pilot, while his hosts opened up the bar behind him, was able to get an angel's eye view of the vast country over which they were flying.

If Tam had imagined that he'd gained some grasp of the awesome magnitude of the state of Texas when he'd taken to its roads, nothing had quite prepared him for the actuality. It was as if a whole world was spread below him, an endless land with no visible horizons, just a vast expanse of pasture and mountains, waterfalls and plains. Tam began to experience a feeling of almost hysterical excitement, excitement that he had never felt before. It was as if he was being born not just into a whole new experience, but into a new existence. It was as if he was shedding a skin and growing into something entirely different, emerging from his childhood and early youth into life proper, and all because of the vast expanses below, this infinite immeasurable land rolling on and on beneath the smart red and white painted aircraft.

Naturally there was dread too for the longer he stared out of the window the less he wanted to actually arrive at his destination. He wanted to stay at twenty thousand feet, flying high, flying over everything, never entering into real life again. But then all too soon he could see an outline of a city as the plane tipped its wings, tilting at forty-five degrees as the pilot began his descent and approach to the airport, bringing the Lockheed into Dallas, unaware that within less than a day it would be the focus of every nation on earth.

Lionel saw it all happen on television. Mattie and John had left him for the evening, and since it was too early to eat, and he had already had several drinks, he switched on the television, and drawing his dear old dog to sit up beside him he waited for the news. Minutes later he was fast asleep, for what with the fire in the sitting room and the restful sound of the dog's snoring there was little to keep him awake.

He awoke much later. The fire was out, and he was hungry. He wandered through to his immaculately kept kitchen, prepared himself a grilled lamb chop, a grilled sliced tomato, a grilled mushroom, and some fried potatoes, not to mention a generous helping of mint sauce, and wandered back with it all neatly set on the tray. It was only as he sat down that he heard the news, and only when he turned up the sound that he realised that once again the world was teetering on the edge of a crisis.

He frowned at the screen, finding himself unable to quite take in what the newsreader was saying, wanting to say to him 'I say, old thing, would you mind repeating that?', staring in bewilderment at the images being presented by the news teams.

Tam was staring at a delicately beautiful glass bead necklace with matching earrings shaped like butterflies when the crowds that were shifting and passing behind and beside him appeared to become frozen. Sue Sue was nearby, absorbed by an infinitely more expensive pair of earrings which she was trying on, turning this way and that as the assistant held a mirror for her to look at her reflection.

'Mrs Dysart?'

'Yes, darlin'?' Sue Sue turned away from the mirror towards Tam.

'A lady behind has just said that President Kennedy has been shot.'

'Darlin'.' Sue Sue smiled at Tam and patted his cheek. 'You have to get used to Texas, honey. Even the rumours are bigger.'

'No, really, Mrs Dysart, someone's just come in and told her he'd heard it on his car radio, and she's just run out of here, crying. Look!' Tam pointed.

'Ah, darlin', her husband's probably just taken her cheques away. You know how some men can be – they don't unnerstand a woman's wants, dear.'

Sue Sue turned back to the mirror, and it was only when the assistant put down the glass and turned away to try to cope with yet another tearful shopper that the dime started to drop, and she realised that Tam was perhaps not inventing everything, that the President of the United States of America had indeed been shot.

It was then that the panic set in. People swayed to and fro, turning this way and that, always demanding, over and over, and over, was it true? Could it be true? Where was he? Was he dead? If shot was he dead? Was it possible?

Tam watched in muted fascination, feeling that he too had lost all colour, as they all had, that he had no blood in him, feeling that he too would like to cry, but feeling also that, since it was not his president, it might not be quite right. It was as if, like when he played music, everyone at that moment had welded together in this moment of grief, struck down by bewilderment and infused with panic. As if everyone was looking round feeling that they would never find their wives and husbands ever again, such was the sway, the to and fro of the first silent then loquacious crowd of shoppers, and he was a part of it, and yet not a part of it, just like them, just flotsam and jetsam, not really mattering much at that moment, yet mattering too, and more than they knew.

'We must find mah husband, honey.' Sue Sue grabbed Tam's sleeve. 'We must get the hell out of this city. I reckon if they've shot the president, who will they shoot next? Could be the Russians invading us. I have a gun in mah purse, but it's only a small one, and I doubt that will help us overly.'

She started to run towards where they had already arranged to rendezvous with R.J. and the pilot, and Tam started to run after her, as did many others, all of them running, only Tam had the feeling that maybe they would be running towards trouble, because that was what so often happened when you thought you were running away.

Thoughts flashed through his mind: his home, Bexham, Flavia, Kim and Jenny. He started to pray as he ran, remembering moments in his life as he heard his own breath coming out in little gasps. Pictures of his life – his mother pushing him on a swing on a sunny day with Mr Astley seated at a table, the Bexham sky bluer than he ever remembered it since. His father coming to fetch him from the fields, swinging him up and around before walking him home singing some old Sussex pub song. Eating lardy cake with Flavia while sitting on a wall watching the fishermen and the boats.

He knew at that moment he might never see any of them again, but that if he kept Sue Sue's pink scarf, now fluttering behind her, in front of his eyes, he might.

Lionel must have been dozing in his chair for a long time. He was certainly enjoying where he was. He was upstream somewhere on a beautiful stretch of river with what felt like a good-sized salmon on the end of his rod. The banks of the river in which he had been wading were covered in flowers, which was strange for the side of a river. The blooms were of soft colours and the shapes of the heads were graceful, the outlines gentle. A warm sun had made the crystal clear waters around him dance and sparkle as though they were baubles thrown from some eternal Christmas tree. He could see fish swimming, rhythmically, watching him with their large, doleful eyes as he flicked his fly back and forth across the water, yet even as he caught one he knew it was not on his line, that it was no more on the end of his line than its companions, that they all remained swimming and playing about him, teasing him with their lazy antics, playing at being caught, taking the line in their mouths and, as Lionel pulled this way and that in the clear waters, jumping and spinning in the air.

Laughter from the bank opposite him made him look up to see the familiar face of a handsome young man watching him while his feet dangled in the water too, splashing to and fro as lazily as the teasing fish.

'How's it going, Lionel?'

'As you see, Jack, as you see.'

They both laughed in delight, and finally Lionel sighed from pure exaltation, at the sparkle of it all, at the clarity. It was all so simple really.

*   *   *

'Is there something the matter, Daddy?' Mattie shook Lionel gently by the shoulder. 'Daddy? *Daddy!*'

But there was nothing truly wrong, and no real need for Mattie to cry, especially not if she could have seen Lionel at that moment strolling with his new friend Jack among the flowers and the trees, the two of them talking about every imaginable and some quite unimaginable things, all of which, should she have heard them, would have made her smile and laugh quite as much as they.

1967

'There never was such a crowd, some walking shoulder to shoulder, some on their own, some jostling each other in their hurry to go forward. But where they were all going no one could have said, least of all they. More than that, where was it all to end?'

INTERLUDE

'Women can be anything they want this Season, that is the stunning news, for following the geometric fashions of last year Paris is bringing us the news for which we long. We can wear Regency waistcoats over velvet knee breeches. We can be Feminine and Starry, Zhivago-like in our long coats with vast fur hems and matching trimmed hoods. We can be Sirens in navy blue velour with endlessly long mufflers which we can toss over our shoulders as we stroll the boulevards. In short the choice is ours. Cat suits worn with long coats, Regency velvet trouser suits worn with long floppy hats. We are what we want to be this Season. That is the wonder of Nineteen Sixty-Seven. The choice, ladies, is yours, the look is yours. We are not at the feet of Paris, Paris is at our feet. We have led the way with British boutique fashion, and now they are hard on our heels. In the daytime we can stun in Yves Saint Laurent's trouser suits, the masculine cut adding to our feminine allure, in the evening we can seduce with the frills and spills of lace and velvet. Either way we will be unstoppable – as time will prove. Nineteen Sixty-Seven is here to stay!'

Susie Sissingford for *My Style* magazine

Chapter Eight

To anyone approaching London eager to take part in a revolution that involved everything from fashion and food to interiors and sexual morals, the sound was unmistakable. It was the insistent rhythm of thousands of young people moving forward, silently chanting, *This is our time*.

'The young have money to spend, let them spend it,' the bankers murmured.

No sooner had the new revolution started than it filtered out to the provinces, cities and towns, all of which seemed to be instantly transformed into a sea of chaotic conflicting fashions, so that, unlike previous generations, the young of every class could no longer recognise each other instantly from the way they dressed. Tweeds and pearls were no longer worn except by those poor souls who had been married off and quietly dumped in the country; and even they were known to be putting up their hems to skirt the tops of their knees, to the less than quiet consternation of their country-loving mothers-in-law.

No one needed to tell Flavia Sykes any of this, not after selling endless Laurel Cottage fisherman's knits, knitted stockings, and seafaring pullover/dresses to an astonishingly wide variety of customers. She had modelled more Laurel Cottage Dolly Fashions than she cared to think about. Finally, as the business expanded and no longer needed her to promote their already popular designs, she had moved to London, where she was already finding work. This particular afternoon was her first assignment for a premier manufacturing house. As she stood about waiting to be sent flying down the catwalk to what she hoped would be gasps of appreciation, she was finding that her twenty-one-inch waist, far from being a cause of admiration, as it had been in Bexham, was now a reason for considerable grumbling by the backroom staff.

'At least twenty-two for Susan Ball fashions, dear, yes,' said one of them, frowning at the cause of the problem standing in front of her, 'not twenty-one. We're not Paris, you know, love.'

Despite the fact that she had very little experience outside her mother's fashion business, part of Flavia wished to goodness they *were* Paris. After all, if the clothes were French, perhaps they would be a mite more exciting.

She picked up a cigarette packet and her lighter preparatory to going out of the stockroom into the street for a breath of fresh air, and a good gasp of nicotine. Once outside she leaned against the wall, and stared up at the small piece of sky that she could see between the buildings.

She had already told her mother and father she was on her way, and it was true that she *was* being employed by the best of the second eleven, but Paris, and a life as a top photographer's darling, was realistically still a long, long way off, and she knew it.

She watched a small spiral of smoke drifting up to the narrow band of blue above her, and thought with some pride about her mother and Laurel Cottage Dolly Fashions, and how they had set about launching the business. Together they had turned it from silly gifts, and mugs, and tea towels with pictures of seagulls sitting on the sides of boats, into a profitable fashion enterprise. But now it seemed that the upshot of the huge success of Laurel Cottage Designs was that her father had just taken off for a long holiday touring Australia with a male friend, leaving her mother alone at home just as Flavia, and Sholto too, had left for London.

'Good luck this afternoon, darling.'

When Flavia had spoken to her earlier Rusty's voice seemed to be echoing around the family kitchen, bouncing off the Formica cupboards full of expensive china that would now be neatly stacked for Rusty's sole use. Flavia imagined that when Rusty woke up every morning at Lowfield House she must feel she was rattling around, a pathetic figure in a cotton wrap making her coffee and single piece of toast for breakfast, tidying an already tidy house before leaving for her office, and then coming home in the evening to a lone steak and salad and watching the television news before going to bed quite alone, except for the cat.

Flavia would have adored to ask Rusty up to stay with her at the flat she shared with three other modelling hopefuls, but Laurel Cottage Designs had really taken off and Rusty couldn't be spared, even should she have wanted to be.

'Flavia Sykes! Flavia Sykes!' a woman's voice close by called.

Flavia immediately flattened herself against the bricks, taking instant advantage of a nearby jut in the wall.

She didn't know why she was doing it. It was just something she'd always done. The moment someone called her, she always hid.

'Flavia Sykes!'

The vendeuse, whom Flavia could now just see, strictly corseted and costumed in black, put her head once more out of the twin doors that led into the alleyway.

Flavia heard the doors close behind the vendeuse again, and promptly stepped out of her niche and followed her into the back rooms that eventually led through to the front showroom, the catwalk, and all the other paraphernalia. She didn't like working for someone else. She didn't like the clothes she was about to have to hoof out in front of the dull, grey faces of the buyers, but she was at least in London.

They put her in a grey flannel coat and skirt. Flavia stared.

OK so it's manky and boring, she told herself, *so I'll pretend it's St Laurent!*

The curtain leading to the catwalk was flung aside. She was on her way.

Rusty had left Bexham for her Bournemouth shop before he slipped from behind the wheel of his car to step out on to the quayside, ignoring the No Parking sign that had been painted on the stone in large, white letters.

Of course he was aware of eyes watching him, but he made a practice of not noticing, for apart from anything else caring about what other people thought of him was not a preoccupation of his. A great many eyes were watching from the windows of the old inn that gave on to the harbour, but although he took this in, and enjoyed the attention, he never so much as glanced at them. After all, parking his Rolls-Royce Silver Cloud always did attract crowds: gawpers, starers, minnows, people whom he took great pleasure in ignoring. Today he'd left his chauffeur in town, preferring to drive himself and his wife to what was, essentially, a private visit.

A small boy sidled shyly up to him. Poorly dressed, his hair cut in the traditional pudding basin style of country village barbers everywhere, he smiled up at the man in the camel-hair coat smoking the large cigar.

'Could I have your autograph, please, sir?'

'And what would you want that for, sonny jim?'

The small boy's eyes drifted towards the large car and back to its expensively clad owner.

' 'Cos you're a movie star?'

The man laughed, and slowly took out a visiting card case, signing one of the cards with a silver Parker fountain pen, which he then replaced in his inside pocket.

'There you are, sonny.'

The boy stared at the signature, happy to be the owner of something so valuable, but before he could pocket the card a hand came out and seized him by the scruff of his neck and dragged him away.

'What've I told you 'bout talking to strangers!' The fisherman whose son it was looked down at the card before the boy could smuggle it into the pocket of his short trousers. ' 'Ere, you give me that.' He stared at it, and then, turning back to the man still standing by his magnificent car, he very slowly and deliberately tore it up, allowing the small pieces to catch the wind and thereby be tossed eventually into the harbour waters.

The visitor, watching all this, showed no emotion, but turned as the passenger door in the limousine opened and a small, blond woman in an overlarge mink coat emerged. She stood momentarily surveying the scene before her, and looking remarkably unimpressed.

The fisherman stepped forward.

'You can't park 'ere,' he informed the man as he locked up the Rolls-Royce.

He turned and smiled. 'As you can see, I am parked 'ere, as you call it.'

The fisherman stared at him, dropped his eyes, and moved off, dragging his son after him, as Waldo turned from the window seat in the Three Tuns overlooking the harbour, drink in hand, cigar in the other.

'I think you have a visitor, pal,' he called to Richards, who was sitting up at the bar marking his racing selections for the day. 'Looks like Mr Big has arrived.'

Richards glanced over his half-moon spectacles, took them off, shut them, and slipped them into the top pocket of his immaculate blue sailing blazer.

'In that case perhaps we should batten down all the hatches?'

Waldo smiled. 'Mmm. Might be a good idea, while you're at it,' he agreed, before lowering his voice. 'Looks every inch what you would call a bounder, Richards.'

The door at the top of the steps swung open and the visitors walked in, removing their top coats and strangely new gloves as they did so. They looked round as if expecting someone to take them, failing which they hung them up in the usual way on pegs by the door, and turned their attentions to the bar.

'I'm looking for a Mr Richards.'

There was a small pause before Richards nodded.

'I am Mr Richards, sir.'

'Ah. I'm Martin Markham, and this is my wife Mrs Markham.'

Richards allowed another pause.

'Ah, yes, that would follow,' he said smoothly. 'How do you do?'

'Quite so.' Markham nodded towards a back room. 'I wonder if we could do business, Mr Richards, somewhere private?'

He lit a cigar from a gold lighter and blew the smoke in leisurely fashion over Richards's head before turning to the barman.

'A glass of champagne for my wife, please.'

Perhaps feeling Waldo looking at him from behind his newspaper, he turned and smiled at the man seated in the window overlooking the harbour. Waldo appeared not to notice, but, as he watched Richards preceding the newcomer into the back room behind the bar, in spite of the sunny day, the boats bobbing on the water, the bar filling up with locals, in spite of everything, he felt his heart sinking. He knew the rumours, he knew the facts, and now that he'd seen the man in person, he knew his enemy.

At that moment Jenny was deep in conversation with her tutor at the Guildhall. The subject was her playing of Schubert's Unfinished Sonata in E major. She had her hands on her lap, placed there like a pair of gloves, one hand on each knee, to stop them shaking.

'You have improved.'

Jenny knew this was about the best she could ever expect from Geoffrey Donaldson.

'Any questions?'

'Where did I go wrong?'

The music teacher stared at her while at the same time thoughtfully pushing his spectacles up his nose. Normally he would lambast his pupils at every opportunity, but he knew that Jenny Tate had already been through overmuch in just one young lifetime. Rather than shake her confidence, he paused, thinking carefully, knowing that for some students one wrong word spelt the end.

'Schubert has these quirky spacings, and figurations too – passages that can sound empty if the player is not up to them.'

Jenny's eyes were still fixed on her two carefully placed hands. She looked as if she might be praying, or meditating, but he knew she was listening hard, as hard as she seemed to like to push herself, never finding anything that she did quite right, always seeing the bad, never the good.

'I thought so,' she said quietly. 'I made such a mess of that middle passage.' She looked directly at him now. 'Actually, I was thinking that it might be better if – if – well, if I stopped wasting your time, Mr Donaldson.'

There was a pause.

'Please yourself, but what I was actually going to

say was that you filled Schubert's spaces more than adequately. Surprising really, particularly for someone of your slender experience.' He always avoided any reference to age, as age never seemed to make much difference to musical depth. 'The Andante for instance was filled with surprising energy and colour. Delicacy too. I quite liked it.'

Jenny nodded, her eyes dropping to her hands stilled on her knees once again. Donaldson allowed a longer pause, staring at the music as if he himself was about to begin to play, knowing her as he was beginning to do.

'I think I might be really too nervous to go on, Mr Donaldson,' Jenny finally told him. 'I will never perform well, I think we both know that. Never. I will always – I won't be good enough.'

Yet another long pause, after which Donaldson nodded.

'Not to be nervous would be a great pity,' he said evenly, frowning at something in the middle distance. 'I know of an international soloist who used to get so transfixed with nerves he couldn't get his hands off his knees. Once, in Russia, his hands stayed glued to his knees for quarter of an hour, until finally the audience started to throw things at him.' He smiled. 'You can imagine the scene – hats, gloves, sweet papers, in the hope of getting him to play. Fired up by being hit by their missiles he finally started to play the Schumann. You can imagine the poor old conductor waiting for it to happen – baton raised, baton down, baton raised again. At any rate, it didn't matter. In the end he played so well, so brilliantly, that they wouldn't let him go, a standing ovation, in fact. So, nerves are good, must have nerves, much better than not having any.'

'Even so, I don't think I'm cut out to be a concert pianist. I just want to play well, that's all. Just.' She paused. 'Play *well*.'

'Why not leave that, the performing side then, let's say, to the fates? Now, much more important – do you want a cup of tea?'

'That would be lovely.' Jenny looked surprised. Tea was not usually on offer.

They sat together in a companionable silence drinking the tea the professor had brewed in a secretive sort of way in a small cupboard at the back of the room. It tasted strangely good to Jenny, exactly as tea had tasted after she'd had one of her many operations.

'I myself had a bad time in Russia, once. The piano they'd supplied had freewheeling castors. You can imagine?' Donaldson raised his hands and started to mimic himself trying to play at a disappearing keyboard, and Jenny started to laugh. 'I spent the whole concert dashing after it, and no standing ovation at the end of that, I'm afraid! Just PA.' As Jenny looked questioningly at him: 'Polite Applause.'

She laughed again and as she did so it seemed to the teacher that the few scars left on her face, minute but still visible, disappeared. The surgeons might have done their work, but he sensed that it was up to music to actually heal Jenny Tate, although because she gave not just all but everything to her playing, because she was hypercritical of herself, he knew that they would always be walking the high wire with her. That was OK. What he didn't want was to be the cause of her falling off.

'So.' Donaldson took Jenny's cup. 'See you next week.' As Jenny stood up and gathered her music together, he added, 'And don't forget to embrace your nerves. They are your blessings, you know, and definitely not in disguise. By the way, thought for the day.' He waited until he held her interest. 'Have you ever noticed that we always speak of composers in the present tense? Schubert does this, Chopin does that? As if they were alive today? That's because they are, and always will be. Great art is always alive, so to be part of great art is to be permanently alive.' He turned, still talking, and started to rearrange some papers. 'When we play we become part of someone far greater than ourselves. That is one of the marvels about playing music, entering the soul of someone wondrous.'

'I never thought of that.'

'Good. I leave the idea with you.'

Of course it might just have been Donaldson's imagination, but as he watched the slim, navy-blue-skirted figure leaving the room to make way for his next pupil, it seemed to him that Jenny Tate had grown just a little taller.

*   *   *

Later Max picked Jenny up from college in his Mini Cooper. He was full of himself, or rather, as Jenny noted to him with light sarcasm, even more full of himself than was usual with Max.

'I've only gone and landed a part in *The Avengers*,' he told her exultantly. 'In the hit TV series of all time! Well, maybe not of all time, but still *The Avengers*! Filming starts next week at Elstree. You are looking, my dear Jennifer Tate, at a future starker, a starker of all starkers! I am about to crack it.'

Jenny, who was worried about the exam she faced in a fortnight's time, tried to look both fascinated and impressed, and failed. Somehow music always seemed more important than acting.

'I expect you'll be going out to dinner to celebrate,' she asked, trying to keep the hope from her voice.

'Yes, and you're coming.'

'No. No, Max, really. I'll only be a gooseberry with you and the face of Poppet Stockings.'

'No, love, not. Patsy Gordon of Poppet Stockings has broken up with me.' Max drew up at the traffic lights and shook his head woefully at Jenny while his eyes still sparkled with the marvel of having landed a plum part in a hit series. 'Didn't I tell you? Yes, that bastard David George, he only comes into the Thirty One Club while we're having dinner, does the round of the tables, and only goes off with Patsy! I mean talk about hard-edged. Buys her a drink, chats her up, and voilà she's gone from under my nose. Not that she wasn't boring, poor Patsy, but boy, her legs! Let's face it, though, you can't have a good time with a pair of legs however long and brilliant. So, you're coming out to dinner to celebrate with me tonight. We are going to have ourselves one helluva celebration, because, as Granddad always used to say, "there's no taste in nothing".'

The car moved swiftly forward, dodging in and out of the traffic, and as it did so Jenny found herself shutting her eyes, her head turned firmly away so that Max couldn't see that she was still nervous in cars, still hated being driven.

'Actually, Max, I really do have to go and practise at Teddy's. I go there twice a week.'

'Today is not that kind of day, Jenny.' As Jenny turned and stared at him Max went on, 'Today is B for Big Day For Max. You gotta come, that's all there is to it. You gotta come and celebrate. Not to would be criminal, love.'

Jenny turned and looked out of the back window. As she did so, her eye caught a piece of food half wrapped in a page of the *Daily Mirror*.

'What on earth . . .'

She picked up the piece of food.

'That's my breakfast, pay no attention. I just didn't have time to finish it,' he ended feebly, trying to keep his eyes on the road and away from Jenny's horrified expression.

'I don't believe it, Max Eastcott! A green pea

326

sandwich? I don't believe what I see, truly I don't. Green peas in a sandwich.'

Max banged his wooden steering wheel lightly. 'I know it sounds a funny mixture, green peas in a sandwich, but it can be very nourishing, at the right moment in the day, of course. Tell you what, let's go and buy you a birthday present at Biba's?'

'It's not my birthday, Max.'

'Every day's your birthday. I know, I'm your half-brother. That is what half-brothers know about, birthdays. I can just see you in one of Biba's great purple hats with a long feather boa.'

'No, thanks, really, Max. I'd rather go home and change if you don't mind, if you're serious about dinner, that is.'

'Oh, for goodness' sake, let me at least buy you a hat. Everyone's wearing hats out to dinner nowadays, it's *de rigueur*, *chérie!*'

Max stopped the car outside the shop.

'You can't stop here, Max, it's double yellow lines.'

Max stepped out of the car.

'I won't be a moment,' he told her, bending down and talking to her through the car window. 'Not a moment. Just sit behind the wheel, would you, oh and keep the engine running! We're allowed five minutes to load and unload. OK?'

Before Jenny could refuse Max had vanished inside the dark interior of the purple-painted shop, leaving Jenny in the Mini with the engine still running. After a few minutes of looking out anxiously for both policemen and traffic wardens Jenny spotted a policeman walking slowly and most deliberately towards the car, a sight which filled her with instant panic. Scrambling over the stubby little gear stick and slipping into the driver's seat, she tried to sit behind the steering wheel looking as casually relaxed as was possible. Two cars equally badly parked, but without anyone behind their steering wheels, were duly ticketed by the affable bobby, before he bent down to Jenny's window and told her she'd better move on before she suffered the same fate.

Jenny smiled at the policeman and swallowing hard put one very shaky hand on the short gear stick and pushed it forward while still attempting good humour.

'Try using the clutch, miss,' the policeman said, in a kindly tone. 'It does help.'

'The clutch, right, yes, sorry. Of course. Silly of me. My glasses, you know.' She reached into her handbag, taking care to look vague.

She had watched Max drive enough, she ought to know how to shove your foot down, and then put the stick into gear. Pressing the accelerator pedal once again she took her foot off the clutch and closed her eyes. The car shot violently forward in a series of terrible lurches, but somehow, heaven only knew how, and only heaven would ever know, failed to stall. Jenny at once saw trees rushing towards her, heard her own voice crying out to Tam, heard something else, and then nothing. She started to laugh. Perhaps to drown the sounds, perhaps because against all possibilities the Mini was inching slowly away from the Law, the pitching and heaving having ceased as she pressed slightly harder down on the accelerator, not too hard, just a little. Finally the little black and cream car proceeded evenly, cautiously, but proceeded none the less down the road, yard after yard, until finally the baffled policeman was less than a dot in her driving mirror.

At that moment Max rushed out of Biba's clutching various large bags, only to witness his car heading firmly towards the Kensington Odeon, watched by the tall policeman, who was slowly shaking his head.

'Cor,' Max said, delight and astonishment equally represented in his voice.

'I know, sir, quite. How some of these girls ever pass their tests I don't know. I think they asphyxiate the examiners with their perfumes. I mean, if you hadn't seen it.' He shook his head in amazement.

Max didn't stay to hear any more but bolted after Jenny and his car, the Biba shopping bags swinging from his hands as he did so. When he caught up with her Jenny and the Mini had slid to a standstill on a single yellow line outside the cinema.

'Jenny?' Max wrenched the driver's door open. 'Jenny, what on earth happened? Jenny. Are you all right?'

There were tears on Jenny's cheeks but Max

couldn't see them. All he could see was her head, long hair tumbling about her shoulders, her shoulders shaking. Finally she turned her face towards him.

'Oh, Max. That was such a laugh, wasn't it? Me. Driving. You. The policeman.' She slid over to the passenger seat, still laughing. 'I mean if that isn't funny, what is?'

Max and Jenny were sharing a small flat off the King's Road, so it was only a short drive back from outside the Odeon to their front door. So far they had managed to combine their very different lives without too much conflict. Max's private life was ruled out of bounds after midnight, and Jenny, for obvious reasons, was forbidden to turn up the telly while he was learning lines, or talking, endlessly and often it seemed to her pointlessly on the phone. To avoid claustrophobia Jenny often took her studies to a café along the way where she would sit, nursing an endless cup of espresso, and the occasional doughnut.

She was loving her new life, and would not have swapped places with anyone, her only difficulty being finding somewhere to practise. On an off-chance she confided this problem to Waldo Astley, who immediately, as was his wont, came up with a solution. He had an unmarried bachelor friend who owned a large house in the Boltons. He would ask him to give Jenny the freedom of one of his three grand pianos.

'After all, he can't want to play them all at once, can he?'

Teddy Overton Handley was an extremely languid Anglo-American. An authority on early ragtime – Scott Joplin in particular – he took an instant dislike to the idea of anyone's playing *any* of his pianos. Waldo was persuasive. Jenny Tate was a shy girl. Jenny Tate had very quiet ways. She wouldn't disturb Teddy, any more than Teddy would disturb her.

'Besides, Teddy, you know you owe me one. Remember? Paris? 1945?'

'Oh, very well.'

As it happened Teddy took to Jenny from the start. In fact he fell in love with her, as elegant, confirmed bachelors sometimes do with young girls, in the nicest possible way. So much so that far from locking himself away in some distant room the moment he knew her to be arriving, unbeknownst to her he would lie in his best silk dressing gown and monogrammed slippers on a day bed in the room adjacent to where Jenny was practicing, listening. Finally he confided to her that he was going to exact a fee for his generosity.

'Friday evening of every week you're going to come down and play for me on my best Bechstein.'

Against her better judgement, but mindful of what she owed him, Jenny agreed to this one condition. Every Friday she played for Teddy and his friends. Sometimes she even played requests, but because Teddy was an old friend of Waldo's and she knew that Waldo loved him, it didn't seem like performing in public at all.

Now, however, both having changed at the flat, Max and she were sitting in a candlelit corner of Carlo's, one of Max's regular haunts, a first class, if somewhat boisterous, bistro run by a northern Italian whose other interest was driving in car rallies. This meant that the restaurant was more than usually filled with an interesting, cosmopolitan clientele ranging from racing car enthusiasts to pop singers and models.

Max was shaking his head, smiling.

'I still can't believe that you, of all people, sat behind that wheel and drove my Mini Cooper. And now I suppose you want to learn to drive?'

'Yes, sir.'

'Are you really that – cured?'

Jenny sipped her wine, thoughtful for a moment.

'Yes, I think I really must be. Otherwise, surely, otherwise I couldn't be so sure, could I? I mean I am totally sure that I can drive now, that . . . it's all behind me, in the past, doesn't matter.'

'Not nervous?'

'Oh, I expect I will be, but not like that. Not the way I have been, properly nervous, you know, so you feel as if you're melting, your insides are melting.'

'I know that feeling. Acting's like that.'

'Oh good, that's better.' Jenny smiled, lightly sarcastic. 'We're back to you, Max. That is much, much better. I mean.' She looked at her watch. 'It must be fully five minutes since we spoke about you, old thing.'

'Acting is,' Max stated, not paying the slightest bit of attention, 'acting is, I always think, like being a soldier. You're going over the top, and before-hand you go green and quite pass out—'

'Yes, I've seen you go green—'

'Yes, you have, and I shall doubtless continue to do so.' Max nodded, serious for a moment. 'It's when I stop going green and thinking I'm going to pass out that I shall start to worry.'

'That's more or less what my teacher says to me. We need nerves to be good. But back to you, love.'

'Oh, God, thank heavens for that. Now. What do you really think about *me*?'

They both laughed.

'As a matter of fact,' Jenny went on, 'and just to finish what we were saying, I think I will drive, and if I do I'm going to make sure I do it really well.'

Max nodded. 'And what *else*, Miss Tate?'

'Play the piano, as best I can—'

'And what else?'

Jenny put her glass down too quickly, spilling some wine on the cloth. She immediately began pouring salt over the stain as a distraction.

'What *else*, Jenny?'

'I don't know, what else is there?'

'Stepping out of the shadows, that's what else. You know what I mean. You are – now – back to how you were.'

'I'm not, Max, you know I'm not.'

333

'Yes, you are, Jenny. And that's official. You're going to drive again, and you're going to step out of the shadows and start looking in mirrors again.'

Jenny sat back in her chair, at the same time throwing him a furious look, but she said nothing. She couldn't, because Max was right. She never looked in mirrors unless she could help it, not since the accident. Just brushed her hair, cleaned her teeth, usually in the dark, and bolted out of the door, clean, tidy, but definitely not glamorous.

'For a start I've booked you in for a make-up course,' Max told her grandly. 'It's my gift to you.'

Jenny went to say something but then stopped. What *could* she say, after all?

'It's only a day, and it'll be the greatest fun. If you don't go then I shall know that you're not the person I know you to be. A girl I met the other day has done it, and it's fantastic; really. They teach you everything.'

Jenny was proud, but she was also realistic. She felt wounded by Max's lack of tact, but when had Max ever, ever been tactful? She took a deep breath.

'Thank you, Max.'

This particular evening Teddy was in no mood to let go of Waldo. He wanted to discuss Jenny Tate and her playing.

'I've been talking to her half-brother – Max, isn't it? And apparently she's what the kids nowadays call really "hung up" about her looks. So I suggested to him he sends her for some kind of make-up course. You know, there are these professionals who give women lessons. It's not that her scars are so bad, d'you see? It's that she *feels* that they are. I think she carries the image of how she was, just after the accident, around in her head the whole time. You know her grandmother, has she spoken to you about it?'

'No.' Waldo paused, and he shook his head. 'No, Teddy, I'm awfully afraid that Jenny's grandmother is out of bounds as far as I'm concerned at the moment, or rather I am as far as *she* is concerned. The problem being that I helped the boy who was driving when Jenny had her accident. I sent him out to the Big U – you remember the Big U?'

Teddy started to laugh.

'My God, just before the war, wasn't it? I was told to take you there, by your uncle, I think, to make a man of you. Make a man of you? It made a *wreck* of me! I had saddle sores for weeks afterwards. Now I come to think of it, I think that so-called holiday at the Big U got me out of the army. March, sir? I can hardly *walk*.'

They had just started on their second martini together, but Teddy was drinking his so quickly that in order to give the impression that he was keeping pace, Waldo had started to tip his glass surreptitiously into a nearby pot plant. Teddy was an old friend of Waldo's bachelor uncle, elegant, and unrepentantly life-loving.

'We must do something for Jenny Tate and her talent, Waldo, really we must.'

'The last time we did something for someone and their talent, Teddy, we regretted it for months after. Remember, if you want to make an enemy, help someone?'

'Sure, and isn't that the dreariest adage in the whole world? No, of course we'll do something for Jenny. Even if her grandmother never ever speaks to you again in this world, we must do something for Jenny.'

'Is she good?'

'Very.'

'In that case, we shall try to be of assistance, on one condition – she never, ever knows it's us. We will sponsor her, quite privately, when she finishes at the Academy.'

'I knew you'd see my point. Another martini?'

'I would love it, but one more of those, Teddy, and I will be walking back to Bexham on all fours.'

Wrenching himself free of Teddy's company Waldo walked quickly along from his house doing up his mackintosh a little too tightly, as if punishing himself for having drunk two martinis so early. He was actually weighing up the possibility of going to fetch his car and driving back down to Bexham when he passed the front of the Hyde Park Hotel. He stopped, at once tempted by the idea of dinner. He would go in, and he would dine all alone, in splendour, relishing every moment of the meal, and after that he would take himself off to his flat where he would fall thankfully into his own very comfortable bed, and when morning broke he would drive home.

He was about to step into the hotel when what he thought was a familiar voice spoke his name. Long before he turned he found himself longing for it to be a familiar voice. It had just that hint of uncertainty in it to make it appealing, just that hint of shyness that made him turn. As soon as he saw who it was, he stepped forward and drew the owner of the voice towards him.

'Judy.'

It was one of those moments which, had he planned it, which he very definitely had not, Waldo would actually have hoped would turn out to be exactly as it was now. He would have had Judy looking pretty as paint in a bright blue coat and dress, he would have had the evening sun around Knightsbridge playing tag among the façades of the shops and houses, he would have had the sound of other guests' voices laughing and joking fading to a strange kind of background music as he took her hands, and he would have had her lift her face up to him in a way that made her seem quite different. Not Judy as she always was in Bexham with all her worries, her children, her husband, but Judy quite alone, looking younger than he ever remembered her looking day-to-day, looking, for once, completely and astonishingly carefree.

'Waldo.'

Had Judy planned bumping into Waldo this way she would have had him looking just as he was now, casually dressed, his greying hair setting off his summer-darkened skin, a look of ruffled delight about him as if he too had just come from a bit of a celebration, as she had, but not squiffy or anything, just delighted, and delightful.

'Is Walter with you?'

'No, Walter's away, all week, until next week.'

Later Waldo would find himself wondering why he had said this and realising that it had been the only thing on his mind.

'Have dinner?'

'Why not?'

He held out his arm for her to slip her hand through, which she did feeling oddly wicked as she did so, which was ridiculous. After all if they were in Bexham she would walk along with Waldo and everyone would see them talking their heads off and not think even the tiniest thing, but here in London such a simple act seemed somehow all at once both exotic and sinful.

'Life can be wonderfully appropriate at times, can't it?' Waldo stated as they walked along, neither of them really thinking too much about where they were going, or why. 'Here am I escaping from Teddy Overton Handley's martinis, and here are you coming out of a wedding, and now here are we both, feeling ravenously hungry.'

Judy stared in the shop windows as they strolled along Knightsbridge and from there down Sloane Street. Men were always hungry for food, women were always hungry for clothes. Just to look at the beautiful dummies in the windows, their plastic hips thrust forward to show off the latest in dresses and coats, their nylon wigs styled in the endless romantic curls that were becoming so fashionable, was quite enough nourishment for her. She wanted nothing more and nothing less than to press her nose not up to a restaurant window, but up to the windows of the clothes shops past which they were strolling. She would love time to stare at the frills and flounces on display, at the tightly tailored trouser suits with their starched shirts, before sighing over the embroidered boleros, the diaphanous blouses, the waistcoats, the gypsy dresses, but Waldo was intent on finding a restaurant, and was even now standing outside a chic-looking place with a menu card on display. What was more it was a menu written in the kind of large, purple, continental writing that always seemed to promise so much. In fact it was a menu that declared it was going to not only feed them, but feed them excellently well.

'Table for two?'

Once they sat down Waldo raised his eyes to heaven.

'Why do waiters always ask that?' he wanted to know. 'If there are two people standing waiting for a table, would you really be wanting a table for twelve?'

Judy took off her tightly buttoned jacket, arranging it carefully around her shoulders. It was as deep a blue as the dress underneath. Waldo's favourite colour, although she wouldn't possibly know that, any more than she would know that he had kept the lace handkerchief she'd left by mistake the last time she'd called round at Cucklington House, when she was so worried about Kim.

'Don't let's talk about anything ordinary, shall we?' Waldo asked her, after a short pause.

Judy shook her head. She knew that what he was really saying was 'don't let's talk about Bexham or anyone we both know.'

'No, don't let's,' she agreed.

Once they had both ordered, and Waldo was busy choosing the wine, Judy's eyes wandered round the restaurant. It was fashionable, it was beautifully decorated, and it was everything that she had never known. It was neither hotel grand, or café simple: it was, in effect, perfect. Perhaps Waldo always brought women he knew to it? A stab of jealousy shot through her, at the idea that Waldo must know many other women, London women of whom she would know nothing, that just as he knew Teddy whatever his name was, he must also know women whom she knew nothing about. She had hardly embraced this idea when she felt instantly ashamed. How could she possibly dare to entertain a single jealous thought about Waldo when she herself was married to Walter? Walter who, as far as she knew, was at that moment somewhere in the north of England, attempting to defend some poor benighted man who stood accused of embezzling his firm's funds.

What would they talk about, if not their interests

and concerns which all centred around Bexham? What would they talk about if not Waldo's concern with the rich man who had designs on building cheap housing around the harbour, and perhaps even caravan sites, as Richards had suggested to Judy only the previous day. But that was a forbidden subject, so Judy searched around for another.

Her mother had always said, 'If you ever find yourself stuck for a subject to talk about when you're at dinner with your husband, darling, just tell him the story of the Three Bears, or Cinderella, anything rather than sit in a growing silence. It works a treat.'

Judy didn't think that would work with Waldo. Besides, he wasn't her husband.

'Now that you've lived in England so long, Waldo, do you feel at all English?'

'No. As a matter of fact, if anything I feel much less.' Waldo laughed. 'Teddy and I were discussing it only the other day, and we both agreed that nowadays when we're in England we feel American, but that when we're in America we feel English, so how's that for confusion?'

They went on to discuss nationality, which led to exile, which in its turn led to Europe, and how different it was from America, until, as Waldo called for the bill, Judy realised that they had been together for over three hours and not mentioned one mutual friend or acquaintance.

He hailed a taxi outside the restaurant. Judy

climbed in while Waldo stayed holding the door open.

'I've told the driver to take you to Victoria Station, but you'd like me to accompany you, wouldn't you?'

This time the stab that Judy felt was one of ridiculous disappointment.

'No, no, at least, yes, of course. Yes, I must take the late train back. Yes, of course.' Even now she managed to avoid the word 'Bexham', sensing that it would somehow spoil the moment.

As Waldo stepped into the cab and sat back, the light from the street lamps catching first the top of his head and then his face as he stared ahead, Judy turned away, making sure to gaze out of her passenger window, wondering at the shape of an evening, how it would make one sort of shape at one point, and quite another a minute later. Other couples were walking down the streets, other people were catching cabs, or climbing down from them, and their evenings must also have made different shapes at different times, and yet to Judy it seemed that she was the only person in the whole world to be feeling a calamitous sense of put-down, as if she had somehow or another been snubbed, sent on her way, and of course the fact that Waldo was so silent, he too staring out of the window on his side, only served to underline her sense of sudden isolation.

'What a wonderful evening, Waldo. Thank you so much,' said Judy as they arrived at the station.

She lifted up her cheek for him to kiss, which he did, and made to walk away from him, crossing carefully on to the main concourse of the station, only to turn back and find him following her.

He caught her arm.

'I can't leave you alone on the station, not at this time of night.'

'Why ever not?' Judy started to laugh. 'Don't worry about me. I did live through the bombing, you know.'

'Yes, but that's different. Ticket?'

'It's OK, I've got a return.'

'Pity.'

'Why – pity?'

'Oh, I don't know.'

As they walked down the platform, ostensibly looking for first class carriages, Judy could sense that he was feeling as cast down by the fact that their evening had ended as she was, that he too hated the idea of saying goodbye, hated the knowledge that once they were both back in Bexham, he driving there the following morning, she already back at Owl Cottage, 'it' would be over – 'it' being that funny thing that happens, that moment of utter, singular joy when it seems impossible that anything would be able to come between two people who for a few hours have been innocently at ease with each other.

Finding an empty first class carriage Waldo opened the door and handed Judy up to it. She pushed the window down after she had stepped in

343

and he'd shut the door, reaching down for his hand. She wanted to kiss him on the cheek again, but they were on a station, and that would not be her way. She wanted him to kiss her, but that would not be his way. Besides, the guard had blown his whistle for departure and so with a sudden lurch the train began to move forward, throwing Judy into the carriage. She went back to the window.

'Waldo—'

'Safe home, honey! Safe home!'

He kissed his fingers to her. Seconds later he stopped running after the train and fell back to a walk as the trail of carriages accelerated away. A minute later the dark, swaying noisy object had gathered speed, heading south.

Alone in her carriage Judy sat back in her seat staring out into the darkness. Tomorrow she would be herself again, but tonight she was someone else, someone whom, if only she was truthful, she would secretly adore to be able to remain. She glanced at her watch, dreading arrival at Churchester in an hour or so, dreading the transformation that would have to take place the moment she set her foot on the platform, the person who would resume her place at the centre of her being as she slipped into her car and drove back to Owl Cottage, and all the familiar problems crept up to settle themselves at her feet, staring up at her with helpless eyes, begging her to allow them to be dependent on her.

The door of her carriage slid back and Judy turned back from the darkness outside the carriage window to face forward again.

'Hallo, Mrs Tate. I didn't know you were on the train.'

Judy started, turning to see who it was.

'Flavia.'

She stared up at Rusty's daughter for a moment, not really registering who it was, and then realising that she was back down to earth, she smiled. It was real life again.

Chapter Nine

They had so much to catch up on neither of them knew quite where to begin, so the first sequence of their conversation was, for them, almost monosyllabic.

'Hi,' Max said with difficulty, taking one of Tam's two heavy bags. 'How was the flight?'

'High. And long. Boy, that is some long flight. Big head wind.'

'You got an American accent! Hey man. You speak-a American!'

'Like hell I do, man. I just maybe picked up a bit of a hint – I have been away rather a long time, old thing,' Tam ended on an English note.

'Tell you something else, you've grown. What did they give you – some kind of injections?'

It was such a long time that they could both be excused for being embarrassed. Max now stood looking at his younger friend, someone he had still thought of as a boy until the moment a tall young man in a cowboy shirt with mother of pearl buttons, well washed Levi's and half-boots strolled through Customs, his eyes hidden behind a pair of sunglasses, a thick gold chain hanging round his neck. Judging from the confidence that Tam exuded Waldo's plan to send him to America for a few years, both to forget and to mature, appeared to have been justified.

'So you really are this big a pop star, man?' Max wondered as they drove away from the noise and bustle of the airport. 'That is something, isn't it?'

'Nope, not a big pop star, Max, no.' Tam paused, and still thinking Texan in his head, he refused to hurry towards his next sentence. He tapped a cigarette from the pack of Chesterfields he had taken from his shirt pocket and offered it to Max, who gladly took it, knowing that nothing was much cooler. 'The group's pretty successful, but then so are a lot of other groups.'

'Yes, but The Bros. I mean, they're up there, aren't they?' He leaned towards Tam for a light as they paused at some traffic lights. 'You are looking at someone who is hoping that you've brought him a prezzy of your last LP, man.'

'Course I brought it for you, Max,' Tam stated, sounding more like his old self. 'Course. And. It's doing well. Went straight to number eight.'

'You are going to be one rich boy.'

'And you? Acting's taken off, hasn't it? You're a big star, aren't you?'

'Huge. Hence the big new flash car, and all the girls in the back.'

'Seriously, man. You doing OK?'

'I'm doing all right. Just finished a part in *The Avengers*. With Diana Rigg.'

'Wow. Did she fall for you?'

'Over me, but give her every due, only if I got in her way. Not *for* me, alas.'

'Even so. *The Avengers* – that's cool, Max – that's real cool.'

There was a long reverential silence.

'It's going out, next month. Will you still be here?'

'Depends on what the boys have planned for Christmas.'

'Meanwhile, you're going to be on *Top of the Pops*. Imagine.' Max turned quickly and grinned at Tam. 'I mean when you left four years ago, you would never have imagined that you would be coming back to that, would you? I mean for God's sake, never could you have imagined that, surely?'

Tam raised his eyebrows, shrugged and then suddenly grinned, the grin Max remembered so well, the boyish, impish grin that lit up his features and told Max that somewhere in there the severely un-cool, Bexham, car-mad Tam was still lurking.

'Course I didn't, Max,' he replied, and then his smile vanished. 'As a matter of fact I never thought – I didn't think I was coming back at all. You know, after . . . after the—'

'By choice, you mean?' Max interrupted quickly.

'By – everything, Max. How could I? I imagined the door would be closed for ever. That England, for me, was a no-go area.'

They drove on for a while in silence, Tam staring at a countryside that had already become unfamiliar to him, a landscape so different from the broad sweep of Texas, a scenery that seemed suddenly makeshift and drab compared with the magnificent country to which he had grown so used. The thought occurred to him that had it not have been for the television booking he would never have bothered to return.

'She's OK, you know,' Max said suddenly, breaking the silence as they approached the flyover at the end of the motorway.

'Who is?' Tam asked, playing for time, trying to sound disinterested.

'You know. Jenny. She's fine.'

'Oh. Oh good.' He paused. 'She's OK then, is she? Jenny's OK?'

'Oh, for God's sake, Tam.' Max groaned, shaking his head. 'You don't have to pretend with me. I'm your friend, remember? Max, Jenny's half-brother, we can talk about these things, more than that we *should* talk about these things. You're going to have to talk about it *some* time so you might as well start now. Talk about it with me, who knows you both, understands just a bit. I mean we're not strangers, are we? After all this time you know you have to talk about it, and then forget it.'

'How can I forget it?' Tam asked, with sudden passion. Then, after a pause during which Max said nothing he added, 'Mum wrote to me about it, all the time. After each operation, she wrote in detail.

I couldn't have forgotten what was happening over here, even if I had wanted to. I think it was Mum's way of saying you're not running away from what you've done, my son, not if *I* have anything to do with it. And she was right. I had to keep facing down what I had done, showing off like that – acting the goat. Consequently, I did. You know my mother, she's one helluva lady.'

'Yes, she is, and so is Jenny. She's come through the surgery fine, she's OK as far as that goes, and OK as far as studying the piano goes, but to paraphrase – OK is as OK does. And things are a lot more complicated than that. Jenny is, I mean. She's bound to be, isn't she?'

Tam shrugged. 'I don't know. How should I know? I haven't seen her since the day I ruined her life, for ever.' He took out another packet of cigarettes and lit one without offering one to Max. 'I don't know,' he said again. 'I don't know why we're talking about it, really.'

They both knew Tam meant he wished he'd never agreed for Max to pick him up from the airport.

'Because I thought we *should* talk about it. Because actually—' Max's voice changed as he lost a bit of bonhomie remembering Jenny after she emerged from her day on the make-up course, how she had seemed to have grown as tall as Harrods now that she realised she could artfully conceal what remained of her scars. 'Yes. I do. I believe passionately that you should talk about it.'

Tam was silent, looking down at the floor of the car, then leaning back with a sigh to stare at the headlining.

'I didn't know how to get there, Max, I'm sorry. I mean, if you really want to know, not a day has gone by since that awful day when I haven't thought about Jenny and wondered how she was doing. But how can you make it up to a girl when you've destroyed her face, put her through agonising operations? However great the time I've been having over there, there still isn't a day that hasn't gone by when I would have given my own life for it not to have happened to pretty Jenny, of all people.' He opened his side window and threw his cigarette out into the night. 'I shall regret what I did for the rest of my life, and it still won't be enough. Jenny was always – so gentle.'

'She's not so gentle now, Tam.' Max turned and grinned at him. 'And I don't think she would give a tuppenny damn for your regrets. So we can leave regrets out of it from here on in.'

'Just trying to tell you – you asked, man.'

'Yup, I know, it's just that I've had to live with it, so I have to fit the pieces together. What were you planning on doing tonight?'

'After that flight? Taking a pill and going to sleep for a day, what else?'

'No dice. You have a date.'

There was little Tam could do to resist Max's persuasion. To refuse would have looked churlish and mean-minded, and yet the idea of having to go through the experience Max had planned for him filled him with acute anxiety.

At least one of his pleas was heard, namely not to sit anywhere he might be seen. It seemed that Max had that covered and intended to sit them both right at the back. So, arriving just before the recital was due to begin, and the lights were already dimming, Max and Tam took their seats in the back row of the audience, the taller Max sliding well down in his seat, his long legs stretched out in front of him, so that his easily recognisable head would not be prominent. Tam followed suit, hating every minute of the whole thing, feeling tired out of his skin, and completely out of place. But what could he do? Max was his hero, had been his hero, and Jenny was Max's half-sister. What could he have done to get out of it?

A man introduced as the principal made his way out on to the concert platform, to scattered applause.

'Ladies and gentlemen,' he began. 'Students of the London Conservatory of Music – friends. As those of you who attend this place of study are aware, it is the custom during the first term of each academic year to hold a recital during which the four most outstanding students of the previous year, the winners of the medals awarded for excellence on their particular instrument, entertain us with a programme of their choosing. I stress the word entertain, because this is the whole point of this evening – to celebrate the success of those graduating from here and to be entertained by them. Music is made for us for our enlightenment, but above all for our entertainment – and that is something none of us should ever forget, most particularly when we find ourselves taking ourselves too seriously – or, worse, someone else taking us too seriously. So to begin this evening's recital, Sophie French is going to sing for us – and I shall leave her to tell you her choices.'

Tam began to sink lower in his seat at the thought of the evening he was going to have to face, which seemed to include the sort of music – man! – about which he knew less than little, such as the Schubert Lieder chosen by the first performer. To his surprise, and against his very best judgement, such was the sweetness of her young voice and the intelligence of her phrasing, he found himself enjoying the German love songs.

The soprano was followed by a clarinettist who predictably enough played some Mozart, and unpredictably a tune composed and made famous by Duke Ellington's one-time clarinet player, Barney Bigard. The penultimate performer was a sixteen-year-old female violinist who took everybody's breath away with a pyrotechnical per-formance of one of Kreisler's showstoppers, leading Tam to remark somewhat dolefully that having heard that, he would have to review his conception of himself as a musician.

As he was chattering away to Max during the

generous applause the last performer was announced, and hearing Jenny's name Tam immediately fell silent, sliding well down in his seat while staring at the young pianist in the deep midnight blue tightly waisted satin dress with pinch pleats above the belt leading to a boat neckline that showed off beautiful shoulders, a slender neck and a head that carried itself with just a hint of defiance.

'That isn't Jenny,' he whispered to Max.

'No it isn't,' Max whispered back straight-faced. 'It's Jennifer Tate. Didn't you see on your programme, mate?'

'It can't be.'

Tam frowned with astonishment all the way through Jenny's first piece, the Invention No. 8 by Bach, and was still frowning as he joined in the applause.

'Well, matey?' Max grinned at him. 'Do ye still ha'e your doots?'

Tam shook his head, still applauding absentmindedly long after everyone else had stopped.

Jenny followed the Bach with a simple and graciously flowing performance of Mendelssohn's charming *Frühlingslied* and, to conclude, astounded the audience with a very powerful and passionate rendering of Chopin's Revolutionary Etude.

'Workers of the world!' Max laughed, as he applauded and others cheered. 'Music to mine ears!'

'Do put a sock in it, Max,' Tam grumbled. 'You're

at a concert, not the barricades. And you might have told me she was this good.'

'I didn't know!' Max protested, as everyone around him started to leave. 'I've only ever heard her practise! And if you don't want to bump into my mum and stepfather who were seated in the front row with a clique from Bexham we'd better disappear.'

The two young men hurried out of the hall and across the road into the nearest pub to have a beer until Max reckoned it was safe to go and try to find Jenny. In vain Tam protested that she was bound to have gone out with her parents, only for Max to contradict him and say he had promised Jenny to come and take her out for a celebration since her parents had to get back home as soon as the concert finished, because there was no one to look after the dogs.

'I should know the form, Tam,' Max continued. 'She does lodge with me, old love.'

'I still don't think it's a good idea,' Tam muttered. 'I don't think it's a good idea at all. I'm the last person she's gonna want to see.'

'You're going to have to face her sometime, Tam.'

'Why?' Tam shrugged feebly. 'And why tonight?'

'Why any night?' Max grinned. 'Come on – knock back your beer and we'll go and find her.'

Tam hung back as long as he could, hoping that sensing his reluctance Max might have a change of heart, or if the worst came to the worst when they went to look for her they would have missed her. For the life of him, even though such a moment had never been far from his thoughts, he had never had the slightest idea of what he would say to Jenny if and when he ever met her again face to face, and now that moment had come he was even further from having any inspired notions.

But, unfortunately, Max wasn't in the mood to be sidetracked. Finally confiscating the all but empty beer glass from Tam, he took his friend by the elbow and steered him out of the pub and back towards the large Victorian building opposite, which now that they reapproached it seemed all but deserted. None the less, and in spite of further pessimistic mutters from his companion, Max hurried them both along the well polished corridors, past the recital hall and down a short corridor which led to a green room behind the stage where a small group of students and their friends were still holding court, and from there on to a small labyrinth of dressing rooms.

Tam looked away from the door on which Max was knocking, as if hoping to make himself invisible. A voice he knew all too well called for them to come on in, at which point Tam found himself firmly rooted to the spot. As he stood there he heard Jenny wondering to Max who it was he had got with him, to which Max told her to wait and see, at the same time leaning over and putting a hand on Tam's jacket collar to wheel him round and into the dressing room.

Jenny was still wearing the dark blue dress in which she had played and was standing brushing her long fair hair in front of the mirror when she saw Tam reflected behind her. It was a moment she had imagined, but never fully realised, even in her imagination, most especially as she had never really liked Tam the way her cousin Kim had liked Tam. As soon as she saw his face behind her, in the doorway, her smile vanished, and she stopped brushing her hair.

'Hi, Jenny,' Tam said awkwardly, he at least attempting some kind of bonhomie, however false. 'Hi.'

'You might have told me, Max,' Jenny said, turning away from Tam. 'That was the least you might have done.'

'Before your recital?' Max replied. 'I don't think that would have been very clever.'

'You didn't have to bring him.'

'No. No, that's perfectly true, I didn't.'

'Look,' Tam interrupted. 'It's perfectly OK. I can just disappear.'

'No you can't,' Max said, keeping a hold of him. 'That isn't going to solve anything.'

'What are you trying to solve, I wonder?' Jenny said with little interest, turning back to her looking glass to check her hair and then pick up her belongings from the tabletop.

'I thought it might be – well – nice for you to see each other again,' Max offered lamely.

'OK,' Jenny said, turning back and looking at Tam dispassionately. 'So now we've seen each other – now that's been achieved, I'm going home.'

'I'll give you a lift,' Max said quickly. 'The car's just outside.'

'I'd prefer to take a taxi.'

'You can't afford to take taxis, Jen.'

'It's OK,' Tam said, glancing daggers at Max. 'I can take a taxi. OK? 'Bye, Jen. And sorry – OK? It wasn't my bright idea.'

Tam turned and went, giving Max no chance of stopping him, hurrying down the corridor at a fast trot which turned into a run as he crossed the now deserted green room, along the corridors and out into the cool of the night air.

For a moment he stopped to try to regroup, but his mind was still racing, just as his heart was still pounding as much from the emotional impact of the meeting as from his sudden sprint. It was just as he had imagined it would be, only much, much worse.

In one of his many re-enactments of such a meeting Jenny had shouted and cursed him, and now that he had finally come face to face with her again how he wished that she had done. It would have been infinitely preferable to that terrible coldness. He leaned his head back and closed his eyes, trying to expunge the image. He could still see the look on her face – and why not? he wondered to himself, as he began to walk down the street in search of a taxi. He shouldn't be in the least surprised since it was exactly what he had expected.

But it hadn't been what he had hoped. Before he had returned to England, when he had thought about Jenny his hope had been that sooner or later some freak chance of circumstance would bring them together, and when it did, after an initial moment of discomfort and awkwardness, somehow a point of forgiveness would be reached and they would become friends. In his imagination he had always skirted over the exact logistics of this all-important moment. What had happened instead was that Jenny had looked at him as though she never wanted to see him again.

And what made it infinitely worse was not what she obviously felt at that moment, but what *he* felt at that moment. It wasn't fear – because all fear vanished the moment he looked into her eyes, and it wasn't sadness, because a part of him had all at once felt uplifted; neither was it pity because when he looked at her he could hardly make out any scars on her lovely face, and nor was it remorse. It was a strange, unwarranted exhilaration, as if, having heard her artistry, he could not be as remorseful as he should be. As if, after all, something marvellously good had come out of the awful accident that he'd caused her, because, having put her months of acute suffering into her art, Jenny was now able to produce something that might almost turn out to be great.

In time he caught a taxi, but not until after he had endured a long dismal walk made worse by the onset of rain. Having no raincoat he pulled the collar of his jacket up around his neck and looked round desperately for a taxi, sudden exhaustion adding to his inner misery. He fell asleep in the taxi when he finally caught one, drifting in and out of an uneasy slumber during which he dreamed that he was flying as a passenger in a private jet just like R.J.'s, only this one was being piloted by Jenny, who looked over her shoulder at him directly into his eyes with just the same expression she had shown in her dressing room before putting on a parachute, opening the door and jumping out, leaving him in an aircraft spinning helplessly out of control.

He woke up with a startled yell just as the taxi was pulling up outside his hotel.

'What's the matter, mate?' The taxi driver laughed at him through the open compartment window. 'Incher never been in a cab before?'

Whenever Judy collected Walter from the station she would become mesmerised by the sight of the wives who drove late and too fast into the station, their hair looking as if it had last been brushed with the pony's curry comb, or tied up any old way under an old horse-festooned silk scarf. Drawing to a halt, usually under a No Parking sign, they would jump out of their wooden-sided estate cars and run towards the station buildings in jodhpurs and bedroom slippers, or sometimes slacks and evening shoes, an inevitable half-smoked tipped cigarette sticking out of the sides of their mouths. How Judy envied them their carefree, possibly careless attitudes to life, their husbands and children. She knew herself to be as different from them as it was possible to be.

She would never meet the train without allowing at least ten minutes' grace to pick Walter, or one of the children, up from the station. By the same token she would never arrive dressed less than immaculately, however old and pre-war her clothes, her hair newly shampooed, her make-up as perfect as possible, her nails freshly varnished. Lady Melton had been so strict with her, possibly because she was an only child. Judy had never been able to ignore what her mother always referred to as 'the rules'. The rules governed Judy's life.

Just for that moment in London, though, she had forgotten the rules, and perhaps but for that chance – and it had been chance – meeting with Waldo, she might never have known how close she could come to actually breaking them. How easy it was to keep to your mooring when no other craft came near, but set up a storm, break your mooring and find yourself out in the wild sea, and you could forget what it was like to be in harbour.

'Hallo, Walter.'

Walter kissed her on the cheek. It was a little like a child's kiss, half fond, half dutiful. Judy smiled. He put his weekend case in the boot, and she moved to the passenger seat as he took the wheel of the car, as he always did.

She always tried to avoid saying 'How was your week, darling?', seeing it as most possibly being as irritating as saying to a child 'I bet you're looking forward to going back to school?'

Tonight she glanced at him, once when he arrived and then again as she settled back into the passenger seat. First glance was always to see his expression, for she would know straight away whether or not he had won his case. Second glance tonight was to make sure that she was right, and he had lost his all-important case in the north.

'Hubert rang just before I left,' she said, over-brightly.

'Did he just?'

Walter always brightened at the idea of Hubert, just as he became gloomy at the mention of Kim's name.

'He's having a grand time in Scotland with the Ogilvys. Fishing and walking, not too many mosquitoes. Food's great. It's a marvellous place. He wants to stay.'

'Hubie wants to stay wherever he is. He's that sort of chap.' Walter smiled fondly. 'Just such a shame about—'

'I know, I know, but your mother says that if he doesn't want to go to university, prefers to go into the City, much better to let him do just that. Loopy maintains that university is—'

'Don't tell me!' Walter jammed the brakes on so

suddenly at the traffic lights that Judy was flung forward, saving herself only with a swift hand to the dashboard. 'Don't tell me, Mother's favourite subject – university is an *indulgence*. If you ask me I think she's influenced Hubert against it.'

Judy paused, taking a deep, inward breath.

'No, Walter. What she says, actually, is that university is a luxury, and that if Hubert wants to go into the City – that is, if he doesn't get into the cricketing team at Oxford and feels he would just find himself marking time there, then that's what he must do. And I agree with her.'

'Of course you do.'

'Not "of course", Walter, but in this case I do.'

Judy stared out of the passenger window, as she often did when Walter was driving, trying to suppress a strong desire to jump out and run off into the fields they were passing, run away from the endless torture that marriage sometimes seemed to inflict. Everything took such a toll: other people's decisions, your children's ideas about life, everything asking more of you than you sometimes felt you could possibly give.

'Your mother and father's cocktail party for the village is this evening. You know, their "Save Bexham Party".'

'I can't go, Judy. Really, I can't.'

Walter's expression was so mulish she knew at once that he must have lost his case by a wide margin, that the man he had been defending had gone down by a great deal more than had seemed

363

possible at the outset. It kept happening to him lately. She looked down at her gloved hands, knowing better than to argue with him.

'I have so much work to do – you go.'

Judy found herself making the shape of a church and its spire with her index and little fingers, and then turning her hands over and waggling her middle fingers – 'open the doors and there's the people'. It was what they had used to do at school when waiting to go in to see the headmistress. It was meant to calm their nerves.

'What shall I tell Loopy and Hugh?'

'They won't even notice. Say I'm coming on later, I've been held up. By the time the party's over they won't remember whether I've been there or not.'

There was a certain truth to this, which Judy had to accept. Nevertheless, as she walked ahead of Walter up to their front door, the front door that had been theirs for so long, the front door to the cottage that Loopy had found for them on the outbreak of war, it occurred to her that it was most unlike Walter to refuse to go to a cocktail party at Shelborne. He never missed a family occasion. He must know. He had to know.

She dressed slowly and carefully, laying out her clothes on their bed, as her mother's maid had used to do for her, before the war, when she was young and going to her first dances. Everything laid out in order of dressing, everything just so. Downstairs she could hear Walter had turned up the radio, some comedy programme that he always liked to listen to on Friday evenings when he came home. It was as if he wanted to drown the sounds of her dressing. Or perhaps, if she but knew it, he was trying to drown his feelings of jealousy and anger? Perhaps that was why he was refusing to go to his parents' party, perhaps that was why he felt unable to face his mother when he knew what he knew about Judy?

The truth was that ever since Flavia had slipped into her carriage on that late night train to Churchester, her imagination had been torturing her. Flavia, if she had seen anything that night, would surely have told Rusty? Everyone she knew must all now know how she felt about Waldo.

'Do I have to go to the Tates' this evening?' Flavia groaned.

'Yes, you do, and not for Bexham, for me.'

Rusty appeared at her daughter's bedroom door, brushing her thick auburn hair into an attractive shape in the nape of her neck and skilfully tying a large silk scarf around the result. She was wearing one of her own Laurel Cottage designs – a long black velvet skirt filleted with lace flounces, and a matching jacket with lace at the sleeve edges.

'You look great, Rusty,' Flavia told her, turning and smiling. 'The look of the moment as modelled by Rusty Sykes.'

Flavia had started to first name her mother when they'd thought it better not to let on to customers and business contacts that they were mother and daughter; and even though Flavia no longer worked with her mum she still first named her when they were alone. It put them on a one to one footing, letting them off playing their long-burnt-out roles of difficult daughter and long-suffering mother.

'OK, boss, for *you*, but not for anyone else. I couldn't care a fiddle about the Yacht Club, you know that.'

'*I* know, but just don't let anyone *else* know, for my sake. Promise?'

'Sure.' Flavia looked surprised at her mother's sudden intensity.

'Feelings are running high in Bexham, Flave. You know what that can be like in a small place.'

'Sure,' Flavia said again, as she snatched up her evening bag. Her skirt was about the same length as one of her mother's handkerchiefs, but since she was wearing long suede boots the gap between the skirt's hem and the top of her boots seemed almost decorous. 'So, who else is going to be there, do you think?'

Flavia followed Rusty down the stairs to the hall. Nowadays her mother smelt deliciously of French scent, and, more than that, looked amazing. She had no idea how, or indeed why, her father could have taken it into his head to go off to Australia leaving behind such a lovely woman, but then, thank God, that was none of her business, and never would be.

'I think there'll be the usual Bexhamites – the

366

family, and, you know, Judy and Mattie and all of them, and then just about every member of the Yacht Club. Waldo Astley, everyone like that.' Rusty tossed Flavia her car keys. 'Come on, drive your poor old mother.'

Flavia followed Rusty out to her new, flashy red convertible, and settled into the driver's seat. She knew – because of Tam's accident and all that – her mother always went out of her way to trust Flavia to drive her, which was flattering, and kind, but as it happened, this evening, Flavia didn't particularly want to drive, but she also knew to refuse would be to hurt Rusty's feelings in some indefinable way.

'Oh, I forgot to tell you I saw what's his name on Victoria station the other weekend.' Flavia backed the car too quickly on to the road, not really checking whether anything was coming towards them.

Rusty was so busy keeping her eyes firmly on the road she hardly heard her. 'Who d'you say?' she asked, vaguely, her hands tightening on her evening bag.

'Yes, you know – what's his name . . .' Flavia clicked her tongue. 'Yes, that friend of yours and Dad's – Bruce Kingsley.'

'Oh, Bruce.'

Rusty sounded so disinterested Flavia immediately became suspicious, and glanced at her mother briefly.

'He's looking quite groovy for his age, bless him.'

'Knowing our Brucie, I expect he was putting half Bexham on the late night train.'

'Well, as a matter of fact he was. Half of a wedding party, it looked like, a ton of them.'

Rusty still kept her eyes firmly ahead of her, at the same time struggling not to say 'mind that van' or 'there's a car coming out of that turning'.

'It seems to me you can't go anywhere without meeting someone from Bexham.'

They drove on towards Shelborne, and had soon moved on to a much more interesting topic of conversation than Bruce Kingsley, namely the new collections, and the shocking price of crushed velvet.

Loopy and Hugh looked at each other and then raised their glasses.

'Here's to Bexham, here's to Shelborne, to everyone, but most of all tonight – beloved Bexham.'

They sipped at their drinks and waited for Gwen to come to the door with the first of their guests. The marquee covering the garden was filled with warmth and flowers, with glasses and champagne, and halfway through the evening Loopy knew that Hugh would be inviting all their friends and acquaintances to make the same toast. Everyone was agreed, whether or not they were members, that the Yacht Club had to be saved from the man they had all now nicknamed The Beast and His Wife.

'Mr and Mrs Bryn de Badout.'

The first of the guests to arrive, the de Badouts, were practically founder members of the Yacht Club. Loopy hurried forward to greet them. They were only two of dozens of friends that she and Hugh had known over many years, and in whose company they had delighted.

'So good of you to come.'

It would be the first of many times that Loopy would be saying as much, but she did not care if she wore herself to a shadow saying what she truly meant. Both she and Hugh felt passionately about Bexham, about the harbour, about the place where they had lived all their married life and where their children had grown up, where their grandchildren were now growing up. It was for places such as Bexham they had all fought the war. It was from Bexham that so many of them had sailed to Dunkirk to rescue their army. They were not going to give up Bexham for anyone or anything, let alone a man in a camel-hair coat and pigskin gloves who was convinced he could buy anyone.

'Judy, darling. You look wonderful.'

'Thank you, Loopy.' Before Loopy could say any more Judy told her, 'Walter's coming along later, he's been a bit delayed.'

'That's Walter. He never stops, does he?'

Loopy smiled at Judy, but her eyes had already passed on to greet the next group of guests as Judy moved off towards the marquee where Mattie and John were the first people to wave to her. Judy found herself shrinking from going over to them, but she went, finding when she did so not a shred of discomfort in their manner towards her, that is until Waldo arrived.

'Oh look, Waldo's here! Cooee, Mr Astley, over here!' Mattie waved Waldo over, at the same time saying to Judy, 'We must grab the old darling before everyone else does.' She pulled Waldo over to John and Judy's side, kissing him quite openly on the cheek, both arms round his neck in Mattie's old enthusiastic manner. 'I told Judy we were going to grab you before everyone else does,' she said triumphantly to Waldo, 'and we have!'

Judy kissed Waldo just as enthusiastically, copying Mattie, putting both her arms round his neck, hoping against hope that by doing so she would allay all fears that he meant any more, or any less, to her than he meant to Mattie.

Only surely Mattie's heart couldn't be beating quite as fast as Judy's nor could she be feeling quite as faint, not outwardly faint, but that deep down faint that simply won't go away.

Waldo turned to John. 'How about I kiss *you* now, John? You must be feeling so left out.'

Judy thanked God for Waldo's wonderfully carefree manner.

'No, I think I'll pass, if you don't mind, Waldo.' John laughed. 'There are many things that I will do to raise money for the Yacht Club, but kissing you is definitely not one of them.'

They all laughed, and Judy tried to make sure that she didn't laugh more than anyone else, that she didn't sound hysterical, that her eyes didn't hold his too long. And it was all fine, and she was fine, until John and Mattie moved off, and Waldo offered her a cigarette and Judy took one, and her hand was shaking.

'Waldo! Over here, please. Time for the speeches.'

Judy watched Waldo walking off, feeling immense relief that he had sounded so confident, that no one would know about them, and turned immediately to a couple of friends from her sailing days.

'Wonderful to see the whole village united, isn't it?' she asked mechanically.

'Yes, it is,' they agreed enthusiastically. 'We were saying it's just like the war. All for one, and one for all. Best time of our lives, Graham and I always say, the war, strange but true.'

Judy hardly heard, which wasn't surprising. All she knew now was that Waldo must feel just as she did, because as he was lighting her cigarette she couldn't help noticing that his hand was shaking quite as much as hers.

After that she could hardly bear her life. It's only natural that when something overwhelmingly exciting happens to you nothing else seems to matter, and things weren't helped by Walter's being called away on yet another case, telephoning her that he would not be able to get down to Bexham for some days.

'Pains in your chest are not good,' Dr Farthinghoe told him, when Walter struggled to his London surgery, despite the pain in his head which had seemed unwilling to leave him for the previous God only knew how many days. 'I will send you on to a specialist. These we must not ignore.'

'Not a word to my wife, will you, Dr Farthinghoe? I don't want her worried. She's had quite enough to take from me already.'

'Understood.'

The doctor turned away, sighing inwardly. It was always the same with decent people, they always wanted to keep worry away from their loved ones, but the truth was they could only delay it, they couldn't actually prevent them from knowing, not in the end, not finally.

'Other people's love affairs are always ludicrous,' Lady Melton announced, as she lowered the newspaper and stared at Judy over the top of it. 'I was telling Ellen only the other morning, it seems so sad, to me at any rate, that people nowadays are so eager to tell all, not reticent at all. They publish their diaries and their love letters, and while I'm quite sure that they're utterly sincere, I'm also only too sure that by doing so they're making complete asses of themselves. "I love you, my little gooseberry" written by a former prime minister to his mistress – and I know it's not fair or logical – but it makes him seem just as silly as his little gooseberry. What we feel when we're in love is overwhelming,

372

I'm sure, but it has to be concealed from the outer world. Not to conceal it leads to ridicule, I'm afraid.'

Lady Melton stirred her coffee vigorously. Judy meanwhile lowered her eyes to her mother's newspaper before raising her own cup of coffee to her lips.

'Gracious, here's Mathilda, trotting up the garden path, looking for all the world like Little Grey Rabbit with her basket of goodies.'

They were all meeting to make yet more plans to save Bexham from The Beast. Judy waved to Mattie as she started to pull on the brass bell pull to the side of the door. Mattie, fresh-faced and looking unfairly young for her age, waved back, and kissed her fingertips to Judy. Lady Melton had learned to love Mattie, despite her having had what her ladyship always called 'an unfortunate little baby', but now the little baby was an adult she seemed to have forgotten all about Mattie's little mistake.

Next came Rusty. Lady Melton and she were old friends, not just because of the war, but because Rusty had come to her for what they both jokingly called 'speaking proper lessons' when Peter had moved her to Churchester. Nowadays Rusty looked happy and relaxed. Judy couldn't prevent herself from envying her. Rusty had taken a gamble with her boutiques, and as a consequence was now busy and fulfilled. By comparison what had Judy ever done?

As they all sat down to make new plans to help

the village fund, Judy suddenly became aware that she was the odd one out, the only person in the room who seemed, in her own eyes, to have achieved little or nothing, except perhaps to help Kim, who it seemed had now become involved in some sort of animal sanctuary.

'Kim finding herself again, I suppose?' Walter would ask every now and then, lightly sarcastic.

Judy would turn away, knowing that Walter was missing his only daughter, and knowing that it was all Judy's fault that he was, but insisting that Kim must be allowed to do as she wished, make her own life. People should be allowed to follow their bliss. Otherwise what was life about, for heaven's sake?

She was so caught up in her own thoughts it was some time before she became aware that everyone was waiting for her to say something.

'What do you think, Judy?'

'Oh, I think, definitely.'

'Good, well then, we're all agreed. We'll give a charity luncheon on the day of the Regatta, take over the Three Tuns for a luncheon buffet and drinks. Richards will be all for it, I know.'

Inwardly Judy sighed. *They* would do this, and *they* would do that, but at the end of the famous day what was *she* going to do?

Finally after some days it came to her. She would do something quite simple. She would go away, all by herself, and she would think. Away from all domestic ties, away from everything that reminded her of little grey areas of failure, and large black ones of even greater failure. Away somewhere quiet, where no one knew her, or cared about her in the least, in some place where she could, as she had been in London, be just anyone. There, in an oasis of anonymity, she might have a chance of finding her centre again.

As soon as everything was arranged Judy put all thoughts of home away from her, wishing only to recapture that intoxicating ozone of freedom she had enjoyed when she was with Waldo in London. But that was back there, and back there didn't matter, couldn't matter, at least not for the moment. Now, as she drove away from Bexham towards a small family hotel in the Cotswolds, it seemed to her as if she was young again, as she had been in London those last few months before the war. It seemed too that she was enjoying that particular state of mind which sees everything in a different way.

As she saw it, the pub where she stopped for lunch was filled not with red-faced farmers but with smiling locals, the sandwiches she ate were not just ham sandwiches, they were the best ham sandwiches she had ever eaten, the gin and tonic she drank was the most thirst-quenching. The view of the countryside from the bar window was the best view from any window. It was ridiculous. She was alone, quite alone, and yet she was happier than she had been for months. How could that be?

More than anything she exulted in that feeling of freedom. Everything anyone had ever told her now appeared to her as having been wrong. You *could* run away from everything, you *could* throw your hat over the windmill, if only for a few days; you could leave behind the cares of a few hours before.

The small family hotel was run by a man of ancient lineage who came out to greet her personally, dogs around his feet, eyes calm. Everything about Robert de Gray spelt reassurance from his thatch of thick white hair to his old, much-mended cricketing shirt. The house, or hotel as it now was, was old, graceful, three-floored, Queen Anne, and covered with a patina that only comes with time. Judy was grateful for its air of inconsequential charm, its rows of tennis rackets clustered in the hall, its numbers of family portraits, some of which hung crooked around the stairs and halls. She didn't want to stand out in some homely way among sophistication that would be too smart for her, among riches that would laugh at her really rather worn clothes. Instead, as the staff took her luggage and showed her to her suite, she felt instantly at ease.

While she was taking in the rose-strewn chintzes in her bedroom, the large chintz-hung fourposter, appreciating everything about what seemed to be a perfect bedroom, what with the bowls of roses and the old leather-bound books, there was a knock on the door, and Robert de Gray stood in the entrance wondering if everything was to her liking?

'It's a beautiful room.'

'It was my mother's. Anyone coming here on their own, I try to arrange for them to stay in this one. It has such a lovely atmosphere, I always think.'

He smiled at her, all calm kindness, a little like a doctor, as if he knew that she had much to work out, and was not in need of too many words. After which he left her.

Judy laid out her clothes, ran a bath, and undressed. She stood in front of her mirror and studied herself. She was still slim, she was still quite pretty, even in her own eyes. What she was not was young again.

'You are not Cleopatra,' she told herself, and, turning away from her image, went to put the radio on.

The dress she had chosen to wear for dinner was new, navy blue silk, three-quarter length, with a boat-shaped neck and short sleeves. She fastened a string of pearls round her neck, for some reason remembering, as she did so, that Meggie had used to say that as soon as you wore a new dress the waiters always felt compelled to spill cream down your back. She smiled. Meggie was always so *funny*.

As she walked down the stairs she couldn't help imagining what it might be like if there was someone waiting for her at the bottom.

'You look stunning,' she hoped he might say.

377

He might take a step back as she reached the bottom step, admiring her, holding her hand lightly as if they might be about to dance. And Judy would float towards the drawing room and the drinks, towards the whole evening, as if it was her birthday, or as if she had never felt quite so pretty before, and might never again. She still bought so few clothes, the fact that her dress was new was exotic enough. It all came from the war. She, and Rusty this time, had laughed so much about that.

'Times they are-a-changing, Judy. Nowadays clothes are for wearing, and then chucking away. Thank God! I mean thank God if you're in the rag trade like me, that is.'

But a new dress was still so novel to Judy that once she arrived home she'd spent the whole evening taking the dress out of her cupboard and putting it back again. Now she was actually wearing it, not just holding it up to the light, but she knew, far from ever chucking it away, she would always treasure it. She knew that from the way she was trying to imagine him looking at her, as if she'd never looked quite so pretty before, as if perhaps he hadn't quite appreciated her before, which of course he might have done, but only as a friend. Now, though, he wouldn't have to pretend to be an old friend. Now he could be her lover, and she his.

Dinner was by candlelight, naturally, little tables set about what had once been the library, discreet couples dining. Every now and then Judy's eyes slid round the rest of the room, wondering if they were all about to embark on an affair, or whether they were safely married to the people they were with, and if they were, if they still felt the same about the people they were meant to love?

A part of her really rather wanted them all to be having affairs, a quite large part of her wanted them to be about to tear up their pasts, and yet another part of her hoped that they were all safely in harbour. She inched her slender hand across the table until she imagined it resting against his hand, and then she left it there. It would be so comforting, so real, to feel the side of his hand resting against hers. Perhaps he might now be telling her all about his life in America, or about his war, about all those things that she'd never had time to ask him?

'Liqueur and coffee in the drawing room?'

She followed the waiter through, choosing to sit in a dark corner away from the main part of the room, hoping to be left alone.

'Come over here, my dear. You play the piano, don't you?'

Robert de Gray was already seated at an old Steinway grand, beckoning to her, inviting her over, as he started to play a medley of old tunes.

'You do play? You look as if you play,' he told her over the sound of the music.

'Only a little.'

'Like me to play anything special for you?'

It would have taken a less kind personality than Judy possessed to refuse.

'I . . .' Of a sudden she couldn't think of a thing. 'How about . . .' Her mind blanked.

'How about "The Nearness of You"?'

'Of course, of course, that would be lovely.'

'You sing, don't you?'

Judy shook her head. No, she didn't sing, at least not in public.

'I'll turn for you, but I won't sing,' she murmured, smiling.

She stood by the piano as Robert de Gray played a host of favourite numbers, and one or two of the guests started to drift over, determined on joining in, and then, inevitably, demands started to be made, and requests had to be met, and one or two of the guests turned out to have awfully jolly voices, the sort that make up very good church choirs everywhere. And so all the guests started to give their all, and drinks having been ordered, and consumed, the evening crept towards midnight, and after midnight and on; until had it been summer it would have still been light enough for them all to go for a swim, but since it wasn't, and they were all reluctant to give in to the early hours, the party around the piano remained around it, with Robert finally sitting happily in front of a closed piano lid, his private concert at an end, happy to be talking and laughing with all his guests.

'I think it's such fun, don't you?' The young woman next to Judy smiled enchantingly at her. 'Robert's so clever, never lets anyone in he doesn't know, so it always sashays into a house party at this time of night, so un-hotel-like, don't you think?'

She raised her chilled glass of wine to her flushed cheeks, pressing it against them.

They were all leaning, one way or another, against the piano, which had myriad silver-framed photographs scattered over it. In company with everyone else, Judy had long ago forgotten to mind about the time. The young woman next to her picked up one of the silver frames from the old mahogany lid.

'Gracious, I know that face,' she said, frowning. 'And it's not the wine speaking, no. Yes, I know that face.' She turned the photograph towards Judy. 'This is the face of the famous beauty of her day, Elinor Gore-Stewart.'

Judy stared at the photo, convinced that she was wrong. It wasn't Elinor Gore-Stewart, it was Meggie Gore-Stewart. She took the old sepia-tinted photograph from the young woman, who had already moved on to others, picking them up and putting them down in swift sequence, murmuring to Judy as she did so.

'Queen Mary. Of course she was Robert's god-mother, wasn't she? Oh, and look, a house party before the war with Lady D. Cooper. Was there ever a house party without her, one wonders?'

Judy held the photograph closer. In the event it actually wasn't Meggie, but it might as well have been. There was Meggie's cool look, there was

Meggie's aloofness, and there the way that she stared out at the world, as if challenging it to be a great deal more entertaining than it wanted to be. No wonder Madame Gran had loved her grand-daughter. Meggie had been Elinor Gore-Stewart born again, from the top of her blond head to the bottom of her elegant feet. Meggie – the love of Waldo's life, the woman he still missed.

'She was the grandmother of my best friend,' she heard herself say to the young woman, who was already turning away, calling to her husband.

'Vigo! Dear! It is way past our beddy byes. This stay was meant – I say *was* – meant to be a rest we were having!'

The gaiety of the party gradually fractured, as guest after guest finally filtered away, reluctant to leave, but too tired to stay, leaving only Robert, now playing once more, and Judy watching him.

'One last one for the road?' he suggested.

'You choose.'

'Only one song does for this time of night—'

Robert sorted through his music, and beckoned to Judy to sit down on the double piano stool beside him.

'Come on now, both together.'

'*The party's over*,' they sang. '*It's time to call it a day . . .*'

Robert stared at the music, smiling occasionally.

'You have a very sweet voice – shouldn't be so shy.' He stopped. 'Now, once more with feeling.'

There was no need for him to call for it. He knew

from the expression on Judy's face that it was there anyway.

'Such a beautifully sad song.' He closed the piano lid, and stood up. 'Goodnight, my dear.'

He turned to look back at Judy, who was still lingering by the piano.

'And don't worry, everything will work out. It always does.'

'You know my mother's asked us for drinks at lunchtime,' Judy groaned from her bed.

'Yes?' Walter replied without much interest, once again, following the failure of yet another defence case, this time in London, having retreated back behind his psychological guard. 'So?'

'I have the most awful migraine, Walter. I'm sorry, but I don't really think I can go.'

'You're getting a lot of these migraines lately,' Walter observed, slipping a tie under his collar and beginning to knot it. 'Don't you think you ought to see someone?'

'I've seen the doctor two or three times about them,' Judy muttered, closing her eyes and pressing the icepack she had fetched herself even harder to her temples. 'He's given me some pills, but they don't make a jot of difference.'

'I'll go and ring your mother,' Walter volunteered, looking at the reflection of his wife lying supine on their bed through his dressing glass. 'Give her our apologies.'

'I feel doubly awful,' Judy groaned. 'She was so

looking forward to seeing you – she said she hasn't seen you in an age.'

'I've been rather busy.'

'You've been rather away. And it's her birthday tomorrow, but she hates celebrating it on a Monday.'

'Your head really is too bad?'

Judy eyed him, this time catching his eyes in the glass.

'What do you think?' she said quietly, before lying on her side, icepack still pressed to her forehead.

By the time Walter had finished speaking to Judy's mother on the telephone he had agreed to go and have a lunchtime drink with her anyway, even though Judy was confined to her bed. It was actually no terrible hardship for Walter, because over the years he had grown more and more fond of Lady Melton.

Besides, it would also mean he would be able to escape the house for a while, and the sense of claustrophobia Judy's migraines induced in him.

It was a crisp November day and he would enjoy the walk up through Bexham to the older part of the village, where no doubt there would be several other Bexhamites drinking Lady Melton's birthday health, and if that was the case there would be little call for any taxing conversation. He was in no mood to talk about his career at the Bar, since like most people when they feel they're failing he sensed that his recent poor performances were common knowledge to all his friends and neighbours. Sunday drinks and particularly birthday drinks at the Manor never degenerated into inquisitions. On the contrary they were gentle affairs dominated by the older generation who preferred to discuss their gardens, and ailments in rose and herbaceous border, rather than nose around in the affairs of the young.

So as he approached the fine Georgian manor house, lit by a weak but welcome November midday sun, a few of the autumnal leaves of its great trees still fluttering pensively to earth, Walter's mood was considerably better than when he'd first left Owl Cottage, and he was actually looking forward to one of Lady Melton's famous long, strong gin and tonics.

'Have I got the time wrong? Or even the day?' Walter smiled as he looked round the empty drawing room, populated only by his mother-in-law in her favoured weekend rig of long, loose, dark blue cashmere sweater over a crisp white shirt, dark tartan skirt, flat shoes and a single strand of her very good pearls at her neck.

'Not at all, Walter,' she said affectionately, kissing him gently on one cheek before turning him towards the drinks tray. 'You can mix for us both.'

Again, somewhat taken by surprise by the change in routine, Walter looked at Lady Melton a few seconds longer.

'It's all right.' She laughed. 'I'm not going to give

you Grim Tidings. Or suddenly collapse into a chair clutching my chest as I saw someone doing on television. No, actually, old Doctor Farnsbarns says I am in extremely good fettle. Much better fettle than a lot of his patients half my age, so he says, but then he would, the dear old thing, he does so love to flatter.'

Lady Melton sat herself down by the roaring log fire, waving one long index finger at the chair opposite for Walter to follow suit while he placed a perfectly made drink beside her.

'Happy birthday for tomorrow,' he said, raising his glass before sitting. 'Many happy returns.'

'Thank you, Walter dear. Do you know, I've always rather enjoyed birthdays, even more as I've got older. A lot of one's friends start forgetting to celebrate them, which I personally think is rather a shame. Or else they start telling fibs about when exactly they were born, which is so silly, really. Heavens above – can you imagine? The only person who is interested in their age is the person themselves. How's poor Judy? I was sorry to hear about her migraines. I went through a spell of having migraines, so I know what they're like. Perfectly beastly. Did you hear tell, by the by, that young Tam Sykes is back in England?'

'No,' Walter said, surprised that this piece of news hadn't yet filtered through to Judy – or that, if it had, she had neglected to tell him. 'When did that happen?'

'Not sure. Not that it matters – the thing is he's back in England, and by all accounts he's been doing rather well for himself in America. Joined some sort of band, or pop group, would it be? Which the young tell me is *hot stuff*.'

'Well,' Walter mused. 'I don't suppose he'll be coming down here, will he? That might be a bit awkward, even now.'

'Oh, I don't see why not, Walter,' Lady Melton replied. 'I've never thought Tam Sykes was wholly to blame, and I don't think anyone else does, not now. There was even some rumour about some wretched youth boasting about how he'd doctored young Sykes's car in revenge for his taking five pounds off him at darts, or some such nonsense.'

'I'm sure,' Walter replied curtly. 'But that doesn't take anything away from what he did to Jenny.'

'Oh, but I don't think he *did* do anything, Walter.' Lady Melton reached into a worn crocodile handbag, and lit a cigarette with a small slim gold lighter. 'Even if no one had doctored the car, and even if he did make an error of judgement, we have to learn to look on accidents as just that – as accidents. Things happen, either of their own volition, or maybe because we want them to, or perhaps they simply just happen.'

'I don't doubt it, but it's still difficult for those nearest to Jenny. After all she's been through, it would be difficult to take Tam back into the bosom of Bexham, as it were, as if nothing had happened. I know it's not right, but it is only human.'

He swallowed the rest of his strong drink gratefully if somewhat too quickly and held up his glass.

'May I?'

'But of course, Walter. You don't have to ask. You know that. How are your young?' she asked, turning round to watch him as he went past her to the drinks tray. 'According to John, if Hubert goes to Oxford and gets his Blue then he's going to become a cricketer.'

'Yes – but an amateur. There is a very big difference between the Gentlemen and the Players. As we all know.'

'Well of course – understood – quite. I do know what you mean, Walter dear.' Lady Melton laughed. 'I've been married to your father-in-law for long enough. Come summer, like every old cricketer he hardly ever has his head out of Wisden.'

'I'm sure what John means is that if Hubie gets a Blue—'

'Which given his talent they say he well might.'

'He'll play for Sussex as an amateur. If they'll have him. Young men like Hubert don't turn professional. I know they're getting up to all sorts of things nowadays, but cricket's quite different. One of the last bastions of the true amateur, and a particularly good one, too, because amateurs can play alongside the professionals which is as it should be. Just like horse racing – where a good amateur is perfectly entitled to take his place in the field, but you don't see them turn pro, however good they may be.'

'Hmm. Well, we'll see. By the way, your papa-in-law sent his apologies for not being present. He's dreadfully tied up with this Save Bexham business, rarely leaves the committee rooms, even for my birthday.'

Lady Melton glanced at Walter, then threw a couple of small logs on to the fire, before prodding the latter into greater life with a long brass-handled poker.

'I heard a song on the wireless the other day – I always have the wireless on now. Jolly good company, too, and much better than the television which is inclined to shout at you. It was rather a good song actually – a lot of these new songs are really rather good, you know.'

'I've yet to hear one.'

Walter stared moodily into the fire. He had really rather hoped that at least his father-in-law was going to put in an appearance.

'The times they are a-changing was the song, though don't ask me who was singing it. Rather a miserable-sounding fellow actually. And of course they are. The times they are a-changing.'

'Always have. Always will.'

'Yes, but not at such a breakneck pace, Walter. And not for the reasons they are *nowadays*. We do live in pretty stern times, you know.'

'You mean *we* didn't? Good Lord – I can't think

389

of sterner times than the ones we lived through in the last war.'

'Yes, quite, and I've lived through two of them, Walter dear.'

'Precisely. Two world wars, and their quite awful aftermaths – the austerity, the strikes, the unrest. *Those* were stern times. The way they go on about the Bomb you would honestly think the atom bomb was the end of the world.'

'Which it might well be.'

'They're making the atom bomb an excuse for – terrible clothes and worse music.' He shook his head. 'Honestly, I look at them and I think were we all ready to die to make a world for the likes of you? When you think of what we did, how much we sacrificed, quite frankly, I don't think they were worth it, I don't really. In fact I find most of them, for me, are a crashing disappointment, and that's when I'm not finding them crashing bores.'

'They're young, Walter.' Lady Melton laughed. 'Gracious heavens, you were young once. Even I was!'

'I certainly didn't behave as they do.'

'And you certainly *did*, Walter, or at least your version of it. When you were young, you did what you thought was right, and you thought your papa-in-law and I were the most awful old stick-in-the-muds. And we thought you were the *bottom*. Gracious heavens, you rode motor bikes and wore Oxford bags, and went round everywhere with your hands in your pockets and cigarettes in your mouths, and you danced the most extraordinary dances to the most extraordinary music, when we all wanted you to dance waltzes, and quadrilles. No, we thought you were quite ghastly, if that's any comfort.'

She laughed again, but Walter only shook his head, not wanting to admit to remembering his younger self, concentrating only on his grievances.

'It was different then, life was more innocent. The young today seem to think they have some God-given right to do whatever they choose – to think whichever way they want, to talk how they like, say what they like, and to do what they like. All they do is criticise their elders – blaming us for the Bomb, saying we're going to blow the world up – or poison it. They don't know what they're talking about. If they'd had to go through what we had to go through, I might be able to show them a little respect. But no, all they seem to see fit to do is to sit on pavements and hold up placards and expect us to change a world all our friends gave their lives to save.'

'They're only doing what they *think* is right, Walter,' Lady Melton told him, more gently, wondering at his quite visible misery. 'Just as we when we were young did what *we* thought was right. That's what they're doing.'

'I'm sorry,' Walter said, putting down his drink, and taking out a cigarette. 'But for once I can't agree with you. I think for once we shall have to beg to differ.'

'May I have one of those? I haven't tried one of those for ages.' Lady Melton leaned forward, her elegant hand stretched out for a cigarette. Walter promptly offered her one, then got out of his chair to light it for her. 'I gave them up years ago, as you know. But now I am of a certain age, I think oh blow it. Mmm.' She inhaled, enjoying the sensation. 'Lovely choice. Thank you. Which brings me to Kim.'

Walter, back in his chair, looked sharply back at her.

'What about Kim?'

Lady Melton carefully tapped her cigarette on the edge of an adjacent silver ashtray before replying.

'I went to see her, you know. In Ireland.'

Walter stared at her.

'Did – did Judy know?'

'I don't know. I don't know whether Kim told her or not, but go I did. I went, all on my own.'

'If Judy did know, she never mentioned it.'

'Afraid you'd go off the deep end, probably. You yourself haven't seen Kim since – when?'

'Does it matter?' Walter got up from his chair decidedly rattled by this latest revelation.

Mentally he cursed women and the way they always just went ahead and did things without any reference to anyone else. Certainly to his way of thinking not even his mother-in-law – grand-mother though she might be – had any right at all to take herself off and go and visit his daughter

392

without a say-so. And as for Judy – ever since she had proposed sending Kim to Ireland she had quietly but very positively taken control of their daughter's future, to the extent that now anyone and everyone could go and visit Kim without as much as a by his leave, or even his knowledge.

His head began to swim and he felt a cold sweat breaking out down the middle of his back, even though he was nowhere near the fire. He began to shake from head to foot as if he had run from a steam room into an ice house. Nothing made sense any more, nothing – and least of all this. Everyone was ranged against him.

He collapsed back on to the sofa with a groan, wiping his forehead with a handkerchief, trying to ease from his neck a tie that now seemed to be strangling him, before leaning forward and sticking his head between his knees.

In a second Lady Melton was beside him, taking one of his hands.

'Walter?' she was saying. 'Walter, are you all right?'

'Yes,' he said slowly. 'Yes, thank you.' He looked up and smiled a short smile at her, seeing at once her concern. 'It's all right, I promise you. Nothing to worry about. It's just that I've been working very hard. Too hard really, far too hard.'

He wanted to add 'and not very well either – or successfully' but with an inward sigh he assumed that his mother-in-law already knew, which was why she was being so kind to him. It really was all so pointless, all of it. Everything they had done. Everything he had done in his life.

He put his forehead back in the palm of one of his hands, resting the elbow on his knee, and stared at the floor.

'I didn't sleep last night.'

'Would you like me to call the doctor? I know it's Sunday, but he is only round the corner after all.'

'No,' Walter said suddenly over-brightly, at the same time getting to his feet. 'No thanks. I'm fine now. Really absolutely A1. Really. See? I think I was sitting too close to the fire. It did get awfully hot in here suddenly.'

'My fault. It's my age. I do feel the cold dreadfully. I never used to, you know. My blood's thinner than it was.'

Walter smiled, a smile he hoped would reassure his mother-in-law while secretly praying she couldn't hear the pounding palpitations of his heart.

'Tell me about Kim,' he said, walking to the French windows and staring out at the garden where in turn a blackbird was staring at the frost-bitten grass. 'I'm interested, I really am. And you're right – I should go and see her.'

'She's not the same,' Walter.' Lady Melton paused. 'She's gone a bit – well, what my generation would call feral.'

'Feral? *Feral*?'

'A bit native – but then that's only to be expected. She's been in Ireland for how long now? She's been there for over four years, hasn't she? So she's bound to have changed a bit.'

'She hadn't changed much when I saw her. A bit less neurotic perhaps, a bit tongue-tied, but otherwise back to her old self, really.'

'That was nearly two years ago.'

'She hadn't gone feral then.'

'You'll be quite surprised at the change that has come over her.'

'Tell me about it. Save me a trip.'

'No, Walter, I'm not going to, I'm afraid. Because I really think you should go and see her.'

Lady Melton was quite insistent, and remained surprisingly so. And the reason she was so insistent was not that she thought Kim ought to see her father, but that she thought her father ought to see Kim. Nor did she imagine the meeting would be an immediate success. What she hoped for was something quite different. What she hoped was that Kim could help her father, because he was certainly in need of it.

Chapter Ten

In her imagination, but only in her imagination, once he'd made up his mind to go to Ireland, Judy drove Walter to Fishguard to catch the ferry to Rosslare. What actually happened was that Walter drove himself, and they said goodbye in the hall of the cottage.

They embraced first, and then for a second clung to each other.

'Don't forget your pills are in your sponge bag, and the socks in the white plastic bag haven't been aired, Walter. They're still damp.'

Walter nodded, feeling sad, and lonely, and somehow completely unnecessary to everyone, most of all his beloved Judy.

'I'll phone you when I get there.'

Judy shook her head. 'No, don't, Walter. That's just what you mustn't do. You must forget all about here, just go. Forget about work, about me, about Hubie, about Bexham, about everything, just be on your own. It's best. Truly. Believe me, I know.'

She kissed him again with sudden passion, and

then opened the front door and held it open until he very slowly walked through it, and down the path to his car.

When Walter arrived at the harbourside he found a winter sea blowing a force six that drove needle-sharp rain off the water and into the faces and the innards of anyone foolhardy enough to try to brave it out on deck. Being an old salt, the conditions were meat and drink to Walter, who, well wrapped up in his grandfather's old doeskin Navy sea-coat, sat up on deck facing fore, letting the weather do its worst. His pipe was still stuck in his mouth although the prevailing conditions had long since put paid to the tobacco fire in the bowl, but still he sucked at it as he thought about the journey he had been on over the last few years, realising more and more that he had, for some reason, ended up in a cul-de-sac.

He'd suffered a miserable time recently, losing two cases that he knew he should have won, and losing all belief in himself. It was not a loss that could be reversed easily either. It was not a profit and loss sort of loss, you couldn't turn the page and find 'loss of confidence' and transfer it to another column. This was a transforming loss. It was as if he had lost his ability to join in anything, even earning his own living. It was as if he could see right through everything and everyone, and none of it, or them, was worthwhile. Perhaps years of living in London during the week, or being away for sometimes months at a time on some case or other, had taken its inevitable toll on him. It certainly made it heartbreakingly difficult for two people, no matter how much they loved each other, to maintain the same level of intimacy.

But now, as England became a faraway island, her shores finally obliterated by the sea, and the gulls following the ship screeched out their ancient street cries calling for bread, or fish, or scraps, or just a free journey to Ireland, and other passengers went below in search of a warming drink, Walter remained on deck, thinking.

Being left by Walter had a shocking effect on Judy. Suddenly, with Kim and Hubert away, she was quite alone. At first it seemed to her that being alone at Owl Cottage was just like the war, and then she realised it was not at all like the war. During the war she had been out most of the time driving about in the dark, attending accidents, taking town children to place them in country homes, driving everywhere and anywhere where she might be needed: hospitals, bombed-out cinemas, burning houses. She had not been alone at Owl Cottage either, for after Walter went missing Loopy and Dauncy had come to live with her there, and she had loved having them, setting up a jolly little household who all needed each other, cared for each other, but never once seemed to tread on each other's toes, such was the urge for survival. So being alone at the cottage now was not at all the same as the war. Finally she realised that she must now know what it was to be lonely. It was to be without any particular purpose. If she had a purpose she would be busy, but she was, at that moment in her life, without direction and she hated it, feeling useless and unwanted.

Walter reached Waterford easily in time for lunch, eating a lonely meal in a small white-painted hotel while the rain still bucketed down in torrents outside, before heading southwest for Cork where he planned to stay the night before setting out on the last leg of his journey. He had booked into the Majestic where he drank and dined alone, glad of his solitude and happy to retire early to his bed where to his surprise he found that for the first time in months he fell asleep immediately.

Much refreshed after a splendid cooked break-fast, and a stroll down the main street of a city whose charms he found growing on him by the minute, he threw his bags into the boot of his car and in greatly improved weather set his course for Loughnalaire, which he had discovered to be along the coastline between Skibbereen and a landfall known as Mizen Head, just south of the famous Bantry Bay. The rain had stopped altogether overnight, leaving the late November skies a pale blue-grey with cloud higher than was normal at this time of year. By the time he had crossed the Bandon a weak sun was shining, but even had it not been Walter realised that he was already in love with this mysterious country of rocks and sky, of water and lakes, and few people.

He wondered what he might find on the coastline along which he was now driving, his speed dropping ever lower as he realised the wonder of the landscape he was passing through.

Below him on the left the Atlantic, still swelled by the recent gales, was landing dramatically before splintering on granite rocks, while to the right of him and ahead rolled unbroken and unspoilt miles of rough green pasture, dotted with tiny cottages, some whitewashed and still inhabited, to judge from the curls of peat smoke rising from their chimneys, others long abandoned and derelict, their thatches either collapsed or removed, the windows just dark stone apertures, their doorways open and empty, inviting only listless abandonment.

On distant hills men were cutting peat by shovel and hand, while donkeys in the traces of carts piled high with fuel waited patiently to make their next journey. Other donkeys roamed free, some with floppy-eared heads hanging over loose lines of broken barbed wire watching Walter driving slowly by, others standing in small groups on the edges of the bogs, their tails swishing rhythmically and their shaggy coats twitching spasmodically as some hidden scrounger took yet another bite of their undernourished flesh. A black collie chased his car for a good half-mile, running alongside the driver's door and barking at Walter, while casting him a doleful glance every time Walter looked his way. Finally he stopped and fed the scrawny animal some biscuits he had in a tin on the back seat and the last four squares of a bar of milk chocolate that the half-starved dog swallowed seemingly without even chewing. As a consequence he accompanied Walter for the next half-mile, until, worried that he might unwittingly be abducting some farmer's working dog, Walter accelerated away, leaving the dog behind, watching its image in his driving mirror until it was a speck, and finally vanished completely.

It was then he got lost, and there was no one around to give him directions. There were few signposts, and those he had passed seemed in retrospect to have directly contradicted each other. The first one had signposted Loughnalaire to lie northwards of his position, then the very next sent him straight back on his tracks. Doubling back he lost his bearings and found another signpost that showed Mount Glen lay due west, although the way the finger was pointing seemed to indicate the traveller must drive over hill and bog since beyond the sign there was no road. With a sigh, Walter stopped yet again, relit his pipe and made another study of his map which seemed on this reading to bear no resemblance whatsoever to the countryside in which he was parked. He got out of the old Riley and stood surveying the great finger of land on which he had stopped, the Atlantic Ocean breaking in huge white rollers both sides of him, wondering how on earth the signpost behind him could indicate that Loughnalaire now lay out to sea.

Hearing a sound from down the road Walter turned and saw a tall gaunt man slowly driving a tiny cow slowly along the road, an animal whose rump every now and then the driver gave a swish with what looked like a bundle of ferns. The small cow appeared to take no notice whatsoever of its chastisement, stopping where it so wished to chew a bit of the scenery, while its driver swished without interest at its quarters in between puffs at the white clay pipe he was smoking.

'I'm looking for Loughnalaire!' Walter called to the newcomer, who paid him scant heed. 'I said I'm looking for Loughnalaire!'

'Then look away!' the man called back. 'Don't let me be a-stoppin' you!'

'No,' Walter explained, going over to the man. 'No, what I mean is I can't find Loughnalaire.'

'Sure you wouldn't, would you? Not if ye're lookin' for her.'

'Her?' Walter wondered. 'Loughnalaire is a place.'

'Do ye think that is somethin' I'm not knowin'? Sure I know Loughnalaire 'tis a place, as I knows ye can't be findin' her, wouldn't you say?'

'Then perhaps you could help find it?'

'Why? When I knows where she is?'

'Help *me* find it?'

402

The man stared at him thoughtfully over his clay pipe, which he puffed strongly and deeply until his head was swathed in thick blue smoke.

'And sure what would I do with Veronica here while we went lookin'? She's the very divil of a walker.'

'There's no need for you to accompany me. All you have to do is point out where Loughnalaire is,' Walter suggested.

'How can I do that so? When I cannot see her from here?'

'Perhaps you could point me in the general direction.'

'You're in the general direction, sir. Loughnalaire is, as ye say, situate here generally speaking, wouldn't you agree?'

'Fine. Thank you,' Walter replied. 'But I wonder *where* exactly.'

'So ye do, so ye do. For if ye did not, ye would not be askin', now would you?'

'Absolutely.' Walter stopped and drew a patient breath. 'So if you could just perhaps be kind enough to tell me where she lies specifically . . .'

'*Specifically* is it?' The man tilted his cap to scratch the side of his head with the stem of his pipe. 'I can't do specifically. I haven't done specifics since when I was at the school, do ye see. Specifically ye want. Well now, let me see. Let me see.'

The man turned his back on Walter and stared back down the road. Then he turned half right and stared that way, before turning right round to stare the other. Finally he turned back to Walter and looked beyond him over his head.

'Ye've tried most of these ways, I'll be thinkin', so you would, wouldn't you?'

'You'd be right, too,' Walter assured him.

'Then the best thing ye can do is try this way so, wouldn't you say? Turn the car around, and then to the left. Go up the hill foreninst ye, then go down the other side. Turn the car to the left of ye, even though the sign says to the right and to the left No Through Road. Go down the No Through Road till ye can go no further then turn the car about and go to the right.'

'Why turn the car about?' Walter wondered. 'Couldn't I just go down the No Through Road and simply turn left?'

'There's a reason, but now it's gone for ye have me quite lost again. Turn the car around, and then to the left,' he began again, in a kind of chant this time, as if it was something he had learned by rote. 'Go up the hill foreninst ye, then go down the other side. Turn the car to the left of ye, even though the sign says to the right and to the left No Through Road. Go down the No Through Road till ye can go no further then turn the car about and go to the right. And the reason why ye have to do that is because ye cannot just turn to the left because there's this big rock in the way. Ye'll see. Then ye'll come to a man with a dog and ye'll need to turn to the right again.'

'A man with a dog? Why should there be a man with a dog there?'

The man looked at him and shook his head as if Walter had lost control of his senses.

'What time do ye have, sir? Isn't it a quarter of one hour after four? Of course it is, even my watch has that.' The man was looking at a large pocket watch he had pulled on a great length of string from one trouser pocket. 'So if it's a quarter of one hour after four there'll be a man with a dog by the turn so turn right be him and travel on till ye come to a sort of a crossroads.' He fell silent.

'What do I do then?' Walter asked, anxious to prompt his guide out of his silence.

'Whatever you please, sir. For isn't that Loughnalaire? Loughnalaire there at the crossroads will be all around ye. Sure ye can't miss her so.'

'Thank you,' Walter said, trying to memorize the instructions but unwilling to ask for a recap in case it led to further modifications. 'Thank you very much for your help.'

'Something tells me ye're not from these parts,' the man said. 'Don't ask me *what* – just something.'

Sticking his pipe back in his mouth, the man swished at his little cow who this time to Walter's amused amazement broke into a trot and disappeared off down the road, while her keeper stood staring after her, shaking his head.

'Isn't that another in need of guidance? For isn't that the road back to the market?'

Parking his car in a badly potholed area at the top
of the beach that spread out before him in the
gathering November dusk, Walter grabbed his
overnight bag and made his way down to the large
house surrounded by what looked like a small
village of cottages that lay at the foot of the steps
cut in the side of the cliff. There was no sign of
much life as he walked up to the front door, other
than a large lurcher dog fast asleep under a hand-
written sign that said, DO NOT RING BELL OUT OF
ORDER.

At a slight loss, Walter nevertheless knocked on
the door, at which sound the dog barked, but no
one came. Walter opened the door and called, but
no one answered. Following this he pushed the
door open further and found himself in a hall full
of large pots stacked with old fishing rods, broken
umbrellas and a variety of walking sticks. On a
long, slender hall table were a variety of hats in
which slept a variety of cats, while an enormous
stag's head hung precariously at an angle on one
wall, its antlers ringed with coloured hoops,
making the creature obviously the target of some
rainy day game. At the end of the corridor through
a half-glazed door Walter could see lights, but no
figures. He called once more but still receiving
no response began to make his way to what he
assumed must be the kitchens. En route he passed a
half-open door through which he could glimpse
a large drawing room where most of the furniture

seemed to be either upholstered in well-worn velvets or draped with faded multicoloured shawls. Pushing the door wide open he peered inside to see if it contained any sign of life but there was none.

Beyond the drawing room was a huge conservatory, again lit up, although again seemingly unoccupied. Beginning to think he had wandered into some sort of tragic scenario where everyone who lived in the house had been body-snatched by unknown forces, Walter eased over to the conservatory and opened the door. At once he heard definite signs of life, the unmistakable sound of extremely heavy snoring coming from the far end of the large glasshouse, which was kept at a fine heat. Looking down to the end of the room he could see a pair of very large feet clad in a pair of very large laceless boots sticking out from behind a groaning and rumbling boiler. Tiptoeing down further Walter discovered the owner of the feet, an enormous red-bearded man fast asleep in a deck chair, dressed in red flannel underwear clearly visible under a wide open tartan dressing gown whose string girdle at some point had become undone, the top half of his face covered with an open copy of *The Life of Sophocles*.

Unsure of what red-bearded men did when suddenly and rudely awoken from their late afternoon siesta, Walter preferred to retrace his steps to the hall and thence to the half-glazed door, on which he knocked. In spite of the blaze of light from the other side and the murmur of what sounded like conversation, there was no reply, so once again Walter entered unbidden.

This time he found a tall woman fast asleep in a huge armchair that was set by a black iron Victorian kitchen range. She had a mountain of pepper-and-salt-coloured hair that was half pinned up and half down, a long purple satin dress under a vast hand-knitted cardigan in what he would soon come to recognise as the Aran weave, two pairs of thick knitted grey fisherman's socks over what looked like black nylon stockings and a beautiful hand-embroidered silk shawl draped round her shoulders. On her lap, equally fast asleep, sat a big black chicken.

Walter coughed politely at first, but that failed even to wake the chicken. So he coughed again and this time followed it with a solicitation.

'Excuse me,' he said. 'Excuse me?'

The louder repeat woke the chicken who stared round at him with quick, sudden movements of its head, as if wondering who had dared to interrupt its reverie?

'Excuse me?' Walter said once more, hoping this time successfully to wake the sleeping woman. 'Excuse me – are you—'

'I am, I am, I am,' the woman interrupted him, although to Walter it sounded more like *yam yam yam*. 'And isn't this a terrible time to be sleeping? The Romans were right now, were they not?' She stretched out her arms and yawned expansively, but even that failed to dislodge her pet, which merely squawked. 'Never slumber at the hour of sundown. And sure weren't they right as per usual? Can I help you now?'

'I'm Mr Tate. Walter Tate,' Walter volunteered.

The woman nodded vaguely at him, pinning up some loose strands of long hair. 'Is that right? And I'm the Widow Hackett.'

'I thought you might be.'

'Grand. Grand. So what can we be doin' for you?'

'I'm Mr Tate?' Walter repeated, as if that was sufficient. After all, he was expected.

'The name is ringing the bell, Mr Tate now – ah yes to be sure! Mr Tate! You'll be Mr Tate who must be married to Mrs Tate now! You'll be dear Mrs Tate's husband! Whom I was forever calling Lyle, would you believe? Heaven forfend us, what can you be thinking? And here's me asleep with old Puck-Puck – what can you be thinkin'?'

The Widow was up on her feet by now, placing her beloved hen in a dog basket by the range and picking the feathers carefully off her velvets.

'And how is lovely Mrs Tate?' she asked, with a flash of a green-eyed glance at Walter, who was already enchanted. 'We have heard neither hide nor word from her since God knows when. But then mind you when you have no postman, sure you have no post.'

'Something is telling me you didn't get Judy's letter.'

'Ask me my name and on most days it'd need a

push to tell you, so ask after letters and you'll get no better answer. No, no – we've had no letter from anyone for a while since, but then, as I said, sure we have no deliverance.'

'You have no postman?'

'You'll not want to hear about that now,' the Widow said with a frightful grimace. 'Oh God no, you'll not want to be hearing about a saga such as that now. For that you'd need a jug of stout and a good bowl of stew at the very least. That's not for the cold telling. Suffice that we have no deliverer, and the good thing is sure – that means no bills. So what can I be doing for you, you sweet man? You look worn, I'll have to say. Can I get you a drink? I'm about to start in meself, so why don't we have a ball? A couple of balls of malt and you won't know a frown from a smile.'

The Widow expertly took down two whiskey glasses in two fingers of one hand from the dresser behind her, tucked a bottle of Powers under her other arm, and nodded to her visitor.

'Come along, Mr Tate – we'll be away now into the sitting room because you'll not want to be in here when they return.'

Walter followed on obediently, as the Widow rattled on about how everyone had taken the house bus into Bantry to catch some film or other, a work of which to judge from the rumblings and tongue-clucking going on in front of him the Widow did not approve.

'Cleopatra indeed,' she said, pushing the

drawing room door open with one double-socked foot. 'If that was Cleopatra then me – I'm James Bond. Any barge that she sat in sure would sink straight to the bottom of the Nile – and with all hands. Ah, and to think I used to fancy that Richard Burton – but then the eejit went and took the money. Lovely voice. Make the hair stand up on a hedgehog. Here – slainte.'

She handed him a well-filled glass and raised her own.

'Here's to us. There's few like us and them that are is dead.'

'If you didn't get Judy's letter, you really won't know why I'm here,' Walter said, walking round the dimly lit room and peering at what paintings he could make out on walls that appeared to be covered in hessian. Meanwhile, the Widow suddenly dropped to her knees and crawling across to the fireplace began to build a fire.

'I'll light a few lamps up in a cat's tail,' she said from somewhere below him. 'Soon as I have this lit. Bloody old Rufus was meant to do it but then the sea was meant to go backwards for Canute. Isn't that right? You might as well call view hulloo in a fog.'

'Are the lamps oil? If so, I can light them.'

'Then light away, light away. I won't stop you.'

Walter lit four large antique brass oil lamps and soon the elegant room was bathed in a soft warm glow, each lamp as it was lit revealing yet another remarkable painting or drawing on a wall somewhere. Once all the lamps were alight Walter could see there was hardly a free space left anywhere.

'Good gracious,' he said. 'Are you a collector?'

'Me? What of? I can barely collect me own thoughts let alone anything of value. If you're talking about the pitchers, now that's nothing to do with my taste or not. I just get given them – and I just get to hang them. I take no credit. These is all the work of the family.'

'Your children? These wonderful paintings and drawings are all done by your children?'

The Widow laughed, getting to her feet now the fire was alight and searching the fireplace for her box of cheroots.

'My family aren't my children, you dear man, gracious me, no,' she said. 'My family's them that I have here. My family's my guests.'

Walter looked at her, then back at the paintings. Above the fire was what he thought was a particularly fine painting of cliffs and sea, quite modern for Walter's usual taste, and wonderful in its use of colour and light. Looking round the room he saw there were another three or possibly four paintings by the same artist.

'I don't know very much,' Walter offered. 'But I'd say these were quite remarkable.'

'And wouldn't you be right?' the Widow approved. 'Sure they have two of his in Dublin's National Gallery now. Sweet man, he was. He was here for two years before he spoke a word, and God

412

wasn't he forever trying to throw himself off the cliffs or something daft. He's fine now, in case you're wondering. Lives up in Clare and often comes to see us all. Lost all his family in a fire when he was two. Two years old and straight into the orphanage. Sometimes I don't think this world deserves us, that's a fact. That's how much we care. We take a nipper like that and put him in an orphanage – where I have to say they told him the most dreadful things. No wonder he never spoke. You can hardly stop him now. Another ball of malt?'

His hostess, having finished her first drink, took Walter's only half empty glass and refilled it to the brim.

He turned away and looked at another picture on the wall, a lovely line drawing of a sea bird executed in what looked like charcoal.

'You know who I am, don't you?' he said after a moment, when his replenished glass had been handed back to him.

'You're Mr Tate, Judy's husband – sure I know that. Didn't you tell me in the kitchen?'

'No. No, I think you knew before that.'

'Wasn't I asleep before that? So how could I?'

'It was as you woke up. There was a look in your eyes. I saw it. I'm very good at recognising looks in people's eyes.'

'So is your daughter. Of course I knew who you were. I knew it the moment I came to. I'm quite handy too at seeing what's in people's eyes – and I could see Kim there in yours.'

'Did you get Judy's letter?'

'I did not. She telephoned me neither since the lines have been down in all the storms. Kim's not here, you know that. She left here some time ago, but then you'll know that too.'

Walter shook his head. 'All I was told was that she was working here. So I assumed she was still at Loughnalaire.'

The Widow looked at him, veiling her surprise, and sat down on the sofa opposite the fire.

'You may be in for a surprise, Mr Tate. I have to tell you that. You do know that trees are not the only things that change, and shed their leaves?'

'I'm beginning to find that out,' Walter replied. 'And please call me Walter.'

'And you're to call me Atlanta. Although I don't object to "darling" once we're on to the wine!' She gave a great throaty laugh and lit up a cheroot. 'Your daughter's very direct, you know. Probably more so now – but then she has been doing remarkable things.'

'She always was pretty direct,' Walter replied, remembering how whenever he had been vexed with her even as a little girl she had stood up to him and fought her corner.

'She told me I was an old fraud,' the Widow continued, giving another laugh. 'We were having words one day, and she said I was a lot of hot air and a fraud. I axed her why she thought so, and she said I was nothing but one great act – a bit of typical Irish baloney was what she said. Imagine that, a bit

414

of typical Irish baloney. And I told her she was absolutely right, so she was. That I wasn't always as I am now, do you see. That this has all grown as this place grew about me, but then I said to her well sure, but then it had to, didn't it? Because how could a bit of non-baloney run a place like this? A place like this had to have someone like me at its – you know.'

'Its helm.'

'Its helm. But then I'd never have bought ordinary. I doubt if I'd even recognise it. And your daughter has certainly not bought it either. She's doing great things, you know. *Good* things. Good things is better. I think you'll see quite a girl in your daughter. I hope so anyway, or else I'll have failed you – and more importantly I'll have failed her. Now for God's sake get into your drink, man, so as we can get an evening going. Or are you too exhausted for a bit of craic?'

'Craic?' Walter wondered. 'Craic?'

'My, my,' the Widow sighed. 'We don't have to guess who's never taken the ferry before.'

Max had left Jenny and Tam in London and driven down to Bexham for the weekend. He sang all the way down in the car, looking forward to seeing his mother and stepfather, to having a pint at the Three Tuns, perhaps taking a boat out for some freezing cold fishing, or going for an equally cold walk on the Downs.

As he turned into the road that led down to the

harbour his heart rose, as it always did when he saw the inlet with all the fishing boats bobbing, the cottages and houses set about the estuary, the sea-gulls circling, the rush of water lapping up the sides of the old walls. Somehow, for him, always and ever, Bexham would be his England. It was his grandfather, now lying at rest in the churchyard, it was his mother who had played with him on the green, it was all his friends, old and young, who would even now, like him, be thinking of their Saturday beer, and all those other dear things that seem to make up the ideal country weekend.

The first person he bumped into in the Three Tuns was Waldo.

'Young Max, back to see the old folk no doubt?' Waldo asked delightedly. He put both arms round Max and hugged him. Max was quite happy to hug his grandfather's best friend back, not caring what anyone thought.

'A pint, Richards, for the prodigal son come back to the fold!'

'I'm too old to pull pints, Mr Astley,' Richards grumbled, but he pulled one for Max, and pushed it across the bar. 'Lovely to see you back, young Max. Going to stay down and help rescue Bexham, I hope?'

'Of course,' Max agreed, hastily remembering the Cause. 'Yes, of course. How is it all?' he asked, turning to Waldo, who was paying for his beer.

'I have to say that I think that it is not going at all well, Max.' Waldo looked momentarily gloomy, and started to drink his gin and tonic a little too quickly. 'It is David against Goliath, and at the moment all the weight is on Goliath's side, so we may have to rewrite the Bible.' He lit a cigar and breathed out. 'I have no idea how we're going to win, but we do at least have to try. Vested interest, you know, vested interest is so real, I sometimes think it is more real than war. They want to build Lego houses around the harbour, and put a bistro where the boatyard is, and don't let's even contemplate to whom they're going to lease the Yacht Club site. Rumour is that it will be Donald Short, and as you know the design for Short Marinas is usually done by a man who is more used to drawing up factories on the outskirts of industrial towns. It is such an uphill battle, the fight for beauty against business interests, for nature against monied interests, for health against everything. But fight we must, and we will. Whether we will win is quite another thing.'

All the time Waldo was talking Max's mind was dipping in and out of the problems that Bexham was facing. The most serious was obviously money. However much money they scrounged from each other the residents would be hard put to reach up to the knees of the people moving in on their village, unless something spectacular was organised.

'I have an idea, Waldo. I won't tell you, in case I can't bring it off, but if I could it would make thousands and thousands for the Fighting Fund.'

'I have an idea too, Max, and it too will make thousands and thousands.'

'Good man.'

Max punched Waldo lightly on the shoulder and then turned his attentions once more to his favourite beer, but as he did so he couldn't help wondering why it was that the look in Waldo's eyes was so sad. He suddenly seemed older, less Waldo-like, less ebullient, thinner.

Mattie was waiting anxiously by the window overlooking the green, watching for Max.

John watched her from afar feeling that particular mixture of impatience and jealousy he always felt when Max was expected home, feelings that were only natural since Max was not his son. God knows he tried hard with him, but somehow Max never could live up to Sholto, who was such a straightforward sort of chap, more of a man's man, less complicated than Max, less peppery, if you like. John had never asked Mattie much about Max's father, but he knew from what he had seen of Max as the boy was growing up that the father, an American apparently, must have been quite a character, and good-looking, because Max was good-looking, but not easy like Sholto.

'Ah, there he is.' Mattie's worried mother's frown was replaced by a look of relief and she hurried off to the front door.

'Darling.' She embraced Max at the door, and as she did so she smelt the familiar aroma of the well-brewed beer from the Three Tuns, not to mention nicotine.

'Sorry I'm late, Ma. Stopped off to have a pint with Waldo at the Three Tuns and discuss the Bexham Fighting Fund.'

Max made it sound as if he'd driven down especially to have a pint with Waldo and discuss the Fund. He thought it quite a cunning ruse, until he saw his stepfather's face.

'We've been waiting lunch for you, Max. Your mother's been worried.' He looked pointedly at the sitting room clock.

'I say, I am sorry, John.' Max always found himself playing the part of a 'jolly good chap' when he was confronted with his stepfather, the kind of young man who could always, even nowadays, be found in a Terence Rattigan play, the kind of fellow who would never stray very far from his tennis racket. 'But you know how it is, I got held up on the way down, late for Waldo, couldn't get to the pub phone, such a queue for it on Saturdays, et cetera, et cetera.'

Max smiled disarmingly at his stepfather, but John turned away.

'It's always something with you, Max, always something.' He looked back at him. 'And can't you afford to go to a barber, old chap?'

Max stared after him, half closing his eyes, his suitcase still by his side. He felt like driving straight back to London. His mother came back into the room.

419

'Lunch isn't ruined, love, really. Leave your case right there, and come straight through to the dining room. I've done a new Robert Carrier recipe for you. Don't know what it tastes like, but it smells simply delicious. although I say so myself.'

John followed Max into the dining room. It was never a new recipe for *him* when he came back from the pub on Saturdays, it was always quiche and salad.

Late that night, after trying to toe the line with his stepfather, Max retired to bed exhausted. He never could get it right with John, although he knew his stepfather did love him, but just lately he was getting it even less right. His mother on the other hand was sympathetic to the point of indulgence, rarely criticising him, but on the other hand seemingly not very interested either. It was at these times that Max missed his grandfather, to whom he had been so close. Lionel had such a sense of humour. He could always jolly Max along, dig him out of the black holes into which he sometimes disappeared. Lionel it was who had encouraged him to play golf, to take an interest in politics, all the things that, Max felt, his own father would have done, should he have known him.

It was a subject that Max had raised on the walk around the estuary with Mattie. Should he get in touch with his own father? Should he be told who his father was? Would it be of any interest to him?

Mattie had immediately become agitated, begging Max to do no such thing.

'It wouldn't be fair on either of you, especially not him. Leave in peace what should stay in peace.'

Max had accepted this and they had both returned to the house for tea in the kind of spirits that should lead to a pleasant evening and a good night's sleep.

Now Max was lying in his old bed, staring up at the whitewashed ceiling of his boyhood room, and letting the whole evening pass through his mind, as if it was a piece of film. His stepfather had nearly had a coronary over dinner, and it was all Max's fault.

Poor John, he just couldn't see it, that was all. And not just 'it' – he couldn't see anything. He couldn't see why Max thought bullfighting was cruel, or hare coursing, and worst of all – and it was here that John nearly keeled over with suppressed indignation – he couldn't see why nuclear weapons were wrong. Just couldn't see why Max wanted to join an anti-nuclear weapons organisation, or why the horrific results of dropping the bomb on Hiroshima just had to lead to pacifism. For heaven's sake he couldn't even see why pacifism was right.

There was no arguing with the man, and no centre of real discussion. John had just kept shaking his head, wordlessly, as if he couldn't believe that Max was in his house, seated at his table, eating his food and expressing such views.

If only John would just try to understand, but like so many of the middle-aged he didn't seem to want to even attempt to see another point of view. He clung to his daily newspaper, and its views, as if it were a cliff, and he a barnacle.

'I am actually trying to see your point of view, John,' Max had told him, as gently as he could. 'Really I am, I just can't follow it. I can't follow why making more and more nuclear weapons is going to bring about a peaceful world.'

'If you are strong, you keep the peace. If you are weak, you are attacked. Look at what happened in the last war. Europe collapsed because we were weak.'

'I know, that's what Granddad used to say, but he also said that it was to the shame of the Conservative party that they had sat about not listening to the warnings. He said Cynthia Asquith was warning Churchill as long ago as the nineteen twenties about the rise of the Nazis, but that no one would pay attention to her. Because she was a woman. Granddad used to say that if you are strong in a non-nuclear way, if you are prosperous and trade well, you won't need to drop bombs on people. You can buy them with trade agreements, share your prosperity, and that way everyone stops hating each other. He also used to say that it would be better if people fought each other on the sports field, in games, took out their aggression that way.'

'Your grandfather was a very clever man, I'm

sure.' John had breathed in and out, very slowly. He was a mild-mannered man, but if his beliefs were in any way criticised he became cold and unapproachable. 'Shall I get the pudding, darling?'

While he was out of the room Mattie had stared down at her place, as if it was the only thing of which she could be quite sure.

'Sorry, Mum. I really didn't want to upset John. I keep thinking he's Granddad,' Max whispered.

Mattie stared grimly down the table, this time to Max.

'Well, don't.'

The following morning, to Mattie's consternation, Max decided to go to church. It was the last thing she really wanted, all her friends staring at Max's long hair – it came down a good eighth of an inch over the top of his ears – not to mention his sideboards. Very well his sideboards were not long, but even so the short back and sides 'army haircuts are best' brigade would curl up when they saw him, thinking that she'd brought some sort of long-haired hippy to worship.

'Do you really want to come?' she found herself asking anxiously. 'Wouldn't you rather go golfing, or something?'

Max shook his head, and then he smiled and touched her on the arm. 'It's all right, Mum, I've brought a suit down. And I'll wear a tie.'

Mattie and Max walked to church together, their heads bent against the icy wind. It was just like when he was a little boy, and Mattie, despite not being married, still went on attending church with her father and young son, in defiance of the disapproval of her non-marital state that she knew was rife in the village.

'I always liked coming to church with you when I was little, snuggling up to you and Granddad to keep warm, and then going to put flowers on the graves and all that.'

Mattie relaxed at last. Of course, that was why he'd really wanted to come to church, not to worship so much as to touch the past. By accompanying her to church Max was putting out his hand, as he had put out his hand for the flowers that he'd brought down to place on his grandfather's grave, and taking them from the water in the scullery had carefully wrapped them around with string and ribbon again.

'I miss Granddad, a lot.'

Mattie nodded, staring down at the gravestone. She did too, but she was more reconciled to his going than perhaps Max was. Lionel had been Max's father figure, his counsellor, his best friend in a way that John could never be, however kind.

'Grandfathers are very special,' she said simply.

After that everything seemed to get better, and Max drove back to town resolved never to talk to his stepfather about anything real, because it made for such trouble with his mother. He would keep to trivial things, like golf and sailing. Not that they were trivial, but they were, or at least he hoped they were, a great deal safer. But it was his mother's voice as they walked back to the house after church that stayed in Max's head for the next few weeks. Whenever he felt a bit low he would hear Mattie's voice saying, 'Your granddad was very proud of you, Max. Never forget that.'

On Monday evening an emergency meeting was called of what was now called SABEX – an acronym for Save Bexham, which Loopy thought a bit pompous, but everyone else thought was clever. Not that it mattered now that everyone realised that their whole way of life was being seriously threatened by the development plans of the company owned by Martin Markham, otherwise known as The Beast.

'Has anyone noticed?' Loopy wondered idly as she took her seat next to Mattie on one side and Hugh on the other. 'Has anyone noticed The Beast has no real back to his head? *I* think he's an alien, I do.'

'What he's planning to do to Bexham's certainly alien,' Rusty said, turning round from the row in front where she was sitting. 'What I don't understand is how it has all got this far. It seems incredible. I don't know how the authorities could even contemplate these plans.'

'Money. The sort that slips easily into back pockets.' Hugh leaned across Loopy to speak to Rusty. 'You know he's been letting it be known that anyone who stands in his way will regret it? He's been canvassing a lot of the people in the Crown and the Three Feathers.'

'They're hardly locals to us, surely?' Loopy wondered. 'What possible good could that do?'

'To get as much support on his side as possible,' Rusty put in. 'The planners take notice of such things, even if it's marginal. He's promised a lot of employment in the area, if he gets his permissions. You can imagine the work it'll bring. A new marina where the Yacht Club is, redeveloping the Three Tuns into some great big fancy hotel, a housing development on the south shore of the estuary – heck, the place will be swarming with constructors, and constructors need labour.'

'You should know, Rusty dear,' Hugh said. 'Peter's developed enough sites in your time.'

'But none that weren't garages already,' Rusty said in his defence. 'It's not as if Peter's been putting up garages and showrooms where there weren't such things already.'

'Hugh didn't mean that, Rusty,' Loopy interposed. 'He meant, like us all, he's glad to have you both on side with your experience, Peter with his car businesses and you with your shops. If anyone knows about planners and their ways and means then you two must do.'

'Yes, I know. Peter's flying home tomorrow.'

Rusty tried to look happy about this, when in actual fact a part of her dreaded sharing her life again. She had been independent for too long, and she knew it. On the other hand, it might well be that

426

once Peter was home she would find that she'd been lonely for too long.

'Ladies and gentlemen? If I may have your attention, please?' Waldo called, from his position on the dais at the end of the village hall where he stood behind a green-baize-covered table in the company of those actually on the official committee. 'Ladies and gentlemen, I shall try to be brief,' he continued. 'We are at a crucial stage of the proceedings and the omens are not good. We have received unconfirmed reports that Markham has redrawn his plans after the initial refusal, and the planning officer in charge of the submissions is now going to recommend acceptance. If this is so, then we will have to take our case to appeal. Markham has already let it be known that come what may he will get his permissions to develop Bexham, even if it means going to the High Court. If he did, then we would have to find yet more money to employ the best Silk to oppose him. As you know there is very little we can do about it once permission is granted.'

Waldo paused, took a drink of water and then a deep breath.

'From the first, it seemed the only way we were ever going to succeed against this threat to Bexham was prepare as good a case as possible to show why this development would prove to be such a disaster for the area. To do so wasn't cheap certainly, but I think the money that was so generously donated by so many of you has been well spent, and it certainly helped to get the plans thrown out first time round. But I don't think there's very much more we can now say – at least not on paper. We've argued every argument there is to be argued, and we've had them expressed by all the best people – to whom we owe our gratitude.'

Waldo waited for the round of applause to die down before continuing.

'So we have to ask ourselves what else is there we can do? Nothing, alas – short of buying up Bexham.'

Everyone in the crowded room who had come to the meeting still with some hope intact now sat forward to stare at Waldo in surprise, while others looked helplessly from neighbour to neighbour, exchanging looks of bewilderment and disappointment until Waldo was forced to drop his gavel on its base to call the meeting back to order.

'To make myself plain.' Waldo paused, looking round. 'I know I'm not a true Bexhamite and never will be, alas – that I'm an interloper, someone who's only lived here for twenty years, so who am I to say? But I do say and I do believe – I believe the only way we save Bexham is to *buy* Bexham. And when we have done that – when *we* have bought what Mr Markham wants – we shall then refuse to sell Mr Markham the sites on which he wants to build his version of the dark Satanic mills.'

The mixture of sounds in the hall now changed. It changed from apprehension and concern to hope.

Hugh was among the first to hold his hand up.

'This is all very fine and large, Mr Chairman,' he said, getting slowly to his feet, one hand steadying himself on the back of the chair in front of him. 'But how do we buy Bexham when Markham already has most of his deals in place? Secondly, even if we manage to shake him down and somehow get these deals rescinded, where's the money going to come from? We're looking at the Three Tuns, the Yacht Club with its ancillary buildings and mooring rights, and four acres of land that is or was being offered for sale with building consent. Surely Mr Markham isn't the sort of entrepreneur who would go into a project of this scale without first securing the properties he needs?'

The faces all turned from Hugh back to Waldo.

Waldo cleared his throat, and nodded. 'That would seem to be the case, I will agree. I mean, if it were me, I wouldn't go out for a drive unless I had a car, but then people do business in some very funny ways – and nowadays some very funny people do business, as we know. We owe Mr Jeremy Michaels from Michaels, Michaels and Lamont here for the information I'm about to impart to you.' Waldo indicated the small, rotund and shiny-faced man sitting on his left before continuing. 'Should Mr Michaels ever think of forsaking the Law, he would make an extremely good detective. It appears from his "researches" that everything that should be in place is . . . not quite. As we all know, the lease on the Three Tuns runs out in six months' time, and, as we also all know, our much-treasured landlord, Mr Richards, has so far failed to obtain a renewal. But then neither has anyone else. There are some interesting little refinements in the lease with which – it appears – the new applicant has not yet found fit to agree. I won't stipulate what these are at the moment – all I can say is that the deal is by no means signed and sealed. As for the Yacht Club, we understand that although a price is in place not all the signatories have agreed to Mr Markham's proposition. But in spite of a great deal of pressure's being brought to bear on the board by the Club's new chairman, who just happens to share business interests with the purchaser—'

At this a sound came from the audience, a sound made of part disbelief and part shock, but it was a sound that grew into something more, as everyone began to talk at once, requiring Waldo once again to tap his gavel.

'Despite the new chairman's trying to force the resignations of three of the standing directors so that he could railroad the deal through, the ink is a long way from dry on the contract. As for the acreage of Bishops Fields – again this is unfinished business. The vendors have agreed, Markham has agreed, the contracts have been drawn up and duly presented to the purchaser, but – so far – these have not been signed either, no deposit paid.

'So it may be that Markham is hedging his bets. Perhaps he is waiting until the last moment to part with his company's money – or perhaps, ladies and gentlemen – perhaps, as rumour has it, his company is suffering from a shortage of cash. If this is the case, while far from saying that Markham is not a genuine threat because he is not a genuine buyer, I think we must appreciate his business methods.

'He offers, he agrees, he waits for his permissions – and once they are granted he pays, but *not* before. We know he pays because there are Markham projects all along this beautiful coastline, many of which have recently been completed, alas. But what we do see here is a chink of light – our man has left the door open, and if possible the foot that should be in it must be ours.'

'Fine,' Rusty agreed, having been granted the floor. 'Excellent sentiments, Mr Chairman. But as Hugh Tate has just pointed out, where is the where-withal? We are talking quite a sum of money here, because in order to thwart Markham in advance of any permissions we would have to put in higher bids than his, and quite frankly I can't see how we could even afford to match his bid on one of these properties, let alone three.'

Rusty sat down to disappointed applause, after which all eyes turned back to Waldo. But the magician wasn't quite ready yet to perform any further tricks. Instead he lifted up a pile of typed sheets from the table and nodding to a young boy who was standing ready to help gave them to him to hand round.

'You'll find a few facts and figures here,' he told the audience. 'How much money we have been able to raise so far, how much we could call in from our benefactors if needs be, and lastly how much I think we should need to pull this off. Once you have read through everything, you may recommend we take for our motto – *Never Say Die*.'

Chapter Eleven

Despite his commitment to saving his adopted village, Waldo was feeling more than restless, he was feeling sad – missing his bridge games with old Lionel, missing his lunches with Loopy. In fact, he felt he was missing almost everything. Outwardly of course he remained quite the same. He went to committee meetings for the SABEX Fund, he was looked after by the goodly Maria and her husband. He sat in front of the fire and stared into it, or stared up at Meggie's portrait and reminisced to himself, recalling the fine times they'd had together, but nothing helped to fill the void that he now knew was central to his life. He was empty, and he knew it. He was lost for how to go on from day to day. Everything he did, he did mechanically, because that's what you do when you're lonely. Everything he once thought mattered now seemed not to matter in the least. Everything he had ever loved seemed to have gone.

Above all there was no gaiety left in his life. No

ne calling round unexpectedly, or phoning out of the blue just out of passing interest, wanting to talk about something inconsequential, wanting to share a joke, wanting to tell him something that he didn't know. Nothing like that had happened to him since his dinner with Judy, since those few hours when a brighter future had seemed to open up only for the curtain to fall once again. His world was closing down.

So when the telephone rang in his drawing room one Saturday evening and it was Loopy asking him round for drinks and Sunday lunch, Waldo felt as if his life had been transformed.

He tried not to sound excited about going to Shelborne, because to sound excited might be to turn himself into something pathetic, someone to be pitied. Not that he hadn't been to Shelborne recently for various fund-raising events, but this was different. Tomorrow he was going to have lunch with Loopy alone, because Hugh was away on business with John, and she said that she was lonely, and needed company.

And that was so typically Loopy. Where Waldo avoided publicly admitting that he was in just such a state, Loopy, in her still attractively husky voice, said it.

She opened the front door herself.

'Oh, good, you're quite on time, so that means I won't be in a state of delayed excitement before we mix the first of many martinis.'

Waldo and Loopy alone could be not only truthful, but very much themselves. Loopy loved to remind Waldo that whether or not they liked to admit it they were both still Americans living abroad. Bexham didn't feel like abroad, but it was. Although on a good day it could be quite like Cape Cod.

'Shall I?'

Waldo stood by the newly installed bar in the old conservatory, his hands raised over, but not touching, the sacred instruments for martini making. There the ice box with the cubes, there the cut glass cocktail jug with accompanying long silver spoon, and next to it the small pieces of lemon on a plate, and beside the plate the perfectly shaped glasses.

'Shall you? Waldo, if you don't,' Loopy stated, lighting a Menthol cigarette, 'I personally will not speak to you again, ever.'

The gin was poured over the ice cubes into the bottom of the cut glass jug, and over the gin was passed a few drops, certainly not more than a teaspoon, of martini. They both waited, holding their breath. It was after all a sacred ceremony. Next came the stirring – Waldo did not shake, he stirred, believing that shaking 'bruised' the gin. Finally the curl of lemon placed in the centre of the drink.

Loopy watched every moment of the martini's being built, thinking as she did what pleasure there was in simple things. If you made a martini in a hurried fashion, you broke the sacred trust between enjoyment and consumption. It was necessary, if you were not to dismiss life, that everything enjoyable must be done in an unhurried fashion.

'Perfection.'

They both sat down together in front of the fire.

'Gwen is making lunch today,' Loopy said in a low voice. 'Please, therefore, don't expect too much, will you? Heaven only knows I've tried to teach her how to make our kind of food, but the moment my back's turned she boils everything within an inch of its life and forgets to add salt. The pudding should be good – I made that – and at least she can't boil it.'

'I'm sure it will be sensational. It smelt sensational.'

'Roast pork, apple sauce, roast potatoes done in that blackened way that she so favours, sage and onion stuffing, and a rich brown gravy. Very English.'

'And very delicious, my mouth is watering already. I have had nothing put paella all week, and there is a limit to how much paella even I can eat. Maria overdoses me on it. It's all the shellfish around here, she can never stop thanking God for Bexham and its fish, alas.'

Loopy smiled, suddenly and brilliantly.

'Oh, hark at us, Waldo. We're like a couple of old maids discussing our servants and their funny ways. Next thing we'll be complaining about the manners of people nowadays.'

'Never!'

They both laughed, and sipped their martinis.

Waldo knew that Loopy could be counted on not to say 'How's things?' or 'Everything going along OK?' or any of that sort of nonsense. He knew that she could be counted on to know just what the state of play of all her friends might be, and to shut up about it. She was too wise to go to people with their problems, only waiting until they came to her with them. Not that she was above prompting them to come and see her for what she called 'a mild jolly', or above listening when it was needed. In other words, Waldo knew that he hadn't been asked round for nothing. He had been asked to Shelborne, to have lunch alone with Loopy, so that he could talk if he wanted to, or not.

He had actually resolved not to say anything about his life, but once they were embarked on their second martini he found he'd forgotten his resolution.

'This is so nice, the fire, the drinks, the drinks – and the, er, drinks! No, but most of all the conversation. I only wish I could meet a woman like you, Loopy.'

Loopy looked startled.

'Come, come, Mr Astley, this is going too far! And Hugh would certainly warn you off women like me, I promise you. He finds me difficult, temperamental, and inclined to be self-absorbed, or so he told me the other day.' She laughed appreciatively. 'I told him he was right, on every count.'

'Still jealous of your painting, eh?'

'No, not jealous, but he does find it gets in his way. And you really can't blame him. It's that faraway look that comes into my eyes when I'm embarked on a canvas. It's terribly annoying to anyone remotely civilised, and let's face it, Hugh is civilised. He does like to think that when he talks, someone is listening. It's just a fact. He says he'd do better living with Gwen – at least she likes listening to the same radio programmes!'

Waldo smiled. He knew that Loopy was deflecting from the fact that he was hoping, so hoping, to end his loneliness somewhere, with someone.

'I thought I might have fallen in love you know, a few weeks ago,' he said suddenly, out of the blue, not caring that she might have guessed with whom.

Loopy fell silent for a second, lighting another cigarette, and slowly breathing in before replying.

'Falling in love can be quite painful, I always think. Sometimes one just doesn't want it to happen, but it does. Like the flu, or measles, but then it goes away again, and one is quite relieved, don't you think?'

'This won't go away again. I keep trying to make it, but it just won't. It hangs around, like a double dose of the flu, and it's making me very, very miserable.'

'That's not Waldo-like.'

'No, it isn't. I'm glad you said that, by the way. But, no, I don't think it is. So what do you think I can do about it?'

Loopy stood up. She had always found that two martinis were dangerous, most particularly when it came to people confessing to emotions to which they might not have admitted when drinking water.

'A friend of mine once told me that when she was seventeen her father asked her into the library to tell her the facts of life. When it came to it, his fact of life was "Never forget, dear, you're just not the same girl after two dry martinis."' As Waldo laughed Loopy quickly stubbed out her hardly smoked cigarette. 'Therefore, dear, let us lunch first, and exchange intimate confidences second. Personally I think falling in love is nothing but a pain. I mean do you see where it got me? Three pregnancies and Hugh – not to mention Gwen, glowering at me from the door—' she added, turning as Gwen, who was becoming more eccentric by the minute, appeared in the sitting room doorway, pinny spread about her now ample figure, in her hand the luncheon bell out of which no sound was coming.

'It's lunch, Mrs Tate,' she said, above the sound of the bell now being shaken loudly and silently in her own ear. 'Roast pork and all the trimmings, but

439

I won't take responsibility for the pudding, and hope that you told Mr Astley as much?'

'Of course, Gwen. I wouldn't want you blamed for making it, not in any way.'

Loopy turned back to Hugh and raised her eyes to heaven.

Later, after a magnificent lunch, they sat back down in front of the fire and returned to the subject of the day.

'You see,' Loopy explained, 'it's not much fun, being in love I mean. It's all agony, with or without the loved one, that's why one has to get married, to stop the rot. I think you feel you need a wife, and I think you may be right.'

They both laughed. It was that serious.

'This is a very fine car,' Atlanta Hackett remarked to Walter, having accompanied him to the top of the steps where he had left his Riley. 'This is a very fine car altogether.'

'Hardly,' Walter smiled. 'It's only a Riley.'

'Only a Riley, do you hear,' the Widow repeated as she walked round the shiny dark green vehicle. 'She's very fine all the same. And just the thing.'

'Just the thing for what, Mrs Hackett?'

'Atlanta, you daft man,' the Widow scolded him. 'Didn't we agree last night on the intimate?'

'I remember very little about most of last night,' Walter admitted. 'And I've been in the Navy.'

'Ah the Navy's full of boys when it comes to

enjoyin' themselves. 'Tis being in Cork that learns you. Now you have your directions – and don't go stopping to ask, for the nearer you get, the more wrong they'll send ye. 'Tis the absolute way of the world when you're travelling, and no denying it.'

Despite his sizeable hangover, Walter had prepared the ground for his journey thoroughly. At breakfast he drew himself a detailed route map, even going to the trouble of noting grid references and compass bearings to pinpoint a house called Culoheen near a lake by the name of Cumeenduff which lay to the west of Knocknabreeda Hill, which was where he was headed.

It was a clear morning as he drove away, the mists that had been hanging now dispersed by a fresh sea breeze that brought some rain as he passed through the town of Kenmare before bearing northwest into Kerry and the lee of a range of mountains known as Macgillicuddy's Reeks. The countryside was fearsome, with rough-hewn hills and rough mountains rising behind blue-mist-shrouded lakes and bogs, serpentine roads twisting up rock-strewn mountain passes only to zigzag down the other side, past stone memorials of fallen soldiers and the occasional huge crucifix immortalising martyrs, into valleys watered by teeming rivers, wild high waterfalls that tumbled down granite rock faces or crystal clear springs that gushed down from the mountains along stony beds to tumble under the stone bridges that spanned the narrow winding roads.

His spirits lifted by the country through which he was driving, Walter tried to recall as much as he could of the conversation he had enjoyed with his hostess after a riotous dinner in the huge kitchen with several members of the Family who had returned from what they all jokingly called 'the fillums'.

'She has this sponsor now, do you see?' the Widow had stated.

'A man is keeping her, you mean?'

'Do you listen, not at all. Very grand he is too – the Lord of Tara, no less. He's sponsoring her to the tune of as much as he can afford which is not a lot since he's no rich man. But at any rate, it all started with Poor Puss.'

'A sick cat?'

'Ah, will you listen? Kim was out fishing one day and she came back with this injured dolphin – and let me tell you, the fish are all but sacred here, do you see. But didn't young Kim get us all to fill the old swimming pool with sea water? And didn't she put old Poor Puss as he got to be christened into it? And didn't he get better with her love and care? And wasn't he then returned to the seas, God bless her. Him too. Lordy was here or hereabouts when all this was happening and wasn't it the very thing. He's not a well man at all, God help him – but after the high old times with Poor Puss and the three-legged sheep after that and then the old blind owl, didn't he take such a shine to young Kim and her works that he shrugged off his sickness and was

442

lepping about the place like a five-year-old. So
that's where she is now, up on his land – at least a
part of it for he has bits and pieces here there and
everywhere. But that's where she is – up at one of
his old houses where with his money and her
energy – and some help from one or two others of
the Family – she's running this sort of sanctuary I
suppose you'd have to call it. And that's where
you're to go to see her.'

And that was where Walter was now, in the wilds
of Kerry heading up a rough potholed drive over-
hung with wind-bent trees, past fields where
donkeys were happily grazing with sheep and a
few cattle, until he came to a large stone house
painted in pale yellow turning light green with
mildew, its roof half thatch and half tile, and
with half its large Georgian windows shuttered
against the weather – with good reason, too,
Walter observed as he drew up outside it, since
most of the shuttered windows were very short of
glass.

It had now begun to rain in earnest, so pulling
his old doeskin naval coat from the back of his car
Walter threw it on and went in search of some life.
There was no answer to his ring on the rusty old
bell hanging outside the front door and no sign of
light or life within. Finally, pulling the big collar
of his coat up around his neck, he bent his head
against the driving rain and hurried his way round
to the side of the house.

Here at last there was life, to judge from the lights that were shining in the gathering gloom as the November skies emptied on the land beneath and a marrow-cutting wind sprang up, whipping piles of old black leaves into the air and banging any half-open door or window to and fro. As he approached a line of stables and sheds two fox terriers suddenly appeared and made for his ankles, barking furiously. One managed to seize one of Walter's trouser legs before a bellow from the nearest stable called him off. The two dogs turned at once and ran back to their master.

A young man dressed as if it was a warm day stood regarding Walter, an old small briar pipe stuck upside down in his mouth. He was thin, tall, with a mop of straight white hair and bright pink albino eyes, dressed in a pair of faded jeans, an old-fashioned short-sleeved Aertex shirt and a sleeveless Fair Isle pullover.

'May I help you?' he called. 'Are you lost?'

'I'm looking for Kim Tate!' Walter replied, a hand over his eyes to shield them from the rain. 'This is Culoheen House, isn't it?'

'She's busy now! Sorry!' the young man replied. 'Who shall I say it is?'

Walter waited, wishing they had been able to get through on the telephone to warn Kim that he was coming. But thanks to the vagaries of both the Irish telephone system and the changeable weather, let alone the remoteness of Culoheen, the Widow had failed to make contact. Or – as Walter suddenly

444

thought – so she'd said, which was perhaps a different thing.

'Tell her . . .' Walter began, then hesitated. 'Tell her it's someone from England! Family!'

'I will so!' the young man replied with a nod, ignoring the pelting of the rain as he turned and wandered back inside the building. 'You'd best wait in the house!' he called back over one shoulder.

Hurrying back to the house with the wind and the rain at least behind him this time, Walter pushed his way in through the heavy front door that seemed to be held in place by only half its hinges and looked for a light switch. He found one adjacent to the door but it failed to ignite any electricity. In the gloom of the hall he stumbled against something, something which grunted and then scurried away. Walter promptly lit a match and peered into the gloom, just in time to see what looked like a badger's brush disappearing ahead of him into the room at the end.

Finding another switch, one that worked this time, lighting a clear glass low-voltage bulb directly above his head, Walter found himself the object of several pairs of curious but apparently unfrightened eyes. On top of a tallboy, held upright by a pile of books under its one missing leg, sat a barn owl, its talons gripping the edge of the ancient mahogany, its eyes wide open and unblinking. On the shelf below a cardboard box contained a nonchalantly sleeping hare, stretched out to the full

445

with one of its hind legs stiffened by a splint. A moment later a three-legged collie dog wandered out of a side room wagging its long tail in greeting. Walter returned the salutation with a pat to the dog's head as he headed for the room at the end of the hall.

The door was open, and led through to a flag-stoned ante-room which in turn led on to a large kitchen with a high vaulted roof, on the rafters of which sat a medley of birds, including a one-eyed raven which, disturbed by the light which Walter put on as he entered, shrieked a defiant warning before jumping off its perch to flop casually down on to the table below where it sat with its head on one side, balefully regarding the intruder with its one good eye. Thanks to a range of stoves and ovens not unlike those at Loughnalaire, in the centre of which glowed a fire fuelled with peat, the room was warm and welcoming, with its large scrubbed table surrounded by a collection of widely differing antique chairs, on the back of one of which perched some sort of bird of prey, possibly a kestrel, but obviously still too sick to make himself a dinner out of any of the small mammals housed in the huge kitchen.

Walter stared at the scene, shaking his head wearily as he realised that far from being a chimera the kitchen obviously was some sort of haven for sick and injured creatures, and he thought he knew just the person who might be responsible for the chaos.

After such a long journey he thought he might forgiven if he made himself a cup of tea, whr he duly did, having washed up a mug and dried r on his handkerchief. He dusted off one of the many chairs and sat himself down, only to find his legs knocking against something under the table. He bent down quickly to see who, or what, he had inadvertently kicked, only to set startled eyes on a small badger who promptly disappeared into a dresser cupboard. Walter bent down to the cupboard to find two tiny bright eyes staring at him.

'Don't worry, old thing, I won't let on,' Walter told him, straightening up.

Some time later the young man from the stables, but without fox terriers, reappeared, but looked startled when he saw Walter, already on his second cup of tea, at the head of the kitchen table offering an arm to the one-eyed raven, which gladly accepted the invitation.

'She can't see you now,' he said to Walter, helping himself to a raw carrot from a large bowl of fruit and vegetables that sat on the table. 'She said you're to wait. That is if you want to wait.'

'I'll wait,' Walter said. 'I'm in no hurry. There's tea in the pot if you want some. Or I can make some fresh.'

'Let's do that. I'll make a fresh brew.'

'I'm Walter, by the way,' Walter remarked, washing out a mug for the young man and rinsing out his own. 'And you'd be?'

Gabriel,' the young man returned. 'I'd be
Gabriel Ryan, and you'd be Kim's father.'

'That is correct. Will my daughter see me now?
I've come a long way.'

'I know that.' There followed a small silence.

'What I'm trying to say . . .'

'I know what you're trying to say, Mr Tate,'
Gabriel replied, turning his pink eyes to look at him
not unkindly. 'And what I'm saying is Kim has her
hands full and that's all I know.'

He sat at the table and poured himself a mug of
tea, spooning in two sugars, which he stirred with
another carrot selected from the bowl before
feeding the carrot to the raven.

'It's a soft old day, is it not?' he said. 'And have
you journeyed far today?'

'From Cork. From Loughnalaire.'

'Of course.' Gabriel nodded another couple of
times and sipped at his tea.

'Were you at Loughnalaire?'

'Of course.'

'Of course,' Walter agreed. 'Of course. And this
place . . .'

'The Widow will have told you about this place,
surely.'

'She told me about Kim's benefactor, but she
gave me no idea of what this place was like.'

'This is a grand place. This is a very grand place.
This is a very grand place indeed.'

'Are there many of you here? You seem to care
for a lot of animals, which can't be easy. So – so how

many of you work here? And are you all from – a
you all Family?'

Gabriel smiled for the first time, a long,
languorous smile that curled his small, childlike
mouth upwards into a delighted grin. Then he
laughed and shook his head.

'No, sir – no, Mr Tate, no – no, we don't work
here. No one works here. This is not work. We live
here – and there's only the three of us. Kim, myself
and the Dandy Man. And this isn't work. This isn't
work at all.'

'No,' Walter said thoughtfully, understanding
that, far from work, what happened here was
something entirely different. 'The Dandy Man
sounds intriguing.'

'Intriguing indeed.' Gabriel took another sip of
tea and fed a wizened grape to the raven. 'You'd be
right there. He thought he was Beau Brummell, do
you see. And he thought that for a good while.'

'Any particular reason?'

'Is there ever, I wonder? I've a notion it's not
something one chooses, but something that
chooses you, when you're in the state.'

'The state.'

'The state of mind that comes on you after a
disturbance, let's say. They call it – sometimes – the
balance of the mind, and I always have a feeling
that has an aptness about it. The balance of the
mind is a fine thing, and if it tilts, that is when
the state comes upon you. The Dandy Man had
a bad state. Very bad. He had three daughters,

449

. loved them all, and they all died on him.'

'It is wisely said that there's nothing worse than for a parent to bury a child.'

'I'd say that would be so, Mr Tate. It's a hard enough thing, I should say, to be a parent and to have the children, without having them to die on you.'

'Three girls.'

'Three girls, and didn't he love them all?'

Walter put his cup of tea down and reached inside his pocket for his cigarette case, finding himself in urgent need of a smoke. He offered one to Gabriel who looked at the case with his head on one side, as if considering whether or not to accept, before declining with a shake of his head.

'The Dandy Man was near dead, do you see?' Gabriel sighed with the recollection. 'Even the Widow was near despair, and there wasn't one of us who could ever remember the Widow anywhere near such desolation. Perhaps she had feelings for the Dandy Man, who can say? But she was driven to distraction when he stopped eating, and when he stopped drinking, and when he took to his bed. It was such a thing when he came round, it was such a thing, Mr Tate, we ceilidhed for a week I'd say.'

'You say he came round,' Walter said quietly, his cigarette now alight.

'Isn't that what he did? Isn't that what you do when you come out of the state? It's what I would say I felt when I was recovered. That I'd come round. It was the oddest thing with the Dandy Man, the very oddest.' Gabriel smiled his strange childlike smile again as distance came to his eyes with the memory. 'It was Poor Puss that did it I'd say – and some of the others would too. The Dandy Man saw it from his window, saw what was going on, and he says Poor Puss called to him – which was why he left his bed that day and got in the water with him. When Poor Puss was returned to the sea, Kim used to take her boat out with whoever was keen on it, and Poor Puss would appear and we'd all swim with him. The Dandy Man, too . . .'

Before he could go any further, the kitchen door opened and a small, slight man in his middle age appeared dressed in baggy thornproof trousers, a shapeless Aran polo neck sweater and large wellington boots, yet from the way he carried and presented himself he could have been wearing the best of suits from Savile Row and hand-made shoes from Lobb. He had, Walter observed, a pair of the saddest-looking eyes he had ever seen on anyone, and yet a moment later, when Gabriel introduced them to each other, his smile banished the tragic look in a second.

'Monsieur,' he said, presenting himself in the traditional manner of a French gentleman, heels together and with a nod of his head as he offered his hand.

'This is Kim's Da, Jean,' Gabriel said. 'Mr Tate, this is Jean Bouchet.'

'Monsieur,' the Dandy replied, with a different

inflexion now he knew who Walter was. 'You are to be congratulated. You have ze most remarkable daughtaire.'

After yet another cup of tea accompanied by a delicious bacon sandwich, the Dandy Man and Gabriel were about to return to the stables when a whirlwind blew into the kitchen. Kim's dramatic and noisy arrival seemed to surprise no one except Walter who found himself up on his feet the moment she burst through the door.

'Dandy?' she was calling. 'Gabriel! It's great! Listen! Wonderful news! He's come round! He's come round and I think he's through it!'

She had thrown her arms round Gabriel, hugging herself tight to him, and then around Jean without even a look in Walter's direction.

' 'Er ottaire,' Jean explained over Kim's shoulder. 'She fine 'im in a trap.'

Walter nodded, waiting to see if his daughter was going even to acknowledge his presence.

'Quickly!' she urged everyone. 'It really is fantastic. I really thought we'd lost him.'

As she reached the door she half turned and beckoned to Walter.

'Come on, Da, you don't want to miss this, really you don't.'

Walter would hardly have recognised Kim. It wasn't so much that she had changed as that she was so very different. Gone was the aggression and in its place was the confidence of a secure young

452

woman. Not that anyone would have been bowled over instantly by either her beauty or her appearance. She wore a pair of dark flannel men's trousers with big turn-ups and deep-looking pockets that were at the moment full of unseen objects, what seemed to be the regulation Aran knit sweater, this one a crew neck in a charcoal wool over a skinny black polo neck jersey, and heavy brown men's walking shoes, designed for hills and bogs rather than the pavements of a city. Her hair was pulled back from her face and held in place by a piece of farm string. Yet, it had to be said, she looked mesmerising, possibly due to her flawless skin and sparkling eyes, but most of all due to the warmth of her expression.

'It's real good to see you, Da,' Kim went on as she began to lead him briskly out of the kitchen and down the hall. 'But you have to come and see this. We found this otter in a blasted snare, wouldn't you know – and we was total sure he was dead. But he wasn't – just all but – then we get him back here and he's only half gone – and now I think we may have him back altogether, thanks to the wonderful work of Dandy here.' She turned to Jean who was following on and blew him a kiss.

Jean shrugged. 'I was a vet – once, before my head he blew up.'

'He's totally brilliant, Da,' Kim assured him, urging them all on. 'Just the best in the entire world.'

She led her father out of the front door and into

.he driveway on which a watery sun was shining apologetically in place of the fierce rainstorm that had been sent to all but drown the countryside. As they hurried across towards the stables and outhouses, Walter noticed they were being followed by a selection of the rest of Culoheen's residents. Obviously he was not the only one who was going to be privileged to see the recovering otter.

They were to eat dinner in the kitchen that Gabriel, Jean and Kim illuminated with a variety of oil lamps and candles, the need to conserve electricity being paramount.

'And besides,' Kim had laughed as she had lit another half-dozen candle stubs and fixed them to saucers with a knob of their own wax, ' 'tis a whole lot more flattering. And don't I need all the help I can get? Will you just look at me. What can you be thinking, Da. Your daughter's gone native on you.'

'Nonsense, you look well, that's all that matters.'

'And that has to be just the nicest thing to say.' Kim stopped and stared at him, her head on one side. 'And you don't, do you know that?'

Walter looked startled.

'No, you look to me as if you're badly in need of a drink!'

She pulled a bottle of John Jameson out of a cupboard, followed by three relatively clean glasses, and placed them on the table.

'You do the honours, Da. While I set the table and prepare the feast.'

Walter and the two men sat down together at the table, the whiskey soon making their conversation easier.

The room was still full of wildlife, either roosting, recuperating, or wandering at will in and out through a large flap specially cut in the back door. For some reason the raven had taken a special interest in their visitor from the first, and very shortly after had developed a special liking for him, either sitting beside Walter on the table or perching on his shoulder. He felt strangely honoured, while pretending not to notice.

Dinner was a stew, but a delicious one, served with fluffy potatoes and some of the carrots Gabriel was, it seemed, so happy to use as teaspoons. The talk was all animals, their ways and curiosities. Walter was content to listen, partly because he found himself wearier than he could have imagined, but also because he realised that the three seeming eccentrics with whom he was dining obviously knew so much about the nature of the animal life on which they doted. Not all their stories were happy ones, and it would take the hardest of hearts not to be moved by their accounts.

'So how long are you staying?' Kim asked him as he helped her wash up.

'A day or two if that's all right with you.'

'A day or two, so? Well, that's fine, you'll have enough time to make a nuisance of yourself, then.'

Walter smiled, his back to Kim. Far from being irritated by Kim's Irish accent, for some reason he found himself charmed by it, perhaps because it confirmed the change in her in a way that nothing else could.

'Just enough time for that,' he replied finally, putting the dishes up on an old wood draining rack. 'I've brought a few things.'

'If you're to stay, you'll stay as long as you want. There's enough room.'

'You can have an entire wing to yourself, if you don't mind sleeping without windows,' Gabriel told him.

'He means glass in the windows,' Kim laughed. 'But pay no attention – there's a choice of good dry rooms, though they're not the Ritz.'

'If I won't be in the way . . .'

'In the way? In the way?' Kim sighed. 'You'll not be allowed to be in the way at all! We need you for slave labour!'

Once all the animals who were being housed within the kitchen were bedded down, and a tour had been made of the wards of the makeshift animal hospital outside, Walter was heading for the stairs, overnight bag in one hand and candle in the other, when the near silence of the house was suddenly shattered by an enormously loud telephone bell, amplified so that it could be heard ringing from everywhere within the house as well as the immediate environs outside.

'That'll be her, don't you bet,' Kim said, finding the telephone under the clutter on the hall table. 'That'll be Atlanta, or my name is Pansy.'

'The telephone's back.'

'Since when was it ever out?' Kim replied. 'If the phone's out here, it's a national emergency. Here – it's bound to be for you, Da.'

Walter frowned in good-humoured bewilderment and took the phone. 'What makes you say that? Why should it be for me, Kim?'

Kim looked at her two friends and shook her head sadly.

'He doesn't yet know the Widow, boys,' she sighed. 'My poor da still has a bit to learn.'

She lifted the receiver and held it out to her father, without bothering to take the call. Walter blinked, put the receiver to his ear and said hello.

'Ah then ye've arrived then!' He heard the Widow's unmistakable tones. 'After that storm I was saying ye might have been washed out to Dingle Bay and beyond.'

'It's a nice night now, Atlanta. The rain's stopped, and the moon's out.'

'And what do you make of the place then?'

'I think – I think it's absolutely remarkable. Quite remarkable.'

'And that's good. That's very good. And what else do you think?'

Walter thought for a while, frowning as he looked at his daughter, her face lit by candlelight, her friends beside her, one with a raven perched on his shoulder, and the other the lugubrious-faced saint from France.

'I think I might have got it all wrong.'

'Ah, well isn't that just the ticket?' The Widow sighed in deep pleasure. 'Goodnight now.'

Chapter Twelve

It was Max's idea. It would never have occurred to Jenny, but she said she'd go, although only out of curiosity because she had never before seen inside a television studio. All he was suggesting was that he could get them both in to see The Bros recording their spot on *Top of the Pops*, and that was it. The bass guitarist wouldn't even be aware of their presence since they would be watching the performance from high up on the gantry that ran round the studio.

'I've sussed it all out,' Max told her. 'The floor manager on this play I'm doing at the Beeb used to work on *Top of the Pops* – in fact I think she did more than work in it, I think – in fact I know – she had an affair with the producer – and she can get us in through the gallery. It's not as if we're going to be on the floor with all the trogs, shaking our heads about and screaming. No one will know we're there.'

After sensing resistance he'd left it be for a while, still having a few days in hand. He said nothing of his plan to Tam. He had seen the look in Tam's eyes that night, and he had seen the pain. Nevertheless, Max could not resist trying to heal the wound. Not just because Jenny was his half-sister, but because he had always loved Tam like a brother.

Besides, he had other things on his mind. He wasn't always pre-occupied with the lighter side of life. The death of Che Guevara, which had saddened the hearts of boudoir revolutionaries everywhere, had certainly got to him, as had the growth of the anti-Vietnam war feeling in the US. He was still determinedly supporting the campaign for unilateral nuclear disarmament, despite the increasing withdrawal of the Labour Party. Perhaps because of this lack of sympathy he found himself increasingly attracted to the Workers Revolutionary Party, whose views were being readily disseminated within the profession by a number of leading actors.

As it happened Max's apparent indifference actually increased Jenny's interest in going to watch The Bros. She agreed to accept Max's invitation, but she also raised the possibility of having to audition on the day of the recording.

'Fine,' Max said. 'OK – great. Don't worry if you can't make it – it's not as if I've had to pay for the tickets. I shall be at the BBC that day anyway, so if you don't show, it doesn't matter. It won't be the end of the world. It'll just be your loss, that's all.'

'You're right – it won't be the end of the world.

It won't even be the beginning of one. Besides, I can see them on telly.'

'Sure. Not the same as seeing it live, though. I mean to say you actually saw The Bros live on their first British gig. Not bad, is it? They've got Julie Felix on as well – and Eddie and the Tramps. Just let me know the night before.'

Max was leaving for Television Centre when she caught up with him.

'I can come . . .'

'Oh good,' Max mouthed at her through his bacon sandwich, his car keys dangling from one finger as he sidled out of the front door.

He bumped into Tam almost as soon as he arrived, going to get a coffee from the snack bar between their two studios and spotting him ahead in the queue. They stood and talked for a while, eating their Club chocolate biscuits and sipping over-hot milky coffee from ribbed plastic cups.

'How is it?' Max asked. 'Is it as boring as our technical? It can't be. I'm in a long-running costume serial at the moment, playing a minor part who's always on, and in the heaviest costume. Oh boy, have I grown to hate tech runs as a result, all sweat and no fun.'

'It is boring.' Tam nodded. 'I mean really boring. I hate hanging about at the best of times, but hanging about and pretending to play while some guy hovers around shoving a steel beanpole up at some clanking great spotlights is not my idea of fun.'

461

'You're not going to mime? I thought you said you guys were really going to play.'

'Of course we're going to play – if they can cope with us.'

'It's just when you said *pretending to play* . . .'

'That's because we can't make a sound while they're doing all this technical stuff. Lighting, camera angles – you name it, they do it. Give me a stage show any day.'

'This isn't the first telly you've done, is it?'

'No wây,' Tam grinned. 'We were on Ed Sullivan the week before we flew over. Now *that* was cool.'

'Hey – this is going to be cool too, man!' Max exhorted. 'It had better be – or I'll throw BBC doughnuts at you from the gantry!'

During the afternoon, not being needed for half an hour, Max sneaked in to the *TOTPs* studio with the connivance of his friend the floor manager and hung around in the shadows at the side of the set just as The Bros were preparing to play for the first time. As soon as he heard the first crackle of Lonnie Dysart's snares and the snappy splash of his cymbals, the languid, deliberately idle practice licks on the electric guitars by Lee and Tam, and Brewster giving the director the first couple of lines of the song they were to sing in his odd, high tenor while sound tested for levels, Max thought he felt his hair begin to stand on end. Here was a group that was already legendary in the States, and reaching cult status in England, who were actually about to play live, and his childhood friend Tam

Sykes was a member of the band. Now that it was happening Max found he couldn't handle it. He thought he might pass out from excitement.

He heard the whole song through, the band being able to perform it with only one late interruption towards the end, when one of the cameras missed his shot and the group were asked to go back to the beginning of the last chorus. By now it was time for Max to return to work as well, so moving as quietly as possible he made his way back to his own studio where they were now ready to start the dress run for the half-hour drama in which he was appearing.

It took all his concentration to empty his mind of the great sounds he had just heard and apply himself to the part of the youngest son returning home to his estranged family to attend his father's funeral. By the time he had finished his first major scene, there was no doubt in Max's mind in which studio he would rather be, and with which particular group of people. He could hardly wait for his next chance to hear The Bros. By contrast the play and his part in it seemed suddenly mundane.

'I wasn't actually thinking of going home for Christmas as it happens,' Walter told Kim as they did their best to hold a rather wild and very woolly sheep while the Dandy Man attended to one of its feet, which had become badly infected. 'I was thinking of Christmas here – if you'll have me.'

Kim barely glanced across at him. 'Sure. Course.

But what about Ma? And Hubie? It wouldn't exactly be fair on them now, would it?'

'You can hardly leave this place and come to Bexham for Christmas.'

'Hardly!' Kim laughed, tossing some hair that had got loose back out of her eyes. 'Gay has to go home for a few days because his ma's not too good, and I could hardly leave Dandy Man here in charge. That wouldn't be on at all.'

'Hokay!' Jean announced, having finished with the animal's foot. 'We can 'ave him beck in 'is stibel now, please!'

Walter and Kim lifted the sheep down and, retaining a good hold of its thick coat, steered him out of the surgery and into the stable he was sharing with two other lame sheep.

'You're more than welcome to stay here for Christmas, Da,' Kim said as she bolted the door.

'I'll pay for the food, don't worry. I'll look after all that side of things. It's just – it's just I'd like to stay on here a bit longer – as long as I may in fact – and I thought Christmas together, you know? I thought it might be rather nice.'

'Sure.' Kim shrugged again, knowing that any decision would finally be her father's to make, and not hers. 'Long as it's OK with Ma and Hubie. You know . . .'

She stopped and gave a small sigh, looking out across the windswept landscape, fixing her errant hair while pulling a little wistful face.

'You know, I wouldn't a bit mind seeing my

brother as it happens,' she said. 'And Ma. I've sort of missed home at times.'

'You must have.' Walter nodded. 'But you have to make sacrifices for all this. It's worth it.'

'You really think like that? That it's an achievement?' Kim turned an anxious eye on her father.

'If this isn't an achievement, Kim, then I never sailed a sea – nor no man ever loved.'

There was a short pause while they remained looking at each other, broken by Kim clapping her hands once in delight.

'Hey!' she laughed. 'You're getting the gift of the gab, Da!'

Walter laughed, took his pipe out of his pocket and began to fill it as he wandered after Kim back towards the surgery.

'So look,' he called to her. 'If you want to see your brother and your mother, and since I do too, why not all of us have Christmas here? Might be quite fun.'

'Quite fun?' Kim had stopped in amazement and turned back to look at him once more. 'Great *fun*? What are you saying? It'd be truly enormous. No other word for it.'

Jenny had been abandoned at the eleventh hour by Max who, having got his timings wrong, found himself called to his own tech run at the same time as The Bros were being called into action.

'My fault entirely!' Max had confessed, as he had guided Jenny up to her permitted position on a section of a steel gallery that ran right round the studio walls above the battery of huge lights that lit the set below, positioning her at the perfect spot bang in front of the rostrum on which the band were to perform. 'Time sheets are always in those wretched military hours, and I'm always getting them wrong. After the show's over wait for me in my dressing room. OK?'

With a wave he had left her and clattered back down the two flights of steel stairs before disappearing into the crowd of people already flocking on to the floor of the studio below. But he hadn't left her alone – there were several other fans and interested spectators lining the gantry as the floor manager and his assistants began to bring some order to what a moment ago had seemed to be chaos on the floor below. Jenny leaned forward and looked down, her hands gripping the rail in front for safety, as the musical guests took their place to perform the first number. A big bearded man in a checked shirt had already been introduced as the presenter to much screaming, shrieking and whistling from the fans on the floor. He now stood by, microphone in hand, and after half a minute of enforced silence, the last five seconds being visibly counted on the fingers of the floor manager's hand, that week's edition of *Top of the Pops* was under way.

Walter put the telephone down in the hall of Culoheen House, relit his pipe and walked back to the living room, which over the last few days whenever he had found himself superfluous to needs he had set about making a little more ship-shape.

On a fine winter's day he had driven around the Upper Lake and along the east side of Lough Leane and down into Killarney to collect what he needed for repairs, to augment the store cupboard and to place an order for what he had worked out in detail would be required to feed, drink and entertain the house party at Culoheen, now that both Judy and Hubert had leaped at the idea of having an Irish Christmas.

So far he had concentrated most of his efforts on trying to reglaze the windows. There was little he could do about the incipient damp, other than sweeping as many of the chimneys that should be in use with a set of brushes he had found in one of the outhouses and lighting as many fires in as many of the rooms that were to be occupied as was possible. In front of roaring wood fires he aired mattresses, cushions, chairs and blankets, and on yet another trip into town he purchased fresh linen and a dozen new pillows for the beds.

On exploring the attics he found several sets of once rather fine curtains wrapped up in brown paper and placed in sea trunks. They were filthy and full of dust, as well as moth-eaten in places, but they were good curtains, properly lined and inter-lined so that once they were brushed, aired and cleaned they would not only help to keep out the winds that whistled through the living room and the main bedrooms in rough weather, but also help add warmth to the eye as well as the body. Jean, Gabriel and Kim, all delighted with Walter's transformations and discoveries, couldn't wait to lend a hand with whacking the dirt out of them with old-fashioned beaters before hanging them at the windows of the rooms that required them. Finally, exhausted and half choked with dust, they downed tools and sat in the kitchen, quenching their thirst with several bottles of Guinness Extra Stout that Walter had thoughtfully provided.

'This is great gas,' Kim announced. 'I votes we install my da as resident housekeeper.'

'Here, here,' Gabriel agreed, raising his black bottle of beer.

'*Absolument*,' Jean echoed. 'Although I rarzer 'as my eyes on 'im as my assistant.'

'Here,' Walter said to Kim when they were alone, the other two men having taken themselves off to enjoy a shave and a good hot bath now Walter had conquered the water-heating system. He handed her a small half-folded piece of paper. 'It's not a Christmas present in advance. It's just simply a present.'

Kim, who was busy letting down her long dark hair from the constriction of its bands, prior to washing it when it was her turn for a bath, took the piece of paper, with a look of curiosity at her father.

'Ta,' she said. 'What is it?'

'I told you, Kim. A present.'

468

'Ta again.' Kim laughed, then stopped as she unfolded the piece of paper. 'Jeez. Jeez, Da – *five hundred quid*?'

'I don't see why old Lordy should be your only benefactor,' Walter replied. 'I think you're doing wonders here – all of you.'

'Jeez, Da.' Kim shook her head. 'You are a right whiz and that's for certain.'

The Bros played their hit single 'The Tide's Comin' In', Brewster's fine, sweet, high tenor voice cruising the melody line over the forward sweeping beat of Lonnie's gentle drumming and the surging beat of Lee's and Tam's guitars. The kids on the floor were doing their half best to stifle their squeals and sighs as the number progressed, and even Jenny standing high above the band found herself held by the slowly building and insistent rhythm and the atmosphere of land, sea and sky the song was creating. Most of all she found herself watching the neat, elegant figure of the bass guitarist, standing swaying to the beat as he laid down his line, along with Lonnie to the left of him driving the band along its musical road, insisting on the beat, changing the harmonic lines and increasing the pulse and thrust just at the right moments. At one moment he looked up and it seemed to Jenny he was looking straight up at her, particularly since he suddenly smiled, but then as he resumed looking down and back at his left hand she realised that it simply could not be possible for him to have seen anyone, let alone her, through the massive battery of blinding lights that hung between them.

Yet he had actually looked up right at her and smiled.

She carried this picture away with her in her mind's eye as she made her way back down the gallery steps at the end of the recording while the studio slowly cleared. The Bros had long since vanished, somehow smuggled away somewhere through the screaming fans, without any doubt the hit of the night and as far as Jenny was concerned deservedly so. Like many people she was only too well aware that there were far too many pop groups about who were nothing more than cheats, bands of pretty and sometimes not so pretty lads collected together by unscrupulous managers who saw themselves getting rich quickly on the backs of bands who could barely mime to backing tracks laid down by a totally different set of musicians. So when a real group hit the scene, a band that could not only play and sing but also compose, the discovery of their sound, their style, could often be one of the moments in a musical life to treasure – and to Jenny's catholic ear, which took in and enjoyed all sorts of music, this was one of those moments.

Finding her way back through the green room, she was making her way down the narrow corridor that led to Max's dressing room as instructed when another dressing room door opened and she found herself once more face to face with Tam.

For a moment neither of them spoke.

'What a surprise,' Tam said, recovering his composure. 'Hi.'

'Hello,' Jenny said, looking suddenly down at the ground, all her insecurity returning with a rush.

'You look great.'

'Thanks,' Jenny muttered, still staring at her shoes.

'What are you doing at the Beeb? You here to see Max?'

'No.' Jenny looked up briefly then down again. 'No – no, I'm not here to see Max.'

'To play the piano or something? I mean – I don't know – it's just such a surprise.'

'She's here to see you,' a voice from behind Jenny announced. 'Or rather more precisely to see The Bros.'

Jenny turned quickly in relief. 'Max. How did it go?'

'Here to see – to see the band?' she heard Tam wondering, while Max smiled over her head. 'That's great. I mean fantastic. I mean that's great. Really. So what did you think?'

'She thought you were rubbish, Tam,' Max said, straight-faced. 'Absolute garbage. It's just not her kind of thing.'

'Oh.' Tam's face fell, because Max, being an actor, was good at teasing.

'I didn't at all,' Jenny said quickly, glancing at Tam to reassure him. 'That's not at all what I thought.'

'OK. OK – so what did you think? Please tell me, Jenny. I'd really like to know.'

Jenny paused.

'I thought you were terrific. Amazing, in fact,' she said finally.

'Really?' Tam was looking at her uncertainly, while at the same time thinking that he really shouldn't be minding so much. 'Did you really?' he asked again, sounding lame, even to himself, and quickly taking a drink of water from a nearby carafe.

'Yes. Yes, really.'

'Oh. Good. Good.'

He turned away, wiping his palms down the sides of his trousers like a schoolboy. It was ridiculous but he had a sense of *déjà vu*, and at the same time one of unreality.

'I actually thought "wow, wow, wow". All the way through,' Jenny went on proudly.

'Wow is about right,' Max agreed. 'You are part of one pretty groovy band, man.'

'It isn't groovy, Max,' Jenny sighed. 'It isn't anything like that. It's a very good band – a terrific band. Musically – presentation – everything.'

'That really means a lot, especially coming from you.'

'It shouldn't – I'm just like anyone else. I just know what I like.'

'And you liked The Bros.'

'Yes, and I was wonderful too, thank you.' Max

sighed over-loudly. 'Absolutely brilliant in fact, darlings.'

'As a matter of fact you were pretty good, Max,' a tall man in a beard put in, as he ambled by. 'Coming up to the bar?'

'Try and stop me.' Max nodded at the departing figure. '*Mein Herr Direktor*. Better go and keep him sweet. You two coming?'

'I don't think so, Max,' Tam said carefully, not wanting to point out that the difference in their status now might lead to a few embarrassing scenes. 'The band are going back to the hotel. Think I'd better stick with them.'

'Jenny?' Max turned to his half-sister. 'You want to come and wet the whistle?'

'I don't think so, Max. You know me and crowds.'

'OK. You're a big girl now. They'll get you a taxi at Reception – if there isn't one waiting out front. Be good.'

With a cheery wave Max disappeared, leaving Tam and Jenny standing alone in the corridor. Their solitude wasn't long-lived, however, because suddenly a handful of young girl fans appeared screaming and waving autograph books, having somehow slipped through security, to judge by the expressions of the men in hot pursuit.

'Here,' Tam said, quickly opening his dressing room door to Jenny. 'Till they've got rid of them.'

Once they were inside, Tam bolted the door

and stood with his back to it, while Jenny stood a little sparely in the middle of the tiny space, clutching her handbag in front of her like a maiden aunt.

'Sorry about that.' Tam smiled, apologetic.

'It's not your fault – quite something, this amount of popularity, though, isn't it? I mean quite difficult to handle, I would have thought.'

'They can be quite scary. When we arrived at Heathrow, we all thought no one would have heard of us. But there were masses of them up on the roof, screaming and yelling and jumping about all over the place.'

'A bit like the Beatles.'

'I have the feeling that it doesn't matter who we are – if they find they're within screaming range of a pop group, out they go and scream.'

'Still, must be a bit – well, disconcerting, I suppose.'

'Frightening. Weird. Freaky. I suppose you wouldn't like to come out to dinner?' he added in a sudden rush. 'I mean – you know – we could go and have a quiet dinner. If you'd like, that is. If you don't, it doesn't matter.'

'Doesn't it?' It was Jenny's turn to pull a straight face.

'Yes of course it does!' Tam retorted, all at once annoyed with himself. 'I didn't mean that. I just meant . . . I was trying to be polite.'

'Don't be.'

*   *   *

Once in the taxi Tam realised he hadn't an idea as to where to take Jenny for dinner. The driver suggested a place that simply defined itself as Number 28.

Tam peered at its doors as they arrived.

'It looks a bit smart. And I'm not exactly wearing smart.'

'You look just fine, mate,' the driver assured him. 'And so does she.'

Jenny smiled and climbed out of the taxi.

'It looks just fine,' she told Tam. 'But maybe a bit quiet.' She put a hand up to her ear. 'No sounds of anyone screaming.'

'Mockery is the sincerest form of sarcasm.'

Tam paid off the cab, and they walked into the restaurant together feeling oddly, as Tam observed suddenly, as if they had been doing just that for as long as they could remember.

Afterwards it was difficult for them to remember just what it was that they'd ordered for dinner. Jenny remembered Tam had just begun to describe the Big U and R.J., complete with hilarious imitations, when the door of the restaurant burst open and four large men in wide-shouldered mackintoshes stepped over the threshold in swift succession. They didn't run in shouting. One of them simply kicked the door open with his foot, shattering the glass and splintering the frame, and then all four simply strolled in and stood looking round the half-full room.

Seconds later the three members of the trio

took themselves quietly off the bandstand and disappeared into the gentlemen's washrooms, thoughtfully locking the door behind them, as crockery and glass started to fly in every direction.

Tam, who was seated just behind the intruders' eyeline, nodded to Jenny who was watching him closely and pointed with one finger downwards, indicating that the safest place to be at that moment was on the floor and under the table, well out of sight. Jenny immediately slid herself down slowly off her chair and joined Tam in the darkened privacy underneath the heavily clothed table.

'What is going on . . .' Jenny began in a whisper, because even now, no matter how hard she tried, she still hated the sound of breaking glass. Tam put a finger to her lips, pressing his mouth to her ear.

'I think someone might owe them some money,' he whispered. 'Don't worry. They're not concerned with us.'

'They've a funny way of collecting it, haven't they?'

Together they sat holding each other's hands as tightly as they could while the incomers kept chanting the proprietor's name.

'Peter!' they called, in exaggeratedly tired cockney tones. 'Peter – Peter – Peter? Be a good boy and come on out, right? Come on out and see us right – and we'll be off, OK? You really don't want to have to redecorate the *whole* of this lovely joint, do you?'

Tam was dying to lift a corner of the cloth to [see] for himself exactly what was happening, but cho[se] discretion instead, listening out for mutte[red] instructions, voices murmuring assent and dissent, while he carefully placed a reassuring arm around Jenny.

'You're going to think that you've only got to see me and something terrible happens,' Tam said, sighing, as the general cheering from around the restaurant denoted that the gang had obviously left, at which they both started to laugh so much that, inevitably, it was some time before they eventually emerged from their hiding place.

'How are we doing, my old friend?' Waldo wondered as he settled down by the bar with Richards to have a warming whisky Mac, the December weather having suddenly turned from mild to bitter, the heavy frost of morning still unthawed, icicles still visible on the shiny black capstans, and frozen puddles of sleet still catching the unwary as they picked their way across the quays. 'How's the Save the Three Tuns appeal bottle doing?'

He tapped the enormous glass bottle that stood on the bar, happy to see it full to the very brim with silver coins and folded notes.

'We intend to count it tonight,' Richards replied. 'I doubt if one could get another sixpence in there.'

'Must be a few hundred quid, wouldn't you say?'

few hundred will not be enough to stop this ace going under, Waldo.'

'Added to this it might.'

Waldo produced a small leather-bound account book from his coat pocket, searched for the right page, then bent the stiff-spined ledger open and laid it on the bar. Richards put on his reading glasses slowly and carefully, as if about to consult a menu rather than a column of figures that might decide the fate of his beloved public house one way or the other.

'These are projections, are they, Waldo?'

'These are pledges, old pal. Some of them have coughed up already.'

'Who on earth is Wesley Atloda when he is at home? If indeed he has one?'

'I'd say a guy as generous as Mr Atloda can afford to have a couple of homes, if not more,' Waldo said a little hastily, turning over the page, only for Richards to turn it back again.

'Why should a total stranger want to pledge that kind of wampum?' Richards demanded. 'I for one have never heard of anyone so oddly named in these parts.'

'As it happens he's a very private guy – and that's just his nom de plume.'

'Well, well,' Richards sighed heavily. 'I would never have guessed – *Wesley*.'

Waldo glared at him and drained his drink. 'Let's have another. My shout.'

'No, I think it's mine, Wesley,' Richards said,

poker-faced, as he got up to go round behind tr
bar.

'Richards.' Waldo sighed, reaching for his cigars.
'It is my money, and I can do what I like with it.'

'You can't save the whole of Bexham, Wesley –
and you know it. That is beyond even your super-
human powers.' He gave Waldo the famous
Richards *eye* and sat down back next to him, both
their glasses recharged.

Waldo sighed again, and set his cigar to one side.

'I can't save Bexham single-handed, you're right,
old chum, but then thank God I don't have to – the
rest of these signatories are perfectly *pukka*, as you
would say, and they have genuinely plighted their
dibs.'

'How near to salvation are we, Waldo? Or how
far from it? Much as I appreciate your immense
generosity -- and believe me, I most certainly do.'

'Hell, I know that, old man.'

'The point is that even if we do save this place—'

'This place is as good as saved.'

'There'd be no point in this place going on being
this place if the rest of Bexham is no longer going
to go on being Bexham.'

Waldo nodded, picked up his unlit cigar and
stared at the end of it.

'I know what you mean, just as I know things
have to change. I just don't see why they should
change this way, and this suddenly.'

'*Que sera*, Waldo. *Que sera*.'

'In that case we might just as well roll over now.'

'It's probably me, Waldo – I'm getting old. The light's gone out of me.'

'This is the moment I wish I could show you a vision of the future, old pal. I wish I could take you forward to a time when you could see how and what this place is going to be – if someone doesn't take steps to try and prevent it.'

'You mean the new version of *It's A Wonderful Life*? *It's A Terrible Life*?'

'If you like.' Waldo smiled and lit his cigar, slowly and deliberately. 'It won't be long before there aren't inns like this any more, believe me,' he said, extinguishing his match with a wave. 'All sorts of things will come to bear on places like this – all sorts of influences, alternatives, laws, you just wait and see. These big brewery chains buying everything up and making them all uniform. The independent British pub is a statement on your way of life, and if we don't fight to keep them independent the future doesn't bear thinking about. The village pub is the hub of its social life – you can't imagine Bexham without this place.'

'You don't have to. This place would still be here.'

'But not like this, Richards, and you know it. The Beast wants to turn it into an hotel – somewhere to house all these tourists he's going to bring here. And with them will come gift shops and all those other tourist traps – and Bexham will no longer be Bexham. It will be dominated by one damn' great long marina, with an ugly second rate hotel standing right here, and a mass of little box houses springing up everywhere.'

'And you're going to stop it.'

'We all are, for God's sake! It's our duty to stop this kind of rail-roading tactic!'

'I suppose it doesn't occur to you that some people in Bexham might welcome that sort of change? A change that brings more trade and greater prosperity to an area that has after all relied on fishing for far too long?'

Waldo looked at his old friend, pondering on what he had just said. Perhaps there was some truth in it – perhaps he really was fighting to preserve a place that was in dire need of change. Perhaps he was simply indulging himself? Most of all, perhaps he was trying to preserve Bexham simply for himself, to keep it as it had been when he had met and fallen in love with Meggie?

Shortly afterwards he left the Three Tuns, walking slowly back to Cucklington House, deep in thought. He had already come to the conclusion that there was no point in spending Christmas at home. Better to be somewhere quite other, because Christmas could never be the same again once you lost the one person you loved. He would do the decent thing, and go away for Christmas, sitting quietly in the corner of some large, anonymous hotel, letting the world go by without him, carrying along with him the memory of the only Christmas he'd spent with Meggie, most especially since the only other person he had imagined he could spend his particular time with was on her way to Ireland, speeding through windswept glens and past cloud-topped mountains with her son in the back of the car singing happily at the top of his voice, the boot of the Riley packed with presents and her husband at the wheel, leading the singing.

Chapter Thirteen

Christmas passed, January blew by, February froze and March stormed in. A fortnight was all that was left to stump up the amounts still needed to buy Bishops Fields and the Yacht Club, Richards having already and finally more than happily accepted the gift of Mr Wesley Atloda, a gentleman whose real identity he promised Waldo most faithfully never to reveal, pretending instead that he was an old acquaintance from his days in service, a fellow servant of Portuguese extraction whose long-time master had finally fallen off the perch, leaving an unmentionable amount of money to his ever faithful butler, a man who had now, albeit somewhat late in life, become a keen entrepreneur and investor.

So with the Three Tuns saved from the jaws of Martin Markham, and the board of directors of the Yacht Club refusing to bow to the pressures of Markham's puppet chairman, and safe in the knowledge that the contract for Bishops Fields still remained to be agreed let alone signed, the committee were of one mind: all they needed now was another miracle.

For Waldo Christmas had been less of a miracle and more in the nature of a disaster. He had chosen the wrong hotel, a place exaggeratedly called the Grand when all that was grand about it was the hauteur of the staff. As soon as he could get a flight, he took himself off to Paris for the New Year, staying with friends instead in the *16ième arrondissement*, only to find when he arrived that the whole family had flu, to which he also succumbed. Struggling in poor shape back to England after a week spent in bed rather than in celebration, he found the weather so unwelcoming that he again took flight, this time to the Caribbean where an unfriendly hurricane took the roof off his hotel, and storms destroyed what was left of his holiday.

So when he finally returned to Bexham in the middle of February he could not have cared less about the freezing conditions and the foot of snow that lay covering the ground. It was only what he had come to expect. Seated alone at Cucklington House in front of a roaring log fire, comfortable in his own home once more, it could have been hoped that he would have at last found some kind of tranquillity, and yet he had not. All he felt, day after day, was loss and regret.

'What in God's name am I going to do with the rest of my life?' he wondered aloud, as he drew the drawing room curtains back and stood staring out at the frost already bleaching the grass. With the sky appearing to spread like some sort of sparkling dome above the still high water of the estuary, and the water below it reflecting its beauty, Bexham was surely, if not a heaven on earth, at the very least a haven.

The truth was that there was only one person who *would* have missed him if he left Bexham, and she was gone.

He turned and looked at the portrait of Meggie that hung over the fireplace. No sooner had they come together than she had been taken from him. He stood below the picture, looking up into eyes that always seemed to be looking into his, remembering what he had used to call her pilgrim soul, her easy, careless laugh, the rapture of her smile and the passion of her love.

And as he did he knew that he must move on. But when he woke in the morning, and felt the sudden light of the sun on his face as it sprang at him, spiralling up from the frosted garden below, it was as though he had felt the earth tip just slightly under his feet. It was as if it was spinning itself around towards spring, and as the world tilted, so too did the light change, and the very nature of that moment filled his heart with a rush of hope, just as it always did the moment he realised winter was over. The moment the faint thin light of February turned to the clearer, brighter light of March, bringing with it hares, high white scudding clouds, swaying daffodils, and the first sticky buds, and green came back to colour the dull grass, he once more believed in Eden.

Soon there would be swallows, cuckoos, house martins, the lazy drone of bees, the bright green leaves on the beeches and blossom everywhere, white, pink, red and yellow, covering trees and shrubs, ready to turn to fruit later as the skies filled with summer visitors and gardens echoed to bird-song once more, instead of the hollow cawing of the big black birds of winter.

He could not prevent his heart from lifting as he looked out on his fine garden, the pretty unspoiled harbour, the fishing boats setting out on the morning tide, the yachts bobbing on the deepwater moorings, seemingly as anxious for the arrival of spring as everyone awakening that fine March morning, and as his heart lifted Waldo saw that he had one more thing to accomplish before he left.

It was Tam who was the harbinger and finally the redeemer, arriving as he did down to see his parents, back in England once more with The Bros to appear in what he happily described as a 'junk heap of a film' about some band on the run.

'Another classic example of Swinging Sixties garbage,' he told his mother, who was overjoyed to see him, because she realised that despite his huge success somehow Tam hadn't allowed any of the things that were happening to change him. He was still Tam, but better.

486

He brought Jenny back down to Bexham with him, having attended Jenny's first lunchtime recital at the Wigmore Hall, through which she had sailed with satisfactory colours.

They'd duly celebrated that night, and, as they danced once more at Number 28, despite her relief that her first concert was behind her Jenny couldn't help wondering whether Tam was as nervous as she was about going back to Bexham. The mutual conclusion was that since it was something they would both have to face sooner or later, much better to face it together.

Even so, when Jenny and he eased themselves into the crowded saloon bar of the Three Tuns for a drink shortly after their arrival in Bexham and found that instead of being surrounded by the usual sea of happy faces they were marooned on an ocean of gloom, both of them thought that somehow the news of their new association had preceded them and this was their reception committee.

There would seem to be good reason to believe this since even the ever-optimistic Waldo was sitting grim-faced in his usual seat in the window at a table that he was sharing with Jenny's equally grim-faced grandparents, while her parents sat at the bar looking as if they were arranging each other's funerals.

No one noticed their entrance as the running conversation between the table in the window and the group round the bar continued.

'So it's a lot more serious than we thought?' Hugh Tate was saying. 'I don't in all honesty see what we can do now – the whole thing's out of our hands.'

'Perhaps we should all sit round a table and make a new plan?' Mattie suggested, her back to the door. 'We still have time.'

'*I* think Hugh and I should follow Waldo's fine example in selling Cucklington, and sell Shelborne.'

'Really, Loopy darling, what a whizzy idea,' Hugh said, looking at her through weary eyes. 'And where would that leave us? Can't see where that'll get us, not for the life of me.'

'There'll be no point in going on living here if we lose this one, Hugh, so to my way of thinking we might as well sell the house.'

Mattie, suddenly catching a look in John's eyes, turned round on her bar stool and following his gaze spotted Tam and Jenny still standing in the shadows by the door.

'Well, well, well,' she exclaimed, putting out her hands. 'Look who it is! Jenny darling!'

'Hallo, Mummy,' Jenny said carefully, coming forward to kiss her mother while her father continued to stare past her at the figure behind her, still standing in the doorway.

'Hallo, darling,' Mattie said, returning the kiss. 'And hallo . . . Tam.'

Tam stepped out of the shadows and looked round the bar with a fixed smile.

'Hi everyone,' he said to a suddenly silenced room. 'What can I get anyone? It must be my round, surely.'

Before he could even reach into his pocket for his wallet, it seemed as if the whole of Bexham, and most of Jenny's relations, had engulfed them.

'Jenny, darling,' Loopy said, getting up carefully and extending both her hands to her grand-daughter. 'I didn't know you were expected. No one told us.'

'It was a bit last minute, Grandma,' Jenny replied. 'Tam's doing this film with the band, and he didn't know whether or not they might be called.'

'Jenny, my dear.' Hugh beckoned Jenny over to his table, and she leaned over and kissed him, but his eyes were still fixed on Tam.

'Hallo, sir,' Tam said carefully. 'May I buy you a drink?' he added, glancing down at the older man's empty glass.

Hugh was about to shake his head.

'Of course you can, Tam,' Loopy put in quickly. 'Hugh'll have a whisky and soda – a lot of soda. And gins and tonics for Waldo and me, please.'

Hugh said nothing, only nodded and took his old silver cigarette case out of his pocket, extracting a Senior Service which he carefully tapped on the case before putting it in his mouth and lighting it.

Tam smiled, picked up some empty glasses and went to the bar to place his order.

'How are you, Tam?' Mattie asked. 'We hear

great things of the band – that you're going from strength to strength.'

'Their latest album went straight to number six in the States,' Jenny announced proudly as Tam turned to John Tate.

'Can I buy you a drink, sir?'

'Thank you, Tam.' John nodded, after a small pause. 'I'll have another pint if that's all right. I'm drinking the Pedigree.'

'Best draught in the South.'

There was a small silence, while John searched around for something to say.

'Oh, by the way, Tam. Congratulations on what you've done. Never thought little Bexham would throw up a famous pop star.'

'Very kind of you,' Tam replied modestly, 'but it's not really the case. I'm just the bass guitarist. Bass guitarists don't get to be stars.'

'Oh, come on, bro!' Flavia, who had burst through the bar room door in time to overhear her brother's modest statement, now hooted, throwing her arms round Tam's back and pretending to try to lift him from the floor. 'The Bros are only one of the biggest bands! And you're a *Bro*, bro! Whether you dig it or not!'

She let go of him, fished out a packet of cigarettes from her overcoat pocket and handed them round to anyone who wanted a smoke.

'What was all the earnest discussion, Dad?' Jenny wondered. 'As we came in everyone looked *so* serious.'

490

'It is pretty serious, Jenny. You know what been going on – with this awful man.'

'You mean this guy who's trying to buy up the place?' Tam asked, taking the tin tray that held the senior Tates' and Waldo's drinks from the barman. 'Is that still a big thing?'

'Getting bigger by the minute,' John Tate said, accepting his pint. 'Cheers.'

'Cheers,' Tam returned. 'I'll be back in a minute.'

He took the tray over to the table by the window, Loopy and Waldo toasting his health and continued success while Hugh nodded, pretending momentary deafness.

'Don't pay any attention to him, Tam, he'll come round,' Loopy murmured.

'Daddy was just saying,' Jenny said, putting Tam back in the picture. 'They've so nearly succeeded in saving Bexham, but because of—'

'The time factor, mostly,' John put in. 'The whole business has been so protracted – which was in our favour at first. I mean that's how *this* place was actually saved.'

'This place? The Three Tuns was going to be bought up?'

'Was very nearly bought up, Tam,' Mattie said. 'And guess who came to the rescue as usual? Our American knight on his great charger.'

'So what's gone wrong?' Tam asked, looking round at Waldo who mock-bowed back to him. 'I mean what else is at risk and why's it all too late?'

'The people who are selling Bishops Fields.

491

his plot with planning permission for a housing development – they got fed up with The Beast—'

'The man who's trying to buy Bexham,' Mattie explained. 'We call him The Beast.'

'Anyway, they got fed up with his prevarications, which we thought was good for us – only to find that when we tried to move in they'd jacked up the price.'

'They maintained that so much time had passed since The Beast's first offer that the value of the land had gone up that much, particularly with all the increased interest in Bexham,' Waldo explained, joining the group. 'So now there's a shortfall. And there's no good looking in this direction, because the cupboard is bare.'

'No one's looking at you, Waldo,' Mattie said. 'No one could have done more to help. Waldo's even sold his house—'

'You did what?' Tam asked in amazement. 'You sold Cucklington?'

'Too big. It was just too big. Neil?'

Waldo held up his glass to the barman. At that moment Walter and Judy appeared at the door and, seeing Tam and Jenny, went straight over.

'We were just hearing of your problems, Mrs Tate,' Tam said. 'They say things have to get worse to get better, but I guess in this case you feel it's gone far enough.'

'I have to admit it could be better, Tam,' Judy replied. 'I mean for a moment this week we really did think we'd won the war, but no.'

492

'How short is the shortfall, Waldo?' Tam asked discreetly taking Waldo aside.

Waldo shrugged, before turning to look out of the pub window, down one of his favourite views of the quays and the waters of the harbour and the estuary, now at high tide.

'Let us say, Tam, it's big enough to be too big for me to throw it in, even if I could take any more out of the States, which I can't.'

'There could be a way,' Tam said quietly. 'There just might be.'

Excusing himself, he went to the bar and asked if there was a telephone he could use. The barman was about to direct him to the public phone in the back bar when Richards beckoned to Tam.

'You'll stand a much better chance of hearing what the other person is saying if you go through there to the back room.'

Tam stood in the back room, which was filled with crates of empty bottles, and yet more crates of full ones, and stared round him. He remembered being allowed to help Richards, sometimes, as a treat, when he was younger, and the excitement and mysteries that seemed to be part of backstage in a pub.

The persistent ringing of his call must have woken Brewster Dysart because at long, long last Tam was privileged to hear a sound at the other end of the phone – a groan.

'What do I want at *this* hour, Brewster? To bring you into the real world, which is filled with

..asty guys who want to ruin my home town. It was my friend Max who first put me on to it, and now I realise how things stand.' Sitting down in Richards's swivel chair, Tam leaned forward until his head and the telephone receiver were practically between his knees, as if afraid someone might overhear, and began putting his proposal.

'You're mad,' Hugh was saying to Walter, as Tam got through to London. 'You must have drunk something very strange over in Ireland, that's all I can say. You're going to give up a thriving career at the Bar to build boats? You've gone barmy.'

'Potty actually,' Judy corrected her father-in-law. 'What's more, we've already made an offer for the boatyard.'

'We?' Hugh looked at his daughter-in-law with increased astonishment. 'Oh, so you've lost your senses as well, have you?'

'We're all in this together,' Walter interrupted. 'It's something we all believe in.'

'The family who builds ships together,' Hugh muttered, 'goes to bits together.'

'What about those poor people running their little café?' Loopy wanted to know. 'What did you do? Just buy them out?'

'They were having a bit of a struggle,' Judy explained. 'And although it takes time to get a place like that going, I have a feeling time was fast running out.'

'But you don't know the first thing about bu[...]ing boats, Walter!' his father protested. 'Anythin[...] you built would sink in dry dock!'

'I can learn, Papa. I do know a little about boats, and an awful lot about sailing – and as far as *building* boats goes, that is something I am going to learn.'

'And Walter's had a very good idea who from,' Judy said. 'He's coaxed Rusty's father, old Mr Todd, out of retirement.'

At that moment Tam exploded back into the bar, his eyes searching for Jenny. He found her gossiping with Flavia and immediately interrupted, wanting to know what time lunch was set for.

'Your mother said half past one and don't be late.'

Tam looked at his watch, bit his lip and then took Jenny's hand and began to drag her out of the pub.

'If we hurry we'll only be ten minutes late.'

Bexham being such a small place, the journey in his rented car didn't take long, his destination being, happily, on the way to Churchester.

'The old iron works?' Jenny wondered as Tam swung the red Fiat to park it in front of a large pair of heavily padlocked mesh gates. 'What on earth do you want to see the old iron works for?'

'That shed,' Tam replied, pointing to a huge building which had once been the heart of the ndry. 'All I know is, when they closed down ere, they stripped that shed bare – took all the machinery and stuff out of it, just leaving the four walls and the roof and that's about it.'

'So?' Jenny said, getting out of the car to follow Tam along the fence line. 'What are you thinking of doing? Buying it?'

'I wonder who owns it now – I mean it's been empty for how long now? Years. I remember they closed it down when I was still a nipper.'

'Tam – Tam, we're going to be not just a little late for lunch with your mum and dad, but very late.'

'OK, OK – just one last question. How many people do you reckon you could get in there?'

'How many *people*?'

'How many people,' Tam repeated. 'What do you think its capacity would be?'

Peter Sykes knew who owned the old iron works. He happened to be a fellow Rotarian and a good business friend. Peter also thought that Tam's plan, while being a top plan, was also doomed to failure since as far as he knew the old iron works had been declared a no-go zone for some time now, and the old foundry in particular.

'Problem is the overhead rails – all those huge, heavy blocks and tackles which it would be practically impossible to secure and make safe, let alone the vast cooling pits on the floors which would also present a possibly insoluble problem.'

'Couldn't you fill them in, Dad?'

'With the amount of people you want to let in?' Peter shook his head, laughing, which he found he did a great deal nowadays. 'Filling in means concrete and that would cost a small fortune. Then you'd have the problem of fire exits, and adequate ventilation. The council are very strict about these things, as far as entertainment licences go – and while I think it's a great notion, son, I think it's a doomed one.'

'What a pity.' Jenny sighed. 'I wonder how many it could have held?'

'I don't know.' Peter scratched the beard he had been proudly sporting since Australia. 'Say two and a half – three thousand maybe.'

'As many as that?' Jenny gasped. 'Good heavens.'

'Lot less than we get at Park Road of a Saturday.'

Jenny frowned and shrugged at Tam, unsure what his father was referring to.

'Park Road,' Tam said. 'The home of Churchester United.'

'Who have done a bit of all right this season, thank you,' Peter said smugly. 'Thanks to their brilliant newly elected chairman.'

Rusty cuffed her boastful husband on the back of his head with her table napkin as she sat down again.

'And how many does Park Road hold, Mr Sykes?' Jenny enquired. 'I'm afraid I've never been there.'

'Fifteen thousand,' Tam said. 'There or thereabouts.'

'Twenty thousand I'll have you know, son,' Peter corrected him. 'You're forgetting the new stand.'

'Twenty thousand,' Jenny echoed. 'Wow.'

She looked at Tam, who got the message.

'Wow is about right. What do you think, Mr Chairman?' Tam turned back to his father, who was looking serious.

'We'd have to take a cut. Can't all go to Bexham Fighting Fund, you know. Fair's only fair.'

One of fame's greatest assets is the ease with which the word can be spread. The bookings for the concert began to pour in long before the first proper formal advertisement in any national let alone regional newspaper, leading Tam jokingly to remark to Jenny that since word of mouth was all that was needed they could have saved on the promotion. Not that there was any shortage of promotion either; as soon as the media learned The Bros were to play an impromptu gig in aid of some tiny heritage charity the papers, radio and television all carried stories. Within five days of opening the bookings, every seat in the stadium at Park Road was sold.

'Which all goes to show *something*,' Tam said, wryly, to Jenny.

All the Tates, bar none, were invited to the Directors' Box as Peter Sykes's guests. Since none

of them had ever experienced such a conce.
before, the sense of excitement was electrifying
The crowds were vast, the roads around the
stadium packed not only with fans who had tickets
but also with those who had arrived in the vague
belief that somehow they would either find themselves a scalper's ticket or be able to hear something
from outside the ground.

'I think you're the most excited of us all,' Waldo
said to Loopy, who was sitting beside him in the
back of one of the limousines Tam had laid on for
the Bexham contingent. 'Why, I think you might
even be turning into what I believe they call a
groupie.'

'I think it's heavenly, Waldo,' Loopy confessed.
'This just has to be one of the very *bestest* of days.'

The young of course tried to play it cool, as if this
was the sort of thing they experienced every
weekend when they went to a party, but keeping
cool soon proved to be a bridge too far for both
Sholto and Hubert, who became completely transfixed by the girls who pressed their over-painted
young lips up against the car windows whenever
the traffic slowed down. Flavia found the whole
thing a bit of a shriek – but when they actually got
inside the stadium and up into the Directors' Box
and heard the terrifying volume of noise that was
rending the night air over the sedate city of
Churchester, she was actually silenced.

There was a large stage set in the middle of the
pitch, canopied on top in case of rain, but open on

ll the sides, and pitched high enough for the fans even on the tops of the terraces to have some sort of sight of the performers. Finally, after an interminable wait during which several dozen young girls were carried out fainting in the grateful arms of cheerful young policemen, a voice announced over the PA system that this was the moment they had all been waiting for.

'Ladies and gentlemen!' the voice boomed. 'Here they are! Here they are in person! The fabulous, fantastic . . .'

The rest of the announcement was simply drowned in hysteria as the spotlights picked out four tiny figures running out between a cordon of security guards towards the raised stage, where their instruments were already set. For five minutes they stood on stage while their fans screamed and they stood smiling and waving, turning round and round so that everyone could see them. When they realised the mayhem was not going to cease, Lonnie climbed behind his set of Rogers drums and beat them hard into their first number.

Even then the noise continued, but the fans hadn't come to hear the music. The fans had come to see these four gorgeous young men from America who were setting the world dancing and grooving, swinging and singing with their rhythmic, sweeping, insistent rock. At long, long last the noise died down enough for Brewster's tenor to rise above the screaming, for the licks of

Lee's guitar to be heard, for Tam's bass to swi᷄
along and Lonnie's drumming to beat them all up

The ends of most of the songs went unheard, such was the crescendo of sound that built with the climax of every number, and the beginning of each new number was drowned in hysteria from the moment Brewster announced it, yet enough could be heard to savour the unmistakable sound of the now world famous group.

It was a fantastic night, with no frills other than the performance of the band. There were no fancy lights, no fireworks, no girl dancers – just the music.

But it wasn't just the music they all took home with them, the twenty thousand fans who had come from everywhere and anywhere to experience something they would remember for the rest of their lives. What they took home was the whole occasion, the sense of celebration, the extraordinary moment, the entire happening.

'I must say,' Hugh's voice came from the back of the vast car he was sharing with Loopy, Waldo and the Walter Tates, 'I have to say I wouldn't have missed that for the world.'

'Of course you wouldn't,' Loopy agreed. 'I've never seen your feet tap like it.'

'Not quite Rodgers and Hart,' Hugh continued, determined to qualify his admiration. 'But damn' good all the same.'

'So now perhaps you'll say something nice about Tam. Or even to him.'

'I already have.' Hugh looked round at the others, a smug expression on his face. 'Sent him a note.'

'Which said?'

'Mind your own business.'

And so it was that Bexham came to be saved – or rather those parts of Bexham that were under threat came to be saved. But then it can be argued that by saving those parts the whole of Bexham was saved, so perhaps the first part of the sentence may stand uncorrected. Bexham was saved.

The concert raised more than enough money, as it was bound to do, once the idea of filling the Park Road ground was realised. The shortfall was made up easily, even after Churchester United FC took their commission, and there was money to spare which went a long way to help local causes.

The Three Tuns was already safe, so all that was left to accomplish was a *coup* at the Yacht Club to rid the board of its irksome chairman. This, it was rumoured, was masterminded by the Club's patron, Captain Hugh Tate, Rtd. Once the *coup* had been effected, and the chairman replaced by John Tate, the shareholding members at once voted that the new bid for the Club, tendered by a private local cabal, should be accepted.

So it was too that when spring finally turned to summer, Loopy suggested to Hugh they should give a thanksgiving party. Hugh agreed that this was an excellent idea, and while remembering how

much he had enjoyed the now famous pop conc
thought it might not be such a good idea to as
them back because 'they might disturb the neighbours'.

Loopy reassured him that the band were well
and truly back in America, where their success
continued, but she did express the hope that Tam
might be persuaded to fly over for a week, if he was
not too busy.

'Of course it's not really up to me,' she said. 'But
even so I've already suggested it to Jenny, and
she'd already suggested it to Rusty, who'd already
thought of it anyway.'

'What size of party did you have in mind? If I'm
going to be expected to sing, which I dare say I will,
I mean if it's going to be a large party then I might
have to ask John to fix me up with a microphone
like he did at Christmas.'

'It will just be family and friends. We won't have
to hire Park Road.'

In the end over a hundred people filled the
gardens at Shelborne on a warm, fine and sunny
June evening that took everyone by surprise,
emerging as it did after a week of persistent drizzle
and grey skies. All the Tates were of course present,
young and old, including Kim who, having heard
about the success of their campaign, found a return
air ticket in the post a few days later, and so was
able to leave Culoheen for a long overdue break.
The entire Sykes clan were represented, Joe Todd
rejuvenated by having been dragged – with no

eat difficulty let it be said – out of retirement by
the new owner of his old shipyard. Richards naturally refused not to be allowed to serve drinks
and food, if and when he felt like it. Hugh sang, and
Jenny played. Sholto ran a very good disco in the
basement, and Waldo took Judy down for a dance.

'You know I'm leaving Bexham.'

'Yes, Loopy told me.'

'To return to my native land – where I belong.'

'You belong here too, you know.'

'I know, but here's not home, not finally. I
brought you a farewell gift, left it in Loopy's studio.
By the way, it's the one that's wrapped!'

Judy stopped dancing and took a step back from
Waldo.

'You can't give me that—'

'How do you know what I'm giving you?'

'Because, Waldo, I know *you*.'

'I'm leaving my Meggie in safe hands, with her
best friend, Judy. And who knows? One day I may
come back for her. Now let's go join the others
upstairs. I find I'm getting too old for discos.'

'Never.'

They both laughed. It was, after all, all that they
could do.

Later, when some of the non-family guests had
departed and the dancing had finally stopped – not
because everyone was exhausted but because as
they wandered out into the garden to cool off they

504

saw what an enchanted night it had become and so stayed outside, some of the older guests wrapping sweaters or cardigans around their shoulders against the very faint chill but none the less determined to enjoy the beauty of such a star-filled summer's night – gradually everyone who was left congregated on the terrace outside the drawing room, where they sat on the walls or on the loungers, talking and drinking and smoking, or just watching the sky above them and the waters beyond. Finally, it was Jenny who disappeared inside, reappearing with an ordinary six-string Spanish guitar that she handed to Tam.

'Wow.' He smiled. 'You're full of surprises. My very first guitar. I haven't seen this fellow since I was seventeen.'

They looked at each other. The accident, the flight to America. It might be a hundred years ago.

'Have guitar, now sing for us, and that's an order.'

'Hey, man!' Tam teased. 'I'm a bass man, man!'

'No you're not, Tam Sykes, don't obfuscate,' Jenny insisted. 'Now sing for your supper.'

'Only if you'll play along.'

'Only if you tell me what you're going to play.'

She sat at her grandfather's piano, which was only a step inside the French windows, while Tam sat on a stool in the opening, and they set about playing everything from the Beatles to The Bros, from Barbra Streisand to Joan Baez. Everyone was captivated, and the party turned into an enchanted semicircle that arced around the two performers.

'That really is enough, surely?' Tam protested at last. 'Don't you people *ever* sleep?'

'Are you a man or a mouse?'

'Very well, Captain Tate. Anything in particular?'

'We'll leave that entirely to you, young man.'

'Then let's finish with Pete Seeger's famous song.'

He looked at Jenny who knew at once, and after a short pause started to play a simply lyrical introduction before Tam came in with an eight bar lead and launched into the song itself.

At first no one else sang, and there was only Tam's fine, sweet but oddly original voice to be heard, until he got to the second verse, when one by one the younger generation started to join in, their sad lament hanging in the night air and drifting slowly away from them towards the estuary, and eventually, and at last, the distant sea, to be drowned by the sound of the envious wind.

When the third verse of the song asked *Where have all the young men gone?* it seemed everyone joined in, quietly but carefully, afraid to be found singing out of tune.

By the time they got to the last verse, and found that all the graveyards were covered with flowers, every one, some of the singers had taken each other's hands, while others preferred to look up at the sky, or over to the trees where the music of their

voices was drifting away towards other garden.
and from there to the dark fields, where the grasses
swayed, and nature for once stayed silent, perhaps
because she too was listening.

When will we ever learn? When will we ever learn?

Epilogue

Loopy and Hugh had just settled down to enjoy a drink in the conservatory overlooking the estuary. It was what Hugh always called a 'springish sort of day' which is to say there was a blue sky, a fast breeze, small clouds and small sailing boats dashing about on the horizon in equal quantities. There was much about which they could be thankful, most of all the idea that Bexham, at any rate for the time being, had been saved from the forces of evil commerce.

Despite his father's best advice Walter had indeed resigned from the Bar and with Hugh's help was buying the old Todd boatyard, his declared intent being to start making sailing boats in the old way, re-employing many of the locals who had long ago been forced out of the business. Not to be outdone, Judy was now designing dresses for Rusty's ever growing chain of shops, for which Peter had managed to find backing in the City, while Peter had sold up his business and joined Walter in his father-in-law's old boatyard.

Waldo having returned to America immediately after the party, no one knew exactly what kind of person the new incumbent at Cucklington House might be, but the feeling was that they must be someone of substance, since the house had changed hands for what was rumoured to be a considerable sum.

'Wouldn't it be terrible?' Loopy asked, laughing suddenly. 'Wouldn't it be terrible if Waldo had sold his house to Markham by mistake, Hugh? I mean if we have all been duped, after all that?'

'Anything's possible, my darling, but as it happens I very much doubt it. This morning I called on the new people to ask them to drinks after church on Sunday morning.'

'That was certainly very previous of you, Hugh. They've hardly moved in.'

'It certainly was very previous of me,' Hugh agreed. 'But it means I am in the privileged position of being able to tell you that the new occupant of Cucklington House is a woman, and . . .' He paused. 'Very beautiful. So beautiful, in fact, that I fear a great many noses are going to be put out of joint whenever, or if ever, she pops to the village shop or attends the Yacht Club Ball. She is tall and dark-haired with large blue eyes of a fascinating hue, and, from the brief time I spent with her, sweet-natured too.'

Loopy sighed with sudden satisfaction. She had been feeling rather low, since Waldo had left Bexham. Now the very idea of a great beauty moving into Cucklington House seemed just what was needed. For a start great beauties nearly always caused excitement, and very often envy. And then, too, if the great beauty was single, or divorced, she would be certain to be in need of some sort of male company. Loopy started to run through in her mind any single men in the village who might be interested in a rich beauty. For a few hilarious seconds she realised that the only person she could think of who was currently not spoken for was Richards at the Three Tuns and he could hardly be expected to be interested. She frowned as the name of a man came to her. He was handsome, rich and single, and most certainly, as far as she knew, in need of a wife. She put down her martini glass, and made a note on the pad she kept on the table beside her chair.

The note read *Write to Waldo*.

THE END

Charlotte Bingham would like to invite you to visit her website at *www.charlottebingham.com*

If you enjoyed *The Moon at Midnight*, look out for
Charlotte Bingham's next novel *Daughters of Eden*